## Praise for Vicki Lane's Mysteries

### IN A DARK SEASON

"Vicki Lane writes of Appalachia as if she'd been driving up our hills and through our hollows her whole life. *In a Dark Season* richly blends past and present into **a suspenseful tale of love and lust.** In showing us how memory lingers like a smoky mist across the mountains, Lane reminds us again that the past never completely dies."
—Margaret Maron, award-winning author of *Hard Row*

"Vicki Lane fashions a gripping tale of despair and sorrow in an Appalachia she understands and loves...**Lyrical and compelling.**"
—Carolyn Hart, award-winning author of *Death Walked In*

"**Vicki Lane is a born storyteller** in the finest tradition of Sharyn McCrumb. Lane's best yet, *In a Dark Season* is a haunting, lyrical tale of the Appalachians, as heartbreaking as it is magical. **Brooding, suspenseful and superbly written,** Lane's Marshall County mysteries rank among the best regional fiction anywhere today."
—Julia Spencer-Fleming, Edgar finalist and author of *I Shall Not Want*

# OLD WOUNDS
## A Book Sense Notable Book

"Vicki Lane's gift as a storyteller is to grab her readers, plop them down on Elizabeth Goodweather's Appalachian front porch, and involve them in **a brilliantly detailed, exciting double tale of mountain life. Wonderful characters with heart-breaking secrets, past and present.** You won't want the book to end. You'll want more!"

—Rita Lakin, author of *Getting Old Is to Die For*

"A story so **exquisitely written and perfectly paced,** you will not want to put this book down. *Old Wounds* is a powerful and very personal mystery for the thoughtful Elizabeth Goodweather to solve."

—Jackie Lynn, author of *Down by the Riverside*

"Vicki Lane is quite simply the best storyteller there is. **Her books, like her Appalachian home, have everything: mystery, suspense, beauty, heart and soul.**"

—John Ramsey Miller, author of *Smoke & Mirrors*

"Vicki Lane weaves **a rich, intricate tapestry of secrets and lies** in *Old Wounds,* the third in her compelling series featuring Elizabeth Goodweather. This vivid portrait of life in Appalachia is charged with suspense, proving that Lane continues to perfect her talent of putting an unsettling twist on 'write what you know.'"

—Karen E. Olson, author of the
Annie Seymour mystery series

"Vicki Lane's done it again. **She's opened the door to Elizabeth Goodweather's Appalachian Mountain home and stitched for us a quilt with fabric from childhood tragedy and new love.** With an unerring ear for the language of the mountains—new voices and ancient ones—she sends us racing to a dramatic and surprising end. Her voices are the mountain voices I know so well, **haunting and authentic.** She's crafted a keep-us-guessing mystery, people we care about, and a poetic vision of a place apart—a truly memorable read. Pull up a rocking chair and visit awhile."

—Cathy Pickens, author of *Hush My Mouth*

"Vicki Lane is a superb storyteller. Her Appalachia series with heroine Elizabeth Goodweather is revelatory, and her newest offering, *Old Wounds,* is chillingly entertaining. I especially love the characterizations—so vivid and memorable. Elizabeth is the kind of person most women would want as a best friend—smart, wise and compassionate—and in this edition Elizabeth's love life heats up considerably and deepens the complexity of this well-told tale."

—Gammy L. Singer, author of
*Down and Dirty: Another Landlord's Tale*

"**A new Elizabeth Goodweather book is like a vacation.** In addition to mystery and mayhem, Elizabeth brings us into the rich life of Appalachia. And whether her creator Vicki Lane is reawakening a 20-year-old mystery, or showing us how Elizabeth weaves a wreath from rosemary and bay, her smart, clear writing makes the experience immediate, lively, and real. With *Old Wounds,* Lane has only gotten better. Welcome back, Elizabeth."

—Clea Simon, author of *Cries & Whiskers*

# ART'S BLOOD

"Lane mixes the gentle craft of old-time quilting with the violence of a slaughtered innocent."

—*Greensboro News-Record*

**"Lane is a master at creating authentic details while building suspense."**

—*Asheville Citizen-Times*

"An **engrossing** tale."

—*Tampa Tribune*

**"A true solid winner, an original adventure, heart thumping**...Lane has done something far beyond the genre of the mystery/suspense novel....Lane nails Asheville's local color....Lane charms readers with her knowledge of Appalachian dialect and ways."

—*Rapid River Magazine*

"A well-conceived mystery with a fascinating setting."

—*Mystery Lovers Bookshop News*

"*Art's Blood* is an especially satisfying read. The mystery is as complicated and textured with secrets as a handmade Appalachian quilt. The characters are complex and real. Best of all, the writing is rich, clear, and intelligent. Vicki Lane is a brilliant storyteller and I can't wait to read her next book."

—Nancy Thayer, author of the Hot Flash Club series

"Lane's sharp eye for detail gets put to good use in this second installment of her Appalachian series.... The widow Goodweather is a wonderful character: plucky, hip and wise. **The dialogue sparkles with authenticity, and Lane generates suspense without sacrificing the charm and mystique of her mountain community.**"

—*Publishers Weekly*

## SIGNS IN THE BLOOD

"*Signs in the Blood* turns the beauty of the Appalachian hills and a widow's herb and flower farm into the backdrop for modern menace. This clash of the traditional and the modern makes for an all-nighter of satisfying suspense."

—*Mystery Lovers Bookshop News*

"Vicki Lane shows us an exotic and colorful picture of Appalachia from an outsider's perspective—through a glass darkly. It is a well-crafted, suspenseful tale of the bygone era before 'Florida' came to the mountains."

—Sharyn McCrumb

"**A well-crafted, dramatic tale of murder, miracles and midlife romance.** Evocative detail brings the supporting characters vividly to life.... Also admirable is the sensitivity with which Lane utilizes exotic religions to intensify the book's dark-toned suspense, while resisting oversimplification and insult. Her heroine's open-minded fascination with beliefs not her own should appeal to an unusually wide readership."

—*Publishers Weekly*

Also by Vicki Lane

*Signs in the Blood*
*Art's Blood*
*Old Wounds*

And coming soon from Dell

*The Day of Small Things*

# In a Dark Season

Vicki Lane

A DELL BOOK

IN A DARK SEASON
A Dell Book / June 2008

Published by
Bantam Dell
A Division of Random House, Inc.
New York, New York

This is a work of fiction. Names, characters, places, and incidents either are the
product of the author's imagination or are used fictitiously. Any resemblance to
actual persons, living or dead, events, or locales is entirely coincidental.

Dell is a registered trademark of Random House, Inc., and the colophon is a
trademark of Random House, Inc.

ISBN 978-0-440-24360-1

Printed in the United States of America
Published simultaneously in Canada

www.bantamdell.com

OPM  10 9 8 7 6 5 4 3 2 1

*To John, who heard me say, "I'm closing in on it—almost done—any day now!" for over two months and never once complained.*

# Chapter 1

## *The Palimpsest*
### Friday, December 1

The madwoman whispered into the blue shadows of a wintry afternoon. Icy wind caught at her hair, loosing it to whip her cheeks and sting her half-closed eyes. Pushing aside the long black strands, she peered through the fragile railing of the upper porch. Below, the fieldstone walkway with its humped border of snow-hooded dark boxwoods curled about the house. Beyond the walkway the land sloped away, down to the railroad tracks and the gray river where icy foam spattered on black rocks and a perpetual roar filled the air.

Her hand clutching the flimsy balustrade and her gaze fixed on the stony path far below, the madwoman pulled herself to her feet. Behind her, a door rattled on its rusty hinges and slammed, only to creak open again.

She paused, aware of the loom of the house around her— feeling it *waiting*, crouching there on its ledge above the swift-flowing river. The brown skeletons of the kudzu that draped the walls and chimneys rustled in a dry undertone, the once lush vines shriveled to a delicate netting that meshed the peeling clapboards and spider-webbed the cracked and cloudy windowpanes. From every side, in small mutterings and rustlings, the old house spoke.

*None escape. None.*

As the verdict throbbed in her ears, marking time with the pulse of blood, the madwoman began to feel her cautious way along the uneven planks of the second-story porch. A loose board caught at her shoe and she staggered, putting out a thin hand to the wall where missing clapboards revealed a layer of brick-printed asphalt siding, the rough material curling back at an uncovered seam. Compelled by some urgent desire, she caught at the torn edge, tugging, peeling it from the wood beneath, ripping away the siding to expose the heart of the house—the original structure beneath the accretions of later years.

She splayed her trembling fingers against the massive chestnut logs and squeezed her eyes shut. *A palimpsest, layer hiding layer, wrong concealing wrong. If I could tear you down, board by board, log by log, would I ever discover where the evil lies... or where it began?* Resting her forehead against the wood's immovable curve, she allowed the memories to fill her: the history of the house, the subtext of her life.

*The logs have seen it all.* Their story flowed into her, through her head and fingertips, as she leaned against them, breathing the dust-dry hint of fragrance. *The men who felled the trees and built this house, the drovers who passed this way, the farmers, the travelers, the men who took their money, the women who lured them... and Belle, so much of Belle remains. Her dark spirit is in these logs, this house, this land. Why did I think that I and mine could escape?*

No answer came, only the mocking echoes of memories. The thrum of blood in her ears grew louder and the madwoman turned her back on the exposed logs of the house wall to move to the railing. Leaning out, oblivious to the cutting wind, she fixed her eyes on the stony path thirty feet below. *Far enough?* She hesitated, looking up and down the porch. A stack of plastic milk crates, filled with black-mottled shapes, caught her eye.

*Of course there would be a way. The house will see to it.* Belle *will see to it.*

Snatching up the topmost crate, she lifted it to the porch railing. Dried and mildew-speckled, the gourds tumbled down to shatter on the stones, scattering seeds over the path and frozen ground. The madwoman set the empty crate beside the balusters and slowly, painfully, pulled herself up to stand on its red grating-like surface. Then she placed a tentative foot on the wide railing.

The words came to her, dredged from memory's storehouse. As always, when her own thoughts faltered, one of the poets spoke for her, one of the many whose works she had loved and learned and taught.

Balanced on the railing, the madwoman hurled the words into the wind's face.

*"After great pain, a formal feeling comes—"*

She broke off, unable at first to continue, then, gathering strength, she forced her lips to form the words, speaking the closing lines into the bitter afternoon.

*"…The Snow—*
*First—Chill—then Stupor—then the letting go."*

The house waited.

# Chapter 2

## *Three Dolls*
### Friday, December 1

The three naked baby dolls, their pudgy bodies stained with age and weather, twisted and danced in the winter wind like a grisly chorus line. As the car negotiated the twisting road down to the river, Elizabeth Goodweather saw them once more. They had hung there as long as she could remember, dangling by their almost nonexistent necks from the clothesline that sagged along the back porch of the old house called Gudger's Stand.

The house lay below a curve so hairpin-sharp and a road so narrow that many travelers, intent on avoiding the deep ditch to one side and the sheer drop to the other, never noticed the house at all. It was easy to miss, seated as it was in a tangle of saplings, weedy brush, and household garbage, perched well below the level of the pavement on a narrow bank that fell away to the river.

*I wish I'd never noticed it. It wasn't until the power company cleared some of those big trees that you could even see the house.*

Her first sight of the house and its cruel row of hanged dolls had been on a fall day sixteen years back. *It was Rosie's first year in high school. Sam was still alive. He was driving and our girls were in the back seat. . . .*

The memory was piercing: the sudden appearance of the

hitherto-unseen house with its long porches front and back; the pathetic dolls and the hunched old man sitting in a chair beneath them, belaboring their rubber bodies with his lifted cane. *And a woman just disappearing into the house; I only saw the tail of her skirt as she went through the door. The whole scene was bizarre—and unlike anything else I'd seen in Marshall County. I started to say something to Sam but then I couldn't; it just seemed too awful—those helpless little baby dolls—I didn't want the girls to see that old man hitting the dolls.*

Ridiculous, of course. The very next time the girls had ridden their school buses, ghoulishly eager friends had pointed out the newly visible house and the trio of dangling dolls. As they downed their after-school snacks, Rosemary and Laurel had discussed the display with eager cheerfulness.

"Shawn says it's where old man Randall Revis lives—and that he's had *three* wives and all of them have run off. So old man Revis named the dolls for his ex-wives and he whacks them with his walking stick."

Rosemary's matter-of-fact explanation, punctuated by slurps of ramen noodles, was followed by her younger sister's assertion that a girl on *her* bus had said the old man was a cannibal who lured children into his house and cut them up and put them in his big freezer.

"Like the witch in 'Hansel and Gretel'! And every time he eats one, he hangs up another doll!" Laurel's eyes had been wide but then she had smiled knowingly. "That's not true, is it, Mum? That girl was just trying to scare the little kids, wasn't she?"

"That's what it sounds like to me, Laurie." Elizabeth had been quick to agree, adding a tentative explanation about a sick old man, not right in the head.

*But really, the girls just took it in stride as one of those inexplicable things grown-ups do. I think they even stopped seeing the house and the dolls. I wish I could have. For some reason I always have to look, and I'm always hoping that the dolls or the cords holding them will have rotted and fallen away. Or that the kudzu will have finally covered the whole place. The old man's been dead for years now; you'd think someone would have taken those dolls down.*

Elizabeth shuddered and forced her thoughts back to the here and now. Sam was six years dead; their daughters were grown; it was Phillip Hawkins at the wheel of her car on this particular winter afternoon. But still the sight of the hanging dolls made her shudder.

"What's the matter, Lizabeth?" Without taking his eyes from the road, Phillip reached out to tug at her long braid. One-handed, he steered the jeep down the corkscrew road and toward the bridge over the river at Gudger's Stand. Snowplows had been out early: tarnished ridges of frozen white from the unseasonable storm of the previous night lined the road ahead.

She caught at his free hand, happy to be pulled from her uneasy reverie. "It's just that old house—it always gives me the creeps."

Phillip turned into the deserted parking lot to the left of the road. For much of the year, the flat area at the base of the bridge swarmed with kayakers, rafters, and busloads of customers for the white-water rafting companies, but on this frigid day, it was deserted except for a pair of Canada geese, fluffed out against the cold.

"That one up there?" Phillip wheeled the jeep in a tight circle, bringing it to a stop facing away from the river and toward the house.

She nodded. "That one. It's as near to being a haunted house as anything we have around here—folks tell all kinds of creepy stories about things that happened there in the past—and ten years ago the old man who lived there was murdered in his bed. They've never found out who did it."

They sat in the still-rumbling car, gazing up the snow-covered slope to the dilapidated and abandoned house.

Low-lying clouds washed the scene in grim tones of pale gray and faded brown.

"What's that?" Elizabeth leaned closer to the windshield, pointing to a dark shape that seemed to quiver behind the railings at the end of the upper porch. "Do you see it? There's something moving up there!"

"Probably just something blowing in the wind." Phillip followed her gaze. "One of those big black trash bags maybe—"

"No, I don't think so." Elizabeth frowned, struggling to make sense of the dark form that had moved now to lean against the wall of the old house. "It's a person. But what would anyone ... I wish I could see—"

Phillip was already pulling out of the lot and toward the overgrown driveway that led up to the house. And even as he said "Something's not right here," the angular shape moved toward the porch railing. There was a flash of red and a tangle of rounded objects fell to the ground.

"It's a woman up there." Elizabeth craned her neck to get a better look at the figure high above them. "What's she doing ... climbing up on something or ... ?"

The question in her voice turned to horror. "Phillip! I think she's going to jump!"

The car was halfway up the driveway when they were halted by a downed tree lying across the overgrown ruts. High above them they could see the woman balanced on the railing. One arm around a porch pillar, she swayed in the wind.

Elizabeth shoved her door open and leaped from the car. Pulling on her jacket as she ran, she pounded up the steep drive, skidding treacherously on the frozen mud and ice-covered puddles. Behind her, she could hear the steady thud of Phillip's boots. Ahead she could see the scarecrow form of the woman, teetering on her precarious perch. Black hair writhed around her head, obscuring her face, and a long black coat lofted out in the wind, making her look like some great bird preparing for flight.

"Stop!" Elizabeth's voice was little more than a thin quaver against the wind, and she took a breath and tried again. "Please! ... Wait! ... Talk to us!"

This time her cry reached the woman on the railing, who turned at the sound. Her pale face stared at Elizabeth and her lips moved, but the words, if there were words, were carried away by the pitiless wind.

Elizabeth gasped. "Nola!"

She tried to run faster, even as she shouted to the figure high above her. "It's me, Nola—Elizabeth Goodweather. Please, get down from there before—"

The woman on the railing hesitated, wavered. Then she lifted her head as if listening to a faraway sound.

"Nola! Wait where you are, please! We'll help you..." Elizabeth's side was aching and her voice was a rasping croak, but she forced herself up the road and toward the old house. In the distance, a siren began its urgent howl.

Phillip was at her side now, pointing to the stairs that led to the upper porch. "Keep talking to her; I'll try to get up there."

The siren was louder now, very near.

"Nola, let us help you!" She kept moving toward the porch, laboring to be heard, to be understood, to get closer, to make eye contact with this woman she had met only a few months before. "Please, be careful; that railing looks—"

Above her the black-haired woman slowly shook her head. Elizabeth heard the emergency vehicle turn into the drive behind her. The siren shrieked once more, then died away.

She turned to see a Marshall County sheriff's car stopped just behind her jeep. Its light was pulsing in blue rhythmic bursts as two men, followed by a smaller figure in jeans and a purple fleece jacket, emerged from its interior and began to race up the drive.

Whirling to see what effect this new arrival would have, Elizabeth was just in time to see the black-clad figure release her hold on the post, spread her arms wide, and plunge—a great ungainly raven tumbling from the sky.

"How the hell she survived . . . if it hadn't been for one of those old boxwoods breaking her fall before she hit the stone walk . . ."

The EMTs had responded swiftly, strapping the crumpled, unconscious body of Miss Nola Barrett to a backboard and loading her into the ambulance for the trip to an Asheville emergency room. The young woman in the purple jacket had gone with Miss Barrett.

"She's the one who called us," Sheriff Mackenzie Blaine had explained. "Miss Barrett's niece or something—been visiting her aunt. She said Miss Barrett's started acting kind of squirrelly—obsessing about this house. Evidently the house belongs to Miss Barrett—or she thinks it does. Anyway, the niece—what's her name, Trace, Tracy?—said she went to the store after lunch and when she came back, her aunt was gone. She found footprints on the trail leading down this way and was concerned that Miss Barrett might be going to . . . to hurt herself."

As soon as the ambulance had been loaded, Phillip had led Elizabeth to her car, started the motor, and turned the heat to high. In moments, the car filled with warmth, but Elizabeth, her face pale and drawn, continue to shiver. Phillip put an arm around her as Mackenzie Blaine slipped into the back seat. Behind the jeep, his deputy waited in the patrol car. Clouds of white exhaust billowed from both vehicles.

"It's a sad thing, seeing a woman like Miss Barrett come to this." Blaine stared out the car window at the old house. "Folks always thought a lot of her around here. Funny thing—"

"Mac," Phillip interrupted. "Why'd the niece call you? How'd she know her aunt wasn't over at a neighbor's house or—"

"There was a note—and it worried the niece enough that she called us right away—well, you saw what happened— Miss Barrett was trying to kill herself."

Blaine opened the back door and stepped out into the cold air. "Looks like she may get her wish too—the EMTs weren't sure if she'd make it, with that head injury."

He leaned back into the car and cast a sympathetic brown gaze at Elizabeth. *It's the sympathy that does it, every time,* she thought, firmly quelling the rising tide of tears.

"You knew her, you said?" The sheriff's voice was warm and gentle, full of concern. There was no hint of official inquiry.

Elizabeth gulped and nodded. "I met her for the first time a few months ago. But, Mackenzie, Nola Barrett isn't *squirrelly*... or suicidal... at least not when I saw her a week ago. My god, the woman has a memory like... like..."

She faltered, unable to find an apt comparison. "Her memory's amazing. Just a few weeks ago I was telling her about how Sam and I left suburbia to learn to farm... how we wanted a garden and cows and bees... and all of a sudden she launched into 'Nine bean-rows will I have there, a hive for the honey-bee—'"

Seeing bewilderment spread over the sheriff's face, Elizabeth broke off. "It's from a poem by William Butler Yeats. Nola knew it all by heart. She once told me that she'd memorized page after page of poetry when she was young and still could go on for hours without repeating herself. She was... she was the most..."

The memory of that nightmare figure on the upper porch, the pathetic crumpled form caught in the green-black clutch of the ancient boxwood, and the stricken, bloodless face that had disappeared into the ambulance was too much.

Betrayed by her emotions, Elizabeth choked, unable to go on.

Blaine's eyes met Phillip's and he said gently, "You all go on home now, Hawk. I'll be in touch."

When the sheriff's car had gone, leaving the way clear, Phillip began to back slowly and carefully down the rutted drive. Elizabeth stared up at the old house. The blank windows returned her stare, watching and waiting under the lowering sky, and the entire scene swam and wavered in her watery gaze.

As they pulled farther away from the house, once again she could see the dolls on the old porch, stirred by the chill wind sweeping down the river gorge into a writhing, endless dance.

# Chapter 3

## *Nola Barrett*
### Friday, December 1

Tell me about that house. You said there'd been a murder . . . is that why no one lives there?"

Phillip handed Elizabeth a thick mug of rum-fortified tea. Her call to the hospital had been fruitless—beyond the fact that Nola Barrett had been admitted and was still alive, no information was forthcoming.

He took his seat on the denim-covered sofa beside Elizabeth. She had finally stopped shivering but was withdrawn to some wordless sorrow, staring into the fire.

*Get her talking—otherwise she'll clam up and hold that misery in.* He began to rub the back of her neck and could feel the tension in her body slacken. "The building's overgrown and run-down for sure but it looks pretty sound. At least the ridge line isn't sagging—that's one of the earliest signs that a place is falling apart. With the great view from those porches—the river *and* the mountains—it's hard to believe some Florida person hasn't snapped it up and turned it into a bed-and-breakfast—it's sure big enough."

His fingers moved down to work the muscles of her shoulder. She was still silent; then, with a last sip of the tea, she set her mug on the old chest before the sofa and turned to offer both shoulders for his attentions.

"As a matter of fact, that's what the house *was* years ago—

not a B and B, but an inn. Back before the railroad came through, it was one of the stopping places on the Drovers' Road."

Her voice was low and sad, but at least she was talking. Phillip continued to knead the taut muscles. "Yeah . . . I kinda remember Aunt Omie talking about that—the road through Marshall County where they used to drive hogs and such to market. I'd forgotten . . . it followed the river, didn't it? So of course it would have come right by there."

Elizabeth's head dropped and she leaned forward. "That feels good. You have a nice firm touch."

She breathed a contented sigh and went on. "You're right, the Drovers' Road ran by the river, pretty much where the railroad is now. And every eight or ten miles there'd be an inn with big lots or corrals to put the livestock in for the night. They called them 'stands,' those stopping places. And that creepy old house was the inn at this stand. The park where the paddlers put in and the fields by the river— all that's where the corrals were—"

"—and that's why the area at the bridge is called Gudger's Stand." Phillip beamed with pleasure. She was relaxing and she was talking. *Keep it up.* "That makes sense," he continued. "It never occurred to me to wonder—there're so many odd names here in the mountains."

"I guess it was a Mr. Gudger who built the place and ran the stand. Evidently the house is one of the very few drovers' inns still . . . still standing, no pun intended."

There was a lack of humor in her voice, but at least this was a flash of the usual Elizabeth. He nodded to himself as she went on. "The only other remains of a stock stand that I know of in Marshall County are down the river a little way. Remember on that raft trip we did back in the summer? About halfway between the bridge and Hot Springs, just before those big rapids, the guide pointed out a little stone building. He said that it was all that was left of another stand."

"So the old house is a historic place, huh?" Phillip worked his fingers down either side of Elizabeth's spine. "It really seems like there'd be someone hot to turn it into one of those tourist 'destinations.' The way the county's growing, I can't believe no one's thought about doing something with the only remaining drovers' inn, even if there *was* a murder there."

Under his fingers, he could feel her body tense again as she replied. "It wasn't just the old man's murder—the place has always had a bad reputation. Supposedly there were other murders way back—drovers returning home, killed for the money they were carrying. And then, after the railroad came through and there weren't any more stock drives, the inn turned into more of a tavern and a hangout—lots of drinking and fighting and there were shootings now and then. Miss Birdie still talks about what a dangerous place Gudger's Stand was, back when she was a girl."

The cell phone at Phillip's waist vibrated. He kept one hand on Elizabeth's back, moving it in lazy circles as he flipped open the little instrument.

"It's Mac, Lizabeth. Maybe he'll have some news about your friend."

Mackenzie Blaine's report was terse: Nola Barrett was stable but unconscious. A dislocated shoulder and a concussion seemed to be her major injuries.

"Amazing it wasn't worse." Phillip returned the phone to his belt. "Mac said Miss Barrett's niece is with her and is making arrangements for her care whenever she can be moved. The doctor won't commit herself, but did tell Mac that the old lady had a good chance of a full recovery—physically, anyway."

"Nola's sixty-four." Elizabeth's voice was thoughtful. "Only ten years older than I am."

"Are you serious?" Again he saw the sticklike figure, swaying and gibbering in the wind...and the huddled, broken shape with a death mask for a face, being loaded

into the EMS ambulance. "I just assumed—I don't know...
senility ... Alzheimer's ... something like that."

"It couldn't have been." Elizabeth swung around to face
him, her eyes flashing blue fire. "Not Nola Barrett. Absolutely not."


Absolutely not. But what had taken Nola Barrett to the old
house she had vowed never to enter again; what had sent
her over that high railing in search of death?

As she lay in the steaming water of her pre–bedtime
bath, Elizabeth thought back to her first meeting with Miss
Barrett. It had been only a few months ago, when Sallie
Kate had called. Sallie Kate, whose real estate business took
her over so much of Marshall County and acquainted her
with so many of its inhabitants, needed a favor.

"It's about that old building at Gudger's Stand, honey."
Sallie Kate's voice was excited as she described the various
groups interested in the property—the historic old inn with
its adjacent acreage and river frontage. There were rival developers with plans for an upscale gated community on the
property. And there were preservationists and environmentalists who wanted a nature sanctuary and drovers' museum.

"I'd think you'd be thrilled to have so much interest in
the place," Elizabeth had gently teased her friend.

"Oh, there's plenty of interest, all right. Along with the
developers and the tree huggers, there're the local people
who think gold's hidden there, back from the days of the
Drovers' Road. *And* county gossip says there're a few folks
with something to hide about the murder of old man Revis—
folks who'd be just as happy to see that place burn to the
ground. County gossip *also* says that Vance Holcombe—
you know, the sheriff back then—didn't try very hard to
solve the crime. And that Mackenzie Blaine, our illustrious

current sheriff, may know more about the case than he's sayin'."

Elizabeth had nodded into the phone, wondering vaguely what sort of favor Sallie Kate wanted.

"The thing is, honey, I'm tryin' to get Miss Nola to hire a lawyer—at this point she doesn't have clear title to the place, no matter what the family tree in her Bible says. If old man Revis made a will, no one knows where it is. And here I've got deep-pocket buyers absolutely *slaverin'* over the place and she keeps draggin' her feet.

"*So*, Elizabeth honey, I figure this might be right up your alley. Did I mention that Miss Nola has several trunks full of family quilts? Some even go back to before the war— the *Wa-wahr*, that is—the *Civil Wa-wahr*. You're always so interested in old quilts—let me take you over to meet Miss Nola. I know you two'll get along. And then, maybe you can help her understand that if she doesn't hire a lawyer to sort out this mess and get a clear title to the property, she's not likely to see a dime from that place."

And so Elizabeth had made the short trip, across the river and up the winding road to Dewell Hill. The little settlement, early and briefly the center of Marshall County government, had long ago lost the battle for preeminence to Ransom, where a red-brick courthouse in the neoclassical style shed glory on the modest county seat. In recent years Dewell Hill had lapsed even further, from a thriving village to a somnolent cluster of houses, several churches, and a small convenience store. What had once been a proud two-story school for grades one through twelve had been partially demolished, leaving only a paltry one-story wing to serve as a community center.

*They don't even have a post office anymore.* The low frame building that had, fifteen or twenty years before, housed a general store and a tiny post office had been converted into two rental units. *With a lovely view of the garbage bins,* Elizabeth thought, pulling her car in behind the silver SUV that bore on its front doors the Country Manors logo and phone number.

Nola Barrett's tiny stone house sat on a corner, perilously near the pavement. Across one road was the garbage collection center with its looming green bins; across the other, the erstwhile post office. Behind the house an ancient gnarled apple tree stooped and spread its bare branches over the little lean-to back porch. A wisp of white smoke lifted from the stone chimney and vanished against the sky's deep blue.

"Come in the house!" Sallie Kate's cheerful voice had called out as the front door opened. "Nola's expecting you."

Elizabeth had stepped through the door of the little cottage and stopped in sheer confusion. *But I wasn't expecting this,* she thought as her eyes took in the contents of the room.

Books. Books and books upon books. They lined the walls of the little sitting room, packed tight on simple white-painted shelves. Old books, new books, paperbacks and hardcovers in a kaleidoscope of colors. More volumes were in neat stacks on the end tables that flanked the shabby chintz-covered love seat, and still more were on the sturdy oak table under the window, ranging beside a laptop computer. Next to the boxy oil heater, a sagging upholstered armchair with a matching ottoman was attended by knee-high towers of still more books. The no-nonsense reading light just behind the chair and the worn fabric of the armrests, as well as the permanent sag of the cushion, suggested that this was the owner's habitual seat.

Sallie Kate had been in full realtor regalia that day—gray wool slacks, black turtleneck, and a fire engine–red blazer. Her usually helter-skelter blonde curls had been slightly subdued by a pair of side-combs that she was in the act of resetting.

"I doubt I'll ever get the hang of these things." Sallie Kate peered dubiously over the top of her wire-rimmed glasses into a little mirror on the wall. "The last time Lola cut my hair, she fixed it so cute with these—I mean *très* elegant, honey—"

"I think it looks great." Elizabeth glanced around the little room. "Where's—?"

"She's back there in the kitchen, fixin' some coffee." Sallie Kate glanced at a half-open door and added in a whisper, "Get her to show you the quilts and then ask her about the old inn. Eventually you can get around to the lawyer thing. She won't listen to me and I can't stay anyway; I've got a closin' in Ransom at ten-thirty. Just remember—"

"You'll have time for a cup of coffee before you go, Sallie Kate. It won't take you fifteen minutes to get to Ransom, so just sit down and quit fidgeting."

The woman who came through the door to the kitchen spoke in the firm tones of one who expects—and receives—prompt obedience. She carried a hammered-copper tray with three sea-green pottery mugs, a matching sugar bowl and cream pitcher, and a shining glass-and-chrome French press coffeemaker. Moving without hurry, she advanced on the oak table and deposited her burden in the cleared space to the right of the computer. Then she turned and put out her hand. "Elizabeth Goodweather, I presume." A smile flitted across her thin lips. "Sallie Kate tells me you're interested in quilts."

"Yes, ma'am." Elizabeth took the proffered hand, cool and dry, a collection of fragile bones. "I've made a few quilts and I have some beautiful ones done by my great-grandmother and her sister."

Nola Barrett regarded Elizabeth with an appraising eye, then released her hand and turned to pour the coffee. There had been unexpected strength in that brief clasp. *I was expecting an old lady—but this woman's . . . what, in her sixties? Maybe ten years older than me. What made me call her "ma'am"?*

*I bet she hates hearing that from someone with more gray hair than she has.*

Indeed, Miss Nola Barrett's hair, sleeked back into a classic French twist, was black as the proverbial crow's wing. As were her carefully penciled eyebrows. The older woman's elegantly spare and upright frame was clothed in a crisp white shirt tucked neatly into a flared charcoal wool skirt, while her long, narrow feet were encased in well-polished black low-heeled pumps. A gray wool cardigan, adorned with a silver brooch in the shape of a dogwood blossom, and opaque black stockings completed the somber outfit.

Elizabeth, supremely conscious of her own faded jeans, boots, and flannel shirt, found herself smiling. *I was expecting someone like Miss Birdie or Dorothy—in a little print house-dress or polyester pants and sweatshirt—not this. I'm used to the farm folks of Marshall County; obviously Nola Barrett is something else. Sallie Kate must be mistaken; this woman doesn't look like anyone who needs help understanding the legal system.*

But Sallie Kate was standing, looking at her watch, gulping down the last of her coffee, and saying a hurried good-bye. She was out of the door in a scarlet flurry, and Elizabeth was left alone with her hostess.

"You haven't mentioned the books yet." Nola Barrett settled into the armchair. A cool gray gaze studied Elizabeth through thick lenses set into heavy black frames. "Most people ask if I've read them all."

"I'll bet they do." Elizabeth nodded in smiling agreement. "I have a full wall of books in *my* living room, and I almost always get that question. I've taken to saying that they're there for insulation."

"So you're a reader too." The steely-gray eyes softened. "What do you read?"

"A bit of everything—the classics, Southern fiction, English mysteries, biographies, history—"

"Did Sallie Kate mention to you that I'm working on a

historical novel about Marshall County?" With a nod toward the laptop, Nola Barrett went on. "I taught English literature for many years at Mars Hill College, and when I retired I decided to try my hand at writing."

Gradually Nola Barrett's story had been told. "I was born right here in Dewell Hill—and grew up in this very house, as a matter of fact. My mother had no education to speak of, but she was determined that I should have a chance for more. She kept me at my books—books she could barely read herself—and took any job she could find to keep me in school. Fortunately, I took to learning like a starving man to food—we couldn't afford many extras and, heresy of heresies, didn't own a television. I was an odd bird: I amused myself by memorizing poetry, which, as you might imagine, didn't do much for my popularity with my classmates. But by the time I was through high school, a local church arranged a scholarship for me at a women's college in Atlanta. One of the members was a recent graduate and she acted as a mentor, making sure that I had the right clothes and an allowance that would allow me to fit in with my classmates.

"And at college"—Miss Barrett stood and returned her empty mug to the tray—"I managed to lose my mountain accent. At first my roommates could hardly understand me; later they mimicked and teased me till I learned to speak in the educated dialect I now employ. You, on the other hand"—her head tilted to one side as she regarded Elizabeth with a pensive gaze—"your original speech was undoubtedly educated—oh, Southern, definitely, but educated. *Now*, I think, some of the mountain patois has become part of your habitual language. Am I correct?"

"Guilty as charged!" Elizabeth felt a flush rising on her face but hastened to explain herself. "I love some of the great phrases I hear from my neighbors. So, yes, you'll hear me saying things like 'everwhat' instead of 'whatever,' or 'They're givin' rain this evenin'' for the weather forecast, or

'Back of this' meaning 'before'.... And I guess I've probably picked up a bit of a twang..."

"Yes, you have indeed." It was not, Elizabeth noted, said
disapprovingly; just a statement of fact.

"But you came to see my quilts." Nola Barrett rose, moved
to a tall wooden cupboard, and opened it, revealing three
deep shelves on which folded quilts and coverlets lay. A
scent of cedar, mixed with some herbal aroma, wafted out
into the warm room. A bottom shelf was packed with bright
toys, picture books, and a tall red, yellow, and green plush
rooster, all evidently brand-new.

*Odd. I wonder who those are for?* Elizabeth was opening
her mouth to ask, when Nola Barrett reached for a bundle
wrapped in what looked like an old sheet.

"This is the oldest of the quilts—dated 1860." She
brought it out and gently pulled back the swaddling fabric.
"I'll spread it out on the love seat so you can look at it."

Elizabeth stood and watched as the small, somber quilt
was unfolded. Usually quilts inspired good feelings in her—
awe at their beauty, amused affection at their naivete—but
*this*—this quilt made her uneasy. She frowned at it. The
solemn purples and blacks had been carefully cut and
meticulously pieced into an intricate pattern of linking circles. A wide black border with a quilted motif that resem-
bled a twisted rope surrounded the whole.

"Do you recognize the pattern?" One bony finger traced
the circumference of the central circle.

"I'm not sure ... something to do with a wheel, I think. I
know I've seen pictures but—"

"It's a Wheel of Mystery." Nola Barrett beamed with
quiet satisfaction. "I showed it to a quilt expert at the Folk
Art Center in Asheville. They were quite taken with it—
begged me to consider donating it to their collection."

Elizabeth was bending over the quilt, minutely examin-
ing the tiny stitches of the decorative quilting, the variety of
purple fabrics that had been used, the excellent condition of

the entire piece—but for a stain on one corner of the quilt, it was really almost perfect—no fading, no deterioration.

"You said it was dated . . . ?"

"There's some writing on the back; there on the corner where the stain is. Go on; it's all right to handle it."

Elizabeth gingerly turned back the stained corner to reveal a purple square of cloth affixed to the loosely woven backing. There was writing in a spidery hand, the black ink sharp against the pale violet. *L. G. ~ 1860 ~ A Life for a Life,* followed by more initials—*B. C.*

"A life for a life?" Elizabeth pulled her reading glasses from her shirt pocket and leaned closer. "Is that what it says?"

She studied the quilt, wondering at its odd dimensions—long and narrow. "Was it made for a baby . . . maybe one whose mother died in childbirth? That might be the meaning . . ."

Miss Nola Barrett's eyes had narrowed. "Now that's a possibility I hadn't considered. I've always assumed it was a coffin cover."

# The Drovers' Road I
### Lydy Goforth ~ 1860

When first I seen Belle Caulwell she was standin in the midst of a great drive of hogs, her dark green skirts not swayed a lick as the flood of swine, all a-slaver at the smell of the corn wagons, parted and passed by to either side of her, like as a rushin creek will divide at a tall rock. She stood there not payin the brutes no mind a-tall and just a-starin at me, them dark eyes of hern like fire-coals burnin their way right into my breast.

The lanky youth fell silent. He laid one bony hand over his heart and stared up at the tiny patch of sky just visible through the high barred window, his gaze fixed as if he could see the burning eyes watching him still.

The Professor shifted on the planks of his bunk, picked a bug from the ragged gray blanket that was the whole of his bedding, and cracked it against the wall where a scattering of red dots told the tally of his kills.

Circe, he pronounced, shaking his head. Circe and John Keats's merciless dame, the two subsumed into one. He scratched at an odiferous armpit. Boy, I begin to see why it is you find yourself in such a dire predicament. But, like the blind singer Homer, you have initiated your narrative in media res. Perhaps you would indulge my curiosity and begin at the beginning. I take it that these mountains are your native heath?

The young man frowned and shook his head as if reluctantly

*returning from a happier world to the chill reality of the Marshall County jail. He shot a suspicious glance at his cell mate.*

The Professor brushed at the sleeve of his black frock coat in a vain attempt to remove the dirt ground into it during the unfortunate events surrounding his arrest. His once-white shirt was adorned by the tattered remnants of a dark blue cravat—the garments of a man with some pretensions to gentility. With a soft exhalation, he settled himself more comfortably on the narrow bunk, his head cocked expectantly, awaiting an answer to his question.

The young man, whose blue-checked shirt and rough jeans trousers, though far from clean, looked to be new, lowered himself to the uneven bricks of the floor. He cast a last, longing glance at the little window before replying.

*Well, I see why it is they call you the Professor—all them fine words just a-spewin out yore mouth. Now I don't know nare singer called Homer, nor do I understand the half of yore fancy talk. But I reckon you kin tell me first who it is you are and how come you to be here afore I unburden myself to you. Hit'll do to while away the time till that ole jury kin come to an agreement. And my name hain't Boy, hit's Lydy Goforth.*

The Professor rose and made a little bow in the direction of his companion. *My most humble apologies, Mr. Goforth. Allow me to introduce myself—Thomas Walter Blake, the second of that name, native of Charleston, South Carolina, late of Harvard University, and completely at your service. In view of our enforced intimacy, may I suggest that we dispense with formalities hereafter? If it meets with your approval, I shall call you Lydy and I beg that you will make use of my own praenomen, my familiar appellation, my given name . . . in short, please call me Tom.*

*Lydy's eyes narrowed. Reckon I'll stick with Professor, iffen you don't keer. Hit don't seem fitten fer a body with so many big*

words in his craw to be called by a name any common he-cat might
carry.

The Professor shrugged and sank back to his bunk. *As you
will, my young friend, as you will.* He leaned back and, crossing
one black-trousered leg over the other, assumed the air of a gentleman at his club, about to embark on a leisurely narrative.

*You may ask how it is that I, scion of a distinguished
Charlestonian family and graduate of Harvard University, how it
is that I find myself in this verminous cell, in this backwater of
civilization—*

*Shitfire, Professor!* Lydy broke into the current of words. *Be
damned iffen I know what it is you're talking about. What I
asked is how come you to be in jail?*

*Aah. You prefer a concise account. Very well. It appears that
I am being held for carnal knowledge of a minor.* The Professor
straightened his cravat. *Or breach of promise. The father of the
damsel in question has not yet made up his applejack-befuddled
mind.*

Lydy dragged the rough homespun of his shirtsleeve across his
eyes. *Law, Professor, looks like hit's the love of woman that's
overthrowed the both of us. Hit's a fearsome, powerful thing, that
kind of love is. I've studied on hit but be damned iffen I can make
it out.*

The young man looked down at his big rough hands and
slowly turned them, palms up and then down. His face wore a
puzzled frown, as if the hands were strangers to him. After a
moment's study he wrapped his arms around himself to hide the
hands in his armpits. His voice trailed into a dreaming whisper.

*You know, some of the time hit seems like a hundred years ago
and other times I'd swear hit was only yesterday that I was back
at my uncle's place, way up there on Bear Tree Creek.*

Lydy leaned his head against the wall, once again fixing his
eyes on the little window. *What brung me here . . . I'd have to say
it started back there, back on this one day when I was huntin a*

little spotted heifer what had come in season and had took a notion to travel. Well sir, I followed her trace clear to the top of Old
Baldy. When at last the heifer come into view, I seen that she
had found what she was atter. Hit was a red and white bull what
I hadn't never seed before and he was a-ridin her like one thing.
I seen there weren't no way of turnin her back down the mountain till they was done, so I set down there in the grass to wait.

Hit was in the spring of last year—eighteen and fifty-nine—
and the day was one of them bright sparkly ones with all the
world looking like hit had been washed clean. Old Baldy's the
highest peak on Bear Tree and with the sky so close hit seemed to
me like hit wouldn't be no trouble atall to reach out and maybe
grab God's shirttail.

The bull got done at last but I just set there, thinkin how I
had spent all of my life down in the holler, a-clearin my uncle's
ground, bustin his wood, and choppin his corn, with my eyes
looking at the dirt till it grew too dark to see. Then hit would be
back to my pallet in the loft and up before first light to begin all
over again.

Off in the far distance I could see the mountain humps
a-stretchin out in blue rows till they kindly melted into the sky.
And then it come to me as how I'd like to travel beyond them
mountains someday, maybe see the great ocean that my kin had
crossed, back when they first come to this land. I stared off into
that blue far-away and, like I had heard the preacher say one
time, my spirit took wing.

The young man was on his feet now, still gazing up at the
window and the darkening sky beyond. And then, all to once,
there's my uncle, a-standin over me afore ever I heared his step.
He had come lookin fer the heifer too and when he saw her and
the bull croppin grass and me just a-settin there not doin nothing,
why he commenced to whup on me with his ole walkin stick.
Called me a worthless, loaferin woods-colt and said though he'd

kept me on like his sister had begged on her deathbed, now I had plagued him a time too many. I thought to fight him but he was a stout, full-growed man and I feared I'd be beaten bad.

I left him there, a-shoutin vile curses at me whilst I lit out down the mountain. Weren't none of the others to the house, so I took the blanket offen my pallet and rolled my good shirt in hit, along with my few other bits of plunder. I helped myself to corn-bread from the safe and set out down the creek.

Hit was late evening when I come to the river and the ol' feller with the ferry was just puttin off fer a man and a mule what was waitin on the far bank. I didn't have no money but the ol' feller agreed to put me across iffen I did the haulin.

I'll ride like a gentleman for once, says he, and set hisself upon an empty nail keg. That ol' feller grinned like a fool whilst I hauled his flat-bottom raft across the fast-runnin waters of the French Broad. Hit was a stout rope he had strung over the water and hard though my hands were with the use of the axe and hoe, by the time the far shore was nigh, I had raised me a blister or two.

But I paid no mind to the burnin of my hands for there on the slope above the turnpike was the place I'd been making for—the inn on the Drovers' Road. I looked up at that fine big place with its porches and galleries and its two stone chimbleys reaching up so tall and hit seemed to me that Gudger's Stand had been a-waitin fer me all the years of my life.

# Chapter 4

## *Snowbound*
### Sunday, December 3

Elizabeth wakened slowly in the half-light of early morning. Through slitted lids she could see her breath making little puffs in the frigid air, and she dragged the heavy comforter higher, temporarily dislodging the small dog James from his nest at her feet. Beside her she could feel the long, warm curve of Phillip's back and hear his regular breathing. Keeping the covers well over her shoulders, she lifted her head from the pillows to see what sort of day the weather gods had arranged.

Beyond the big east-facing windows was a world stripped of form or color. A pearly white void that, as her eyes began to focus, became a moving curtain of thick, blowing flakes. She raised her head higher, turning to look at the clock on the chest just beyond Phillip's pillow.

*Seven-fifty and hardly light. I know the sun's cleared the mountains by now, but there's not even a smudge of brightness showing. It's like a scene from* Doctor Zhivago.

Briefly she debated getting up, building a fire, starting breakfast. Molly and Ursa were still asleep on their denim-covered dog beds; James, reestablished in a fold of the soft comforter, had begun to snore softly. *Maybe another fifteen minutes,* she decided.

Sliding back into the warmth of the bed, she turned on

her side and once again pulled the comforter over her ears. Those few moments of sitting up had chilled her and she inched nearer to Phillip and the radiant heat of his comforting bulk. The mattress quivered as the heat source rolled over and reached out to pull her closer to him.

"It's still pretty damn cold out there, Lizabeth. Even if it clears, with this heavy cloud cover I don't think the snow's going to melt any time soon. I know you were planning to go in and see about Miss Barrett, but you might want to wait till tomorrow."

Elizabeth looked up from the stack of Christmas cards and envelopes on the table before her. There was a series of thumps as Phillip deposited a load of logs into the wood rack beside the fireplace. The rough bark of some of the logs still held snow deep in its crevices, and Phillip's navy watch cap was dusted with white that quickly melted as he leaned down to add more wood to the fire.

"Maybe I can go in after lunch." She cast a dubious glance out the dining room window at the snow-covered scene. "The plows and the salt trucks'll be out and the roads should be clear by then."

Nodding toward the phone on the table just beyond the cards, she continued. "I called the hospital again to ask about Nola and to find out about visiting hours. They—"

As if activated by her glance, the telephone rang. The male voice at the other end was unfamiliar—an unctuous, self-assured tone with only a hint of the mountain twang to betray the speaker's origin.

"Mrs. Goodweather? This is Payne Morton. I pastor the church in Dewell Hill and I'm making some calls on behalf of Nola Barrett's niece, Tracy—"

A cold dread began to gnaw at Elizabeth and she broke in. "Nola . . . is she . . . ? She's not . . . ?"

"Praise God, Sister Nola is awake and the doctor seems

confident that her physical recovery will be speedy. In fact, the hospital plans to discharge her tomorrow."

"That's wonderful! I—"

"Ah yes, the Lord was watching over her." The caller paused, sighed, and then went on, his voice slightly lower. "Sadly, however, our poor sister's mind is still wandering and confused and it's obvious she'll require special care. Her niece is making arrangements and she's given me a list of her aunt's friends who might be concerned. Poor Miss Nola, I'm afraid that her mind was badly disturbed to do such a thing. Terrible, terrible..."

The resonant tones trailed off in an incoherent mutter, followed by a vigorous throat-clearing. "But I'm forgetting the purpose of my call. Tracy asked if I would inform her aunt's friends that Miss Nola is being moved to the Layton Facility just outside Ransom. If you were thinking of a visit, Tracy feels that it would be best to wait till her aunt is settled in. Maybe midweek."

The oily flow of words continued as Pastor Morton explained that he had three more calls to make. "And our service begins in less than an hour." He paused, meaningfully, it seemed to Elizabeth. "Perhaps I should apologize for interrupting your own Sabbath preparations, Mrs. Goodweather?"

When Elizabeth didn't respond, the pastor segued with practiced ease into an invitation. "Of course, if you don't have a church home of your own, let me just say that Beulah Bethel is always happy to welcome in our un-churched neighbors...."


"I don't understand, Phillip. Where'd this niece come from? Nola never mentioned any relatives."

Phillip, seated at the other end of the dining table, was absorbed in sharpening her motley assortment of kitchen knives. It was a job he seemed to relish, approaching each blade with the reverence a samurai might accord a fine sword. He had bought an elegant series of ever-finer whet-stones and a special oil of some sort so that he could bring each edge to near-perfection. The slight whispering grind of metal against stone had come to be a familiar and comforting sound.

*We're like an old married couple with these routines: Sunday afternoon—knife sharpening or some little repair job or grading papers for him, bills and correspondence for me, and the local NPR station for both of us.*

Phillip didn't look up as he maintained a steady circular movement of the battered old chef's knife against the wet surface of a grayish-white stone.

"You just met Nola Barrett a few months ago, right? Maybe she hadn't gotten around to filling you in on all her family. I know you've been spending a lot of time with her recently but—"

"But that's just it. I was helping with her research about the county. A lot of what we talked about was her family and its ties to Gudger's Stand. I know she believed that she was the old man's only heir and that it would be her decision alone as to what would happen to the property."

"Did the old man leave a will, do you think?" Tiny ceaseless circles and still he didn't look up.

"I don't know for sure. The last time I went to visit Nola, she told me she had come to a decision about what to do with the stand and the property. But she said there were some papers that she needed to find first. I assumed she meant the missing will Sallie Kate mentioned."

"Nola took care of that nasty old coot for years," Sallie Kate had said. "She says he made a will namin' her as his heir. And she's paid the taxes on the place ever since he died. But the will's never turned up and the title's not clear. I don't know why she hasn't gotten things straightened out before this; I do know she hates the place and hasn't set foot in it since she found the old man dead one mornin'. Of

course, it's only just in the past few years that there's been
all this interest in the property. As long as the taxes got
paid, the county was content just to leave the whole mess
unresolved."

The persistent grind of blade on whetstone ceased.
Phillip looked up, his face somber. "How did Miss Barrett
seem when you saw her—whenever it was you last went
over there?"

"It was the day before Thanksgiving—not quite two
weeks ago. I was taking her some pumpkin bread. And she
was perfectly *fine*—as rational and in control as...as...
anyone."

Suddenly restless, Elizabeth pulled her address book
and the heap of envelopes to her. "If I hadn't been there to
see it happen, I never would have believed it—that elegant,
intelligent woman turned into a suicidal dementia case.
What the *hell* could have caused such a sudden change?"


The clouds had lifted by late afternoon but the teak table on
the deck beneath the dining room windows still bore a thick
mantling of clean snow, untouched but for the spiky embroidery of sharp bird tracks circling its icy perimeter.
Elizabeth watched the juncos and sparrows jostling for
space at the nearby feeder, then gazed at the wintry landscape beyond, struggling with her Christmas letter to her
younger sister Gloria.

*Dear Glory,*

That was the easy part. Everything else required diplo-
matic finesse—Ben must be mentioned without dwelling
on the fact that Gloria's only child had rejected his mother's
way of life in favor of managing Elizabeth's small farm....
No need to talk about the farm...Gloria's lack of interest
in the growing and marketing of herbs and edible flowers
was equaled only by Elizabeth's lack of appreciation for her
sister's ruling passions: designer clothing and pricy resorts

with esoteric beauty treatments. *And do I mention—god, what's the current husband's name anyway? Ben said they were separated . . . maybe I'll just avoid that topic.*

Phillip. Would she avoid that topic too? Elizabeth's pen spiraled a doodle on the notepaper just below the salutation.

For over a year now, Phillip Hawkins had been—*what? My boyfriend? No, I don't think so. I'm a little past the boyfriend stage. Lover? Well, yes, but I wouldn't exactly be comfortable introducing him that way. Significant other? Yuck. What's the word for a man I love, a man I share my bed with—on weekends and holidays?*

Phillip had served in the Navy with Sam Goodweather during the Vietnam War. Though the two had remained in touch, it wasn't until Sam's untimely death *six years ago, seven years on the twenty-first* that Elizabeth had met the man her husband had called his best friend.

The bleak memorial service had been the scene of her first encounter with the burly police detective from Beaufort—*Bow-furt, not Bew-furt*—on the North Carolina coast. Phillip had made the long drive across the wearisome breadth of the state just to attend the brief ceremony. He had introduced himself, one of many during that interminable day, had offered choked condolences, and had disappeared immediately after the service. Elizabeth, deep in her grief, had thought no more about him. Then, two years ago, ex-detective Phillip Hawkins had called to say that he had just moved to Asheville and would like her advice about a place to live.

*And I tried my best to brush him off.*

She looked into the living room where Phillip, deeply immersed in a paperback mystery, sprawled on the sofa in front of the fire, feet propped up on the old chest that served as a coffee table. James was pressed against his side, looking more than ever like a plump sausage that had suddenly sprouted short little legs and a pointed nose. Phillip turned a page; reached down to rub behind the little dog's ears; then looked up, his deep brown eyes meeting hers, his face breaking into an answering smile.

"What?"

"Nothing—just trying to write my yearly letter to my sister."

With a deep sigh, she crumpled up the paper before her, now completely covered with spirals, took a clean sheet of stationery, and began again.

*Dear Glory,*

*We're enjoying a beautiful early snow—just right for getting into the holiday spirit. Ben's thrilled—he and Amanda have been sledding every chance they get.*

Amanda Lucas—the quietly enigmatic daughter of Gloria's best friend. Over a year ago Ben had left the farm to spend time with his mother in Florida—and to recover from an unhappy entanglement. During the three months he had been there, Gloria had done her best to entice him to stay, producing one dazzling beauty after another— the cream of the debutante crowd—for his inspection. Judging from Gloria's remarks in an almost hourlong, late night phone call back in January, Ben, like a picky young pasha faced with a substandard lot of concubines, had rejected not only Ashley and Avery, but Madison, Meredith, Morrison, and Sidney as well, informing his mother that he wasn't interested in airheads who spent more on shoes than books.

"Lizzy, you don't think he's...well, you know...*gay?* Now don't jump all over me; I don't have anything against gay people. I've told you how I just adore Zachary who does my hair, but still..."

And then, not a week later, a second call from an indignant Gloria. "Well, Lizzy, I hope you're happy. Ben's just told me that he's leaving this weekend to go back to your place. I swear I don't see the attraction. He says he's bored down here. *Bored!* Heaven knows, I've done my best to make sure he's met the right people ... Woody—you remember Haywood Carlton, don't you? He was in your graduating class—well, Woody has even offered to take Ben on as a trainee at his brokerage firm—in *spite* of the fact that Ben's degree is only in philosophy, not business. *Philosophy!"* Somehow Gloria had managed to make the word sound obscene. "But, oh no, Ben wants to go back and play farmer and drive a tractor and utterly *waste* his life. Well, I give up. If he'd rather spend his time with illiterate hillbillies and Mexican laborers and ... and dirty *hippies* instead of really *nice* people from good families..."

Ben had returned to Full Circle Farm, happy to be back in the mountains and his little cabin just a stone's throw from Elizabeth's house. He had embarked on an unprecedented flurry of cleaning and refurbishing that had been explained when, a few weeks later, a fresh-faced young woman in hiking boots had arrived—Amanda.

"I met her when I was down in Tampa," Ben had explained one morning over coffee. "She was the only person down there I could actually have a conversation with. Anyway, Amanda's really interested in finding out more about the mountains and this area and she was fascinated by the idea of the herb and flower farm. She asked about an internship and I told her I thought we could work something out."

Elizabeth smiled. *It's a different generation. She just moved in with Ben and that was it. Unlike me with Phillip—two years of telling myself I didn't want to get involved with anyone.*

She looked back at the letter and the vast expanse of virgin paper. Her pen began to move again.

> *You know, Glory, Amanda's been really good for Ben; he's happier than I've ever seen him. And she's developing a nice little business of her own: designing, planting, and maintaining gardens—especially herb gardens.*

*She was busy all during the season—so many of the summer residents in the area want more garden than they're actually able or willing to maintain. Anyway, she's got plenty of customers.*

*My girls are fine—Rosemary will be home as soon as Chapel Hill goes on Christmas break. She loves the classes she's teaching—and she's found an agent for that novel she's been incubating for ages. Keep your fingers crossed for her.*

*Laurel's still in Asheville—bartending and making art. Her latest series of paintings are oils—lovely large landscapes that have gotten some awards and, even better, are beginning to attract buyers. The paintings are almost traditional but as you look at them you realize there's a different sensibility at work—I don't know how to explain it; they're a little unsettling, but really good.*

*Everything is much the same with me—yes, Phillip and I continue to be "an item," as you put it. He's a good man, Glory—funny, kind, undemanding. He's still teaching criminal justice classes at the community college in Asheville. I hope someday you'll make up your mind to come visit and meet him.*

Elizabeth paused and stared out the window at the snow-covered peaks of the Blue Ridge Mountains far to the east. It was late afternoon and though Full Circle Farm and the river valley below were in shadow, those distant peaks were gilded golden-pink with the last rays of the sun, just now beginning its plunge behind Pinnacle Mountain.

*This is the first time Phillip will be here at Christmas—be part of all the family carrying-on. I wonder how he'll like it.*

For the past two years, as soon as AB Tech had let out for

winter break, Phillip Hawkins had returned with his daughter Janie, a sometime student at UNCA, to the Carolina coast, where his son was in grad school. "I rent a little cottage on the beach for a week and the kids stay with me part of the time. Seth and I do some fishing and Janie runs around catching up with all her friends from high school. They have Christmas dinner with their mom and her husband. . . ."

But this year, both Seth and Janie were in Australia: Seth working with a research team studying the Great Barrier Reef, and Janie doing a semester abroad *in whatever major she's switched to now. I hope he won't miss his trip to the beach. I wonder if—*

A bark at the front door broke into Elizabeth's reverie. She stared blankly at the unfinished letter before her, then scrawled a few more lines, ending with a quick *Merry Christmas and Happy New Year with love from Elizabeth*, folded the letter, and shoved it into the waiting envelope.

She started for the entryway but Phillip was already there, pulling open the blue-painted front door to admit a blast of frosty air along with Molly and Ursa, both wagging joyously and shaking the dusting of flakes from their backs. Bits of snow traced their progress across the terracotta tile of the mudroom and on to the wide oak planks of the living room. Ursa was particularly charming, sporting small globlets of ice dangling from the feathery black fur on her legs. The little ice clumps were beginning to melt and drip in the warmth of the room, and the big dog stopped, waiting patiently for the towel that Elizabeth was already going to fetch. As usual, Molly's sleek red coat had remained pristine. The elegant hound headed at once for the hearthrug, where she composed herself to attend to cleaning the last evidences of the out-of-doors from her paws.

The telephone rang again just as Elizabeth knelt to deal with Ursa's wet fur. Phillip picked up the instrument and handed it to her. "You get it, Lizabeth. I'll take over with the Abominable Snowbear here."

"Hey there, honey. I'm not *interruptin'* anything, am I?" Sallie Kate's chuckle was rich with lewd suggestion. "A nice snowy evening like this . . . a cozy fire . . . a good-lookin' guy like Phillip, even if he is mostly bald . . . Lordy, I wish Harley hadn't gone out of town this weekend . . . a snow like this always makes me feel romantic."

Elizabeth grinned. "I think I can spare you a minute or two. So, what's up with the real estate queen of Marshall County?"

"*Empress,* honey, I'm goin' to be the real estate *empress*— if nothing don't happen, as we say around here!"

# Chapter 5

## *The Carrion Crow*
### Sunday, December 3, and Monday, December 4

Phillip finished toweling Ursa and swiped at the wet tracks for good measure. He looked across the room at Elizabeth, seated once more at the dining table and listening intently to the voice at the other end of the line. Apparently Sallie Kate was in full flow; a nod and a brief "uh-humm" now and then seemed to be all that was required of Elizabeth. Her face, which had blossomed into a wide smile at the beginning of the conversation, had grown troubled, and her strong dark eyebrows were drawn into a small frown.

Phillip put another log on the fire, found his book, and settled back on the sofa. Covertly he studied her—this woman in his life. "And a fine figger of a woman," his aunt Omie had pronounced. "No nonsense to her and not afraid to turn her hand to anything a-tall, I'll wager."

*Almost too true,* he thought. *Give her a problem and she won't let go of it.*

Elizabeth seemed to feel his gaze and turned her deep blue eyes on him. The frown softened and she winked.

As happened often these days, he was suddenly bathed in a warm glow of immense and, it seemed to him, undeserved happiness—a glow that was instantly quenched by an icy chill that whispered of the fragility of life and love.

"Okay, Sallie Kate." Elizabeth was standing now and fidgeting as if ready to end the call. "I'll go over there tomorrow morning, if we don't have a lot more snow." She glanced out the window where the light was rapidly fading. "The snow's quit and it's clear as far as I can see . . . Okay, ten o'clock, unless I hear otherwise."

She put the telephone down and came to sit beside him. Phillip laid his book aside and put his arm around her. He drew her closer, feeling the hidden strength of her tall, firm body.

"Problem?" He breathed in the clean, slightly herbal smell—shampoo?—that seemed to be an integral part of her. "You were frowning. What does Sallie Kate want you to do?"

Elizabeth leaned against him and stared into the fire. "Nola Barrett's niece—Tracy—has been in touch with Sallie Kate. Evidently Tracy has been told that Nola's going to require long-term care because of her mental condition. So Tracy's hoping she can sell Nola's house in Dewell Hill quickly to provide some ready cash until the ownership of the property at Gudger's Stand gets sorted out. Decent care is horrendously expensive and—"

"Wait a minute—how can this niece do all that without a power of attorney or—"

"The niece says she *has* a power of attorney. Sallie Kate'll check it out tomorrow before going any further, but she seems to think the woman's legitimate. She's already fantasizing about the fat commission from the sale of the stand property. Anyway, Sallie Kate said that the niece was starting to go through Miss Barrett's things and—"

She broke off and he could feel her stiffen as she fought to hold back the tears so rarely allowed to fall.

"I just can't believe it, Phillip. Three weeks ago Nola and I were talking about the novel she was working on. Her mind was sharp; her organization and her memory were phenomenal. And now...now *that* Nola's gone! It's almost worse than if she'd died."

She pulled free of his arm and stood, her face turned away. "I need to go start supper."

He gave her a few minutes alone in the kitchen. There was the sound of running water, a paper towel being ripped from the roll, a discreet nose-blowing. When he heard the clank of the iron skillet on the stovetop and the opening of the refrigerator door, Phillip nudged James from his lap and went to join her.

Olive oil was heating in the black iron skillet and Elizabeth, her eyes dry but slightly reddened, was chopping onions with manic determination. She looked up and smiled.

"I thought I'd do some shrimp and pasta—quick and easy. And I never answered your question, did I?" She swept the onion into the skillet and began to break cloves off a head of garlic. "What Sallie Kate wants me to do is to go see Nola's niece tomorrow. Evidently this Tracy knows that I was interested in Nola's quilts—she wants to find out where to sell them and what sort of prices to ask."

In rapid succession six cloves of garlic were minced on the scarred cutting board and added to the sautéing onions.

"I hate it, Phillip. It's like crows picking over a carcass. But in this case..." He watched as Elizabeth turned her attention to a bulbous section of gingerroot, quickly and carefully peeling away pale brown skin from the knobby surface. An enticing smell wafted through the kitchen as she cut off chunks, fitted them into a garlic press, and squeezed the pulp into the pan. "...in this case, the carcass is still alive."

Phillip took wineglasses from the Hoosier cabinet and uncorked the bottle of red wine that waited there on the cabinet's pull-out metal shelf. He filled the glasses, handed one to Elizabeth, then seated himself on the cushioned bench in the corner of the kitchen. *Put there so that people can lend moral support to the cook—without getting in her way,* Elizabeth had told him.

"Maybe you can suggest to the niece that she's moving a little too quickly—that her aunt may recover." He found himself starting to run his free hand over his smooth bald scalp—a gesture Elizabeth had teased him about more than once. *I can always tell when you're worried: up comes that hand*—and revised the movement to a quick tug at his earlobe. "Who knows, this may be a passing . . . aberration."

She didn't seem to hear him as she gave the contents of the frying pan a savage stir, reduced the heat, and moved on to the salad preparation, the untasted glass of wine on the counter before her. A few scallions were washed free of grit, shaken dry, and slapped down on the chopping block. Over the staccato tap of the knife, he could hear her saying to herself, "It's that damn house—Nola said it was evil. What was it she told me? It was like a line from that old song— 'It's been the downfall of many poor girls . . .' or something like that. Nola hated that awful place—why would she go *there?*"

*Poor Phillip! What abject nonsense I was thinking and talking last night!*

The menacing clouds and dreary atmosphere of the day before had been replaced by a clear blue sky. Playful sunlight sparkled on the river and winked from the melting snow.

As Elizabeth drove across the bridge at Gudger's Stand, she looked up at the empty house that had always appeared so ominous. Suddenly it seemed different—innocuous, even helpless—a pathetic, moldering hulk in need of vigorous refurbishment.

*Good god! There I was going on to Phillip about it being an evil place. Was I channeling Stephen King or what? It's just a house, for heaven's sake. It's nothing to do with what happened to*

*Nola. There must be some physiological explanation—a brain tumor or... I don't know, maybe an aneurism or something. Surely they'll do some testing. And then they'll find what's wrong and fix it. This niece or whatever she is can't just write Nola off like that.*

A feeling of optimism filled her and she gave a friendly wave to the grizzled old man who was just emerging from a derelict brick building at the side of the road. He jerked his head back in response and continued on with setting out dishes of food for the cats that were pouring out of their hiding places in several junk cars to cluster around his rubber boots. As she passed, Elizabeth smiled to see one particularly bold calico leap onto the man's shoulder as he leaned down to place a dish on the cracked pavement.

Smoke was rising from the chimney of Nola's little stone cottage and a generic-looking car—white, with rental plates— was pulled up beside the back porch. Elizabeth made her careful way along the stepping-stones, wet with melted snow, to the front porch. Just as she raised her hand to knock, the door flew open.

Divested of her heavy jacket, the young woman Elizabeth had last seen climbing into the ambulance with Nola Barrett was painfully thin. Tight black jeans and an acid green sweater revealed an almost skeletal body while lank hennaed hair pulled back in a short ponytail accentuated the bony planes of the woman's pallid face. At the end of her sharp, reddened nose quivered a small, clear bead of moisture. Swiping a crumpled tissue at the emerging drop, the young woman motioned Elizabeth in with a jerk of her head.

"Ms. Goodweather? Tracy Barrett. Come on in; it's freezing out there. Excuse the mess. We're trying to decide what to do with all this junk." She nodded toward the many cardboard boxes piled high with books. From the back of the house came the sound of heavy furniture scraping across the floor.

Fighting back a feeling of intense dislike for this *person* who was acting so quickly to disassemble what was left of Nola Barrett, Elizabeth drew a deep breath.

"It's nice to meet you, Tracy. What can you tell me about Nola? Mr. . . . or I guess it's *Reverend* Morton called and said that she was being moved to—"

"The Layton Facility. Just outside Ransom." The thin young woman's face was impassive as she moved toward a stack of quilts resting on the table where Nola Barrett's laptop had been.

"I was wondering . . . Reverend Morton told me that Nola's not badly hurt, but what about her mental state? How do the doctors explain—"

"The old lady's completely bugshit. Out to lunch and not likely to come back." The speaker loomed in the kitchen door, his massive shoulders almost as wide as the opening. "Trace, what d'you want me to do with all that shit in the cabinets?"

"Just leave it till I can look at it, Stone." A look of annoyance flashed across the thin face and was replaced by a carefully calibrated smile. "My boyfriend's helping me with the heavy stuff. Stone, this is the lady who knows about quilts—Aunt Nola's friend Ms. Goodweather."

*Stone? Can that be his real name? Like Rocky? Good grief, this is one big boy!* Elizabeth tried not to stare at the young man who seemed be built along the lines of a midsized truck.

"Nice to meet you—" she began, but Stone merely glanced at her and turned back toward the kitchen with a bob of his shaven head and an inarticulate mumble that might have been an acknowledgment of her greeting. The sound of heavy objects being scraped across the floor resumed.

"We're trying to get this place cleared out so it can be

sold or rented. And we've got to get back to Raleigh by Thursday night, so we don't have much time." Tracy reached for the top quilt—a green and red pattern appliquéd on a white background. "Is this one worth anything?"

The young woman's impatience was obvious, as was her lack of interest in the quilts. *I could tell her anything—offer her a hundred dollars for the lot of them and she'd probably jump at it,* Elizabeth thought, sorely tempted by the beautiful heirlooms that Nola had preserved so lovingly. *But, as Nixon said, that would be wrong. Oh hell.*

"Well, you need to understand I'm not an expert. But I do know a little about old quilts. This one's a traditional Pomegranate pattern, probably from the 1880s, give or take twenty years. The condition is good . . . some fading in the green fabrics—what they call fugitive dyes and a little yellowing of the unbleached muslin. But—"

"If I took it to a flea market, what kind of price should I put on it? That's all I need to know."

Shocked at the suggestion, Elizabeth was quick to insist, "Oh, no, don't take it to a flea market. You wouldn't get near what it's worth. A few years ago I saw a similar one priced over a thousand dollars in a fancy antique shop in Asheville. But I have no idea what a dealer would pay you—maybe half that. And fashions change—quilts may not be as collectible now as they were."

Elizabeth bent down to study the red appliquéd circles and the faded green crescents that had been delicately stitched onto a creamy white background. With a careful finger she traced the tiny quilting stitches that crisscrossed the fabric.

"Such a lot of work. You know, your aunt—have I got that right?—called this one the Lyda quilt." *My great-grandmother made that one,* Nola had said. "But you probably know that—it being your family too."

The young woman, evidently aware of the unspoken challenge in Elizabeth's words, fixed her with a cool gray stare. "Nola was my mother's sister—but we haven't been close in a long time. If she ever showed me these quilts, I've forgotten."

The icy gaze, Nola Barrett's eyes looking out of a different, younger face, was unsettling. Still, Elizabeth persisted. "Are you sure you want to part with family heirlooms like these? They're undoubtedly worth something to a quilt collector but—"

The younger woman brushed Elizabeth's words aside and unfolded a second quilt. "I'm not sentimental about family stuff anymore. Heirlooms or not, if they're worth a buck or two, they're going to be sold. Do you have any idea how much long-term care for that crazy old woman is likely to cost? If only she could have managed to find the old man's will."

Elizabeth stood in the quiet of her empty house. Behind the leafless trees at the far left of the eastern horizon, the full moon was rising with slow majesty, its great disc looming startlingly large and almost transparent against the rose and lavender of the evening sky.

She had opened her mouth to call Phillip to come look at the moon; then she remembered—Phillip, as was his custom on weeknights, was at his house in Weaverville. *Closer to AB Tech,* he had explained, *and in winter there's less chance I'll have trouble with snow on the roads.*

This was undoubtedly true, but Elizabeth suspected that the chief reason Phillip maintained the little rented bungalow was because some months ago she had declined his proposal of marriage. Their growing closeness had suffered briefly from her refusal.

*You know I love you, Phillip,* she had said. *Will a few words and a license make any difference to the way we feel about each other?*

He had not pressed the issue but had withdrawn briefly,

no longer routinely spending weekends and holidays with her. Gradually, however, and much to her relief, the part-time relationship had resumed. *Thank god, he didn't just bow out altogether. I love him and want him in my life—I just don't see why we need to be married. But I wish he were here to see this moonrise.*

She stood staring out the window, watching the huge pale circle float above the treetops. As the sky darkened, the shadowy globe seemed to shrink and solidify till it was the familiar yellow moon, soaring high above the dark mountain range.

A feeling of vast loneliness swamped her—Molly and Ursa were gone, tempted, no doubt, by the moonlight to prowl the woods till dawn, and James was fast asleep on his wintertime bed in a snug corner of her closet.

And Ben, who for the past few years had been in and out of her house several times a day, was now preoccupied with his new love. *And that's as it should be. Amanda's ideal for him and they're turning his cabin into a real home.* Briefly she thought of calling over to invite the pair to share her dinner, then remembered: *it's the full moon, you idiot, this is the night they were going for that special raft trip with the crew from River Runners—wet suits and all. And Phillip's in Weaverville. Well, hell.*

As she scrambled a few eggs for a quick supper, her mind turned restlessly to Nola Barrett. *She must have been lonely too, living alone in that little cottage for all these years, with just her books for company.*

"So, what was the niece like? And what did you find out about your friend's condition?"

Elizabeth was stretched out on the sofa, Nola Barrett's laptop resting on a pillow in front of her, the telephone cradled to her ear. The feeling of desolation brought on by the rising moon had dissipated with her supper and vanished entirely when Phillip called. *Even if he insists on staying in Weaverville during the week, at least we can talk every night.*

She became aware that Phillip was repeating his question and hurried to answer him. "Apparently there's been no change in Nola's mental condition. She's conscious but not . . . I guess *lucid*'s the word I want. Tracy—that's the niece—said that Nola was just babbling most of the time, didn't know where she was or what had happened. Anyway, I'm going to go see her on Wednesday. Tracy said that the facility requested that Nola be given a few days to, quote, 'settle in' before anyone other than family visited."

She sighed unhappily and Phillip's warm, reassuring voice filled her ear. "Lizabeth, maybe your friend will improve . . . they're probably running tests and looking for some organic cause for this—"

"I don't know, Phillip. The niece is in such a hurry. She says the doctor can't explain the cause of Nola's sudden dementia, if that's what it is, and doesn't think there's likely to be any improvement. Tracy and her boyfriend are hell-bent on getting Nola's stuff packed up so that the cottage can be rented or sold."

"Seems like they could wait a while."

"Which is what I hinted, but evidently they're looking at long-term care for Nola and they need the money now. They're in such a rush that I'm afraid they're tossing out important stuff."

Elizabeth allowed herself a grim smile as she ran her hands over the lid of the little laptop. She had asked Tracy what she planned to do with Nola's notes and partially completed novel.

"Well, it's not going to get written now, is it?" had been the brusque response. "Stone looked at that laptop of hers and he says it's worthless—completely outdated. I told him to take it across to the garbage bins along with that stack of paper she'd scribbled on."

Elizabeth patted the computer again and let her thumb

riffle the sheaf of paper beside it, a mass of pages covered with notes in Nola Barrett's precise, minuscule script.

"I did manage to salvage a few important things. I offered to buy some of the books, mainly ones about the county, and I convinced Tracy to let me bring the quilts here so that I could go over them and see if they need mending." *And when I picked up the pile of quilts and saw Nola's laptop and her notes were underneath them . . .*

There had been a small struggle with her conscience, but Elizabeth's determination to hold on to something of her friend had won. She had asked for a box or garbage bag to put the stack of quilts into, and when Tracy went to the kitchen in search of something suitable, Elizabeth had hastily slipped the laptop and notes between the folds of one of the quilts. *They were going to toss it anyway,* she argued, overcoming the small still voice that nagged in vain. *And I was honest about the quilts.*

# Chapter 6

# *In Hell*

## Wednesday, December 6

Noise. There was always noise. Rattle, clang, clank, loud meaningless voices, shrill mirthless laughter, hoarse whispers. And always the hopeless sound of someone crying. There was no night—night with its blessed concealing darkness and the silence that she had once wrapped herself in like a familiar garment. There was always light. There was always noise. The overheated air smothered her and the dark odor of despair clung to everything.

*I am in hell,* thought Nola Barrett. *I am in hell for my sins.*

Hands plucked at her, pulling at her nightgown. Metal rings slid across a rod. "Nola honey, company's coming today. You want to be a clean and pretty young lady, now don't you? We got to wash you up good."

The thin cotton nightgown was twitched away and there was a spatter of liquid and a sloshing sound. The moonlike face of the attendant grimaced at her and wheezed a smoky laugh. "Like I always say, first we wash down as far as possible..."

A rough cloth, cold and wet, scrubbed at her face, her breasts, her belly. She tried to protest but her tongue, thick with the bewitchment of hell, turned the words into a garble of meaningless sound.

"And then we wash *up* as far as possible."

Nola flapped futile hands at the invasive washcloth that swabbed her feet, then worked its way up her trembling and jerking legs.

"And *then*... we wash *possible!*" The braying voice was loud in her ears and the foul breath of her tormentor made her gag as the relentless hands thrust the wet rag into her most private parts.

They had tied her into the wheelchair, for her own good, they said, and set her in front of a television where mindless people did mindless things. The colors whirled and blurred as her eyes filled with tears.

*I should have died... I wanted to die... I deserved to die...*

Abandoning the hopeless litany of guilt, Nola Barrett concentrated on turning her head to look at the door. The bewitchment of her tongue seemed to extend to the rest of her body: she could *think* an action, but movement, it seemed, was restricted to creaking, shaking slow-motion. As her eyes passed from the flickering screen, over the built-in cupboards and sink, past the open door of the bathroom and so to the second bed with its huddled and silent occupant, there was time to study it all.

Even without her glasses—"You won't be needing these, now will you, sweetheart?"—even though shapes blurred and quivered, the limits of her world were clear.

> *O there's none; no no no there's none*
> *Be beginning to despair, to despair,*
> *Despair, despair, despair, despair.*

Nola Barrett's head slumped forward as the leaden echo of the poem learned in her youth filled her consciousness, drowning out the chatter of the television and the endless, eternal noise of the nursing home.

"No one's there—that Tracy and what's-his-name left a little while ago, hauling off a load of Nola's things. I heard
them saying they'd have to make one more trip at least."

Elizabeth turned from Nola Barrett's front door to see a
pleasant-looking woman pulling a wheeled bin toward the
garbage collection site just a few steps across the road.
Sharp blue eyes under a red knit hat studied Elizabeth.
"You must be the new friend Nola told me about. I've seen
your car here quite a few times. It was here Monday, so I
guess you know what happened. Were you looking for that
niece of hers?"

"Yes, I was." Elizabeth left the porch and started back
toward her car. "I was going to visit Nola at the Layton
Facility, and I thought I'd see if there was anything I could
take to her. That white car was still parked behind the
house, so I thought..."

The other woman abandoned her garbage bin on the
side of the road and came across, smiling and obviously
ready to chat.

"Those two borrowed a truck from somewhere. If they
were taking Nola's things in to one of the secondhand
places in Asheville, they won't be back for several hours—
probably eat lunch in there. It'll be two...say two-thirty
before they're back."

The gray-haired woman stuck out a gloved hand. "I'm
Lee Palatt. That's my place over there." She nodded
toward a house just beyond Nola's cottage. A glistening
white picket fence with an arched gateway surrounded a
white frame house set in a yard that, even in bleak
December, was obviously the creation of a dedicated gardener.

"It's good to meet you, Lee. I'm Elizabeth Goodweather.
I live—"

"I know; you have that herb farm on Ridley Branch.
Nola told me about you and back in the spring I read that
write-up in the paper about you and your wreaths. I kept

thinking I'd try to get over and look at your herb gardens, but I just moved here last year and all my energy's gone into fixing up the house and the yard."

Lee cocked her head to one side and her brow wrinkled. "Now, I wonder . . . what do *you* think about all this carrying on? I would have said that Nola was as sane and well adjusted as they come—this whole thing is just unbelievable. Of course, even though we're neighbors, I haven't seen much of Nola recently."

She flashed an engaging grin and brushed at her blue fleece jacket. A sprinkling of short pale hairs clung to the fabric, resisting her attempts to dislodge them. "I'm a cat person, as you might guess—four of 'em. And Nola's one of those folks who's funny about cats—cat phobia or something. She's never set foot in my house because of the kitties. And that house of hers is so tiny that I haven't felt right dropping in since her niece arrived."

"Nola seemed just fine when I last saw her." Elizabeth looked toward the little stone cottage, remembering the cozy living room piled with books and the quick wit and acute perceptions of the woman who had lived there. "But . . . something must have happened—"

Her new acquaintance gave a disgusted snort. "Phooey! I don't believe Nola would try to kill herself! That Tracy tried to tell me that Nola jumped from the roof of the old house down by the river. Do you believe that story?"

*A nice woman,* Elizabeth thought as she drove away, *if a bit nosy.* In the rearview mirror, she could see Nola's neighbor maneuvering the wheeled bin through her gate. Several cats twined about her legs, complicating the task.

*She never went to the collection center!* The realization spread a grin across Elizabeth's face. *The garbage bin was just an excuse to check me out—to see what I was doing and what I knew. I'll bet Lee Palatt knows everything that's going on in Dewell Hill, not unlike our own Miss Birdie on Ridley Branch. She doesn't seem to like Tracy—that much was obvious. And she sure had a lot to say.*

"Nola never mentioned a niece—never talked about any living family at all. Someone told me there was a sister over in Leicester, but I don't know if that sister's still alive. I suppose Tracy *could* be her niece..." She had frowned and fixed Elizabeth with a troubled gaze. "What I don't like is that Nola was just fine and then this alleged niece and her bald boyfriend come to visit and all of a sudden, Nola starts acting weird."

"How do you mean?" Elizabeth had asked, curious at the vehemence in the other woman's voice.

"You may well ask." Lee had held up her hand to tick off the reasons for her concern. "First of all, the very night those two arrived, I saw Nola, sitting out behind her house on the bench under the apple tree. It was bitter cold and sleeting a little, but Nola just sat there. It looked like she was crying and I started to go over and see what was wrong. I got my jacket and boots on and was walking through my backyard to the little gate between our properties. Just then Nola's back door opened and Tracy called out, 'You won't make things any better by getting pneumonia,' in just the *meanest* tone of voice, and Nola stood up real slow and went inside."

Lee had paused, remembering the scene, then had added in a troubled voice, "Nola's always been so straight and elegant in the way she moves, but that night she was walking like an old, old woman.

"*Two,* when I called Nola the next morning, Tracy told me she was sleeping in. Well, I'd seen Nola through the window at her laptop, not ten minutes earlier when I took my trash across. I'd waved but she hadn't looked up. And I'd seen that she was fully dressed, so how could she have been sleeping in? When I called again later, Nola answered but she sounded kind of *distracted* and said she couldn't talk just then."

A third finger had been thrust out. "And three, why *did* Nola slam the door on Pastor Morton the afternoon of that same day?"


It was a short trip to the Layton Facility, but there had been enough time to decide that the questions raised by Nola's neighbor probably all had some plausible, as well as innocuous, answer. *And if they don't, what can I do? Maybe once I see Nola, it'll all make some kind of sense.*

The one-story complex sprawled on a knoll just off the Ransom bypass, long narrow wings reaching out from the central entry area. A line of pine trees bordered the drive, imperfectly blocking the view of the convenience store and carwash below.

Leaving her jeep in the visitors' parking area, Elizabeth made her way past an inflatable snowman, sagging incongruously on the brown grass by the walkway. To her right she saw the identical windows of one long red brick wing of the building. A few winter-browned shrubs were planted haphazardly along the foundation, and here and there bird feeders provided entertainment for the residents behind those windows.

"Room 167—down the hall, right at the dining room, left at the nurses' station. It's on the left." The receptionist flashed a perfunctory smile and went back to her computer screen. Sitting in a wheelchair by a sparsely decorated artificial Christmas tree, a withered little woman in hair curlers and a pink robe cuddled a worn baby doll. She nodded several times and said something unintelligible. Elizabeth summoned a cheerful expression and stopped. "Hello. How are you?"

"My baby," was the slurred answer as the toothless old woman bent her head over the doll. "This is my baby."

Down the hall, past the dining room, a bingo game was in progress, led by a buoyant, youngish man whose cheerful patter was keeping most of the participants awake. The nurses' station was ahead, with a gaggle of pastel-garbed aides—some pushing carts of cleaning supplies, others assisting frail residents to totter or roll toward the dining room. There was a pervasive smell of disinfectant with an undertone of human waste, and Elizabeth began to feel very depressed.

A heavy man wearing a shiny black helmet lurched toward her, partially restrained by the aide who clung grimly to the belt of wide webbing that circled his jiggling girth. A growing stain of wetness ran down the left leg of his gray sweatpants.

Elizabeth stepped aside as the pair continued their stumbling progress down the narrow hallway. The heavy man's face was expressionless and his eyes were blank.

*Oh, my god, this is a dreadful place. Poor, poor Nola.* A memory of one of Hieronymus Bosch's paintings flashed through her mind. *This is Hell and these lost souls are here for the unforgivable sins of poverty, illness, or old age.*

The door of 167 was open. Under the number were two names: Ronda Mills and Nola Barrett. A beached whale of a woman occupied the bed just inside the door. Her eyes were shut, her mouth was open, and she was snoring loudly. The outline of the coverlet revealed that she was an amputee—half of her left leg was missing. Just beyond this bed the flimsy green privacy curtain was drawn. Two figures were silhouetted against it.

Elizabeth hesitated, not wanting to interrupt whatever was taking place, *visit? care procedure? Should I knock on the door?* A muttered conference seemed to be taking place on the other side of the curtain.

"This is bad, Payne. After all this time—"

A man's hand grasped the edge of the curtain and tugged it back, rings rattling on the metal rod. His dark eyes widened at the sight of Elizabeth. "Yes? Were you looking for someone?"

"I've come to see Nola."

The slumped figure in the wheelchair coughed as the second man lowered the paper cup he had been holding to her lips. He reached into the pocket of his suit jacket, withdrew a pristine white handkerchief, and carefully wiped Nola Barrett's trembling lips as she slowly turned her head to look at Elizabeth.

"I hardly recognized her. Her hair'd been cut—standard procedure for long-term care, the doctor said. And she didn't have her glasses on, or the makeup I'd always seen her in. Her face looked so naked. And her eyes . . . it was as if she was pleading with me, but when she tried to talk, it was just garble. Phillip, I hope I drop down dead before I find myself in a nursing home."

She stretched out luxuriously in her bed, holding the phone close to her ear. Phillip's voice was a pleasant antidote to the bleak memory of her visit to the Layton Facility.

"There was a physician there? That's pretty unusual for a nursing home. What—"

"He wasn't part of the staff. He has a practice in Asheville but his brother's the pastor who called about Nola. They were both there visiting her. Evidently the doctor came out as a special favor. His name's Pritchard—Dr. Pritchard Morton."

The Morton brothers had been a study in contrasts. Payne, the pastor of Dewell Hill Beulah Bethel Church, wore shiny black trousers and a permanent-press white shirt. His dark hair shone with hair cream and his ruddy complexion bore the scars of adolescent acne. His brother, the older of the two, wore a beautifully cut, or so it seemed to Elizabeth's untutored eye, tweed jacket and immaculate wool trousers that broke gracefully over perfectly polished and probably quite expensive loafers.

"So could this doctor tell you anything about the old lady—excuse me, about Miss Barrett's condition?"

"He said she'd probably had a stroke—but they haven't run any tests yet and he's not actually Nola's doctor. But that was his opinion."

"Did your friend recognize you?"

"I'm sure she did, but—"

"She couldn't communicate, right? I know a lot of the time people who've had strokes can't find the right words for what they want to say. But then after a while, maybe with some therapy, they improve."

"Dr. Morton was saying something like that—though he didn't sound as if he believed that it would happen in Nola's case. But listen, Phillip, a really odd thing happened."

She cleared her throat and continued. "After the Morton brothers left, I sat with Nola a while. I'd brought a book of poetry—I told you how she loved poetry. Well, I had the idea that if we couldn't talk, then I'd read to her a bit. And I did and she seemed to enjoy it. But when I got ready to go, I took her hand to say good-bye and she held it in a death grip. She was trying so hard to say something but the words wouldn't come. Then, all at once she began speaking in her old voice—perfect, precise diction. Phillip, she was quoting from *Hamlet*.

"Jeez—I hated that play. We had to study it in freshman English. That guy Hamlet just drove me crazy—couldn't make up his mind." Phillip laid a hand over his heart and began to declaim, " 'To *beeee* ... or not to be ...' "

"Ah ... yeah. And as a matter of fact, that's the speech Nola was quoting from."

The quality of Phillip's silence and then the tone of his delayed reply were carefully balanced between polite inquiry and derisive incredulity. "Okay ... and this woman who we watched try to kill herself ... this woman who's had a stroke or whatever and can't talk... what did she say in her perfect diction?"

"I came home and looked it up to be sure I got it right. Just a minute, I have the book right here..."

Elizabeth reached for the heavy volume of Shakespeare's plays and read,

> "... To die, to sleep—
> No more, and by a sleep to say we end
> The heartache and the thousand natural shocks
> That flesh is heir to—'tis a consummation
> Devoutly to be wish'd."

# The Drovers' Road II
## The Girl at the River

They had wiped the last of the soup beans and fatback from the tin plates with the cold gritty corn pone, and the prisoners' evening meal was but a memory. In the gloom of the cell, the two men settled themselves for the night. All was quiet but for the labored groaning from the other occupied cell—the lamentations of the town's perennial inebriate, locked away to recover from the effects of an epic spree.

The Professor breathed a disconsolate sigh. I could wish for a cigar to settle that repast, he said. Or a dram. But no matter; let us beguile the weary hours till bedtime with story. Pray, continue your account. You left your uncle's farm to seek your fortune in the wide world. And at Gudger's Stand you encountered the siren of the fiery gaze—this Belle Caulwell, I believe you called her. Please, expound further of this enchantress; I am ensorcelled.

Lydy pushed his empty tin plate under his bunk and felt for the dipper gourd. It floated atop the water remaining in the bucket, and he took a careful draught before resuming his story. In the fading light his face was pale and very young.

I see that I have got ahead of myself in the telling of it. And as we're like to have plenty of time, I might as well give hit to you as it come to pass. Belle weren't the first I seen at Gudger's Stand. No, that come later.

He pulled the thin blanket around his shoulders and took up the tale.

*Hit was first dark when the ferry man set me acrost the river. They was a gray mule and a half-asleep man atop him a-waitin at the landing and the ferryman he loaded them on and took off fer the other side. Fare ye well, young feller, he called back. Mind you don't . . . but the words was drownded in the splash and tumble of the river.*

*I looked up and seen the glow of the fires in the windows of the stand and could hear loud talk and laughin. Someone was scrapin at a fiddle, boots was a-thumpin, and I seen a man come out the door. He looked around, then walked kindly waverin-like to the end of the porch. There he took the longest piss I ever seen. He was still at it when two more come atter him and they stood there a-handin a jug from one to the other.*

*Now, not havin a red cent to my name, I didn't want to go up there and play the beggar. In the morning, thinks I, when hit's more quiet-like, I'll find the stand keeper and ask for work. So I went a ways off from the ferry landing and found me a little grassy spot long side of some big rocks. I set there and et my cornbread and listened to the music and all up at the stand house. Hit went on fer quite some time but at last they give over and the laughin and loud talkin begun to die away. I rolled myself up in my blanket and lay down.*

*The fiddler was a-playing one last tune, slow and mournful, and hit seemed like they was voices in the river singin along with hit. I lay there, breathin in the smell of the water and the meadow, watchin the stars in the night sky, and tryin to make out the words.*

*Hit was a girl singin what woke me. A sweet high lonesome song about a wagoner's lad who was goin away and at first I thought that I was dreamin. But then I opened my eyes and seen a heavy mist risin off the river and little drops of dew a-coverin my blanket. I could hear footsteps comin closer and when I looked from*

behind the rocks where I was, I seen a girl totin a big ole bundle
that like to bent her double. She was makin her way down to
where they was a great flat ledge pokin out into the shallow
water.

She clumb careful-like onto the big rock and let that load drop
down. Ooo-eee! she said and straightened up, a-puttin both
hands to the small of her back, like hit was painin her some. The
fog was burnin off now and I could see that she was young and
thin, with yaller hair so pale hit was most white. I watched,
keeping quiet as a cat a-layin fer a bird, whilst she leaned down
to undo that great bundle. She begun to pull at the knot that held
it together and I seen hit was naught but a great pile of blankets
and towels and suchlike. Then she looped up her skirts betwixt
her legs, tuckin them in at her apron strings, and waded a little
way into the river, pulling one of the blankets with her. She had
her a bucket of soft lye soap and she commenced to scrub at that
blanket and beat it against the rock and dip it in the water over
and over. And all the while she was a-singin that song, askin the
wagoner's lad to stay by her.

At long last she had the blanket to where it suited her and she
hauled it up onto the flat rock to begin to wring the water from it.
Hit was a slow task, the blanket bein heavy, and time and again
a corner would drop into the water and then hit would be to do all
over.

I stood up from behind the rocks and used my fingers to set my
hair to rights. Iffen you don't care, says I, speakin soft, so as not
to spook her, iffen you don't care, hit'd be a sight easier job was I
to help you.

Well, she give a little cry and walled her eyes at me, showin a
deal of the whites, but still she stood her ground. I begun to tell
her how come I to be there and afore long, I had took hold of
t'other end of that ol' blanket that was aggravatin her so and we
was twistin it dry and laughin like one thing.

By the time that the sun was full up and the mist all burned *away, ever bit of that washin was done and spread out on the grass to dry. She had told me that her name was Luellen and that hit was her pa what owned the stand. You come up to the house with me, she says. I'll speak fer you and I know he'll give you work. We're in need of a hired hand as our last one has went off with a wagon haulin goods to Warm Springs.*

There was kindly of a hitch to her voice when she said that and she pulled on a big ol' poke bonnet that clean hid her face, saying something about the sun hurtin her eyes. I thought of the song she had been singin. *Well,* says I, *he must have been a rank fool to go off and leave such a fine place—and such fine company.*

She ducked her head and didn't say nothing. We walked slow on up to the house. My stomach was growlin like a new-woke bear but she commenced to tell me all about herself and her family. I seen that iffen I wanted her help, I had better listen. Women-folk always do want you to listen.

Howsomever, she told me that she was her pa's only child but for a brother what had run off with a cattle drive some years back of this.

*My mommy died whilst I was still a lap baby,* says she, and her voice begun to tremble again. *And then my daddy married Belle, so as to have someone to look after me. She weren't but only a servant girl, for all she gives herself such airs now.*

At last we had come to the house with its long porches and tall chimbleys. The smell of fryin bacon was strong in the air and my mouth begun to water. I hoped that Luellen was right about her pa wantin help.

As we come nearer I seen they was two big hounds—great red ones like what they use to hunt bear—and they was chained to either side of the steps up to the porch. They stood up all stiff-legged and the hair on their backs went up. The near one, an old bitch, lifted her lips and showed a mouthful of yaller teeth, some of them broke off, but the light-haired girl just said, *Hush now, Juno,* and led me up the steps.

# Chapter 7

# *Marshall County Voices*
## Monday, December 11

Folks round here is tired of being treated like they ain't of no account. These new people—they come in here with all their money, actin' like they know everything and treatin' us like ignorant hillbillies—"

"It's the God's truth what Mason's sayin'!" A heavyset woman, her head covered with tight, iron-gray curls, broke in, leaning across her husband to speak to the couple just beyond him. "Why, just last week, the morning after that heavy snow, one of them big ol' SUVs with Florida plates on it stopped in front of our house and these folks piled out—there was five of them—and they went right to trompin' round the snow in my nice front yard and runnin' to and fro like crazy people, flingin' snow at one another and mashin' down my flower beds. Now I was upstairs, changin' the beds, and when I happen to look out the window and seen them carryin' on, I rapped sharp-like on the glass—"

The mountain twang resonated in the voices of the group sitting in front of Elizabeth. She didn't know them, but they were familiar just the same—the hardworking bedrock of the county—men and women who often worked day jobs as well as tending the small farms that had been a family heritage.

Now another voice, a woman behind her, spoke. "These local yokels are just a bunch of bluster. When it comes down to it, wave enough cash under their noses and I promise you, they'll sell that dear old home place in a New York minute." It was an accent harsh and unlovely to her ears, and Elizabeth had to resist turning to stare at the speaker.

The auditorium of the Marshall County High School was packed to capacity, with a throng of latecomers standing at the back and along the walls at either side. Elizabeth scanned the audience, looking for familiar faces. Sallie Kate, an uncharacteristic worried frown on her usually cheerful face, was there, as well as many other friends and acquaintances from the newcomer community.

*The old newcomers, that is. Most of my friends have been here at least ten or fifteen years—and most of them were like Sam and me, just trying to make a living and keep a low profile.*

Over there was Dacy, a vet tech who lived "off the grid," as did Sallie Kate and Harley. And beyond her the Nugents, whose organic farm and orchard, together with their herd of Angora goats, had, after years of hard work, become a source of pride for the whole county and a regular destination for school field trips. So many of the old newcomers were like that—all dedicated, in their words, to "living lightly on Mama Earth."

*This all happened so quickly—I guess I thought that the county would go on being the same as always—the local farm folks and our little group of back-to-the-land types, mostly getting along and working hard—and then bam! now there're condos and galleries downtown and gated communities springing up everywhere. It happened in Asheville and now it's happening here.*

Suddenly, it seemed, Marshall County and the very sleepy little town of Ransom were ripe for major development. Wealthy newcomers were pouring in, eager to capitalize on the empty buildings downtown, the acres of empty farmland lying fallow since the end of the tobacco support program, and the hitherto unusable steep slopes of the wooded mountainsides. Property prices were soaring, as were taxes, and many native Marshall County folk were beginning to say they couldn't afford to live on the land their families had held for hundreds of years.

After the spate of letters to the editor published in the county's weekly newspaper had reached a height of incivility unknown in recent years, the powers that be had at last called a public meeting so that interested county residents could voice their concerns.

"We really need to go to this meeting, Aunt E." Confronting her over coffee that morning, her nephew had been particularly insistent.

Elizabeth, reluctant as always to be drawn into the murky depths of county politics, had begun a halfhearted rationalization. "I don't know, Ben. I feel like it's not my battle. I don't want to see all these new developments either, but I'm not a native and it feels hypocritical to want to close the door on any more new people now that *I'm* here . . ."

"That's bullshit, Aunt E!" Ben had begun to pace to and fro in her kitchen, growing more and more angry as he spoke. "Those greedy county commissioners are letting the developers do whatever the hell they please—build on slopes that aren't suitable, pollute trout streams, pack too many houses together . . . all kinds of bad shit.

"And"—he pointed an accusing finger at her—"have you seen the plans that company—Ransom Properties and Investment—has for Gudger's Stand? It was written up in the paper. They seem to think the old lady's good as dead and it's just a formality before they start bulldozing. Shit, I heard that the county is considering doing one of those 'taking' things—condemning the property for 'the greater good' so RPI can develop it."

That final piece of information had raised a red flag, and it was in a spirit of righteous indignation that Elizabeth had claimed a seat near the front of the auditorium for the first meeting of Marshall County Voices—a meeting billed as a forum for *all* concerned citizens, both native born and newcomer. Beside her, Ben and Amanda held hands and carried on a whispered conversation while waiting for the meeting to begin.

The assembled crowd grew somewhat quieter as a cluster of men in dark business suits began to make their way to the raised area at the front of the auditorium. A muffled booing broke out from the back of the room but ceased abruptly as a tall man in jeans and a plaid flannel shirt stepped to the podium and tapped on the microphone. The suited men took seats in a row of chairs to one side of the dais.

"Okay, folks, let's get this meeting underway. We want to give everyone a chance to be heard—"

He broke off as an efficient-looking woman with a clipboard tapped him on the shoulder and handed him a sheet of paper. Glancing quickly at the paper, he began again. "This agenda Miz Worley's just handed me says we're goin' to start with a presentation by Ransom Properties and Investments..."

An angry murmur ran through the crowd but the moderator held up his hand. "Now we all know that the proposed development at Gudger's Stand is the number one issue on everyone's list. And no matter whether you're for or against it, it just makes sense to see what's being proposed before we get down to sayin' how we feel about it."

Behind him a screen was being lowered and the muttering in the audience increased. "They got this all set up aforehand, I make no doubt," Elizabeth heard Mason's wife tell the woman on her right. "They'll use up all the time there is showin' pretty pictures and not let the other side be heard."

At the same time, she could hear the woman behind her. "Hollis is the blond. Is he not to die for? Like a Ralph

Lauren model. Thirty-two years old and a multimillionaire. Of course, he *started* with money . . . his family has developments all over the country . . . my god, they made a *killing* a few years ago on some junky little fishing village in North Florida . . . bought up property for next to nothing, tore down all the ugly little houses and bait shops and tacky little motels . . . and today it's all *gorgeous* condos and utterly *fabulous* beach houses in those pale, pale, Martha Stewart pastels. . . ."

On Elizabeth's left, Ben nudged her with his elbow. "And what do you reckon happened to the *people* who lived in that little junky village?" His voice was pitched low, but as the woman behind them continued with her glowing description, she was in no danger of hearing Ben's answer to his own question.

"I'll tell you what happened: they've got shit jobs, cleaning those fancy houses and condos and taking care of the exotic, water-guzzling landscaping, and they've moved to crappy trailer parks out of sight of this tasteful development 'cause that's the only housing they can afford. If we let these developers rape—"

The moderator's voice rose above the buzz of talk in the auditorium as one of the suited men rose and approached the podium. "Folks, this is Mr. Hollis Noonan of RPI and he's going to show you his vision for the county."

Noonan took the podium to the accompaniment of scant scattered applause and muffled boos. Most of the crowd, Elizabeth noted, simply sat, arms folded, lips pursed, waiting to hear the proposal. *Not the easiest group to make a pitch to. I'm glad I'm not the one up there.*

The one up there, however, seemed completely at ease. Hollis Noonan looked deliberately around the room, as if to take stock of those in attendance, bestowing a smile here and a nod there. He had, Elizabeth noted, an annoyingly boyish mannerism of constantly tossing his head to return his long blond forelock to its proper place. The undercurrent of conversation died away and Noonan leaned into the microphone.

"I'd like to tell you a little story—about a city boy who fell in love with the mountains." His voice was strong, assured, and, it seemed to Elizabeth, without any noticeable accent. "When I was in college, I met a fellow you may have heard of—Vance Holcombe."

An engaging grin spread itself across Noonan's tanned face, and he turned, pointing to one of the men behind him. The sandy-haired Holcombe half-rose with a practiced sweep of the hand at the audience, then resumed his seat. Noonan continued, with another winning toss of that blond hank of hair.

"Don't worry, Vance. I won't tell any stories about our wild college days." Blue eyes twinkled as he confided in his audience. "Now that he's a respectable lawyer, Vance would prefer to draw a curtain over his youth." *See what a good old boy I can be,* Noonan's ingenuous face proclaimed.

"But I will tell you that one year Vance invited me home with him for fall break so I could see the county he bragged on and meet his folks: his brother, Little Platt; his mom and dad, Big Platt and Miss Lavinia; and his legendary uncle, High Sheriff Vance Holcombe."

The atmosphere in the auditorium began to warm slightly as Noonan launched into a rambling account of his first trip to Marshall County—how he had hiked the mountain trails, kayaked down the river, tapped his toe to bluegrass and old-time fiddle tunes at a local music festival, and listened to the many tales his friend's family had to relate of years gone by.

"It was one of the best times in my life. And I always promised myself that someday I'd come back—that I'd have a place of my own, high above that beautiful river, and not have to wait for an invitation from Vance."

Once more the boyish grin swept around the auditorium. Then Noonan's face grew somber. "A year ago I came back to Marshall County and to Ransom, with plans for that dream home and high hopes to be welcomed as a new neighbor. But I was shocked by what I found—a dying town, half the businesses closed and boarded up, a stagnant tourist industry, farming on the wane—in short, *Wasted Potential!*"

The speaker accompanied the accusing words with two sharp blows of his fist on the wooden lectern and another toss of his head. The carefully barbered sheaf of hair fanned out, catching the light before it settled into place, only to begin again the inevitable downward slide. At the same moment, the lights in the auditorium dimmed and the screen at the back of the dais lit up with an aerial photograph of Gudger's Stand. Superimposed on the picture were the words "A New Day Dawns in Marshall County!"

In the half-light of the darkened room, Elizabeth watched the upturned faces of much of the suspicious crowd gradually change, forbidding scowls softening to neutral interest or open excitement. As the presentation rolled on, complete with glowing promises of benefits to the county from an increased tax base as well as a phenomenal projected growth in tourism and jobs, there was a perceptible shift in the mood of the majority.

"Well, Mason, I don't know; looks to me like some good might come of this." The tight gray curls quivered as the woman punched her husband's arm and leaned over to speak into his ear. "What he's sayin' makes a world of sense—and if we was to hold on to that piece you heired from your daddy till some of this building got goin', I reckon we could triple what we was thinkin' of askin'. These Florida people are fools for steep land. And that piece ain't doin' us no good."

Beside her, Elizabeth could hear Ben whispering to Amanda in an angry counterpoint to the lulling patter that accompanied the computer graphics showing the projected development.

"... *garden villas, time-shares, common green space, river-front condos, historic re-creation, clubhouse, Olympic swimming pools, wellness center—*"

An agitated chatter broke out at the back of the room as the door flew open and a husky young man wearing a green and yellow Marshall High School letter jacket, cell phone in hand, burst through the knot of standing latecomers to shout out his news.

"They's someone's big ol' Hummer's on fire out there in the parking lot—burnin' like a summabitch! I called 911 but I reckon—"

"... *wildflowers, peaceful nature trails, pristine sparkling brooks winding through gentle meadows...*" The recorded voice-over continued, accompanying the idyllic scenes that bloomed and then faded on the unwatched screen, as the audience poured out of the auditorium into the cold night air.

# Chapter 8

# *Burn Job*

## Monday, December 11, and Tuesday, December 12

The wail of an approaching siren cut through the clamor of shuffling feet and excited voices as the erstwhile audience re-formed for the unexpected second act of the evening. In a loading zone at the end of the parking lot, mercifully well away from most of the cars, leaping red flames drew the crowd like so many helpless moths. Doors open and interior blazing, a boxy orange vehicle squatted there—a monstrous jack-o'-lantern from hell. The insistent tang of kerosene hung in the air, underscoring a stench of burning plastics.

The watching throng stood at a cautious distance, fascinated by the spectacle of a very new, very expensive car rapidly depreciating as they watched.

"Here comes the fire engine now. That ve-hicle is gonna be a total loss though. Somebody done a burn job on it for sure."

"I believe that's the car the developer folks come in—see there on the front door it says RPI."

"Reckon who could have done such a thing? Someone said they was two big fellers runnin' off."

"What's that writing there on the ce-ment? Appears whoever it was got busy with the spray paint afore they set that car on fire."

Elizabeth craned her neck to try to read the words: yard-high letters scrawled in green paint on the pavement near the wheels of the burning car. At her elbow, Ben spoke, in a voice flat with grim satisfaction. "Looks like not everyone's ready to welcome Mr. Noonan as a new neighbor."

Between the hazy yellow illumination of the mercury vapor lights and the glow of the fire, it was just possible to make out the double set of initials: *R.I.P.—R.P.I.*

"Elizabeth, does that kind of thing happen a lot around here? I've heard some stories about bad feeling between natives and newcomers, but I didn't believe them. I've felt really safe. All the local people I've met have been really nice to me."

Amanda, usually so self-possessed and unflappable, was pale and wide-eyed as Ben pulled the farm truck into the line of vehicles creeping out of the high school parking lot. Behind them the fire truck was still pumping water onto the blackened shell of the Hummer, and a second police car had just arrived to join the sheriff's vehicle and the police car that had accompanied the fire engine.

"Oh, Amanda . . . the people here *are* nice. This was . . . an anomaly . . . or maybe an accident . . ." Elizabeth's words trailed off doubtfully. The smell of kerosene still in her nostrils insisted that the destruction of the RPI car had been no accident.

"Get real, Aunt E—you saw that writing. That was a political statement. 'RIP—RPI' may not be as obvious as 'Death to RPI,' but it makes the same point." Ben laid a hand on Amanda's blue-jeaned leg pressed close to his. "More likely it was some of the so-called radical environmentalists—the rabid tree huggers. But, I don't know . . . they're opposed to pollution, and burning a Hummer, even though it stands for everything they're against in a vehicle, is kind of counter—"

As the truck inched its way to the top of the drive lead-ing down the hill to the highway, Elizabeth broke into Ben's musings.

"Look over there, Amanda. That's Pinnacle Mountain—the one in the middle of the horizon. See that one little light in the middle of all the dark...about a third of the way down? That's my porch light. I always get a thrill out of seeing it from here."

As Amanda leaned forward to peer through the window, Elizabeth was struck anew with the young woman's quite exceptional beauty. *That perfect profile...* Thick, naturally blonde hair pulled up in a careless knot caught the light of a following car and glinted silver-gold. Sometimes it seemed incredible that Amanda, not yet twenty-five, had aban-doned what, according to Gloria, had been a promising modeling career, choosing instead to create gardens and live in a primitive cabin with Ben.

"That's awesome that you can see it from here. I really like the way it looks—kind of a beacon. Like on the raft trip last week, remember, Ben? How they had a battery lantern on the shore so we'd know to take out before those bad rapids."

Amanda snuggled back against Ben, a look of pure hap-piness spreading across those perfect features as an oncom-ing car's headlights briefly illuminated the truck cab, lighting up her face.

*Like the flash on a camera. She probably got used to that.* Elizabeth closed her eyes but the image stayed with her. *High cheekbones, elegant nose, perfect teeth—such regular fea-tures that at first you don't notice her looks, particularly since she doesn't wear makeup. But in that magazine spread Glory sent just so I could see who Amanda "really was"—my god, the girl's a raving, tearing beauty!*

It had been a feature article, clipped from a glossy fash-ion magazine and still redolent of some expensive perfume sample. There had been page after page and shot after shot of Amanda, posed in one improbable designer outfit after another, against the background of the old city of St. Augustine. The text had referred to Amanda's "privileged upbringing" and had dwelt on her stubborn determination to fund her own college education by modeling. *Wonder what that was about? According to Glory, Amanda's family is "extremely well-to-do."*

As they passed a sign giving directions to the River Runners' outpost, Elizabeth was jogged from her reverie. "Ben, Amanda—tell me about that raft trip. I keep meaning to ask—it must have been gorgeous, with the full moon. But weren't you freezing all the time?"

"You would have loved it, Aunt E. It was fantastic!" Ben slowed to a crawl to accommodate a scuttling possum out for an evening ramble. "And with the wet suits and the paddling jackets, we stayed warm enough. But the river's dangerously cold this time of year and we had to be extra careful not to get dumped—that's why we took out before Sill's Slough—even though Josh's made the run hundreds of times, he says it's too tricky at night. There's a hydraulic thing going on there that can be really dangerous. It wasn't too many years ago a guy fell out of a raft and got sucked under. Of course, if he'd had his life vest buckled tight—"

"It was just amazing, Elizabeth!" Amanda interrupted Ben's explanation, eager to describe the experience in her own terms. "The moon was so bright that after our eyes adjusted we could see really well. And Josh told us just when to paddle—he *says* he could do the river blindfolded. It was magic, like . . . like sliding down a ribbon of molten silver with dark woods rising on either side. It was the most beautiful place I've ever been."

*She sounds like someone reciting poetry—or describing a vision,* thought Elizabeth as Amanda continued on, her voice low and dreamy.

"And the sound, the continual low purr of the river and the paddles splashing—it was hypnotic: no one wanted to break the silence. Josh would give directions—you know, 'Paddle left,' or 'Back right,' just loud enough to be heard. And then we began to hear the rapids, a low, continuous roar almost like surf at the ocean.

"And it got louder and louder and we were going faster and faster and down the river we could see the molten silver turning to white foam and then the roar was so loud that we could hardly hear Josh's voice and just when it seemed like we might be going over the edge of the world, Josh pointed to this light on shore and steered for it, yelling, 'Paddle hard if you don't want the Dakwa to get you!' "

Amanda stopped abruptly, breathless with the emotion of reliving the experience. Ben squeezed her knee and said, "You sound like an English major, girl. But you know, Aunt E, there really is something about the river at night—kind of spooky. It's not too hard to believe that there *could* be some big monster lurking there."

"The Dakwa—is that the fish monster that the Cherokees told stories about—the one that would drag people under?" A memory nibbled at the edge of Elizabeth's mind, *something about a river monster in the museum over in Cherokee? Or was there some mention of the Dakwa in those notes I took from Nola's house?*

"Correctomundo! And the way the current and the hydraulics are there at Sill's Slough, you can see how a story like that got started. It's perfectly safe if you know just which way to go, but it's tricky, like a slalom course. You have to stay in this narrow little channel, between these honkin' big rocks and the killer hydraulic."

"Between a rock and a hard place—or like, what's that thing from Greek mythology...Scylla and Charybdis. They didn't tell us all that when we took our raft trip last summer—of course the water was low then so maybe it wasn't as dangerous."

Phillip watched as Elizabeth's finger traced the river's course on the photocopied map from Nola Barrett's papers. A title at the bottom of the page, surrounded by an embellishment of scrollwork, read, *The French Broad River with the Buncombe Turnpike and Drovers' Road, showing all Stands and Inns together with Fords, Ferries, and Bridges. Thos. W. Blake fecit* ~ *1861.* Here was Gudger's Stand, but there had been no bridge in 1858; a spidery *Frry* marked the site of an old ferry, evidently just downstream from the present-day bridge. And here were the rapids with delicate calligraphy noting *Sills Slough.*

"Is that another stand, there at the rapids?" Phillip leaned closer, trying to read the faded lettering. "What's it say—'Flores'... and something in parentheses?" His face touched her ear and she turned, her wide smile embracing him.

"Hey, you, I'm glad you came out for dinner." Her lips brushed his cheek. "And I'm glad you're spending the night—in the middle of the week, you wild and crazy guy."

*I could be here every night if...* Phillip brushed aside the perplexed irritation that always surfaced whenever he thought of Elizabeth's dismayed reaction to his proposal of marriage. He draped an arm around her.

"Well, my first class tomorrow isn't till one, and I'm caught up with my paperwork—plus Mac had some mysterious something he wanted to see me about in the morning. So—"

Elizabeth tossed the photocopied map to the table. "Did Mac mention if they'd found out who burned up that car Monday night?"

"Nope, just the usual cop line about pursuing promising leads. It's pretty obvious, though, that it was someone who doesn't want the RPI folks and their development."

He motioned to the pile of papers on the coffee table before them. "So this is what you stole—excuse me, *rescued,* from your friend's house? The map's pretty cool—what else is there?"

"Lots of great stuff—I told you she was working on a novel about the history of the county and the old house."

Elizabeth pulled the stack of handwritten notes and typed pages to her and began to leaf through them. "Here," she said, offering him several pages paper-clipped together. "This is evidently the beginning of a section on the Drovers' Road. She's describing the old house at Gudger's Stand. It's like some kind of epic."

Phillip stretched lazily and patted at his empty shirt pocket. "My glasses must be in my briefcase. Why don't you read it to me?"

Elizabeth gave him a stern look over the tops of her own reading glasses as he leaned back against the sofa cushions.

"Okay, then. Pay attention now; there may be a quiz."

He closed his eyes and gave himself up to listening, enjoying the soothing cadences of her low voice, the warmth of the fire, the soft embrace of the sofa cushions.

*The logs have seen it all. Giant chestnuts, virgin timber, dragged by ox teams from the endless forest, they had been heaved into place in the year of eighteen hundred and thirty-one. Great fieldstone chimneys had been laid, rock by careful rock, at either end of the long structure, and the gentle flatlands at the riverside had been cleared for field and pasture. The roaming Cherokee who had camped and hunted there time out of mind were sent west on the Long Walk, the Trail of Tears, and the new inhabitants of the land began to shape it to their own uses and desires.*

*The great road whose coming had called the house into being stretched along the river from Tennessee to South Carolina, rugged as the men who had carved it from the rocky cliffs. Along its narrow trace came travelers of every ilk: on foot, by horse, by wagon or jolting stagecoach, they followed the road, seeking land, trade, adventure, or the healing waters of Warm Springs."*

"*Warm* Springs? I thought—"

"Ahh! You *are* listening! I was afraid you might have

dozed off. No, it's not a mistake. The town was named Warm Springs, which is really more accurate, and got changed to Hot Springs at some point. A marketing ploy, I expect, for the hotel there. Do you want me to finish?"

"Sure—I'm enjoying it. It's just that I can focus on it better with my eyes closed."

"Right. Where was I? Oh, here... *In the fall of the year, the road was given over to the great livestock drives. Down from the mountains they flowed, bound for the railheads and slaughterhouses of South Carolina, churning the dirt of the road to reeking mire. Fat with corn and the chestnut mast of remote mountain coves, they came in near-endless streams: horses and mules, cattle and hogs, slow-moving ducks, and majestic, strutting turkeys.*

"Turkeys? Ducks? That must have been challenging—about like herding cats, I'd think."

"I guess so. I read somewhere that the challenge was to get the turkeys to a stand before nightfall, otherwise they'd fly up in the trees to roost and the drovers would have to camp right there by the side of the road and miss all the comforts of the stand."

There was the rustle of paper and he could hear her clearing her throat to resume. "One last page—the most intriguing.

*The house on the drovers' road had welcomed them all, offering food for man and beast, stout corrals for the stock, and a place near the hearth for a man to roll up in his blanket. And if some whispered that those who slept too soundly there might never see the morning, the fiery applejack from the landlord's still and the still-fierier eyes of the landlord's wife convinced many a drover to risk a night at the house called Gudger's Stand.*"

"I'd like to hear more about the landlord's wife." His eyes still closed, Phillip began to move his hand in the direction of Elizabeth's breast. She continued reading, seeming to ignore the lazy movement of his fingers on her arm.

*The house had seen the great drives swell to flood tide and then, with the coming of the railroad, recede to arid memory. But still there had been travelers eager for a meal, a dram, and a place by the fire—and still there had been the whispers.*

*"Time passed. The great fireplaces no longer roared; the smooth fields and rolling pastures gave way to multiflora rose, sumac, and locust. A rising tide of kudzu and grapevine began the green inundation of the long quiet porches that once had echoed with the heavy boots of the drovers. No one visited the old house now; only memories lurked in its empty rooms—memories and whispers."*

Just as his hand reached its destination, her voice fell silent. There was the riffle of pages falling to the floor as Elizabeth turned to him, pressing her lips to his while her hand began an exploration of its own.

# Chapter 9

## *Cold Case*
### Wednesday, December 13

T here were no defensive wounds; the old guy was probably asleep in his bed when he was hit on the head with a chunk of firewood. The firewood likely came from the stack by the fireplace...."

Mackenzie Blaine turned over one of the stack of yellowing pages that spilled from the worn file folder on his desk. "Yep, locust splinters found in the wound were consistent with the remaining firewood in the room. Of course, the weapon itself was presumably cold ashes in the grate by the time the body was found—"

"Hold on, Mac." Phillip shifted in the uncomfortable metal chair opposite the desk. Hard as an ex-wife's heart, with one suspiciously wobbly leg, it was the only seating choice offered a visitor. "Wouldn't it have had to be a reasonably powerful assailant to kill him with a blow like that... not an elderly woman? It just doesn't—"

The sheriff looked up with a puzzled gaze. "Elderly woman? Hawk, Miss Barrett was... let me double-check..." He flipped through the pages on his desk, ran a finger down one and paused.

"Nola Barrett was fifty-four at the time—and not exactly frail. Hell, I wouldn't call her frail now, ten years later.

Besides, it wasn't the blow that killed him—it was the pillow over his face."

Phillip frowned. "Was she ever charged..."

"No, she wasn't. Sheriff Frisby evidently did a cursory investigation and then put it down to murder by person or persons unknown. Nola Barrett's name doesn't come into it except as the person who discovered the body."

"And that's it? The case was just closed?"

Marshall County's newly reelected sheriff was silent for a moment, his shrewd brown eyes studying his friend's face. Phillip waited.

Blaine returned the papers to the file, then stood. "You got a little time to waste?" He was pulling on a jacket and reaching for a hat. "Let's take a ride."

Phillip followed his friend down the hallway, past offices where uniformed men frowned at computer screens or bent over paperwork, into the stifling outer office. A small space heater whirred at top speed, producing a tropical heat in the windowless room. Here a stern-looking, white-haired woman presided over the telephone and reception desk. She detained the sheriff briefly with a litany of questions and reminders. Finally Blaine held up his hand.

"I'll take care of all that this afternoon, Miss Orinda. If Horner calls, tell him the matter's been resolved. Back by one."

As they climbed into Blaine's cruiser, Phillip rolled down his window. "I don't know how you stand it, Mac. A couple of minutes in there and the smell's all over me. That godawful air freshener's bad enough but—"

"You get used to it." Mackenzie was matter-of-fact as he pulled out of his parking place. "She can't help it—it's some kind of chronic condition. She should have retired by now but the job's her life—she's worked here since the dawn of time and knows everything there is to know about the day-to-day operation of the office. Be hard to replace her."

Blaine put his own window partway down, admitting a

crosscurrent of fresh air. "But, yeah, Miss Orinda does fart a lot."

The sheriff's cruiser nosed its way down the unpaved road paralleling the railroad tracks, past three ramshackle buildings and a small rusting trailer, before coming to a halt where the road ended in a brushy meadow. An abandoned school bus, covered with graffiti and resting on concrete blocks, lay ahead, half concealed by the tall, winter-worn scrub.

"You're being awful damn mysterious, Mac." Blaine had evaded his questions during the short drive from the sheriff's office to this dead-end dirt road by the bridge at Gudger's Stand.

Blaine grunted, pulled the cruiser to a stop, and pointed to the derelict vehicle. "Back in the early eighties, a bunch of hippies, river guides and such, used that during the summer. They had it fixed up like a camper—bunks built in and a little galley—pretty slick, from what some of the fellas tell me. This whole field was kind of a campground, tents all over the place during the rafting season."

Phillip peered through the windshield at the rusting yellow hulk. "Okay, Mac. I get the picture. Happy hippie days, free love, grass for the growing, blowin' in the wind, all that Summer of Love crap—what does this have to do with—"

"Well, your song reference is off by about twenty years, but aside from that—yeah, things were pretty loose down here. The sheriff's department turned a blind eye to the marijuana back then—some say the cops were actually part of the supply chain—make a bust in one part of the county, then burn a token amount of the stuff and sell the rest at wholesale to the dealers. The late Sheriff Holcombe—"

Mackenzie Blaine stopped mid-sentence and opened his door. "Let's stretch our legs for a few minutes." Without waiting, he swung out of the car and made his way, limping very slightly, toward the abandoned bus. Phillip fumbled in his pocket for his woolen watch cap and pulled it down over his ears. *Kind of chilly for a walk—this isn't like Mac. There's something's bugging him.*

Zipping his jacket, he hurried to catch up with his friend, who was striding past the old bus and along a faintly defined footpath paralleling the river.

"So this must be where the Drovers' Road was." Phillip gestured down the trail. "Lizabeth's been—"

Sheriff Blaine's rapid pace slowed and he turned to fix Phillip with a look of utter seriousness. "Hawk, I wanted us out of the car for a reason. I was starting to run my mouth—do you know how easy it would be to bug the cruiser? And I can't sweep the car every day without letting whoever it is know I'm onto them."

Phillip stared. *Okay, in a minute he's gonna crack a big grin and say "Gotcha" and we'll have a laugh and get back in the car out of this friggin' wind.*

But there was no grin, no relaxation of the tension. "Mac? I think I missed something. What's the punch line?"

"This is no joke. There's something strange going on in the department . . . maybe in the county too." The sheriff continued along the trail, hands shoved deep in his jacket pockets, shoulders hunched against the wind. "I don't know which of my deputies I can trust—one reason I didn't want to talk about this back at the office."

His strong fingers dug into the heavy sleeve of Phillip's jacket.

"Listen, Hawk, I need another investigator—someone I know isn't part of this . . . whatever it is. We've talked before about you coming to work for me on a permanent basis. I've been kind of waiting, thinking that whenever you and Miz Goodweather got around to—"

Phillip held up a hand. "Don't go there, Mac. Just tell

me what's happening and what you need me to do. God knows, I owe you."

Blaine's hand fell away and he closed his eyes briefly. "Thanks, Hawk. I was afraid you'd think I was crazy. Hell, for a while, I thought maybe I *was*. It started with the letter..."

An anonymous letter, Mackenzie explained, purporting to be from the victim of a brutal gang rape. "She said that they'd kept her tied up and blindfolded for several days and she couldn't be sure but that she thought it was probably in that bus back there. She said she'd been with a crowd that was partying. She admitted that she'd been drinking pretty heavily and must have passed out—anyway, she said when she came to, she was blindfolded and tied spread-eagle on a mattress with a group of men taking turns with her."

"I don't believe this shit—the victim wrote a *letter*? I thought by now everyone knew that coming in and getting the whole rape-kit procedure right away is the best chance for making a case. Hell, with the DNA—but maybe there's still a chance—when did this happen?"

Mackenzie Blaine didn't answer, but turned and began to retrace his steps back along the frozen ground. Bewildered, Phillip turned to follow.

"Mac, does this...girl...woman want to prosecute? Maybe she's just testing the water before she gives her name and files charges. Did she say she knew who the men were?"

"Said she's almost positive of two of them. She also wrote that they were responsible for a death, possibly several deaths, and that she wanted justice and was prepared to name names *if* I would assure her that there was a chance of success. There was a number I was supposed to call at a certain time so I could answer her questions before she decided whether or not to come in and make it formal. If she didn't hear from me at that time, she said, she'd assume the case was hopeless."

The sheriff slowed to study the blue heron on his accustomed rock across the river. The bird stood motionless on the partially submerged footing, his long, cruel beak poised above the frigid, rushing water. In a sudden blur the curved neck straightened, the beak plunged into the rapids and emerged, a silver fish wriggling in its inexorable hold. Another flash of silver, the fish disappeared, the neck resumed its graceful curve, and the heron returned to his silent vigil.

"Jesus, Mac, it's too damn cold for bird-watching. So, when you called did you convince her to come in and file charges?"

"I didn't call her. The time she set for the call was the next day. I left the letter with the phone number she gave on my desk when I went to lunch. When I came back, the letter was gone. I asked the various people on duty and no one had any idea what I was talking about. All I could remember about the phone number was that it was somewhere in Asheville."

"You think someone in the office took the letter? That doesn't make sense . . . what would—"

Mackenzie kicked viciously at a frozen clod. "Now I realize I shouldn't have left the letter out for anyone to see. But I thought it was crank mail. I hadn't believed her when she said that the reason for all the secrecy was because of the 'big people,' as she put it, in the county who would try to keep her from talking. That was why she wanted to set up a meeting with me, rather than coming in to the department."

"And now you think one of these 'big people' has a . . . a friggin' *mole* in the department going through your correspondence . . . maybe even bugging your cruiser?"

Blaine's face hardened and he turned up the collar of his jacket against the wind. "Yeah, Hawk, that's what I think now. You know, I'd honestly believed the bad old days were finally past. You've heard the stories: how the county was controlled by a few powerful families and Sheriff Holcombe was in their pocket—or they were in his. Hell, I don't know... Even when Holcombe retired and Frisby took office, Holcombe was still in charge—the 'shadow sheriff,' was what some people called him. Business as usual—everything just took a little longer because Frisby wouldn't wipe his ass without asking Holcombe if it was okay.

"And Vance Holcombe sat there in his wheelchair in that old house on Center Avenue, keeping an eye on the town, while his brother Big Platt, out at Holcombe Hill, that farm of his just off the interstate, kept his eye on the rest of the county."

As the sheriff spoke, Phillip stared at his friend, wondering if, perhaps, there was more to the story than Blaine was telling.

"Don't get me wrong, Hawk, the Holcombe 'machine' wasn't all bad. If you were a citizen with a legitimate gripe, you could take it to the Holcombes and get a fair deal—as long as you were registered to the right party. There was one old boy—made the mistake of running against Vance one time—never *could* get his road paved after that. Story is the pavement stopped right at his property line, the road turned into dust and potholes, and then back to nice blacktop as soon as it reached the other side of the property."

"Lizabeth told me that story. But she said it seemed to her most of the old-timers she knew liked the Holcombes—she said it was a patronage setup, kind of like the Mafia godfather thing."

"Oh yeah—and without the hit men. If you were on the right side of the Holcombes and a nice county job came up, you'd go see Vance or Big Platt and they'd help make sure your application was 'expedited.' We're not talking major stuff; hell, school custodian or recycling center attendant were prize jobs for some of the folks around here. Still are, matter of fact. And the Holcombes weren't reckoned to be overly greedy—they'd made their money when the interstate

came through. Big Platt had enough influence to see that
the road ran through a good long section of land the
Holcombes owned. I think they just liked the power for its
own sake, being the big men in the county.

"But anyway, Vance Holcombe died of a heart attack,
sitting there on his front porch. Evidently Frisby was like a
puppet with its strings cut—he resigned within the month.
That's when I was recruited from over in Marion to fill out
the rest of his term. I didn't know about the Holcombe machine then—it was the head of the county commissioners
who contacted me. And when I took over as sheriff, never
once did any one try to influence me, in any way. I never
even met Big Platt—he had a stroke and passed away the
year after his brother's death. His sons, Little Vance and
Little Platt—gotta love the South, don't you?—are both
lawyers with their offices in the sheriff's old house there on
Center—and if they're running the county, at least they're
not running me."

"I don't doubt you for a minute, Mac. But—"

"Sorry, Hawk. I'll get to the point. That letter that disappeared said Sheriff Holcombe knew about this rape and
had been involved in a cover-up. It also said that he was responsible for murder."

Phillip stared at his friend blankly, struggling to make
sense of the strange account. "But Holcombe's dead. How
could he have anything to do with the rape described in the
letter?"

"According to Ms. Anonymous, the rape occurred in
October of '95—eleven years ago."

# The Drovers' Road III
## The Professor's Predicament

*Hsst! Hssst!*

Lydy jerked awake and lay listening. In the distance a rooster crowed and another answered. First light—and the little barred window was a pale, glowing square high on the dark wall. He rolled over to see the dark hunched forms of two rats scuttling their way across the floor, noses twitching in search of any stray crumb. Bold and unhurried, they approached the heavy door and squeezed their sleek bodies under the corner where persistent gnawing had widened the gap. As the second naked gray tail disappeared, the sound came again.

*Hsssst!*

*Professor?* Lydy whispered, looking toward the blanket-wrapped form of his sleeping cell mate. *You hear that?*

*Oh god!* came the muttered response as the Professor threw off his cover and swung his feet to the cold floor. He sat blinking and looking up toward the little window.

A rustling could be heard outside and a stifled giggle. Then a woman's voice whispered, *O Tommy, I got something nice for you.* There was more rustling and a small stone rattled through the bars, dropping to the brick floor with a thud.

Lydy started in indignation. *Ay law, hit's a cold heart that would rock two helpless critters that can't run. Did she hit you, Professor?*

But the Professor smiled and reached for the thin cord stretching from the window down to the stone it was tied to.

*Ah, Miss Nettie Mae, a veritable angel of mercy, a raven to our Elijah.* As he spoke, the Professor pulled steadily on the cord and soon a calico-wrapped parcel bumped against the bars. The professor slackened off on the line, gave a sharp tug, and the parcel slipped through the narrow opening, falling into his outstretched hands.

*Tommy, you got to git them vittles out and send the cloth and the cord back through the winder quick as ever you kin,* the disembodied whisper insisted. *If Pa was to wake and find I've slipped off—*

The Professor's fingers moved busily as he replied. *And how is your worthy sire this morning? Still determined to see me flogged and branded? Or does he prefer to welcome me as a son? My ears are open like a greedy shark, as young John Keats so painfully wrote, to catch the tunings of a voice divine.*

The cord that had bound the slim parcel was released and the food removed and placed carefully on the Professor's bunk. He leaned down to retrieve the stone but Lydy snatched it up and began to unknot the cord.

*I believe I'll keep hold of this, iffen you don't care. Gimme that there piece of cloth and the twine and I'll fix it to where I can chuck hit outten the window.*

*Who's in there with you, Tommy? Hit ain't the murderin drover boy, is it? Oh, tell me hit ain't, for I couldn't bear it was he to harm you! You know they found that pore girl's shift, all tore and bloody. And they say the footprints showed he had dragged her down to the river. Oh, Tommy, hit's the awfullest thing!*

*My dear, we are all, in this blessed land of the free, innocent till proven guilty, a quaint concept your family seems not to comprehend. The gentleman who shares my lodgings is a most agreeable companion. I beg you to still your apprehension. It is far more likely that I will suffer injury at your father's hands than those of young Lydy.*

*The napkin was wrapped tight with the cord into a slender cylinder and, after one bungled attempt, Lydy sent it neatly between the bars. More rustling and the girl's wistful voice floated up to them. I'll be back, Tommy, soon's I can.*

*Speaking through a mouthful of biscuit and jam, the Professor mumbled, Always at home to you, dear lady. Then a thought seemed to strike him and, swallowing hastily, he called out, Nettie Mae, my sparrow, what of your father? What steps is he likely to take?*

*Well, now, Tommy. I don't rightly know. Pa's carried on something fierce and he's sleepin it off just now. At first he vowed he'd horsewhip you his own self and not wait for the law to act. And then, ol' Garmon, what was drinkin with Pa to keep him company like, ol' Garmon speaks up and allows that, was it his daughter, he'd geld you like an ox.*

*At these words both men squirmed. The Professor put down the remains of the biscuit, crossed his legs, and took a quick gulp from the little flask that had been in the center of the parcel. The girl prattled on.*

*Hit was just talk, you know. But when ol' Garmon said that hateful thing, I took on so that my mommy spoke up. You uns won't do no such thing, says she right sharp. When preacher comes back through first of the year, says she, we'll see to it that feller weds our Nettie Mae for certain sure. Alls you got to do is to leave him be in the jailhouse so's he don't get no notion about ramblin on afore the words is spoke. That's what Mommy said and she fetched ol' Garman a lick alongside his head and asked him what kind of husband would you make me was you cut?*

*When the girl's soft footsteps had died away, the Professor tossed Lydy a biscuit and a withered apple. The code of the dungeon demands that you, my brother in adversity, accept this. It appears that I shall share your incarceration for a few more weeks at least, till such time as the bridal festivities can be accomplished.*

*The Professor took a thoughtful bite of his biscuit and spoke through the crumbs. I came to these mountains seeking adventure—not matrimony, friend Lydy. But the vagaries of fortune deprived me of my purse and I was forced to take employment. A group of local businessmen and landowners wished their likely offspring to venture beyond the abcedarian fare of Ransom's schoolhouse and so they provided me with lodging and a quiet room above the dry goods store where I might impart the rudiments of a classical education to their sons and daughters.*

*A bit of jam quivered at the side of the Professor's mouth and he pursued it with his tongue. Daughters, he grunted, shaking his head. That was my downfall. He looked at Lydy, who was swallowing the last of the apple. Are you aware of the lamentable fact that flogging and ear cropping are still common punishments in this benighted part of the world?*

*I knowed that. Lydy tossed the apple core to the corner of the cell. And there's brandin too. Sheriff said that iffen the jury brings in manslaughter agin me, they'll not hang me, only hold the iron to the palm of my hand whilst I sing out God Save the State three times over. He regarded his grimy hand with a stoic gaze. Reckon it'd be better'n hangin.*

*The Professor grimaced and shook his head. My dear friend, it was not my intention . . . that is, I never meant . . . in short, I beg your pardon. Please, let us abandon such dire speculation into the unknowable future and return to the account of your peregrinations. You came to a drovers' stand and there you were made welcome by the daughter of the house . . .*

*Hit was Luellen Gudger that I seen at the river. Lydy's voice slid back into the dreaming tone that had characterized his tale on the previous evening. She was the finest gal I ever seen with that smooth yaller hair and white skin and her pink dress for Sundays . . . And she had this little gigglin laugh, put me in mind of the sound of the creeks in midsummer. I thought that her daddy might not want her takin up with no hired man but I seen right soon that he didn't give no thought to that atall—his mind was turned to his wife and the son he was so sure she'd give him atter she got cured at the Warm Springs.*

*His name was Lucius Gudger, called Ol' Luce by most folks, and, just like his daughter, he kindly took to me right off.*

# Chapter 10

## *Cletus and the Bad Boys*
### Wednesday, December 13

Elizabeth rapped on the storm door of Miss
Birdie's house. From within she could hear, not
the usual murmur of the television, tuned to her
neighbor's favorite "stories," but the plaintive strains of an
Appalachian ballad.

> *Come all ye good people and hear my sad tale;*
> *My time it draws nigh and my soul it doth quail.*
> *I'd have you take warning, take warning of me*
> *If murder you've done, then you must pay the fee.*

Peering through the glass of the door, Elizabeth rapped
again. A small artificial Christmas tree was atop the silent
television, lights winking merrily. At the far end of the
room, a shelf full of framed family photographs displayed
dozens of Christmas cards and a glass candy jar in the
shape of a snowman, half-full of red and green jelly beans.

> *While still a young lad I grew restless at home,*
> *Weary of farming and eager to roam.*
> *I followed my fancy, I followed my dream,*
> *All down the high mountain and along the*
> *     broad—*

A plump little woman bustled out of the kitchen, a dish-
towel in one hand. Beckoning to Elizabeth, Miss Birdie

Gentry made for the tape player and stabbed at a button, cutting the singer off in mid-verse.

"Come in outen the cold, Lizzie Beth, and git you a chair. I most didn't hear you fer all the racket." Miss Birdie's eyes sparkled in her wrinkled face as she beamed up at Elizabeth. "Law, honey, hit's good to see you."

"Hey, Miss Birdie." Elizabeth leaned down to hug her old friend. "Who was that singing?" She unwrapped her long blue muffler and pulled off her pea jacket. "They sound really good."

"Why, that's Josh and Sarah Goforth. They was foolin' around at home and their mommy Peggy made that tape for me. She knows how I like to hear them old love songs— my mamaw could sing like one thing; had I don't know how many of them old songs by heart. She tried to teach me but I couldn't never seem to sound tuneful-like."

Birdie dropped onto her vinyl-covered recliner. "I reckon you probably heard of Peggy's boy Josh—they was a piece in the paper just the other day. That young un kin play the banjo and the fiddle and most any other thing you can name. He's a real musicianer, got his own band and travels all over. Now, Sarah, she sings at church and she—"

"Goforth? I've just been reading about a Goforth—back before the Civil War. Something to do with the old house at Gudger's Stand."

"Ay law, Lizzie Beth honey, they's been Goforths in this part of the county long past reckonin'. All up and down Bear Tree Creek, for the most part." Birdie screwed up her face in an effort of memory. "But I don't believe as I ever heared of any at Gudger's Stand. That stand house and land has always belonged to Revises. Besides, the Goforths is all good churchgoin' folk—not the kind to git mixed up with something like that sinful place."

Birdie quivered with indignation. "Why, Lizzie Beth"— her voice was lowered a notch, as befitting secret scandal—

"before old man Revis got hisself killed, that stand house was no better than a tavern . . . or worse."

Elizabeth nodded. Marshall County had been officially "dry" for years, but it was well known that those who lacked the means or the time to travel to the next county could always find a back room somewhere in which beer or hard liquor was sold at inflated prices.

"What else can you tell me about the stand, Birdie? I just recently met a Miss Barrett who lives in Dewell Hill. She's the cousin—or maybe it's the niece—anyhow, the heir of the man who was murdered there at Gudger's Stand—"

"Miss Nola Barrett? The one what lives in the little stone house acrost from the garbage place?"

"You know her?"

"Well, not to say *know*. Of course, they *was* right much talk about her, when she was the one what found old man Revis, but *I* never believed none of it. Nola Barrett's a good-hearted somebody, and that's the truth. It was her what called me about Cletus, that time those no-good fellers done him so bad."

Cletus, Miss Birdie's only child, had been dead for several years now. His last photograph, taken on his forty-first birthday, only months before his death, occupied a place of honor flanked by praying ceramic angels atop the crowded shelf. His simple, childlike face smiled out at his widowed mother.

"What no-good fellows, Birdie? And when was this?"

"Let me see now . . . hit would have been back in '95 and in the fall of the year, for Cletus was out on one of his huntin' trips—you know how that boy roamed—and, as I recollect, he'd been gone several days. Hit was early one morning I got a phone call—I had wrote the phone number on his knapsack, for he couldn't never remember hit—and there was this Miss Barrett sayin' as Cletus was at her house and wantin' me to come git him."

"But how could he have—"

"How come him to be over there acrost that river when he was flat skeered to *death* to walk on that bridge? That's what set me to worryin'. He hadn't told Miss Barrett ary thing and he wouldn't talk to me on the telephone—you know how backward he was about a phone—just couldn't make out how it worked."

So Birdie had driven the short distance to Dewell Hill, where she had found her son finishing a hearty breakfast in Nola Barrett's kitchen. Cletus had refused to answer her questions, by the simple expedient of ducking his head and taking another helping of scrambled eggs.

"Miss Barrett told me she seen him when she looked out her window at first light. He was hunched down there against the gate to the garbage place. Hit worried her so she went out and asked him was he all right, and Cletus told her he was waitin' there for his mommy. Pore thing, he knowed I always come by there everwhen I went to the grocery. But this was on a Sunday and my day fer goin' out was Thursday."

"Did he ever tell you how he came to be there?"

"Not at first he wouldn't, but as we was nearin' the bridge, he begun to tremble like he always done. And like always, I done told him that we'd get acrost jest fine and if he'd shet his eyes, I'd tell him when we was over. But then I seen hit weren't the bridge he was a-skeered of—hit was something down there in the field behind them old shackledy buildings. Cletus was all to pieces and he kept pointing down there and sayin', 'Bad boys! Bad boys!' "

"It's pretty cold but at least there's no wind. I've got a sleeping bag to put around me. And the sky's perfectly clear. I'm going to watch for a while anyway."

"The Geminids, is it?" Phillip sounded dubious but amused. "Are there supposed to be lots of them?"

Elizabeth settled herself into a rocking chair moved from the front porch to the deck below for the occasion. She held the phone to her ear as she scanned the sky to the north. "Well, ten to fifteen an hour is the estimate—so that works out to one every four to six minutes—not exactly a light show but— Oh! There went one!"

A pinpoint of light flared in the soft blackness of the sky's depth, tracing a brief glowing path that disappeared before her sentence was completed. At the top of the heavens' vault, in the deepest darkness, the sky was crowded with a thickly glittering maze of stars, while the eastern horizon was a hazy purple, tinged by a faint glimmering from the lights of Ransom and the surrounding communities.

*Wish on a falling star. I wish that Phillip were here instead of in Weaverville. I wish that that Nola would get well. I wish . . .*

"I wish *I* could see them," Phillip's rueful tone almost sounded sincere, "but with so many security lights in Weaverville, there's no chance. I'll just have to stay here in my warm house and let you describe it to me."

"You seem to be bearing up pretty well under the disappointment." Elizabeth switched the phone to her left ear and shoved her right hand, icy in spite of the heavy glove, into her pocket. "I don't know how long I'll be out here—I always hope that it'll be a real meteor shower—like that song about stars falling on Alabama—with the sky just full of— I think there went another one just at the edge of my vision!"

"How was Miss Birdie? You did say you were going to visit her today, didn't you?"

"Birdie's great—she asked after you." *How is that feller of yours?* Miss Birdie had asked, fixing Elizabeth with a shrewd gaze. *Now I don't mean to be nosy, Lizzie Beth, but seems to me, like my mamaw used to say, you could go farther and fare worse. He's a fine man and a body kin see he thinks the world of you.* "Maybe you could come with me when I take her some Christmas goodies next week. What did Mackenzie want to see you about—if it's not privileged information."

"Well—it's not common knowledge yet, but I trust you not to let this go any farther. You ever noticed that old school bus, parked in the field below the bridge?"

Elizabeth listened with growing uneasiness as Phillip described the anonymous letter and the alleged rape in the old bus.

"Phillip, this is too weird. Birdie was just telling me this story about her son. It was back—I can't remember exactly when she said; I think it was in the early nineties—Cletus was more or less abducted by some young men."

"That poor young un," Miss Birdie had said. "I remember it jest as plain. 'They was bad boys, Mommy,' says he. I finally got it out of him that he'd been over yon side of Pinnacle, sleepin' in an old barn he used sometimes. Howsomever, what he told me was that these fellers come hoorahin' around and when they found him there, they made him drink with them. Now Cletus hadn't never had no whisky and he said he got sick and started to vomick and then they said they'd bring him home."

Miss Birdie's eyes had grown misty and her voice wavered as she said, "You know what Cletus was—one of the Lord's innocent lambs. Well, he got in the truck with those fellers and he said when they got to the bridge he told 'em to turn up thisaway but they didn't pay him no mind. He said they was laughin' and the truck was halfway acrost the bridge and he started to vomick again. They made him get out, right there on the bridge, and he said he got all swimmie-headed and fell down."

Elizabeth shivered in spite of the sleeping bag wrapped around her. "Poor Birdie, she was almost in tears telling me about this. Evidently between the whisky and his phobia about bridges, Cletus passed out. But this is the weird part. He told her that when he woke up, he was in this old school bus—on a mattress with a girl asleep beside him and the 'bad boys' were all gone. He told Birdie that the girl wouldn't wake up and that she didn't have any clothes on and he got real scared. He broke a window to get out and started running."

The slow-moving lights of a distant, silent airplane held Elizabeth's attention briefly. *One more, when I see one more, then I'm going in and get warm.*

Phillip, suddenly sounding very far away, broke into her concentration. "Did Miss Birdie do anything to check on this story—did she believe her son?"

"She believed him—but she figured it was just some drunken kids trying to have fun by seeing what Cletus's re-action would be to a naked girl. *They was more than one whore woman hangin round that old stand and they was as bad to drink as the men. I don't doubt but she was in on the joke. My sweet boy had to put up with a world of hatefulness like that.*

"Maybe that was all it was—or maybe it's connected to this story Mac told me." Phillip's voice was thoughtful. "But unless the one who wrote that letter contacts him again, we'll never know."

"It makes me sad to think of how mean some people can be—especially to harmless creatures like Cletus." Elizabeth silently noted the passage of another meteor. She pushed herself out of the chair and headed for the steps. Her knees felt stiff and arthritic . . . and old. "I'm going in the house now. I've enjoyed as much as I can stand of the Geminids."

The phone still to her ear, she opened the front door, sa-voring the instant, enveloping warmth. Molly looked up briefly from her spot on the sofa in front of the fire, but Ursa, stretched out on the kitchen floor, didn't move. A rapid tattoo announced that James was on the hearthrug.

A welcoming, pleasant room but something was miss-ing. Almost without thinking, she found herself saying, "I wish you were here, Phillip."

There was the sound of throat-clearing and he said, "There was another thing—Mac wants me to come work for him. If I gave up the teaching and went full-time with the sheriff's department, I'd probably have to move out to Marshall County..."

An unspoken challenge hung in the air. When she had rejected his proposal back in the summer, Phillip had said, quietly and without rancor, "I want to marry you, Elizabeth. I'd like that kind of full-time relationship and commitment. But if you're not interested, so be it. I won't keep asking but I won't change my mind; if you change yours, let me know." And there the matter had rested, much to Elizabeth's relief.

The waiting silence grew louder and a bevy of conflicting thoughts raced though her head. *Say something... what?*

"You could move in, Phillip. We could turn one of the guest rooms into an office for you and—"

"And I could keep my sleeping bag rolled up behind your couch?" The words had a bitter edge. "No thanks, I'll find a place of my own if I accept Mac's offer. That way I don't feel like— Oh hell, Elizabeth, forget I mentioned it."

There was real irritation in his voice. "I'll say goodnight now—I've got papers to grade and I need to be up early in the morning."

"Phillip—" A sudden sick feeling swept over her. *Why is marriage so important to him? And why can't I just go along with it?*

"Listen..." She had begun the sentence with no idea of what she was going to say, only hoping desperately to buy a little time. "Please, can we talk about this when you're out here this weekend?"

A chill silence was the only answer.

"Phillip, you *are* planning on coming out, aren't you?" *Oh god, why does it have to be like this? Why can't—*

At last the reply came. "Yeah... I guess so. But we don't need to talk about anything. You know what I want—and I know how you feel."

He hung up just a little too quickly and Elizabeth sank down on the sofa in front of the fire. *This is ridiculous. It's supposed to be the other way around—but I'm the one who doesn't want to commit.*

She reached out to stroke Molly's sleek coat, but the red hound slid from beneath her hand and off the sofa with a languorous grace, stretched, and retreated to the bedroom. Elizabeth picked up a throw pillow, still warm from the dog's body, and clutched it to her chest. *What's wrong with me?* Behind the glass door of the fireplace, the silent flames danced.

# Chapter 11

## *Big Lavinia*
### Thursday, December 14

A unt E, Manda and I are going into the 'ville to do the deliveries and some Christmas shopping. You still want me to get you a tree? I'm gonna be out near the farmers' market."

Elizabeth looked up from the purloined laptop, blinking as she returned to the here and now. She had been lost, fathoms deep, years long gone, in Nola Barrett's tale of the old stand on the Drovers' Road and the tangled lives of those who had passed through its doors.

"Tree?"

"*Christmas* tree. Big, green, pointy on top, lights, doodads, and the popcorn-and-cranberry chain that takes all afternoon to string. Didn't you say Rosemary and Laur would be here this weekend and we'd decorate the tree Sunday afternoon?"

Her nephew loomed over her, regarding her with an amused look. "Or were you just going to skip the whole Christmas thing this year?"

"No, of course not. I was just ..." *I sat down with my second cup of coffee to take a quick look at this stuff of Nola's, and my god, it's a quarter of ten.* A feeling of guilt assailed her.

"Oh, Ben, I meant to go down to the greenhouses first

thing this morning and pack the lettuce for delivery, but I got sidetracked. Let me get my——"

"No worries, Aunt E, Amanda did it while I was taking care of the watering. I seeded some more of the arugula and the red oak leaf too." His smile was complacent. "It's worked out really well, hasn't it—having Amanda helping take up the slack while Julio and Homero are back in Chiapas for the winter?"

*He looks like a big sleek happy tomcat,* Elizabeth thought, watching as her nephew sank into the chair at the end of the dining table. He stretched in the morning sun streaming through the dining room windows, and his long hair pulled back in the usual ponytail glinted, more gold than red, in the strong winter light.

"You're right; she's been a huge help. I wish we could pay her more, but——"

"It's not a problem, Aunt E, Manda's fine with things the way they are." A casual wave of his hand dismissed crass money matters.

"I'm glad she'll be here for Christmas, but what about her folks? Don't they want her home?"

"Manda says her folks always like to go somewhere for the holidays. This year it's Vail so they can ski. They have a house there along with the beach place at Casey Key."

"My god, *two* vacation homes? They must have more money than God."

"Yeah, pretty much. Her father has a bunch of different businesses." Ben had yawned, and added, "They invited Amanda and me to come with them to Colorado but we told them we had work to do here. Besides, she's not into spending a lot of time with her folks."

*I wonder what the story is with Amanda and her family. She's hardly mentioned them or her life in Tampa or her career in modeling. Her interests seem to be totally here—Ben even said she's been spending time at the library, reading up on the history of the area.*

Pulling on her heavy jacket, Elizabeth dug in its pockets in search of her gloves. *I wish I'd known—I would have taken Amanda to meet Nola, the old Nola. She could have told Amanda so much about the county. But it's too late now, unless there's something like a miracle.* The three dogs milled about her feet, eager to be out and doing. As she pulled open the front door, they shot onto the porch, barking with joy, each breath accompanied by a puff of white.

"You dogs, stay," she told them. "I'm going to the store." *And I'm going to see Nola.*

The Christmas decorations at the Layton Facility were drooping and worn, a little limper and a little sadder than they had been the week before. The sparsely decorated tree in the lobby sat at a tilt, its tinsel garland trailing on the floor. And the same frail woman in the wheelchair sat by it. Her robe was blue today but her hair was still in curlers and she still cuddled the worn baby doll.

Down the corridor, past room after room where occupants sat gazing dully at flickering televisions or lay open-mouthed staring at the ceiling. *Please God, don't let me end up like that—a sudden heart attack or something—oh, please—I'll take dying sooner rather than living on like this.*

And here it was, number 167 with the name cards on the door for Nola Barrett and Ronda Mills. Elizabeth took a deep breath and stepped into the room. "Hey, Nola, it's Elizabeth."

The bed nearest the door was empty—not merely empty, but stripped and draped with a single sheet that revealed the rigid and uncompromising angles of the foam mattress. The small clutter of personal items that had covered Ronda Mills's bedside table had been removed.

In the other bed, Nola Barrett lay curled on her side. Her eyes were squeezed shut but her lips were moving. Elizabeth moved closer, hoping for a miracle.

"Nola, it's me. Are you doing better?" She laid a tentative hand on her friend's shoulder.

The sick woman's eyes opened slowly. Elizabeth smiled and spoke in what she hoped was a normal and optimistic tone. "How do you feel today, Nola?"

Nola's head, its short-cropped black-dyed hair now showing a rising tide of white at the roots, rolled to and fro in hopeless negation. The tip of her tongue appeared and moistened her dry lips. Glittering eyes were fixed on Elizabeth's face, and a garble of nonsense syllables poured from the twisted mouth. The woman in the bed struggled, growing more and more agitated, but intelligible phrases would not form. Then, just as she had done on Elizabeth's previous visit, Nola Barrett spoke clearly and precisely—

> *"Like one that on a lonesome road*
> *Doth walk in fear and dread,*
> *And having once turned round, walks on,*
> *And turns no more his head;*
> *Because he knows a frightful fiend*
> *Doth close behind him tread."*

As Nola Barrett completed the verse, Elizabeth listened with a dawning comprehension. *She's using lines from poems she's memorized to communicate! She can't put together new sentences but she can repeat ready-made ones.* The woman in the bed waited, gray eyes intent on Elizabeth's face, willing Elizabeth to understand.

"Nola, you're *in* there, aren't you?" Elizabeth sat down on the bedside chair and pulled it nearer to the bed. She took Nola's hand and leaned closer. "I wonder—"

One of the young aides breezed into the room, bearing a cup of some clear red liquid with a bent straw in it.

"Hey there, Ronda honey; here's you some juice. You got some more company today, I see." The plump young woman thrust the cup onto the tray table and pushed it to the bedside.

"Her name's not Ronda." Elizabeth tried to hide her indignation. *I know how many people this poor girl probably brings juice to but, dammit, at this point her name is about all Nola has left.* "Ronda Mills is gone. This is Nola Barrett."

But the wide-hipped aide was out the door without looking back and on her way to the next room, pushing her jingling cart down the hall. Elizabeth squeezed her friend's hand. "I hope the nurses with the medications are better at knowing who's who. What happened to your roommate, anyway?"

Nola's mouth worked again and this time the words seem to come more readily.

*"No motion has she now, no force;*
*She neither hears nor sees;*
*Rolled round in earth's diurnal course,*
*With rocks, and stones, and trees."*

"That's Wordsworth—but I can't remember the name of the poem."

There was authority in the husky voice that came from the doorway. Elizabeth swung around to see an enormously fat woman, well past middle age, dressed in flowing black trousers topped by a long tunic of the same material. A brilliant red and green silk scarf, secured by a flashing diamond brooch at the left shoulder, hung in artful folds around an almost nonexistent neck. The newcomer's massive legs ended in improbably tiny feet jammed into low-heeled pumps of gold and silver leather that matched the huge shoulder bag she carried.

She made her way toward the bedside, puffing slightly with each step. Nola had closed her eyes—whether in response to the visitor's approach or out of weariness, Elizabeth couldn't decide.

After a swift glance that took in not only the invalid but everything in the little room, the woman cocked her head to one side, fixing Elizabeth with her penetrating gaze.

"Has Nola said anything yet that wasn't poetry—anything that makes any sense?"

"No, not really. But she—"

"I'm Lavinia Holcombe. Nola and I are friends from way back." The new arrival's eyes were back on the woman in the bed, taking in every detail of her condition.

Elizabeth stood. "Please, would you like to sit here?"

"Heavens no, you stay put." With an almost inaudible grunt of relief, Lavinia Holcombe plopped down on the edge of the empty bed. "My lord, what have they done to her hair?" Pale blue eyes, almost buried in doughy flesh, swept appraisingly over the sick woman. "Look at those roots—snow white, poor thing!"

She raised a well-manicured hand to fluff her own ash blonde coiffure. "Are you from Nola's church?"

"No, I'm just a friend. I live on Ridley Branch—the old Baker place." Elizabeth glanced at Nola, whose eyes were still tight shut. "My name's Elizabeth Goodweather."

"Goodweather? That's not a Marshall County name. Is it your married name?"

"Yes, it is. You're right; I'm a transplant. My husband and I moved here back in '84."

"*Did* you?" The pale eyes were assessing her. "And how do you come to know Nola? I don't remember her mentioning you."

*I didn't expect a kind of Spanish Inquisition,* Elizabeth retorted mentally but, exercising a little control, she explained sweetly that she and Nola shared an interest in old quilts. "I only met Nola a few months ago."

Then with a prod from the devil that always lurked just beneath her inherited Southern-lady politeness, she added,

"I guess you all have known each other for years and *years.*"

It *had* been years. Almost fifty. Lavinia Holcombe explained that she had been the mentor Nola Barrett spoke of—the recent graduate who had eased Nola's transition from poverty and rural Appalachia to an exclusive women's college in Atlanta.

"I always got such a kick out of Nola—a scrawny little country girl with big wide innocent eyes. She was as smart as they come—had memorized umpteen hundred poems and parts of poems. You know, English teachers used to be big on making students memorize verse—I still know a fair amount myself. Amazing, isn't it, how some things stick with you and others..."

Lavinia made a pretty flickering motion with her fingers. "Well, they're just gone with the wind. Lord, I couldn't remember a geometry theorem—or is it algebra that has theorems?—to save my life. But ask me to recite verses from 'The Charge of the Light Brigade' that I learned in grade school, and stand back to hear me volley and thunder! Of course, these days, they spend all their time teaching students how to take tests—there's not much time for poetry."

"Did you teach?" Elizabeth asked, warming to this somewhat fantastical personage. Nola lay motionless, either asleep or feigning sleep, and Lavinia Holcombe seemed ready to chat.

"Oh, I taught at the high school for a couple of years when I was first out of college. But then when I married Big Platt, he had other ideas—Platt had the old-fashioned notion that he didn't want his wife working *and* he was set on starting a family right away."

Lavinia's face creased into a wide smile and she gave an irrepressible wiggle of pleasure. "And, lord, how that man went at it! Platt had his office at home, right there in our house at Holcombe Hill, and when we were first married, he counted it time lost if we weren't bouncing in the bed first thing in the morning and last thing at night. Not to mention midafternoon, often as not, if he didn't have a client coming in."

The big woman settled herself more comfortably on the bed, ignoring Nola and continuing her narrative in an uninterruptible flow.

"Well, it was no wonder when our first, that was Little Platt, came along as quick as he did—nine months and one day after our wedding. I can tell you, I would have been *mortified* if that child had been earlier. You know what small towns are and how people used to wear out their fingers counting the months. Of course, it's different now; girls having babies, even announcing it in the paper without a husband in sight. I still call it trashy behavior, but with movie stars carrying on the way they do, it's no wonder young women think it's the 'in' thing to be an unwed mother."

The spate of words paused momentarily as Lavinia Holcombe opened her purse, drew out a package of cough drops, and began to unwrap one with a busy crinkling of cellophane.

Taking advantage of the intermission, Elizabeth ventured, "Well, I—" but Lavinia had already popped the lozenge into her red-lipsticked mouth, lodged it in one rouged cheek, and resumed the story, with a grand disregard of her captive audience's futile attempt at a response.

"Lord, those were hectic years, believe you me. Little Platt was hardly walking before I was expecting again. And the babies kept coming—one every two years, till, after three girls in a row, I put my foot down. 'Platt,' I said, 'I believe four's a gracious plenty. Any more children and people will think we're either ignorant white trash or Roman Catholics.'"

Lavinia looked at Elizabeth, light blue eyes twinkling,

and lowered her voice. "Not to mention that I was putting on weight with every baby—pounds that I could *not* shed no matter *how* many grapefruit and hard-boiled eggs I consumed. Of course, Platt didn't care a lick about that. 'I glory in your flesh, my dear,' that's what he told me. Why even there toward the end, whenever I had to give him his insulin shot, why, here'd come those fingers, grabbing at me. That man never lost interest, old and sick though he was."

As Lavinia ran a preening hand over one voluptuous thigh, Elizabeth remembered illustrations from a recent magazine article. The subject had been the varying standards of beauty at different times and in different cultures. *She's like one of those primitive Earth goddesses—the Venus of Willendorf or whatever. Or a Rubens—"acres of nacreous flesh," who used that phrase?*

Blithely unconscious of Elizabeth's scrutiny, the iconic figure prattled on. "But anyhow, after the fourth, I finally went and got fixed up with some birth control. I was sure my baby days were behind me—gave away the playpen and the baby clothes and all the other odds and ends that weren't family heirlooms. Then, on my fortieth birthday, with all the children off at school, that rascal Big Platt caught me unprepared. He'd brought out a bottle of champagne at lunch and when we wound up in bed I didn't even think about going and getting my diaphragm.

"It was a month later and Nola and I were taking a little trip down to Atlanta for a college reunion when I started feeling sick every morning. Well, of course, that turned out to be my youngest, Vance. When I think that I almost let her talk me into..."

The monologue ceased abruptly and Lavinia Holcombe stood, leaving the bed with two sharp little clicks of her heels on the tile floor. Stepping around Elizabeth, she moved close to the bedside where Nola Barrett lay, eyes closed, rigid and unresponsive.

Her back to Elizabeth, Lavinia spoke again. Quiet and precise, the words were measured out. "They say the last baby is always the one to be spoiled. And it may be true. Make no mistake, Vance is my heartstring. I would do anything for him."

# Chapter 12

## *Arval and Marval*
### Thursday, December 14

The thump of heavy boots and a muttered exchange of angry masculine whispers drew Elizabeth's attention to the door, where two hulking figures were engaged in a restrained tugging match over a potted poinsettia and a large basket filled with assorted tins and brightly wrapped packages.

"Big Lavinia tole *me* to bring this stuff in. *You* was s'posed to wait in the car and keep the heater running."

"Was not."

"Was too. Big Lavinia's gone kick your butt if—"

"Boys!" Lavinia Holcombe's peremptory tones immediately stilled the disputants who stood wedged in the doorway, each unwilling to release his hold on the offerings. "Bring those things in right now. Marval, you take the poinsettia—careful with those long stems—and Arval, you bring the basket. And you two watch your mouths; there're ladies present."

Lavinia Holcombe's tone was sharp but she smiled benignly as the two men, identically clad in the baggy camouflage pants and jackets that had replaced overalls for most of Marshall County's good old boys, lumbered into the room, meekly carrying their designated burdens. The poinsettia was placed on the windowsill to catch what weak rays of the winter sun could make their way between the close-placed wings of the Layton Facility; the basket was set on the empty bed.

"Marval, you open that round red tin and offer Miz Goodweather a ginger cookie. Then you and your brother may take four cookies each and go wait for me in the car. I'll be there in a jiff."

Elizabeth watched as the hulking giant *six and a half feet, I'll bet, and likely over three hundred pounds* pried open the lid of the cookie tin and offered it to her. As she reached for a cookie, she could see his anxious eyes on the remaining goodies, evidently trying to gauge if there would be eight left. Behind him, his equally large brother watched the tin just as avidly.

"That was very nice, Marval. Now let Arval take his... yes, that's right, four is plenty, Arval... and now you take *yours* and you boys may go."

The two hesitated, cookies clutched in their huge fists, identical puzzled expressions troubling their round, small-eyed faces. Arval elbowed his brother and whispered something. Marval cleared his throat and took a step toward the bed where Nola Barrett lay unmoving.

"He wants to know is she asleep or is she dead too?"

Lavinia flapped both hands at him as if shooing a straying animal. "I said, go along to the car. Nola's just resting. I swear, you boys could aggravate the life out of a saint."

As the two jostled obediently through the narrow doorway, Lavinia turned to Elizabeth. "I believe those boys split one brain between them. But they're good with machinery and Big Platt managed it so they got their driving licenses even though they can hardly read a lick. Do you know, they've been driving for us since they were sixteen—that's over twenty years—and neither one has ever gotten a ticket or even a warning."

Leaning again over the figure on the bed, Lavinia put a hand on her friend's bony shoulder. "Nola sweetie, I brought you a nice poinsettia for your window and some Christmas cookies and a few other things. You just have a good rest and get better, you hear? I'll be back soon as I can but you know what the holidays are like around Holcombe Hill. I declare, if I had any sense at all, I'd just lie down on this other bed and refuse to get up till the New Year."

As Lavinia made her stately departure, seeming to swirl, Loretta Young fashion, out the door, Nola's lips worked soundlessly for a few moments, then she whispered into the air, where the heavy fragrance of her recent visitor's expensive perfume still hung, magnificently routing the institutional aroma of Lysol and badly cooked food.

Elizabeth came closer to the bed, in time to hear the precisely enunciated phrase "The devil damn thee black, thou cream-fac'd loon!"

*"The devil damn thee black, thou cream-fac'd loon." Why would Nola say that? According to Miz Holcombe, they were old friends.*

The words had run through Elizabeth's head in a bizarre counterpoint to the saccharine Christmas carols that infested the grocery store. At last she had her cart heaped with the necessities for the coming weekend, including popping corn and cranberries for the traditional chain as well as a bag of oranges and tangerines for Miss Birdie. Waiting in line at the checkout, she leafed through the copy of the *Marshall County Guardian* that she'd picked up on her way into the store.

The Tuesday night meeting at the high school hadn't made it into the weekly paper, which went to press Tuesday afternoon. "SANTA COMES TO TOWN," shouted the four-inch headline, and the front page was devoted to the Christmas parade of the previous weekend. Elizabeth noted with displeasure the prominent photo of a lavish self-propelled commercial float labeled "Ransom Properties and Investments" in the midst of the usual small homemade entries, all pulled by tractors or, in one case, a riding lawn mower.

On an inner page she found a brief article titled "Gudger's Stand Development at a Stand?" The inconspicuous and poorly written piece seemed to say that the county commissioners were suspending further discussion of the proposed development at Gudger's Stand till the New Year. *Well, thanks heavens for that—considering Nola ought to have some say in this if she recovers. And, anyway, nothing's been determined yet about who owns the place.*

"You doin' all right today?" Mysti, one of the ever-changing series of high school girls who manned the registers while carrying on violent flirtations with the bag boys, began to scan the items with languid disinterest. Elizabeth moved quickly to begin bagging the groceries in her heavy canvas carriers before the gawky youth who had just wheeled out the previous order could return to work his special magic, dumping in the fragile produce first, then topping off with cans of dog food or bags of flour.

"Miss Birdie, I brought you some oranges." Elizabeth knocked at the glass-and-aluminum storm door, trying to make herself heard over the sounds of a game show's bells, buzzers, applause, and laughter. At last Birdie emerged from the back of the house and hurried to open the door.

"Lizzie Beth honey, come right in and git you a chair. I heared your vehicle and I was just gittin' that tape of the Goforth young uns fer you to borry." The little woman thrust out a small rectangle, wrapped in a well-used paper bag. "And there ain't no hurry bout gittin' it back to me—Peggy said hit was mine to keep. Ay law, look at them oranges...and tangerines too! Now what do I owe you fer these?"

Birdie's ritual question was met by Elizabeth's ritual answer. "Not a thing, Birdie. Merry Christmas."

Birdie pulled out a glowing tangerine from the bag and held it on her outstretched palm. "Seems like old Santy's come." She beamed at Elizabeth, her wrinkled face radiating a childlike joy. "You know, back when I was little, we didn't never see no oranges 'cept at Christmastime. Oh, we was proud if we could just each one git us a big old orange and a stick of peppermint candy."

She brought the tangerine to her nose and sniffed deeply. "If that's not the finest smell! I thank you, Lizzie Beth."

Handing Elizabeth the tangerine and pulling a second one from the bag, she motioned toward her kitchen. "Let's eat us one right now."

As they sat at the big Formica-topped table, luxuriously savoring the juicy, sweet-tart segments, Miss Birdie carefully put all the pieces of peel to one side, keeping them separate from the seeds and stringy white fibers.

"I always dry my tangerine peel, don't you?" *Don't you?* It was a standard rhetorical question that Elizabeth had come to understand was followed by an unspoken *And if you don't, why not?*

"What do *you* use it for, Miss Birdie? When the girls were little, I'd bake it into raisin bread—they loved it for peanut butter and jelly sandwiches."

"Now, I never thought of that. I generally grind it up fine to flavor my butter frosting for spice cake. I'm not much of a hand at makin' light bread—I allus buy it at the store. Biscuits and cornbread is more to my likin'. Didn't Luther nor Cletus neither one eat enough light bread to keep a bug alive. They just weren't partial to hit, someway." Birdie bit off half of one segment of fruit and stared closely at the remainder. "Hit beats all, how these things is put together."

Belatedly, Elizabeth brushed the seeds and wisps of white fibers from her peels and stacked them neatly beside Miss Birdie's pile.

"I was visiting Nola Barrett again today and a woman

named Lavinia Holcombe came in," she said. "I remember you and Luther always had good things to say about the Holcombes. Didn't they help Luther out somehow?"

"Oh, that was way back of this, back when some fool government woman wanted to take Cletus up and put him in some training school somewheres. She come to the house time and again and talked and talked to us and waved all these papers around and said what a fine thing hit would be and how iffen we didn't sign them papers, why the law could just step in and take my boy anyhow. You know what Cletus meant to me, Lizzie Beth, and how much help he was to us.

"Well, I was in a fine commotion of spirits about the whole thing and my Luther, you know how quiet he was, he just set there a-listenin' to me carry on one evenin' and then he says, 'Miss Birdie, don't you fret none. When I carried the corn to the mill this mornin', me and Cletus paid a call on Mr. Platt Holcombe up to his place. I told him how things was and he asked me some questions about our boy. Atter a while he told me not to worry none, he'd see to it that woman didn't come round no more.' And Lizzie Beth, she never did."

Miss Birdie beamed with smug satisfaction then turned a puzzled face to Elizabeth. "This Lavinia you was namin'— was she a big woman, fixed up all fancy and with a good bit of age on her?"

When Elizabeth agreed that this was, indeed, Lavinia, Birdie's perplexity seemed to grow. "Now that would be Mr. Platt Holcombe's *widow*, if I don't mistake. But seemed to me I heared—"

The telephone bleated and she started to pull herself up.

"Stay put, Miss Birdie; let me get it for you." Elizabeth was on her feet and moving toward the living room, where the cordless phone sat in its dock next to Birdie's recliner. Snatching it up, she carried it, still ringing, and handed it to the old woman.

"Hello? . . . Why, Bernice! I was just now thinkin' I hadn't heard from you yet today . . . yeah, boy, I'm right pert . . . me and Lizzie Beth are just a-settin' here, feastin' on some tangerines she brung me . . . Heared what?"

As Elizabeth watched, her friend's face passed through a series of strong emotions—from incredulity to revulsion and, at last, deep sadness. Birdie began to shake her head slowly, all the delight that had illumined her face a few minutes before erased entirely. At length, she ended the call with a solemn "I'll pray fer his family, Bernice, and fer him too. Ay law."

Clicking off the phone, Birdie laid it on the table. For a long moment she sat staring silently at the neat little piles of orange and white peel. When at last she spoke, her voice was weary and bewildered.

"Lizzie Beth, I've lived a long time and seed many a troublesome sight, but they's some things just beyond my understandin'. That was Bernice on the phone. Her boy was listenin' on his po-lice scanner like he always does and he heared that someone had found Payne Morton—you know, that young feller who pastors up to Dewell Hill? He's preached at our church back of this, durin' revivals. Anyway, Bernice's boy said they found him in his daddy's barn, cold as ice and dead as a hammer, a dreadful great pistol by his side and all his brains blowed out. Bernice's boy said they was callin' it a suicide."

# The Drovers' Road IV
## Luellen

*Hit shames me to say it but I took to Lydy Goforth right off.
Hit seemed a miracle to me, him risin up out of the morning mist
there by the river, the prettiest young man I had ever seen with
his black hair and blue eyes and his ways so pleasing and all.*

*When I went down the river that spring morning, the heart in
my bosom was heavier than the load I was totin. The feller I had
thought to marry had gone off without a word of farewell. To any
that could hear me, I had said Good Riddance and let on that I
didn't care none. But hit had left me all cold and swiveled up inside. Alls I could think to do was to work so hard every day that I
wouldn't have time for rememberin that I had let a low-built,
squint-eyed snake like Mabry Ramsey have his way with me.*

*And there was plenty of work to be done that spring and sum-
mer, what with Mabry leavin and Belle takin herself off in a
stagecoach to Warm Springs to get cured of barrenness. Belle was
past thirty and hadn't never been in the family way, though her
and Daddy'd been wed since she was fourteen. Time and again,
whenever they was a big job of work to be done, she'd act all
puny-like and whisper to my daddy that she thought she might be
breedin. But it never come to nothin. Daddy was a fool for Belle
and that's the truth. Some said, back then, that she had witched
him. There was a time I held such talk to be foolish but now . . .*

*Howsomever, when Lydy begun to talk to me and to help me
with the washin on that first day, all the bitter cold and hateful-*

ness that I'd carried in my breast seemed to melt away with his sweet talk and pretty ways. I could tell he hadn't never been far from that farm he told me of, way back up there at the head of Bear Tree, for he stared up at the stand house like he'd never seen so fine a place.

Ay law, says he, the size of hit! And two great chimbleys!

They's fireplaces in the four main rooms, says I. They burn a sight of wood in the cold times. If you can get wood in, my daddy'll take you on, for certain sure.

This is your daddy's place? He asked it, slow and considerin-like, never takin his eyes from off the house and the barns and the lots and the pastures. The house was lookin back at him, its windows winkin at him in the morning sun.

Why, yes, hit is, I told him. They call this place Gudger's Stand and my daddy is Lucius Gudger. He built the stand back when they first begun to make the Buncombe Turnpike from Flat Rock to Warm Springs. Daddy heired this land from his granny and, soon as he seed the wagons and stagecoaches begin to travel the new road, he set in to build the house, knowin hit would make a good stoppin place. And then, oncet the drives commenced, he fixed all them big lots and contracted with farmers up and down the near branches to grow corn fer him. Folks all round say he's the richest man in this part of Marshall County.

I felt a little shamed to be braggin so, but I had made up my mind I wanted Lydy Goforth to look at me the way he was lookin at the house. I'm all Daddy has, since my brother run off, said I, and led him up the slope to the deep-rutted road that curved around the hill. He followed me like a dog and when I took him to Daddy it was just as I'd thought.

Iffen you can handle an axe and a go-devil, young feller, and ain't afraid of hard work, there'll be a seat at the table for you with me and my family, a place to lay your head, and cash money once a month.

When Daddy named the amount he'd pay, I almost spoke out

*for hit was most double to what he had give Mabry. But Daddy was sizin Lydy up, like he might do some horse he was thinking of tradin for, and hit was plain he was likin what he saw.*

My daddy was right old. He had been born in eighteen and ought five, makin him fifty-four years of age when Lydy come to us. And though he was still a good hand to work, he had slowed up some since that young mule he was breakin had caught him a awful blow to his hip. Ever since that day he had walked kindly bent over though he scorned to use a stick to help him along. I believe that Daddy, even at that first meetin, had the same hopes of Lydy as I did. For he had to know that even was Belle to return, cured of her barren womb, and bear him a boy child the very next year, hit would be a long spell afore that boy, if hit lived, could take on the work of a man.

In the days that followed, I took care that I was in the way, with a clean apron and hair brushed shinin smooth, whenever Lydy come to the house, and I carried him cold buttermilk and gingerbread every morning when he was bustin wood.

Afore long Lydy begun to look at me with that same hungerin look he had give the house and land. All that summer we courted and hit was the sweetest time I ever knowed. He brung me flowers, picked from the wood's edge, and oncet a hatful of the first wild strawberries. Hit was with the taste of those strawberries in our mouths that we first kissed and the taste was there yet when we lay down together.

Time run on like the river, jostlin and endless. Belle was still gone and Daddy begun to treat Lydy more and more like he was a son and not just a hired man. One evening, when I had finished servin supper to the travelers in the public room, Daddy called me to his storeroom where he kept the cherry brandy and applejack locked away. He set there on a keg, smug as a cat what had got at the cream.

Well, girl, says he, when are you and young Goforth goin to come to an understandin? I'll not have my only daughter bearin a *bastard, says he and he leaned close with his eyes hard on me. Lydy's a good hand to work and I'd be happy to welcome him into the family—you best be careful he don't slip away like t'other one.*

*I didn't answer, for Lydy hadn't spoke yet. I believed that he would, sooner or later, but ain't nothing sure in this world.*

*Good thing you didn't waste no time grieving atter that Ramsey boy. He weren't much account nohow. Daddy stood up slow, as if his hip was painin him. He hitched up his britches the way he always done and I could see he was counting the kegs of brandy and applejack.*

*Tell you what, Lulie, he said at last. You and Lydy fix it up for December when the last drive is done. We'll have a weddin feast to beat all—roast a couple of pigs and a beef. And I'll undertake that no man there need go home sober.*

*I still didn't say nothing, just looked down at the floor. Daddy stood there watchin me and at last he said, Lulie, you tell that boy that you'll heir half of everything I own. He took a limpin step toward the door. Or all of it, iffen that stepmother of yourn don't come home soon.*

# Chapter 13

## *The Dark Angel*
### Friday, December 15

"Nola sweetie, time to get you ready-freddy for beddy-bye."

Twisting away from the paper cup of water and the outstretched palm holding the sleeping pills, Nola Barrett growled her displeasure through clenched teeth, willing the proper words to float somehow to the surface of the inky pool that was her dwindling reservoir of speech. Intolerable! Yet another whey-faced minion in childish, pajama-like garb was here to torment her, to address her as if she were an infant, to handle her as if she were a large, insensate rag doll. But without speech, she was powerless. Oh, for the words that had once flowed trippingly from her tongue! The words, the words, where were the words?

"Ooh, look what you got!" Busy fingers prying open the tin of cookies, investigating the contents of the basket, pillaging the items heaped on the vacant bed. "Did Miz Holcombe bring you this nice afghan? Or was it one of the others? My goodness, you're a popular girl with all these important visitors."

Cookie crumbs fell moistly on her arm as moon-faced Michelle, for that was the name on the little plastic plaque pinned to the loose pink-and-green printed top, loomed over her. "Here, I'll just lay it like this where you can see how pretty it is—all them soft blue and purple colors and that fancy fluffy yarn. My sister knits things like this."

The new aide jumped back as, with a heroic effort, Nola worried at the woolly covering till it slid off the bed.

"Now why'd you want to push it on the floor? Too hot? That's all righty; I'll fold it over the back of your chair. We can leave the nice goodie basket right here on this bed. Did you know Miz Holcombe has fixed it where you get to have the room all to yourself? You're a lucky girl to have a nice lady like that for your friend. Now let's just tidy up a smidge."

Nola watched in impotent fury as the horrible helper clattered and clanked and pawed through the two drawers and one closet that contained the sum total of her meager possessions. At last a string of suitable words presented themselves, the title of a children's book—Dr. Seuss, was it? She had read and reread the cheerful, jingling rhymes, hoping to delight Little Ricky with them on that longed-for, and now never-to-be, second visit.

"*'Marvin K. Mooney Will You Please Go NOW!'*"

The words were perfectly formed and spoken louder than she had believed herself capable of, but Michelle ignored her and went on flipping through the pile of cards from well-wishers, paying careful attention to each return address and message.

Nola gathered all her strength and slapped at the mattress. "Anoint thee, witch!"

The woman put down the card she'd been reading and gave Nola a sideways look from under her dark bangs.

"Nola sweetie, you're hurtin' my feelin's. Didn't Miz Holcombe tell you? She's hired you a team of Angel Aides. There's going to be one of us with you all the time, seeing you get taken care of just right."

The Dark Angel moved to the door and pushed it shut, then turned and smiled cheerily at Nola's helpless moan.

"We're goin' to get along fine, Nola, if you'll just be a good girl and help us help you."

Nola watched as Michelle plucked a little satin-cased pillow from the accumulation of objects brought by various visitors, supposedly to add to the invalid's comfort. "Let's tuck this under your head all comfy and then we'll swallow our pills like a brave girl."

As the Dark Angel approached, holding the pillow out like an offering, Nola began to scream.


Phillip Hawkins pulled his old gray car into its accustomed parking spot alongside the corncrib. As expected, Elizabeth was there in her jeep, waiting to ferry him up the steep road to the house. She always insisted that she didn't mind this little extra trip, but increasingly he was beginning to find that *he* did.

Cracking the door so that the overhead light would allow him to collect his possessions, he noticed the faded upholstery and the familiar Texas-shaped coffee stain on the seat beside him. Then there was the odd tilt the driver's seat had assumed. The shabbiness of the car seemed to have increased exponentially since last he'd paid any attention to it.

Well, what the hell, it got him where he wanted to go, didn't it? *Aging but serviceable, kinda like me.* The thought pleased him for a moment, but then a teasing inner voice whispered, *But* does *it get you where you want to go . . . really?*

Phillip took his hand off the door handle. He'd been considering the purchase of a four-wheel-drive vehicle— not to avoid being met and driven up the hill to Elizabeth's house, he told himself; no, it was for increased safety in the occasional icy driving conditions of the mountains. *And if*—he would not let himself say *when,* not yet—*if I take Mac's offer and go to work for him full-time, I'll really need four-wheel drive. But if I buy one now it might seem to her that . . . I don't know, sometimes I get the feeling she really likes living where not just anyone can come calling. A little like there's a moat . . . and she's the one in charge of the drawbridge.*

"Shit." He tried to shake off the brooding thoughts. It had been his intention to come out for the weekend in a cheerful mood, ready to join in the holiday preparations—which were evidently a big deal in this family—and to have a reasonable, rational discussion about marriage with the drawbridge keeper over there. Instead, he was feeling pissed. Pissed and ill-used. Probably do himself more harm than good, the way he felt right now, but it was too late to invent a reason for staying at his own place this weekend.

The door of the jeep opened. In the frosty air, Elizabeth's breath haloed her head, and in spite of the fading twilight, he could see her worried expression. Quickly he grabbed up the little overnight bag from the seat beside him and was out of the car just as she reached him. Trying to let go of the anger and frustration that had been building all week, he dropped the bag to the ground and opened his arms to embrace her.

"Phillip, I'm glad you're here." She flowed into his arms and they stood silently for a moment: two middle-aged people, much encumbered by heavy winter outerwear and vintage emotional baggage, but, for the moment, in perfect harmony.

"I missed talking to you last night. Your message said you'd be unavailable for the next twenty-four hours, so I didn't try to call you today. I started to worry that maybe you weren't coming out."

She grabbed at his hand as they walked toward the house, and he felt a stab of compunction as he remembered the brusque tone of the message he'd left for her.

"I'm sorry, Lizabeth—something came up with Mac. I'll tell you about it later; right now I'd just like to have a beer and find out what you've got planned for the weekend. When're the girls coming?"

"Tomorrow afternoon—tonight, it's just us." As she pulled open the front door, she favored him with a suggestive wink. Then the dogs swirled around them, each one demanding Phillip's full attention.

In the kitchen, a bowl of salted almonds, a wedge of Brie with French bread rounds, and two wineglasses were waiting.

"Let's sit in front of the fire—supper's in the oven and needs another half hour anyway." She ducked into the pantry, opened the refrigerator, and stood pondering its crowded interior. "How do you feel about having some champagne instead of a beer? The last big Christmas order went out today and I feel like celebrating."

"Champagne works—as long as you're not trying to make me weak and silly and then take advantage of me." He moved behind her and, wrapping her long braid around his hand, gently tugged till she turned to him.

"Lizabeth, listen—" Her blue eyes were full on him now, a little wary, perhaps, but she seemed ready to hear what he had to say. "Let's not get into any discussions this weekend about our living arrangements. I'd like to postpone that till"—he made a show of looking at the ceiling and calculating—"till the twenty-first, when AB Tech goes on break. Then *I'll* feel like celebrating. Let's make a date for that day—go somewhere. If the weather's decent, maybe take a picnic and go for a hike. Or just ride around the county. There's still a lot I haven't seen."

She agreed, maybe a little too eagerly, he thought. *Anything to avoid that discussion for a few more days.* The sour suspicion bubbled up, but as they settled onto the sofa, he resolved again to enjoy the weekend without thinking about the unknown future.

*Live in the Now, like Janie's always saying.*

Putting his arm around Elizabeth, he pulled her to him and began to practice his daughter's precept.

"You looked so tired and so...I don't know...so thoroughly *bummed* when you got out of the car I just didn't want to even mention it till later and then the champagne and the...the...."

Phillip looked up from the pile of homework papers he had promised himself he would finish tonight. A golden pool of light from the lamp at her elbow fell on the hoop in Elizabeth's hands, illuminating a square of randomly pieced jewel-tone fabrics. A block for a crazy quilt, she had said. Whatever that was.

He was amused to see a flush spreading across her face as she put down the embroidery. "...the...ah...fooling around put it right out of my mind," she continued, ignoring his knowing leer and Groucho-esque eyebrow waggle.

"See what happens when you give me champagne, Lizabeth? I knew you were trying to have your way with me, you unprincipled wench." *And quite a contradictory wench—the prim and proper widow with her embroidery now but an hour and a half ago—not so very proper and not prim at all.*

"What did my manly attentions make you forget, sweetheart?"

Her face remained serious, unmoved by his teasing. She picked up the embroidery hoop again and resumed the delicate dance of needle and silk floss that she had told him was called a feather stitch.

He rephrased the question, this time matching her mood. "What's wrong, Lizabeth?"

"Your business with Mac last night, was it something to do with Payne Morton?"

He stared. "Lizabeth...what do—"

"Miss Birdie told me that he'd killed himself."

"Miss Birdie?" He blinked, trying to make sense of what she'd just said. It didn't work; there was no way . . . "I don't get it. Mac said he was keeping it quiet till he'd had time to break the news to the family. And when I talked to him right before coming over here, he still hadn't been able to get hold of the brother. How in the name of—"

"Bernice called Birdie and told her. It seems Bernice's boy—"

"Don't tell me. Bernice's boy heard it on the scanner." The wildfire speed with which news spread through remote and straggling mountain communities was a constant amazement to Phillip. Modern technology had been a boon to these isolated folk. Though they chose not to live too close to one another, they were still keenly interested in all that befell their friends and acquaintances. With a sigh, he set aside the papers and quizzes.

"I might as well tell you all about it. No doubt Miss Birdie can fill in any missing details for you tomorrow."

He stretched and, spreading his arms comfortably across the back of the sofa, launched into his story.

"You know Mac had already sworn me in as a deputy back when you and I first met. Well, I never got unsworn, you might say. And Mac is in a kind of a bind right now; he needs someone outside the department to look into a . . . well, an ongoing situation. I can't say anything more about that right now. But anyway, when the call about the pastor came in yesterday afternoon, Mac got hold of me and asked if I could come along.

"I rode with him out to the scene. He was pretty ticked when we got there and found four, count them *four*, of his other deputies, contaminating the scene and blatantly ignoring chain-of-evidence procedure."

Once more she had laid the embroidery aside and was giving him her whole attention, eyes fixed on him.

"Anyhow, just about then another call came through—some domestic dispute up on Spillcorn—and Mac sent two of the deputies off to deal with that. So there we are, securing the scene the best we can, and one of the old boys who's still there sings out that there's a note jobbed onto a nail in the wall. Before Mac can stop him, he's pulled the note down, dropped it on the dirt floor, and managed to step on it, all in the space of about ten seconds. Mackenzie's foaming at the mouth, trying to stop this fool from contaminating the evidence any further but the damage is done."

She leaned toward him. "A note? Birdie didn't mention a note . . . what was in it? Did it say why the pastor killed himself?"

Phillip took his time answering, happy to have beaten Bernice's boy for once. "Well now, that was the interesting part. It wasn't so much a suicide note as a kind of confession. Let me see if I can remember how it went—it was kind of disjointed, but I guess if you're on the brink of shoving an automatic in your mouth and spattering—sorry, sweetheart—I shouldn't have—"

Her pained expression reminded him that she had actually seen and spoken with the pastor recently. Inwardly cursing his own ex-cop lack of sensibilities, he hurried on with the story.

"Anyway, it wasn't so much a note as a kind of series of phrases—'eleven years of agony and guilt . . . pay the price . . . she was willing . . . an accident . . . not right that no one knows . . .' Stuff like that—nothing that made any sense but it was bagged as evidence. But what kept me busy all last night was the piece of the note that we picked up after they'd removed the body and Mac and I were having one last look around. It was just a scrap—a corner of the note that must have gotten torn off when Deputy Doofus stepped on it. The first part was all smudged and illegible—all we could make out were the words 'in the silo at the old stand.'"

# Chapter 14

## *The Silo*
### Friday, December 15

Th he what?" Elizabeth was staring at him, as if he'd suddenly begun to speak in tongues. Then recognition dawned. "Do you mean that old abandoned thing in the field next to the parking lot at the bridge? It hasn't been used as a silo as long as I've been here—it doesn't even have the little dome thing at the top they usually—"

"That's the one." Phillip stood and bent to add another log to the fire. "And I gotta say, going down into that sucker after dark is high on the list of things I don't want to do again." An involuntary shiver ran over him as he remembered the previous night.

"How are you with heights?"

As the ambulance, followed by the unit carrying the other two deputies, had disappeared down the rutted, hard-frozen dirt road that curled away from the sagging barn, Phillip had found himself the object of Mackenzie Blaine's shrewd, assessing stare. The question was unexpected and Phillip's reply was suitably cautious.

"Why? What kind of heights?"

"Oh, nothing major. Say about the height of that silo at the old stand."

Phillip groaned. "You're not thinking of . . ."

The sheriff raised his eyebrows and waited.

"You *are* thinking of . . . oh, *man*, it's almost dark now!" Realizing that his objection was sounding regrettably like a whine, Phillip had switched to reason. "Listen, Mac, if there's anything in that silo—I say *if*—don't you reckon it could wait till morning?"

But Mackenzie was shaking his head and turning back toward his cruiser. "Morton's note said 'eleven years of guilt.' And that letter I got, the one that disappeared off my desk, it was talking about a gang rape eleven years ago. Now"—the sheriff stopped in his tracks and turned to wag a gloved finger in Phillip's direction "—that makes me wonder if maybe there isn't a connection between whatever caused the late pastor to eat his gun and the accusation in the letter. It also makes me wonder why Lester was so damned clumsy handling that suicide note."

The sheriff scowled. "If there's a connection between the silo and that letter I got, then I want to make sure I get there first. All four of those clowns who were on the scene when we got here are deputies I inherited from the previous sheriff. And they had plenty of time to read that note before I got there—for all I know they could have set up that 10-80—a phony domestic disturbance call—to give them time to get to the silo first. But I'm hoping that's not what happened."

Abruptly Blaine stalked off to his car and Phillip hurried to catch up with him. "Mac, what the hell are you expecting to find?"

Mackenzie stopped, his glove resting on the door handle. "I have no idea, Hawk. Probably nothing. If I had reason to believe there was"—he pursed his lips "—anything significant, I'd be obliged to call in the SBI and let them handle it. But at this point, I have no reason to suspect there's a . . . there's anything in there. Matter of fact, this is probably nothing but a wild-goose chase, and you're going to be completely justified in calling me six kinds of crazy. But if there's anything at all in that silo that has to do with whatever it was went down eleven years ago, I want it to be us that find it."

He opened the door. "Get in; time's a-wastin'."

Turning the ignition key, Mackenzie grinned. "I've always wanted to say that."


The silo had glimmered palely in the fading light as they parked at the far end of the riverside park, deserted now, even by the Canada geese. As he followed the sheriff into the weedy field that surrounded the lonely concrete structure, Phillip looked back over his shoulder at the old stand on its ledge overlooking the park, the river, the bridge, and the deserted fields. The last rays of the sun, sliding behind the mountains beyond the river, were caught in the upper windows of the old building, momentarily giving the impression of blazing fire within, then blinking out and leaving the glass blank, as if the house had closed its eyes.

"It doesn't look like anyone's been down this way recently." Blaine's words floated back to him on the icy air. Phillip followed, trying to shake off the memory of Nola Barrett's black-clad figure tumbling from the upper gallery of the old house.

"Maybe not recently, but in the past eleven years there have to have been kids climbing it like kids do, on a dare or—"

"Don't think so, Hawk. Till just a year or so ago, this field was used for pasture—feller in the house down that way kept cattle here. And between the bull and the five-strand electric fence and the fact that the old boy just despised a trespasser—kept a shotgun loaded with rock salt—kids around here had to find some other way of working out their daredevil tendencies."

The frozen vegetation around the base of the old silo was undisturbed, and a thin frosting of snow lay unblemished on the metal rungs that ran to the apex of the concrete cylinder. Phillip's eyes traveled up the meager ladder, lingered at the open top, and then returned to Sheriff Mackenzie Blaine.

"I've got a real feeling that question about heights wasn't just to make small talk. But there oughta be a way in around here . . ." Phillip began to circle the silo, then stopped, seeing the sheet metal that completely sealed off the rectangular opening.

Blaine called after him. "The old boy who kept the cattle here put that up years ago. Probably worried about a cow getting stuck in there. Once the cap was gone, I reckon the bottom got pretty boggy."

Phillip pried at the edges of the rusted metal, but the heavy bolts securing it to the concrete wall wouldn't budge. At last he abandoned the attempt and returned to Blaine. "Okay—so you want me to climb up that ladder—"

"Hawk, I'd do it myself if it weren't for my right knee. It's not back to full strength after the surgery. Still, if you don't feel up to it, I'll just have to—"

Phillip held up a hand. "Please, Mac, spare me. Did you bring a flashlight?"

But the sheriff was pulling something from his jacket pocket. "I've got you a headlamp right here. Free up your hands for climbing."

With the air of one bestowing a medal, he arranged the elastic bands over Phillip's watch cap. When the light was settled to his satisfaction, Blaine gave it a twist. An intense blue-white beam shot out, glancing off the nearby trees and momentarily making them look like photographic negatives.

Phillip swung his head from side to side, enjoying the ease with which he could pick out shadowy objects.

"Dammit, Hawk, watch where you point that thing!" The sheriff jumped back, an arm raised to shield his eyes. "How 'bout you use it to find your way up the ladder? The temperature's gonna drop like a son-of-a-bitch, with night coming on."

The iron rungs of the ladder were mercifully sturdy. *So far, anyway.* Climbing steadily and carefully, his gloved hands testing each rung before trusting his weight to it, his booted feet feeling carefully for a firm purchase, Phillip made his way up the silo's side at a stately pace. *The main thing is not to look down.*

And then he was at the top. Turning his head from side to side to relieve the growing tension in his neck and shoulders, he was startled and momentarily dizzied by the sight of the blue-white beam dancing crazily over the nearby leafless trees and the river beyond. Closing his eyes, he clung to the ladder, waiting for the feeling of nausea to subside.

"You okay, Hawk?" Blaine's voice sounded very far away. *How tall is this thing, anyway? It can't be more than forty, fifty feet.* Phillip tried to concentrate on breathing slowly. *Get a grip.*

He had gotten a grip and, calling down reassurances, laced with a little mild invective, had negotiated the tricky business of getting first one leg and then the other over the open top of the silo to begin the slow journey down.

"And you actually climbed right down *into* that old silo? At night? In the black dark?"

As he resumed his seat on the sofa, Elizabeth moved to sit beside him and he felt a tingle of pleasure at her incredulous gaze. Taking hold of her hand, he leaned back into the soft cushions, determined to make a good story of it.

"Well, I had a headlamp with a powerful beam, and before I started down, I took a good look at what was down there."

He didn't mention the sudden lurch his stomach had given as he stared down, far down into the core of the cylinder that echoed and magnified the clang of his boots on the ladder, amplifying even the sound of his breathing, coming faster and faster. He went on with his story, feigning matter-of-factness.

"From what I could see, the silo was about a third full of god knows what—old silage, leaves—just a bunch of gray-brown vegetable matter. And there was a weird musty, moldy kind of leathery smell—not awful, just not good."

"So, did you find anything?" In the flickering light of the fire, her face was that of a child entranced by a ghost story—apprehension and excitement teetering in a delicate balance.

"From up at the top it didn't seem like there was anything to find. But I kept on coming down the ladder. Then as I got closer to the bottom, I started to worry that all that leafy stuff would be like quicksand or something and I'd just sink into it. So when I got down to its level, I kept good hold of the ladder and eased one foot out onto the surface. The leafy part was about ankle deep but underneath there was a fairly firm footing—a little spongy and wet, but it could hold my weight."

He described how he had shuffled cautiously around the edges of the cylinder and then, realizing that it would have to be done, had gone down on his hands and knees and slowly crawled round and round, tightening the circle to examine every inch of the compost-covered floor.

"I even took off my heavy gloves and put on some rubber ones Mac had given me."

"Just in case," the sheriff had said, and Phillip had been happy to have them as he thrust his fingers into the rotting leaf-duff and scanned the lower level, groping about for whatever it was that the dead man had felt was worth mentioning in his final words.

"And?" The big-eyed kid-around-a-campfire look was still on her face.

"Well, there I was, inching along, pushing the leaves to the side, and feeling around like some obsessed snail who's lost a contact lens. I've got a pretty good rhythm going—sweep, feel, inch forward, sweep, feel, inch forward—and I'm thinking about how I'm going to get even with Mac, when all of a sudden my hand hits something different."

The half-buried, brown-stained object that the last sweeping aside of the leaves had revealed was lying on its side, just inches from his face. The one exposed eye socket was filled with dirt and what looked like a beetle's egg case. And though finding something of the sort was a possibility he'd considered, the sight had jolted him back onto his heels and he had let out a sudden, startled yelp that magnified and echoed within the concrete chamber.

Then, as his adrenaline level eased to normal, the shape of the skull registered.

"It's a friggin' *deer!* Mother of God, is *this* what the late rev felt guilty about—hunting out of season maybe?"

Snorting with disgust, he had grabbed at the forlorn relic to lift it out of the dirt, entertaining a fleeting notion of dropping the skull on Blaine's head.

"And then, just when I'd wrenched this damn deer skull up out of the dirt, I saw what was underneath it—and it wasn't deer bones. I didn't touch anything but I could see enough to recognize part of a pelvic girdle—a *human* pelvic girdle."

Elizabeth closed her eyes and he saw that the little girl listening to a ghost story was gone. This was no longer delightful scary entertainment, her face said. This is death and tragedy and sorrow close to home. Tightening his arm around her, he hurried his tale to its conclusion.

"And that was it. I scrambled back up the ladder in record time and hollered down to Mac that we had remains. By the time I was back on the ground, he had the SBI on his cell."

She opened her eyes and frowned at him. "The State Bureau of Investigation? How come?"

"Lizabeth, the Marshall County Sheriff's Department is fairly limited in terms of investigative resources, and the sheriff always has the option of calling in the SBI. In a case like this, it's more like an obligation. Morton's death was fairly straightforward—ninety-nine percent of the time, a bullet wound of that sort *is* suicide—self-inflicted lead poisoning. But this—remains that may be linked to a suicide, that may have been hidden all of eleven years—that's going to take some expertise. Hell, they'll likely have to figure out the cause of death for the deer too."

He could feel the shudder that swept over her. She bowed her head and he had to strain to catch the words she whispered.

"They'll have to find out about her as well...the girl... the one the pastor said was willing."

# Chapter 15

## *Light in a Dark Season*
### Sunday, December 17

Elizabeth watched as Ben and Phillip coaxed the monster tree through the cramped angles of the mudroom into the living room. The giant fir brought with it a whiff of cold, a spicy fragrance, and an ineffable feeling of the wild out-of-doors that completely vanquished the cozy after-breakfast aromas of coffee and sausage. The two men maneuvered the freshly sawn butt of the tree into a washtub in the corner of the room and wrapped a length of strong black rope once around the trunk halfway up, securing the ends to small hooks in nearby window and door frames.

When the washtub was filled with water, Elizabeth fixed a critical eye on the tree. "I'm not crazy about the way that rope looks but ever since the dogs knocked the tree over one year, I play it safe. And the branches mostly hide the rope, and once all the ornaments are on—"

"It'll be fine, Aunt E, just like it always is." Ben looked at his watch. "Sorry, I've gotta get down and do the watering. Phillip, I guess you're elected to help get the lights up. There's a ladder out back and—Aunt E, what time are the girls getting here?"

"Around three—Rosemary stopped and spent the night in Asheville with Laurel. She said they had some last-minute shopping to do, then they're coming out together. You and Amanda come on over around three and we'll get started on the dreaded cranberry-popcorn chain."

By two-thirty the multiple strands of tiny white lights were in place—on the tree, around the dining room windows, across the mantelpiece, and winding up the steep stairway to the loft guest room. Five fat evergreen sheaves—mixtures of yew, juniper, fir, and holly cut that morning—hung at intervals from the stair's banister rail, each adorned with a red satin bow. More branches had been laid on the mantelpiece, and an assortment of old brass candlesticks with red candles nestled among the fragrant greenery.

"I pop the corn a little ahead of time. If it sits a while and cools off, it doesn't shatter so easily when you try to run a needle through it." Elizabeth set down a huge stainless steel bowl, brimming with fluffy white popcorn, between two bowls of fresh cranberries that were in readiness on the chest in front of the sofa. Nearby was a spool of heavy-duty thread, several pairs of scissors, and a piece of paper pierced by an assortment of long, stout needles.

Phillip was studying the contents of the bowl with an apprehensive eye.

"What's the deal here? I've never done this kind of thing. Sandy always decorated the tree herself—it was a different *motif*, as she called it, every year. But I don't remember anything like this."

"The *motif* here is of the traditional persuasion, I guess—old-timey, country, whatever. We use the cranberry-popcorn chain, red satin bows, candy canes, and all the ornaments that have accumulated over the years, from ones I made when Sam and I were first married to the ones the kids made at school and even ones I inherited from Gramma—the girls would have a fit if they didn't see their old favorites."

She moved to the old trunk at the end of the love seat, gathered up the books that rested on its wood-slatted top, and opened the trunk lid. "The decorations are all in here but the chain has to get done and on the tree before we hang the rest."

Elizabeth watched as Phillip picked up the paper of needles and pulled one free, holding it between his thumb and forefinger and looking at it as if it were some curious new invention.

"Well, okay, give me some string and I'll get started. It's gonna take hours to use up all this popcorn." His face was a study in determination and she felt a surge of tenderness at his willingness to join in this admittedly tedious tradition.

"Not yet, not till the kids get here." Gently, she took the darning needle from him and returned it to the paper. "You'll see, with six of us working, it'll go really fast. Let's take a little walk while we wait for them."


The snow from the previous day was dry and squeaked beneath their boots as they followed the path at the top of the pasture. Delirious with the pleasure of human company, the three dogs romped like puppies, snapping at the fresh snow and making wild forays up the slope in order to hurtle down at one another.

A perfect winter day—bright sun, blue sky, clean snow. And ahead, the dark loom of the woods and the shadowy path lined with elegantly drooping hemlocks, the new snowfall a delicate lacy frosting on the graceful branches.

Elizabeth leaned down to brush the snow from the rustic bench at the edge of the woods. "We can sit here and keep an eye out for Laurel and Rosemary. It's too cold to stay out long but think how good the fire'll feel when we get back."

They sat in silence for a time, watching Molly and Ursa

disappear deeper into the woods. James, whose stubby short legs meant that his undercarriage and tender bits were in almost constant contact with the snow, began to shiver and to eye Elizabeth meaningfully.

"Okay, poor James, come here." Leaning down, she scooped up the little dog, unzipped her jacket, and tucked him inside. "He's just not built for snow; when it's really deep, I have a hard time getting him to leave the porch at all. I thought a sweater might be just the thing and got him one—but when I put it on him, he just fell on his side and refused to get up."

Phillip's perfunctory smile told her that his mind was elsewhere, and she leaned into him. "What's the matter? Do you want to go back?"

"No, this is great . . . beautiful." He hesitated, then enveloped her gloved hand in his. "It's just . . . I was wondering about all the stuff you do for Christmas. I mean, I know Sam's accident was right around this time—I guess I was wondering how . . ." He shook his head as if unable to find the words he wanted.

Elizabeth looked back at her house. Even from this distance she could see the greenery with its red bow hanging from the brass knocker on the blue front door. *The same as every year. And the tree will be the same and the cranberry-popcorn chain the same and the Christmas Eve dinner the same. And the ritual of opening presents, that will be the same too. A yearly renewal.*

But Phillip was waiting, his question hanging unfinished in the frosty air.

"Christmas was always a big deal for us. Not in the amount of money spent—we usually made most of our gifts—but big in the time we took to get ready and in how much we all enjoyed the various traditions we'd developed. And while Sam's accident would have been terrible whenever it happened, having it right before Christmas was devastating."

Phillip started to speak but she plowed ahead. "The decorations were up, everything was as it had always been, and in an instant it was like a particularly obscene joke. Suddenly, I hated Christmas—I would have made a bonfire out of the tree and every single one of the decorations if I'd had the energy."

She closed her eyes, remembering the black bitterness that had assailed her, the crippling anger and inexpressible sorrow. And the hurt in the faces of Rosemary and Laurel and the Christmas Day spent in mute grief while the tree was dimmed and dropping its dry needles on the brightly wrapped, unopened packages beneath.

"It was the girls who insisted that we mustn't lose the joy we'd always felt in the holiday season, the girls who wouldn't let me quit putting up a big tree, putting out the same decorations. And they were right. Eventually I was glad that Christmas hadn't been taken from us along with Sam."

"But it's not a religious thing for you . . . not a Christian thing."

Elizabeth pointed up the slope behind them. "See where the sun is now? It's so far south that it's barely clearing this ridge behind us. And in another hour, it'll be behind the mountain. For us, Christmas is a light in a dark season— the time when the days finally begin to get longer again. And a time to be together and celebrate the past and maybe brace ourselves for the future."

Her face crinkled as she said, "I don't mean to sound all New Age—pagan or Wiccan or whatever—but people have been celebrating the solstice and the return of the sun— that's s-*u*-n—for a lot longer than two thousand years. It was the Christians who grabbed the holiday—according to what I've read, Bible scholars are pretty sure that the historical Jesus was born in the spring. But celebrating the birth of a child is a good symbol too."

Inside her jacket, James was squirming restlessly. "Okay, James says enough lecturing." She unzipped the jacket and the little dog wriggled free, slipped to the ground, and began to bark ecstatically.

On the road below, the familiar farm pickup was crawling up the hill. Laurel was at the wheel, her sister Rosemary beside her. In the back were odd pieces of luggage and several large garbage bags filled with shapes that suggested an assortment of boxes.

Elizabeth grinned and stood. "Let the revels begin!"

As they crunched through the snow on their way back to the house, Elizabeth peered at Phillip. "What about you—what about *your* family traditions? You told me your kids always had Christmas dinner with their mom and her husband; are you ever included? I know lots of divorced couples still celebrate the big holidays together because of the kids . . ."

He made no reply and Elizabeth groaned inwardly. *Uh-oh, be careful here. You may have overstepped a boundary.* To her dismay, she found that she was prattling on. "I mean . . . I guess I've always assumed your divorce was pretty amicable . . ."

Phillip walked on in silence for another few beats. And then, as if commenting on some rather uninteresting fact, he spoke. "Sandy does invite me every year to come to Christmas dinner, but considering that I first met old Don, my soon-to-be replacement, when I came home unexpected one day, walked into our bedroom, and saw his hairy ass going up and down on top of *my* bed, on top of *my* wife—well, it's hard to keep that picture out of my mind. I believe it'd ruin my appetite for Christmas turkey, which Sandy always overcooked anyway. So, no, we haven't had any of those 'Kumbaya' extended family gatherings."

*This is nice.* Phillip looked around the crowded table. To his left sat Rosemary, dark-haired, dark-eyed, usually the quiet one but tonight deep in conversation with Amanda on the dehumanizing aspects of a fashion model's career. Laurel, whose mop of red curls vibrated with energy as she spoke, was giving an account of her latest artistic endeavor to Ben across the table from her. Ben appeared to be listening intently but his eyes kept wandering to the beautiful blonde on his left. *All of them together and the girls chattering like monkeys. Amanda fits right in with this family—she's usually so quiet, but tonight she's outtalking Laurel.*

Opposite him at the other end of the table, Elizabeth seemed to radiate contentment as she listened to the cheerful banter of the young people—*like a mother hen with all her chicks accounted for,* he thought, raising his glass of merlot to her when their eyes happened to meet.

Yards and yards of cranberry-and-popcorn chain—*one cranberry, three popcorn, one cranberry, three popcorn*—had been accomplished and hung in graceful scallops around the tree, a lavish red satin bow carefully tied at the upper point of each swag. The myriad eclectic ornaments had been unpacked, admired, explained, *that's one I made in second grade... I remember how I glued a bunch of sequins in my hair accidentally on purpose,* and dispersed among the tree's branches. Six dozen scarlet-and-white-striped candy canes had been hooked in place. *They have to all face the same way, Ben!* Rosemary had cautioned.

Ethereal music from Elizabeth's much-loved Windham Hill recording, *A Winter's Solstice,* played in the background as they devoured beef burgundy made the day before. There were boiled new potatoes, flecked with parsley, French bread for sopping up the rich gravy, and Laurel's special Painter's Salad: glass plates with a bed of baby lettuce topped by an artful abstract arrangement of orange slices, purple onion slivers, red bell pepper circles, blue cheese, and toasted almonds.

When at last even Ben declared that he could eat no more, he and Amanda began to clear the plates.

"Stay put, Aunt E. We'll make the coffee."

Phillip leaned back in his chair and sipped at his wine. *Nice kids, all of them. And they treat me like a person too—not some ancient geezer. I like that.*

Laurel turned her deep blue eyes on him. *Lizabeth's eyes.* "I'll bet *you* know what's going on down at the river. You're still big buddies with Sheriff Blaine, right? When Rosie and I passed by there this afternoon, there was yellow tape and official-looking vehicles everywhere. I thought maybe someone had drowned, but then we realized that something was going on around that old silo."

"As a matter of fact, I was there yesterday." Everyone looked at him, eager to be told more. *What the hell, it's not like it's some big secret. Might as well give them the straight skinny.* "They've found human remains at the bottom of the silo. They're excavating deeper to see if there might be more."

He had to admit it was kind of satisfying to have all of them paying close attention to his every word. *Who says an old guy can't get any respect!* He described for them the arrival of the SBI team and Dr. Alvarez, the blonde young woman who had turned out to be a well-respected forensics specialist.

Laurel was avid for details. "What could she tell from the remains—was it just bones or was there—"

"Yech, Laur, I'm still digesting my dinner! Could we skip all the disgusting parts?"

Ben was setting cream and sugar and an assortment of mugs on the table. Behind him, Amanda carried a cobalt-blue plate arranged with concentric circles of dried apricots, half-dipped in dark chocolate. Her face had gone pale and Phillip suspected that Ben's objection to gruesome forensic details was on her behalf. Rosemary too seemed less than eager to pursue the story; she excused herself quietly to let the dogs out. Elizabeth followed her daughter and the dogs out to the porch, saying she'd be right back.

But when Ben and Amanda had returned to the kitchen

to get the coffee and the herbal tea Amanda preferred, Laurel whispered urgently, "Was it male or female? Old or young?"

Phillip lowered his voice. "Dr. Alvarez said she couldn't tell till she got the remains to the lab. Some of the bones"— he lowered his voice still more—"had been gnawed. And a few were missing."

Laurel, as enthralled as her mother had been, nodded slowly. "So they don't know anything about who it was."

"Nope, no idea." And then, vaguely aware that he was showing off a bit, he added the sole piece of information the forensics expert had let drop. "Dr. Alvarez did point out something that could be useful in identification somewhere down the road. The right leg had sustained a double fracture maybe a year before time of death."

From the kitchen came the sound of shattering glass followed by Ben's quick "No worries! Just one of the cheap wineglasses."

Lost in speculation, Laurel paid no attention to the sound but pointed a finger at him. "You know who they ought to talk to about those bones? That guy who lives in that old brick building by the railroad track at the bridge. He pretty much watches everything that goes on in that area. And he's been there *forever*—I bet he'd know *something.*"

*Like mother, like daughter.* Phillip had to restrain himself from saying it aloud. Instead, he assumed an air of deep interest. "What's this fellow's name?"

"I have no idea. Everyone just calls him the Troll."

# The Drovers' Road V
## The Wrestling Match

The Professor turned away from the noisome bucket in the corner of the cell, carefully doing up his trouser buttons.

So the damsel Luellen tempted you with her white skin and golden hair and her father's wealth. And you pledged to marry her in December, meanwhile anticipating your union and enjoying her favors. Forgive my impatience, but what of this fiery-eyed Belle Caulwell you spoke of so feelingly? I collect that she was the wife of the innkeeper Gudger—why then was she known as Caulwell? Were they, indeed, wed? Or was it, perhaps, a less formal union?

They was wed, all right. Lydy pulled the thin blanket around his shoulders and settled himself more comfortably on the plank bed. Belle had her a piece of paper that the preacher and some others had put their names to, sayin that she was Ol' Luce's rightful wife. She just wouldn't go by the name of Gudger—said hit was an ugly-soundin name, like walkin in the mud.

An unconventional woman . . . and one with strong opinions, I see. And when she eventually returned home, it was to find you ensconced in the bosom of her family . . .

Naw, I was gone when Belle come back.

The Professor's eyebrows lifted but he remained silent. Lydy took the dipper gourd from the water bucket, sipped, wiped his lips, and resumed his tale.

It happened this-a-way. Back in August, afore the drives

started, they was a train of wagons headed for Warm Springs that stopped at the stand for a night. The wagon boss, a feller named Baylis Martin, was a particular friend of Ol' Luce and after supper they got to drinkin together. Whilst they was puttin down the applejack, they got to talkin about wrasslin matches they had seen and the money they had won bettin on them. And then Baylis went to braggin on this one driver of hisn, sayin as how ain't nare one yet ever bested Red Will.

Ol' Luce tips his chair back against the porch wall and says real easy-like, I got a gold half-eagle says young Lydy there can whup yore man.

Done, says Baylis, and hit was settled betwixt them to hold the match right then and there, as the wagons had to be on their way at first light. In no time atall, the drivers had cleared a spot in front of the house, making sure there weren't no rocks, and drivin in four postes. They wropped a stout rope all around them postes to make a ring and by the time me and the other feller had stripped to the waist, ever one at the stand was circled round that ring.

The sun had slipped behind the mountains just a little while since but they was still light a-plenty for wrasslin. I didn't figure hit to take too long, for I had always been accounted a good catch-as-catch-can wrassler back on Bear Tree, where I had learned enough tricks to let me beat fellers bigger 'n me. I knowed those tricks and what's more, I had bulked up considerable with all the good food that Luellen had been feedin me the past few months.

Red Will was a short, heavyset man with a long red beard. He ducked under the rope and stood in the center of the ring, still gnawin on a beef rib from supper. He looked over at me as I come into the ring, tossed the bone away, and grinned wide. I still remember how there was a little piece of gristle caught on his left eyetooth and how his two front teeth was bad chipped.

He come at me in a bull's rush afore the word had been given, but his hands bein greasy, I slipped out of his grip and took him

*down with a leg around his knee. I was hoping to pin him quick
and so end it, but he pushed free and got me in a choke hold. The
crowd was whoopin and hollerin and Ol' Luce was lookin fearful
for his five-dollar gold piece.*

*Red Will's elbow was squeezin my neck tighter and tighter. I
knowed that I could break loose but I also knowed I couldn't last
out a long match with such a big feller. I would have to make a
move right quick or be beat.*

*In wrasslin, round here most anything goes short of eye-gougin
and ear-bitin. What I done to break free and put the big feller on
his back was said by some to be an old Injun trick and by others
to be unfair. I had learnt it from an ol' boy I used to go huntin
with now and again.*

*Hit was a surprise to that red-bearded feller when he found
hisself flyin over my head. He hit the ground like a big oak fallin
and I was about to fling myself on him when I seen his left leg
was twisted under him in a way that weren't natural. He let out
a great howl and the referee stepped in and motioned me back.*

*Goddammit, Luce, Baylis hollers. That leg's broke. Who's
gone drive Red Will's hitch? I ain't got nare extry man with me.*

*I could see that Ol' Luce was of two minds about the whole
thing. He pocketed the gold piece that Baylis had slapped angry-
like in his hand but he passed the jug to his friend and patted him
on the back.*

*Now Bay, don't take on so. You leave your man here. Lydy'll
go in his place. Come winter, him and my gal is goin to wed but
hit might be as well was he to see a little of the world afore he set-
tles down.*

*He turned to me and said, Son, you stay with Baylis as long
as he needs you. Just see you're back here in December.*

*And so I come to take to the Drovers' Road.*

# Chapter 16

## *Talk to the Troll*
### Monday, December 18

O h, hell! Not *again!*"
At the other end of the bridge, warning lights were flashing and barrier gates were beginning their creaking descent. Resigning herself to a lengthy wait, Elizabeth slowed the jeep to a crawl. A wailing whistle announced the arrival of three locomotives at the head of the seemingly endless 7:40 a.m. freight train.

No other vehicles were on the bridge and she pulled close to the tracks to watch the many-colored freight cars roll by. The proliferation of graffiti *tags, that's what they're called,* was astonishing. *The sophistication of some of them!* Elizabeth marveled. *But however can they paint those intricate designs on the run?* Her inner eye summoned up a lone teenager, pierced, tattooed, and clad in the regulation baggy jeans and hooded sweatshirt, wielding a can of spray paint with each hand, all the while casting nervous glances over his shoulder.

As the train flashed by—boxcars, tankers, flatcars, coal cars—carrying the cryptic tags far and wide, Elizabeth thought of dogs, lifting their legs on automobile tires in what she presumed was canine certainty that now their territory would be extended to wherever the marked tire rolled.

An imposing blue-and-white tag caught her eye. THE MOST DETERMINED, it read, and the skinny teen of her imagining raised both cans in a victory salute as he completed his work and darted into the shadows, just ahead of two husky, sweating security guards who lumbered after him, waving futile truncheons.

The cars rolled on with their hypnotic clickety-clack, picking up speed till the graffiti became a dizzying blur of shape and color. Abandoning her attempt at reading the tags, Elizabeth turned her attention to the railroad itself—*the road of rail. According to Nola's manuscript, the tracks were laid right on top of what used to be the Drovers' Road.*

Her gaze followed the path of the train as it disappeared around a bend, heading for Ransom and, beyond that, Asheville. The history of this old road, as related by Nola's manuscript, was fresh in her memory, and where the present train chugged and hooted, she imagined a broad path, churned to mire by the passage of hundreds of hogs kept in check by drovers whose long, red flannel-tipped whips cracked, urging the weary animals toward the next stand.

*And before it was the Drovers' Road, it was the Catawba Trail, running all the way from Georgia to Tennessee, so Nola's notes said. The Indians used it for hunting and trading.* The vision of the muddy road and the drive of pigs faded, replaced by copper-skinned, buckskin-clad hunters, creeping single file along a narrow but well-trodden path. In her mind she saw the man in the lead raise his hand to signal a halt as a giant buck crashed out of the undergrowth ahead.

*And before there were people,* Elizabeth mused, deep in the romance of the past, *it was probably an animal trail—maybe a migration route. There were buffalo around here a long time ago, weren't there?*

The train had slowed to a crawl now. *Nola said that this part of the Drovers' Road was called the Buncombe Turnpike and it ran from Greeneville, South Carolina, to Greeneville, Tennessee. Who was Greene, anyway? Popular fella. A general*

*or something, the manuscript said. And then the railroad came
and the Dixie Highway followed along part of the same route,
going through North Carolina from Michigan to Florida.*

One of her neighbors *was it Odus?* had described the
Appalachian exodus to Detroit, where there was work in
the car plants. *"Law, Miss Elizabeth, come time school let out
for the summer, they'd be a big old Greyhound bus, just a-waitin'
at the schoolhouse door to carry them young uns straight to Dee-
troit. Hit was a sight on earth, some of them young uns they'd
come out that door with their graduatin' paper in one hand and a
grip in t'other, climb aboard that ol' bus and never look back."*

Yes, it was Odus who'd told her that story. He himself
had gone to the big city, lured from the farm by the accounts of high wages. *"Didn't stay but a day. I flat couldn't
stomach the water they had there—tasted just like that ol'
Clorox. Now that stuff's fine to put in the wash and hit'll flat
cure foot rot in a cow but, aye god, I don't want to drink hit, do
you?"*

So Odus had boarded the bus again for the long ride
back to the mountains, where days were long, work was
hard, and cash was scarce, but pure water bubbled end-
lessly from a mountainside spring above his house. Many
others, not so fastidious where their water was concerned,
had stayed, sometimes marrying Michigan-born spouses,
but always determined to "come home" on retiring. In early
June, when families and churches celebrated Decoration
Day by cleaning graveyards and renewing the wreaths and
floral displays on the graves, these transplanted natives
would return in their big Detroit-made vehicles with
Michigan plates, eager to reestablish old ties.

*Back when I was growing up in Florida we saw lots of
Michigan plates there too. Yankees escaping the cold winters to
walk on the beaches with their chalk-white legs and black shoes
and socks. And then in summer lots of Florida folks headed for
the North Carolina mountains to escape the heat. And now
they're coming to get away from the hurricanes—building their*

*second or third homes in these preposterous communities. A kind
of folk-wandering that—*

A horn's indignant blast roused Elizabeth from her
reverie. The train's caboose vanished around a curve and
the barrier gates stood upright. As she pulled forward
across the tracks, she was surprised to see a crew of surveyors at work below the old stand under the observation of
the grizzled old man her daughters had always called the
Troll.

On the night before, when talk at the table had turned to
the bones in the silo and Rosemary had excused herself,
Elizabeth had followed her to the porch, concerned that the
subject under discussion would inevitably awaken memories of the unhappy events they had endured together the
previous year. But Rosemary had reassured her. "Really,
Mum, I'm fine. I just wanted to see the night sky—it's so
gorgeous here." Then, with a wry twist of her mouth, she'd
added, "And sometimes family can be a little overwhelming
when I'm out of practice."

They had returned eventually to the dining room to hear
Laurel, passionate as always, admonishing Phillip in ringing tones. "Talk to the Troll! He's bound to have seen
something—no, bad idea, not you. He's pretty shy of new
people and particularly men. But he's really nice—I was
painting down at the bridge a few years ago and he eventually got curious—ambled over to see what I was doing and
actually turned out to be pretty chatty. He even invited me
into that neat old building where he lives and gave me a
glass of iced tea. Did you know that place was a general
store years ago? There's this big door on the side that used
to open right to the railroad tracks for trains to offload supplies. He had a bunch of antiques in there—a fair amount
of junk too, but some neat stuff."

"Well, maybe it'd be a good idea—" Phillip had begun,

but Laurel's enthusiastic spiel had run on, stream-of-conscious fashion.

"—I could go talk to him myself but I'm heading back to Asheville early in the morning and I'll be busy with a class for the next three days, then we have an open house at the studio. Maybe Mum could talk to him. She always waves at him when she goes by, so at least he'd recognize her. I bet Mum could find out if the Troll knows anything about the bones in the silo."

And now, here was the so-called Troll, leaning against one of the junk cars that had found a final resting place in front of the derelict building. As she passed by him, Elizabeth slowed, lifting a finger from the steering wheel and nodding in the traditional local mode for greeting someone you recognized but didn't actually know. Lifting his chin in acknowledgment, the Troll continued his rapt study of the surveyors.

The car behind her honked impatiently, and before she knew quite why she was doing it, Elizabeth pulled onto the shoulder and motioned the fuming vehicle around her. The monster SUV roared past, its driver glaring down at her in righteous indignation.

"Florida people!" Elizabeth muttered at the sight of the license plate.

Pulling her jeep farther off the road, she considered what to do. In the rearview mirror, she could see the Troll watching her. At his side sat one of the many cats that were always in evidence around the old brick building.

*What now, Sherlock? You told Phillip you'd see if this guy knows anything about the silo.* Elizabeth looked over to the parking lot and the field beyond, where the old silo stood. No one was there but the structure was encircled with yellow crime scene tape. Fresh tire tracks crisscrossing the parking lot hinted at recent activity, unusual for this bleak season. Along the riverbank, leafless trees inked mysterious hieroglyphics on the lead-colored sky. *What now, indeed?*

The rap of a knuckle against her window made her gasp: she turned to see the Troll's black-framed glasses trained on her. His lips were moving and she punched the button to lower her window.

". . . in need of assistance?"

Elizabeth blinked. "Excuse me?"

Resisting the impulse to punch the window button again as a faint odor compounded of alcohol and unwashed clothes crept over her, she listened in bewilderment as the question was repeated.

"I asked if you were in need of assistance, Mrs. Goodweather. Allow me to introduce myself." The Troll tugged the greasy leather bomber cap from his head and sketched a courtly bow. "Thomas Walter Blake the Fifth, at your service."

Behind the thick lenses, bloodshot gray eyes twinkled in private amusement as Elizabeth, her mouth open but wordless, continued to stare, bewildered. Then, abruptly recollecting her mission, she cut the car's engine off, the better to hear and be heard.

"No thanks, I'm fine. I was just . . . well, I was wondering about those surveyors up there. But how do you know my name? You called me—"

"I called you Mrs. Goodweather. That's correct, is it not?"

"Yes, but—" *Who is this guy? Not what I expected, that's for sure. Sounds educated and, now that I see him up close, he's not as old as I thought. And I'd better stop thinking of him as the Troll. His name is—oh, hell, why don't I ever pay attention to names? He said it was Thomas something something the Fifth. I think.*

"I met your daughter Laurel a few years ago. Quite a talented artist. Her work at that time put me in mind of Gauguin. A charming young woman—we had quite a discussion, if I recall correctly, about the early Impressionists and the Fauves. Of course, I'd seen her coming and going with you and your other daughter for years. But I hadn't known your names."

A little smile lifted the corners of the man's mouth. "Goodweather—a propitious cognomen indeed. Do you know, Mrs. Goodweather, I've taken quite an interest in your Laurel."

"Phillip, I swear, when he said that, it sent a chill over me. I just stammered out something about being late for an appointment and got out of there. Laurel said he was a nice harmless old guy, but you know how utterly naïve she is. There's something weird about him—he looks like a bum and smells like a drunk but he talks like a . . . like a bloody college professor."

She had driven, far too fast, up the winding road to Dewell Hill, pulled over into the parking lot of the old church, and called Phillip on her cell phone.

"So I got no information but now I'm wondering if this Troll guy has ever been under suspicion."

"Because he said he's taken an interest in Laurel?" Phillip's voice sounded amused and this annoyed her.

"Not just that, because he's always *there*—near the silo where the remains were found, near the house where Nola jumped . . ."

"And near the old bus, where the rape was supposed to have taken place. Okay, sweetheart, let me talk to Mackenzie. He probably knows all there is to know about this guy— count on it. I'll get back to you tonight."

On her return trip, several hours later, Elizabeth slowed her grocery-laden car as she neared the bridge. The survey- ors were still at work around the old stand, but the Troll was nowhere to be seen. Elizabeth studied the dilapidated brick building that was presumably his home. *Or his lair.* Once a prosperous mercantile concern, the business had closed long before she and her family had moved to the county. *Birdie said she used to shop there in the forties but it closed when the passenger trains quit running. And that old guy has been hanging out there—I guess living there—as long as I can remember.*

She cast a dubious eye at the rusting cars and trucks resting on blocks in front of the old building. The sight of an enormous tabby cat perched on the hood of a battered old pickup should have been reassuring but instead seemed somehow ominous. *As if it's lying in wait for someone.*

The building's ground-floor windows were covered with plywood, but a curl of smoke from a stovepipe protruding from the flat roof hinted at warmth within. At one of the upper windows, a movement caught her eye, a figure moving past the glass.

*He's completely harmless, Mum. Just an old guy who's kind of sad and lonely.* Isn't that what Laurel had said? Still…

The phone in the house was ringing as Elizabeth climbed the steps, lugging four overflowing canvas grocery bags. Hurrying for the door, she grimaced to hear the ring stop abruptly. But then the door opened and Rosemary, phone in hand, said, "It's for you, Mum—Sallie Kate."

"Merry Christmas and fa, la, la, la, la, Elizabeth honey! Have y'all got that big old tree up yet? I was at the fillin' station when Ben and that pretty lady of his pulled in with it in the back of the pickup. Lordy, it looked as big as the trees they use at the White House! Good thing you have a cathedral ceiling.

"Listen, honey, Harley and I have to go out of town— Harley's mama's taken the notion that this is her last Christmas and she's fussed and carried on till the whole family has to be there. Of course, she did the same thing two years ago. Then she got to feelin' some better and by the time Christmas rolled around last year, she felt *so* much better that she went with a pack of her widow friends on a tour bus to Vegas for the holidays. But now she's back in her 'O Lord, take me now' mode, rollin' her eyes and clutchin' at her heart every whipstitch. She can't fool me, though. Harley's sister told me the old bat's signed up for a cruise to Cancun in February."

"Merry Christmas, Sallie Kate." Elizabeth hurled herself into the tiny breach afforded by her friend's pausing for breath. "Is there anything you need me to see about for you while you're gone?"

"Well, honey, I'm kinda worried about Nola. I went by the nursin' home today and they've put her on oxygen. I visited with her a while but, except for that she was havin' trouble gettin' her breath, she was about the same—still not making much sense. She was sayin' something about fog and little cat feet but I couldn't make anything out of it. Anyway, I asked this girl at the nursin' station and she said Nola'd had a real bad episode of chokin', but that she was stable now, long as they kept her on the oxygen. So then I wanted to know had they gotten in touch with Nola's niece about her breathin' problems and Miss Nurse turned all snippy on me, said that the Layton Facility *always* observed proper procedure and she really couldn't discuss her patient with a nonfamily member. Honey, Nola looks real bad.

"And on top of everything, those RPI people (you know, Ransom Properties and Investments—the big developers) have done a kind of end run around all the rest of us real estate people. They've about got the county commissioners convinced to condemn the property there at the old stand 'for the good of the County' so RPI can get their fancy development underway. Those no-good county commissioners are just rarin' to pull that eminent domain thing. Honey, they're talkin' about a takin'!"

# Chapter 17

# *The Dying of the Light*
## Tuesday, December 19

Why the hell are you still living in Weaverville, Hawk? I thought that you and your lady were—"

"Thanks for coming by, Mac. I figured you still weren't sure how private your phone was, so..." Pointedly leaving the sheriff's question unanswered, Phillip stood back to let Sheriff Blaine into his house. "I wanted to run something by you before I left for class."

Mac held up a white paper bag from which emanated a promising aroma of sage and pork grease. "I brought the sausage biscuits from Sadie's Place. Do you have the coffee ready?"

In the kitchen, Blaine glanced around. "I don't know how you can stand all this pink, Hawk. Of course, the blue curtains *are* a nice touch. Would that be baby blue or sky blue? Or maybe powder blue? I have a hell of a time remembering which is which. And look at those ruffles! Three rows of them! Must be a bitch to iron. Still, if it's..."

Phillip poured the coffee and waited for his friend's humor to run its course. The cutesy country décor of this rented house never failed to amuse Mackenzie. *And I keep telling myself that it's not permanent, that I can live with it*

*another few months. But by god, I'm sick of pink and blue and
ruffles and leering teddy bears.*

"...maybe get some tips from you for spiffing up the
jail. I know I read somewhere that pink walls can make the
prisoners calmer and easier to handle—"

"Mac, what do you know about that guy who hangs out
at the Gudger's Stand bridge? Lives in that old brick
building? Lizabeth was talking to him this morning and
something he said, something about noticing her daughter,
has got her all stirred up."

The sheriff reached for his coffee mug and rolled his eyes.
"I guess I don't even want to know why Miz Goodweather's
talking to Tom. Has she been over checking out the silo
too?"

*God knows,* thought Phillip. "So what about this guy? Is
he a squatter? Local fella or what? Lizabeth said he sounded
educated but smelled like booze. And this was just an hour
ago—a little early for a drink."

"Unless you're an alcoholic. Tom's a serious drunk—
gets up, takes a drink or two to get a nice little buzz going,
then works on it the rest of the day." The sheriff crumpled
up the wrapping from his sausage biscuits and lobbed it
toward the plastic-lined garbage pail in the corner of the
kitchen.

Phillip watched as the wadded paper dropped dead center into the receptacle. "So you know him. Does he have
any history on him? Any criminal record?"

"It's not a crime to be a drunk—as long as you don't
drive. But to answer Miz Goodweather's question: there's
nothing to link Tom Blake with any of these ongoing investigations." He cocked an eyebrow at Phillip. "It *is* her question, isn't it?"

Phillip shrugged. "Inquiring minds, et cetera."

Mackenzie put his elbows on the table. "Tom Blake's
an interesting story. He's the last of a prominent local
family—the family that owned Wakeman's—you know,

that hardware store downtown—and quite a few other businesses in the county. Tom's no squatter—he holds the title to that old ruin he's living in."

"So he's not a bum—just a drunk."

"Yeah, that's pretty much it. I checked him out when I first took office. You know, scruffy-looking guy, no visible means of support, and hanging around that park that's full of kids and paddlers in the summer—I was definitely suspicious. But there's never been a complaint against him—he just likes to watch the river and what's going on."

"No job?"

"None that I've ever heard of. His folks are dead and I guess they left him enough to live on. Story is, he was a career officer in the army in the seventies, and then, all of a sudden, he was back home with a drinking problem. But like I said, he's never caused any trouble—you tell your lady not to worry about it."

"I'm worried about Miss Barrett—the lady in 167."

The woman at the nurses' station looked up from the computer screen, her fingers momentarily paused in the air above the keyboard. "Yes? What's the problem?"

Ignoring the unspoken message sent by those hovering fingers, Elizabeth plunged ahead. "Well, Nola's just recently been put on oxygen but she's still struggling to breathe. Her eyes are red and her nose is runny—does she have a cold? Or could it be an allergy? She seems miserable and I know she can't communicate very well . . ."

"And you are . . . ?" The raised eyebrow accused her.

"Just a friend. But Nola's only relative doesn't live around here and I thought . . ." *I thought I ought to check on her. I even made a special point of coming early rather than the usual visiting times. I've heard of the neglect and sometimes even abuse that can go on in these places. And with Nola unable to speak for herself . . .* "I thought I'd drop in."

♂

Elizabeth had punched the button to let herself in the front
door of the Layton Facility and had hurried through the
hallways, crowded with rattling carts of wan-smelling
breakfast trays. Nola's door had been shut, but she had
pushed it open and peeped in to see her friend gasping for
breath and struggling to sit up in her hospital bed.

"Nola! Let me help you!" Elizabeth had rushed to the
bedside and assisted the wheezing, panting woman to raise
herself. She had placed two pillows behind her friend,
checked the oxygen line to see that there were no kinks in it,
and had readjusted the little two-pronged nosepiece to lie
more easily on Nola's face.

The older woman had said nothing as she was being
ministered to, but, turning piteous, red-rimmed eyes on
Elizabeth, had clutched at her hand, gripping it tight as she
struggled for air. After a few moments, her breathing
seemed to improve and the grip relaxed.

As before, Nola Barrett had summoned up words from
her capacious store of memorized verse.

> *O the mind, mind has mountains; cliffs of fall*
> *Frightful, sheer, no-man-fathomed. Hold them*
>    *cheap*
> *May who ne'er hung there.*

Her dry rasp of despair pierced Elizabeth's heart.

"Nola, please! Just lie back and catch your breath. I'll go
talk to the nurse and see what they can do to make you more
comfortable."

The woman at the computer heaved a little sigh and looked
past Elizabeth. "Miz Barrett's guardian is aware of the situation. Layton Facility appreciates your concern and will

make every effort to provide your loved one with professional, compassionate care in a—"

"Mrs. Goldwater?"

There was a tap on her shoulder and Elizabeth swung
around. The thin, henna-haired young woman was regarding her with ill-concealed annoyance.

"Tracy! I didn't know you were still in town. I was just in
with Nola. She seems—"

"She's failing, Mrs. Goldwater," Nola's niece said flatly.
"The doctor says she's just given up. Of course, that's obvious, considering she tried to kill herself." Tracy's gaunt
face was devoid of emotion as she delivered this pro-
nouncement. "It's kind of you to come to see her, but it's
not necessary, you know. She has round-the-clock care—an
old friend of hers has seen to that. And she's probably not
even aware of you."

Elizabeth stiffened. "Oh, but she is. She talks to me.
Haven't you heard her quoting poetry?"

"Talks to you?" Tracy sniffed. "Is that what you think it
is? The doctor says it's just babbling. There's even a medical term for it—'lalorrhea'—diarrhea of the mouth, he
called it."

She shifted the manila envelope she was carrying to her
other arm. "How about those quilts of Aunt Nola's, Miz
Goldwater? Have you had time to look at them? I'd like to
have some idea of how much they might bring."

"It's 'Goodweather,' actually. But I'd rather you just said
'Elizabeth.'" Struggling to maintain the appearance of civility, she forced her mouth into the semblance of a smile.
"I've started mending them and I've talked to a few places
that deal in antique quilts. If you like, I'll follow through
and try to get you the best price I can. I'd feel I was helping
Nola in some way."

Tracy's eyes narrowed and she was silent for a moment.
Then, with a dismissive shrug, she replied, "Whatever—
one less thing for me and Stone to worry about."

She turned and headed down the hall for Nola Barrett's room. When Elizabeth followed her, Tracy glanced back in apparent surprise but said nothing, merely raising her eyebrows.

Nola was still sitting up but her eyes were closed and she was breathing loudly, with a regularity that suggested sleep.

"Where the hell's that aide Miz Holcombe hired? She's supposed to be here all day till the night duty girl comes on."

With scarcely a glance at her aunt, Tracy whirled around the small room, tidying, rearranging, watering the poinsettia and the other flowers and plants that crowded the windowsill.

Elizabeth picked up her jacket and the book of poetry she had brought to read to Nola. The young woman continued her frenetic activity, her face set in a disapproving frown.

"Tracy, I heard that the county commissioners were talking about using eminent domain to get control of the Gudger's Stand property. Is that true?"

The frenzied movement slowed, then stopped. Tracy's cold gray eyes turned to Elizabeth. "They're looking into it. And it would suit me just fine. If they did that, the house and the land could be bought by RPI right away, without having to wait to figure out exactly who it belongs to. Of course, everyone knows it comes to Aunt Nola—it's just going to take a while to prove it. But if things drag on too long, RPI is likely to take all that money somewhere else. If the county does a taking, the money will go into escrow until it can be proved that Aunt Nola's the owner."

"But that won't help your financial situation now...it could be months or years before..."

"I know that. But an interested party has offered—" Tracy bent to retrieve an empty plastic cup from the floor at the foot of the bed. "You'd think that for what she's being paid that girl could pick up stuff. Anyway, if you want my opinion, Miz Goldwater, the sooner they tear down that creepy old house, the better. It's never brought anything but bad luck to my family—and there's that pretty afghan on the floor." She reached into the narrow space between the bed and the wall and pulled out a beautiful web of soft blues and purples and lavenders.

"Well, I was wonderin' where that had went to."

Elizabeth looked up to see a chubby young woman in bright blue scrubs and an orange-and-pink top standing in the doorway and peering at them from under thick dark bangs. A stale whiff of cigarette smoke clung to her.

"Nola was takin' her a little nap and I just slipped out for a ... I wasn't gone but a ... well, she don't hardly ever ..."

"Michelle"—Tracy's tone was sharp as she cut short the aide's stumbling explanation—"has my aunt had any more of those choking spells?" She cast a chill, accusing eye on the flustered young woman. "And I'd appreciate it if you'd try to keep this room a little neater," she added, folding the afghan precisely and placing it on the vacant bed.

The aide bustled in and made a great show of rearranging Nola's bedcovers and checking the oxygen line. "No, not to say *chokin'*. She breathes easier some times than others but she ain't had nothing you'd call a *spell*. That nice doctor come by yesterday—no, it was the day before that—and he was here when she was took kind of bad, but he got her straightened out and said it wasn't nothing unexpected. It was him ordered the oxygen."

"Who else has been to see my aunt?" Tracy demanded of the hapless Michelle, who was bumbling around the little room in search of something to do.

The aide screwed up her face in an effort of memory. "Well, the juice lady and the speech therapist was—"

"I don't mean the people who work here." Tracy was obviously exerting great control over her temper. "*Visitors*, did Nola have any visitors?"

"Oh, yes." Michelle's pudgy moon face brightened.

"Those twins, Arval and Marval, come by with some more cookies from Miz Lavinia Holcombe. And a nice lady named Lee . . . Nola's neighbor, she said she was. A couple of ladies from the church. I think that was all . . . No, there was one more, a funny old man who looked like one of them homeless people you see."

Michelle wrinkled up her nose in distaste. "He smelled like he might of been drinkin' too. But he talked like an English teacher, more big words than you ever heard."

# Chapter 18

## *Two Sides of a Mirror*
### Thursday, December 21

Phillip came awake to the *whpp-whpp-whpp* of Molly's long ears flapping as she stood, stretched, and shook her head, the opening movement of a morning ritual. *Now she'll come over by the door and wait and if I don't move she'll whine real soft and I can get up now and let her out or I can pretend I don't hear her and she'll keep whining.*

Turning his head, he saw that Elizabeth, as usual, was curled up on her side, the heavy comforter pulled well up over her ears. Deep, regular breathing suggested that she was oblivious to the importunities of her dogs. *She says she never hears them this early—that they're taking advantage of my good nature.*

In the dim, predawn light, he could see Ursa shambling toward the door to join the increasingly impatient Molly. The two dogs stared expectantly at him.

He groaned and swung out of bed, shivering as the chilly air hit his naked body. "Okay, ladies, at your service." Molly began to dance impatiently, but Ursa yawned and sat back down while Phillip pulled on his robe. James, curled into a tight ball at Elizabeth's feet, snored on.

When he returned to the silent bedroom, a barely perceptible glow rimmed the mountains on the eastern horizon. He slipped into the warm bed and leaned back to watch the sunrise through the three big uncurtained windows. *Always different. Makes it hard to go back to a bedroom where all you see is walls or curtains.*

At his side Elizabeth stirred. "What time is it?"

He reached out to tug at her loose braid. "Almost seven-thirty, my love, and you're about to miss the sunrise."

She rolled over and frowned at him. "Seven-thirty? I never sleep that late." Shrugging off the covers, she pulled herself up to look toward the windows.

"There it comes," she said, looking to the right where a deep red shaft of light announced the winter sun, edging its way over the dark mountains. They watched in comfortable silence till the molten ball broke free of the earth. The red became gold and then an unwatchable white heat, and the sun, smaller now, began a slow crawl along its southern boundary.

Elizabeth let out a soft sigh and leaned against him. "Today's the winter solstice—the shortest day of the year. Right now the sun's as far to the south as it can go. It'll just creep along the ridgeline over there and be behind Pinnacle around three-thirty. But then tomorrow it'll rise just a tad back to the north. A few more days—by Christmas—it'll be obvious that it's on its way back to due east."

She turned a wry smile on him. "This is what I was talking about the other day, when you asked about our Christmas celebrations. Watching the sun move across the sky day by day, I began to understand how primitive people might have worried that maybe the days would just keep getting shorter and shorter. And then, when it looked like the sun was coming back, they would've had good reason to celebrate."

"Speaking of celebrating, Lizabeth, are we still on for

that hike? I tell you what, I'm ready to be done with criminal justice classes and overheated classrooms and kids with blank expressions and wires in their ears for a while—and I'd like to see a little more of the county." He rolled out of bed and reached for his jeans. "It looks like the weather's going to cooperate—clear as you could want—and when I let the dogs out earlier, it didn't seem that cold."

She was still staring out the window, seemingly lost in thought, one hand absentmindedly rubbing James behind the ears.

"Something wrong, sweetheart? Don't you want to—"

The shadow of sadness that had clouded her face was swiftly replaced by the full radiance of her smile. "Oh, I'd *love* to go for a hike. And I know exactly where we should go to make the most of the shortest day of the year."


"Max Patch is forty-six hundred feet—pretty high for this area, and there's a 360-degree view. So we'll get all the daylight there is. It's a beautiful spot—one of the highlights of the Appalachian Trail in this area."

"How about Mount Mitchell? It's the tallest, right?" He glanced to the passenger seat, where Elizabeth was flipping through a guidebook. She looked at him over the tops of her reading glasses.

"It's kind of sad and creepy up there—the forest is dying from acid rain and some kind of insect—the woolly whatsit—is attacking a lot of the trees. Max Patch isn't as high but I think it'll be more cheerful."

They were passing through Hot Springs, the quiet little town at the intersection of the French Broad River and the Appalachian Trail. The streets were all but deserted this morning, and some of the businesses bore CLOSED FOR THE SEASON signs.

"Quite a change from the summer. There were hardy

hiking, biking, and camping types all over the place as I re-call."

"Uh-humm." She was still immersed in the guidebook. "This is cool. It's about the big fancy hotel that was built here at the springs. Remember, there was something about it in the bit of Nola's manuscript that I read to you? According to this, in the 1800s, Hot Springs—well, Warm Springs as it was called then—was one of the premier tourist destinations on the East Coast. In 1837 there was a 350-room hotel and people from all over rode stagecoaches for days along the Drovers' Road to get here. Can you imagine? . . . They had a dining room that could seat six hundred!"

"What happened to the hotel?"

"Burned . . . and then another one was built . . . and in 1920 that one burned down too . . . and that was the end of the glory days for Hot Springs. But things are starting to pick up now—no huge hotel, but lots of nice smaller places—inns and B and B's. It's a pleasant town."

Flipping to another section of the guidebook, she ran her finger down the page. "Just stay on this road till we get to Meadow Fork. There're a few more turns and we'll end up on a gravel road that'll take us to a parking area at the trailhead. Then it's just a half-mile easy walk to the summit."

They drove on in silence. From the corner of his eye, he could see that she was caught up in her own thoughts and blind to the passing scenery.

*What's eating at her? I know she's worried about that Barrett woman but she called the nursing home before we left and they said the old lady was hanging on. And Sallie Kate told her that it wasn't likely anything would happen with the property at the river till after the holidays. Lizabeth was fine last night, laughing and carrying on with the kids at dinner and then later . . . but today, I don't know . . . she's in a weird mood.*

As if she had heard his thoughts, Elizabeth reached over

and laid her hand on his arm. "I'm glad we're going. I always try to be out of the house on the twenty-first."

"How come?" He laid his hand over hers and squeezed it. "Because of the solstice?"

Her hand clasped his and one finger traced a spiral on his palm. "Because it's the anniversary of Sam's death. If I'm at home, it's too easy to relive the whole horrible sequence—from watching him go out the door early that morning to the phone call late that afternoon to—"

She stopped abruptly. "Anyway, when I'm outside and away from home, it's easier to let go of all that. Particularly up on the high places where life and death seem like..." She struggled for the right words. "...like two sides of a mirror."

*Two sides of a mirror? What in the world did I mean by that? Poor Phillip—the first day of his vacation and I'm coming over all...whatever it is. Get over it, you fool!*

The road wound higher and higher, through wooded slopes of green pines and gray-brown leafless trees. No sign of snow here, but ahead of them rose the rounded contours of a mountain, its upper third cloaked in soft rime ice.

"Phillip, look up there—where we're headed! It's magical!"

They continued on, steadily gaining elevation. And now the trees on either side of the road were cloaked with the crystalline rime—shining white twigs and branches gleaming against dark trunks. And then they were at the parking area where a brown-and-yellow sign proclaimed MAX PATCH TRAILHEAD: PISGAH NATIONAL FOREST. A vast meadow lay all around them, punctuated by fairy-tale trees frosted with white, by clumps of skeletal weeds transformed to modern art by their coating of feathery crystals, and sagging barbed-wire fences glittering like gemstones in the morning sun.

They were alone in this enchanted place where the deep clear sapphire of the sky came down to meet the bare slopes and whitened trees. Elizabeth felt a surge of emotion welling up at the sight—but whether it was joy or sorrow, she could not have said. *The two sides of the mirror: touching, but worlds apart.*

Pulling on their jackets and shouldering the knapsacks that held a picnic lunch, they left the car to follow the broad grassy trail to the summit. Elizabeth carried the hiking staff Sam had made her years ago, not really necessary on this gentle walk, but a comfort in her hand. *A summer path through a winter world,* thought Elizabeth, as they climbed slowly, pausing every few minutes to take in the changing view. *I could almost believe that it might lead to summer itself.*

And without warning there was an opening in the trees and they were looking out across the tops of a sugar-frosted grove below them and beyond that the nearer slopes, dark but glazed with ice, and farther away the breathtaking procession of mountains, range after range rising one behind another like waves, shading from deepest ocean blue to insubstantial shadows that lost themselves against the sky.

*And the sky itself, pale where it touches the mountains, but deepening to that amazing, almost cobalt blue higher up.* She could feel tears brimming in her eyes and she turned impulsively to Phillip. "I'm so glad to be here today. And so glad you're here with me."

"Me too." He was studying the view intently. "It's funny—I didn't think I'd been here before but it seems so familiar. . . ."

They walked, emerging from the trees onto an open field that stretched out and gently down to show an endless vista of layered pastels in the distance. A little farther and they were at the metal sign that marked the summit.

"It's the top of the world!" Throwing open her arms, Elizabeth turned in a slow circle, her head back and her face to the cloudless sky above. "The perfect place." Catching sight of Phillip's beaming smile, she went to him and hugged him hard. "You thought I was going to break into a chorus of 'The Hills Are Alive,' didn't you? I swear, if I could carry a tune, I probably would. Isn't this *amazing*!"

Without waiting for a reply, she released him and pointed to the footpath that snaked its way across the meadow to disappear into a small dip.

"Want to do a little section of the Appalachian Trail? We could follow it till lunchtime, have our picnic, then head back."

They ate their ham-and-cheese sandwiches sitting on the dry grass of a little hollow just off the trail. The sun was warm there, and in spite of the coffee they had shared from a small thermos, they both felt drowsy and little inclined to move.

"I'm going to stretch out for a few minutes, Lizabeth." Phillip yawned and, shoving the sandwich wrappings back into his knapsack, lay down, using the lumpy little bag as a pillow. "Ten minutes, no more," he promised.

Elizabeth sat quietly, trying to absorb the beauty and the peace that she felt all around her, to let it flow through her and become a part of her being. The soft touch of the sun, the familiar bitter tang of the coffee in her mouth, the scents of dried grass and clean mountain air, the deep, deep, mesmerizing blue of the sky above her, the murmur of the breeze in the trees just below . . .

*There're* leaves *on those trees. That's impossible.*

With the help of her hiking staff, she levered herself up and took a few tentative steps down the steep slope toward the golden-foliaged wood. *I know some trees hold on to their leaves a lot longer than others, but this is unbelievable.*

She blinked. A thin curl of blue smoke was wisping up in the midst of the golden billows below her. She blinked again and saw, through the trees, the outline of a log house with a tall stone chimney that was the source of the smoke. *Weird. I didn't think anyone lived up here.*

Looking back at Phillip, she saw that he was sound asleep, his chest rising and falling, his lips parted in a half-smile. *He must be having a nice dream.* The sight of him aroused tender feelings—maternal, rather than erotic, she noted with amusement.

"You folks picked a good day to come up here."

She dropped her staff. Swinging round, she saw a man climbing toward her from out of the golden grove. A battered black felt hat was on his head, and he wore loose jeans and a brown jacket that might have been fashioned from a woolen blanket. He looked to be in his forties, possibly younger. His face was brown and weather-worn but his eyes sparkled blue and clear as the sky, a webbing of fine lines at their corners.

"You surprised me. I didn't know anyone lived up here anymore. Are we trespassing? We didn't mean to." She stepped forward, hand outstretched. "I'm Elizabeth Goodweather. I have a farm over near Ransom."

"Pleased to make your acquaintance, Miz Goodweather. James Suttles. No, ma'am, you're not trespassing. You and your man are just where you ought to be."

His smile was as warming as the sun and he looked at her, she thought, as if he knew the answer to some question she hadn't yet learned to ask.

"Is that your place down there?" As she looked past him, she could make out more shapes beyond the trees: a barn with a white mule standing in the open doorway, the log house and several outbuildings, rows and rows of small trees and shrubs, and a kitchen garden with covered beds. "You must be quite a gardener, to have things growing at this time of year."

"Anytime's good for growing, if you give your heart to it." He smiled that secret smile again and bent to retrieve her hiking staff. For a moment he held it in both hands, then offered it to her. She took the staff and almost dropped it again. The familiar touch of dry, long-dead wood was gone: the stick in her hand was as cool and moist to the touch as a fresh-cut sapling.

*What is this? Am I dreaming? Phillip's the one who's asleep.*

"Who *are* you?" she demanded.

"I told you, Miz Goodweather, I'm James Suttles. I've lived here for quite some time—time out of mind, as folks say."

He looked up at the sun, now past its zenith and sliding westwards. "You know, to the old people, this was one of those special days. *Solstice,* they called it. In the Latin, that means 'sun stands still.' And when the sun stands still, well, you might say that time stops..."

*Is this man crazy? Or am I? Am I on the other side of the mirror?*

"...and when time stops, past, present, and future are all the same. It doesn't matter which side of the mirror you're on." His smile was gone now and his stern eyes were boring into her. "You need to stop worrying about the past and the future, Miz Goodweather. Don't you see they're all the same?"

Elizabeth stared, speechless.

James Suttles raised his hand and pointed behind her. "Your man's waking. You'd best go to him now."

She turned her head and looked back up the slope to see Phillip rousing and rubbing his eyes. "Go on now," the gentle voice urged.

Without looking back, she obeyed.

# The Drovers' Road VI
## Driving Red Will's Hitch

Luellen took on right much at my leavin but Ol' Luce told her that she could spend the time I was gone readyin her clothes and bedding, for when we was wed.

Lydy studied the grimy cuff of his homespun shirt and ran his hand over the knee of his jeans pants. Luellen made these here clothes for me—they was to be for our marryin. A look of regret passed over his face. Then he shook his head and continued his story.

The Professor, who had been diligently plying a wood sliver in an attempt to clean his fingernails, ceased his exertions. It must have been difficult to tear yourself from the bosom of your intended and take to the road. I can only speculate—

Tell the truth, Professor, I was plumb tickled to be goin. Bein at the stand day atter day and watchin the stagecoaches and wagons comin from places I had only begun to hear of and on their way to places I hadn't never been—well, hit had put a longin in my heart to see some of the world afore I settled down at Gudger's Stand.

Luellen's eyes was red with cryin when she waved good-bye the next mornin. I set up high on that wagon seat with the reins in one hand and a whip in the other and couldn't do more than nod her way. It was a four-mule hitch they had give me to drive, and corn and the night's rest had made them rank. The near leader, a big sorrel horse-mule they called Pete, had danced *around like a unbroke colt when I come to put the gears on him, and they was all of them right mettlesome. There weren't no time for sweetheart good-byes.*

*And when the lead team turned their noses to the road and all the wagons swung in behind, I felt my spirit lift again just like when I run off from my uncle's place, though it remained my firm purpose to marry Luellen in December. I had no doubt that her daddy would keep his word and I figgered that someday hit might be me with the keys to the storeroom and a chest full of gold, like everyone said Ol' Luce had. But Luellen's way of hangin on me all the time had come to seem kindly tedious. And she was bad to take chances, slippin out at all hours to where I slept—ever since that first time, I had gone in fear of what Ol' Luce might do, was he to find us layin together afore we was wed.*

*We set off downriver, following in the ruts of all the wagons and stagecoaches that went back and forth between South Carolina and Tennessee. The road bein dry, hit made for easy travelin. And by the time the sun was shinin full on us, the mules had settled down and I could lean back and take it all in. The clompin of the hooves, the jingle and creak of the harness, and the steady sound of the river filled my ears. Up the mountain to the right I could hear the hammerin of one of them big pecker-woods and then that crazy laughin sound they make when they take wing.*

*I tell you what's the truth, hit were a fine day to be alive. I dug a journey cake out of the poke Luellen had give me and gnawed on it as we went along.*

*It was nigh midday when we come to a stand. Not near to the size of Gudger's, hit had a few lots for stock, a long low log house, and, set back behind a big garden, a little stone house. They was a stagecoach stopped out front and a boy was unhitching the horses. Passengers was climbin out of the inside and down from the top and they was headin for the porch of the log house, where a dark-complected feller waited to bid them welcome. I seen a tall woman, almost as dark as him, coming through the garden with a big basket of greens on her arm. There was flowers in the black hair that fell loose down her back, most to her knees.*

*The feller drivin the wagon in front of me threw up his hand and hallooed but we kept on goin as Baylis was naming to make it to Warm Springs by nightfall. We was haulin dry goods from the mills of South Carolina as well as a world of stores for some big fancy place there at the springs.*

*It's called a ho-tel, one of the fellers told me when we stopped that night at the inn just across the river from Warm Springs. The Patton Hotel. Used to be an inn there, just a regular stage-coach stop like this. But then word got round about the warm springs and how the waters could cure all kindly of ills, so rich and sickly folks begun to travel from the lowlands just to waller in the water that comes flowin out of the ground already hot. Then the Patton family bought the place and built this great fine building, three stories high and beds for near three hundred people. Why, says he, they even got a room just fer dancin, and hit so big the whole of Gudger's stand house could fit inside.*

*Now I found such a tale hard to credit and started to speak, not wantin to be taken for a fool. But another feller who was there at the table—a little feller, travelin alone and headed for South Carolina—he leans over and says real low, What kin you boys tell me of Gudger's Stand? I heared things . . . and he cast his eyes about the room real skeered like.*

*What manner of things? says ol Baylis, starin at the traveler like a bull about to charge.*

*Well, there's some who say folks has stopped there for the night and never been seen again. The little feller drew back from Baylis's gaze. Understand, I don't say it's so. Just what I heared.*

*Baylis flung his big head back and let out a great laugh. Only thing you need fear at Gudger's Stand is gittin tangled up with Gudger's wife. He don't take kindly to that. But I don't believe—and Baylis looked the little feller up and down like he would the runt of a litter and hit hardly worth drownin—I don't beleeeeve, he said, drawin the word out long and grinnin fit to bust, that she'd take to you nohow. She likes em big and young.*

*Ever one there nodded and one said, Now that's the truth, and somebody asked me what had happened to that Ramsey boy used to work there. He went off, I said, and I seen one of them fellers nudge the one next him.*

*That's enough idle talk, boys. Baylis stood up and yawned. We got to get these goods unloaded first thing in the morning and be on our way to Greenville.*

*But before we hit our bedrolls, Baylis come over to me. Lydy, says he, they's a feller here has driven for me back of this and he wants me to take him on. I appreciate you drivin Red Will's hitch today but now's your chancet. I'll pay you fer your time and you can walk on back to Gudger's Stand and be with your sweetheart by tomorrow evening . . . or, if you druther, I can put in a word for you with the folks at the hotel—bein as Ol' Luce ain't lookin to see you till December. Come fall, you could go with a drive and see a little of the world.*

*He looked at me real close and said a quare thing. Might be good for your health, boy, was you to stay here in Warm Springs.*

# Chapter 19

## *Aunt Omie Remembers*
### Thursday, December 21

"WW here were you?" Phillip yawned and looked at his watch. "I feel like I slept for hours, but it was ten minutes, on the nose."

"I went down there a ways." Elizabeth motioned to the slope behind her. "To get a close look at those trees. And then there was—"

He craned his neck. "That's a pretty spot, the way it's sort of set off from everything. Look how the light hits on the ice and makes it look gold instead of white. Of course, with the sun on it that way, there won't be any ice at all in another half an hour."

A strange look crossed her face and she turned slowly. She stood there, her back to him, scanning the wood below as if looking for something. He watched as she shook her head slightly, then raised her hiking staff to examine it minutely, running her fingers along its length. At last she turned and came to sit beside him.

"Are you okay, sweetheart?" He peered into her face, puzzled.

"I'm fine—maybe a little . . . I guess 'mazed' would be the word. Drunk on the day and the scenery."

She grinned and, to his relief, it was the familiar Elizabeth again. Reaching for the knapsack, she said, "I think I need some more coffee before we start back."

He was behind her as they started up the trail to the summit. She strode along with a spring in her step. All traces of the odd mood that had possessed her were gone.

*A spectacular place,* he thought, gazing at the blue mountains folding away on every side. *I can see what she meant about wanting to sing.* He cleared his throat in an exploratory way, then began, quietly at first but rapidly gaining confidence and volume.

> "*We hike along the woodland trails,*
> *And if the way is long,*
> *We drink some booze…*"

She had stopped and spun around at the first notes and was regarding him with an incredulous expression.

> "*…we take a snooze;*
> *And lift our voice in song.*"

It was a decent baritone, he decided, and it rolled out impressively across the open meadow. As he caught up to Elizabeth, he saw that her lips were moving, but he couldn't tell if she was singing very softly or just mouthing the words.

"Happy me! HAPPY WE!" He boomed out the syllables and was pleased to hear her low, slightly off-key, accompaniment.

"Happy *ME!*"

She fell in with him and they strode toward the summit, matching step for step as they swung along in time to the song.

"Happy we-hee-hee-hee-hee-*hee!*" They shouted the line together, and both were instantly seized by laughter—gut-wrenching, deep-welling belly laughs. Elizabeth's long legs folded under her and she sank to the ground, chortling, her eyes streaming. A second later, he joined her. They laughed till the sound of their mirth echoed back from the valleys below, like the calls of a band of lunatic yodelers.

At last, weakly wiping a sleeve across her still-wet eyes, Elizabeth leaned against him. "I can't remember when I last laughed like that...it's been a very, very long time. I had no idea—you obviously have depths of which I was not previously aware. *Where* did that silly song come from? I recognized the tune—that fal-de-ree song about hikers— but somehow I don't remember the words being quite so ... so..."

"Juvenile?" Phillip's expression was innocent. "I cannot tell a lie, ma'am; *I* wrote those words. When I was twelve. Eagle Scout Hawkins of Troop Four. When we weren't annoying old ladies by helping them to the other side of streets they didn't want to cross, we were hiking and singing. Want to hear a verse of 'The Caissons Go Rolling Along'? Or how about 'Be Kind to Your Web-Footed Friends'?"

"If I laugh anymore, I won't be able to walk back to the car. Let me catch my breath."

They sat quietly, his arm draped around her. After a moment or two, she turned to him, lips parted as if about to speak.

*I could happily drown in those eyes.* The thought came out of nowhere and caught him by surprise. *Damn! That doesn't sound like me. This place is getting to me too.*

Her eyes were still on him, somehow expectant. *I wonder... this was the day we were going to talk about where I would live when I take the job with Mac... and if we'd get married. But everything's good right now—why bring up something we might not agree about? And what does it matter, really? If she doesn't want to be married, then—*

"Phillip?"

"Yes, my love?" He *was* drowning, sinking willingly into the deep blue pool of her gaze. "What is it?"

"Will you marry me?"

ॐ

The rime ice had all melted away by the time they walked, hands linked, back to the car. The return drive was through woods of lavender shadows and indigo trunks, rather than the crystalline wonders of the morning. He drove slowly, afraid to risk any disturbance of this newfound perfect harmony. But one thing had to be said.

"Lizabeth?"

"Phillip?" She looked like a child in the midst of a happy dream as she turned to him.

"Lizabeth, I want you to be sure. About getting married, I mean. Today was so . . . I don't know how to describe it. But if you wake up tomorrow and decide that you were high on mountain air and you've made a mistake—I don't want you to feel trapped."

Before she could reply, he overrode her. "How about we keep this quiet for now; give you time to make sure? If on New Year's Day you still feel the same, then we'll tell everyone."

"If that's what you want . . ." She tilted her head at him. "But I won't change my mind."


"So you young uns has been up to Max Patch. I'll just bet hit was a sight on earth! I ain't been up there in the longest time. Phillip Lee, you kin put them packages over yon where a body won't trip over them. Ay law, Lizbeth, look at the color in your cheeks; today you're as purty as a bloomin' rose."

They had taken a detour on the way home in order to deliver Christmas gifts to Phillip's aunt Omie, a tiny, fierce-eyed widow who lived in the little community called Shut In. Somewhere up in her eighties (Phillip didn't know and wouldn't ask her exact age), Naomie Caldwell was the older sister of Phillip's late mother. Phillip had spent many summers with his aunt when he was a child, and now that he

was back in the mountains, he had tried to assume some fil-
ial responsibility for her.

"She's got no other close kin around here," he had complained to Elizabeth, "and I've told her over and over to
call if she needs help of any kind. I had an afternoon free
and I thought I'd ride out and check on her—maybe bust
some stove wood since she won't use that kerosene heater I
put in. So I get there and, not only does she have enough
wood to do her for two or three years, but she's at the top of
a ladder way up high nailing down a piece of tin that had
blown loose on her roof.

"'Aunt Omie!' I holler, 'I *told* you to call if you needed
me!' And that little bent-over woman peers down at me
from the top of that ladder and waves this big framing
hammer. 'Well, Phillip Lee,' she says, 'reckon as how I
didn't need you.'"

Today, however, she had a task for him. "Iffen you don't
care, you can haul off some trash for me, Phillip Lee. I
been going through my plunder and trying to git shed of
some of this clutter. Everwhat'll fit in the back of that jeep,
hit'd be a help to me." Aunt Omie motioned Elizabeth to
the sofa. "You set down, Lizbeth, I'll just show this boy
what needs to get gone, then I got something you might
like to see. You naming Max Patch put me in mind of my
pictures."

When the two emerged from a back room, Phillip was
balancing a stack of cardboard boxes in front of him, his
chin clamping down on the topmost one. He winked at
Elizabeth and shuffled on to the front door that his aunt
was holding open for him.

"Now mind them steps, Phillip Lee," she called after
him. She shut the door firmly, shaking her head as she
muttered, "That boy'll break his neck one of these days if
he don't take care."

Elizabeth scooted to one end of the sofa, making a space for the white-haired little woman and the worn blue cardboard shoe box she was holding.

"Now let me see; it's in one of them yaller envelopes if I remember right." Omie's knobby-knuckled hands picked through the stack of photo-return envelopes and seized on a tattered example. She held it up and peered at the spidery writing.

"Nineteen and fifty-nine—that was the first year Phillip Lee come to stay with me. I thought you might like to see what he looked like back when he had him a full head of hair." Omie's eyes sparkled as she drew out a deckle-edged black-and-white photo and offered it to Elizabeth.

The faded picture showed a sturdy little boy in a plaid shirt and jeans, the hems rolled in a deep cuff. His head was covered with close-cropped dark hair, and he sat, grinning with delight *a familiar grin* on the back of a white mule, harnessed for work. At the mule's head stood a man in faded work clothes and a dark hat.

"He was a fine-lookin' young un and that's the truth." Omie leaned in closer. "And law, was he proud to be settin' up there on that big mule!"

"I love this picture." Elizabeth felt a tug at her heart— a wish that she could somehow have known the little boy in the photo. *The smile's the same, and the way he holds himself. But would I have recognized this as Phillip if Omie hadn't told me?*

"Is this your husband holding the mule?" Elizabeth turned her attention to the image of the man in the hat. She looked closer and blinked. *It's the same man! The one I talked to . . . I think I talked to . . . while Phillip was asleep.*

"Law, no. That picture was took one day when me and Waneeta—that was my sister, Phillip Lee's momma—carried the young un all the way up to Max Patch in that funny little car of Waneeta's. I was wanting to get me some young apple trees from James Suttles and while we was there he gave Phillip Lee a ride on that ol' white mule of hisn."

*Okay, so this James Suttles had a son who looks exactly like him. Or a grandson.*

"And those self-same apple trees I got that day are bearing yet—they's a York Imperial and a Grimes Golden and a Junaluska. Law, James was a good hand to graft an apple. That whole family could raise a garden on a rock and have extry to feed the pigs. And they had the best fruit trees you ever saw—apples what ripened earlier and kept longer, peaches that blossomed late so's not to get hit by a freeze, and the finest cherries you ever tasted.

"Oh, ever one wanted to get their fruit trees from the Suttles. Yeah, boy, they was the finest folks."

Omie's eyes were half-shut and a wistful smile crept across her wrinkled face. Then, recollecting herself, she nodded toward the snapshot. "Yes, that's James all right in that picture. Now his mommy, she was a full-blood Cherokee princess named Rebecca. James was a dark-complected man hisself, but he had the bluest eyes. Him and me was playmates when we was young—we called ourselves cousins."

*Okay, the man I talked to couldn't be Omie's age... maybe...*

"Did you know my Mamaw was part Cherokee?" Omie twinkled up at Elizabeth. "Reckon that's her blood makes Phillip Lee's skin so dark, even in the wintertime. Howsomever, my Mamaw and James Suttles's mommy was kin some ways and when I was just a little thing, Mamaw would take me with her to go a-visitin' up there. We'd stay several nights and oh my, me and James would have us a time."

"Did this James Suttles have a son? I think I've seen someone who looks just like this man." She tapped the pale figure, identical to the man she had spoken with a few hours earlier. "His spitting image, as they say." *Which derives from spirit and image. Oh, lord, this is too weird.*

Omie's brows contracted as she searched her memory. "Let me think about that, Lizbeth ... now, yes, I believe James did have a boy, just the one, far as I kin recollect."

"Was he named James after his father?" *That could explain it.* But even as the thought formed, Elizabeth knew there would be no explanation.

"No ..." Omie shook her head. "I believe they named that boy Larry and last I heared, he had moved off somewheres. I'm ashamed to say it, but I don't know if James is living or not. Could be he is. Suttleses was always a long-lived family."

# Chapter 20

# *Who Are Her People?*
## Friday, December 22, and Saturday, December 23

"Mum, have you heard *anything* I just said?"

"What?" Elizabeth looked up from the book she was reading—rereading, if truth be told, for the umpteenth time—a tattered and loose-paged paperback of Dorothy L. Sayers's *Gaudy Night*. "I'm sorry, sweetie, did you say something? I was just finishing a chapter while I drink my coffee and let lunch settle."

Her thumb held the place *that wonderful scene in the punt* while her face attempted to give the impression of total attention to her daughter's words. "Did you and Rosemary eat in town?"

"Yeah, we grabbed a wrap at the deli. Rosie stayed down at the workshop—she wants to make a wreath to take back to hang in her office."

Laurel dropped onto the sofa and fixed her mother with an unrelenting eye. "What do you know about Amanda's family?"

Elizabeth shrugged. "Not much—they're friends of your aunt Glory; they evidently have a lot of money—Ben says they have several vacation homes. But, Laur, didn't you tell me your generation wasn't into all that 'who are her people?' stuff—that you prefer to judge a person by what they themselves—"

"Okay, I know I said that," Laurel waved off the question and pressed on, "and usually it's true. But Rosie and I got to talking and—"

She stopped abruptly and looked toward the front door. "Someone's out there. Is Phillip—"

With a barely concealed sigh, Elizabeth laid down her book, stood, and went to the door to let in Molly and Ursa. "Phillip went in to Weaverville. He needed to pick up his mail and take care of some other stuff at his house. And, as far as I know, Ben and Amanda are making a delivery. So we're all alone."

She watched the dogs curl up before the fire, then sat down by Laurel. "What's bothering you, sweetie?" she asked, raising one hand to ruffle her tall daughter's red curls.

Laurel pulled her feet in their thick orange-and-purple socks up on to the sofa and wrapped her arms around her knees. Her face was set in an expression of anxiety, so different from her usual carefree exuberance that Elizabeth felt a prickle of cold apprehension.

"Like I said, Mum, Rosie and I've been talking."

Elizabeth waited but Laurel seemed unable to continue. As she wrestled to form a sentence, Laurel began to twist a lock of her hair in the old familiar sign that something was bothering her. Finally, with excruciating reluctance, she got it out.

"Mum, it's Amanda—she doesn't seem . . . Rosie and I, we both think she's . . . well, too good to be true and we don't want Ben to get hurt again. Did you know that Amanda's dad is some kind of big-time developer? We Googled his name and found out he builds these monster resorts all over the country."

Elizabeth leaned back into the cushions, eyeing her unfinished book. "Well, I know we're all kind of sensitive about developers recently, but it isn't actually *illegal*. Besides, according to Ben, Amanda's not close to her family— she can't help what her father does."

Laurel's anxious expression deepened. "It's what *Amanda's* doing that has us worried. She's been spending lots of time at the library—"

"Laurel! *Sweetie!* Since when is *that* suspicious behavior?"

"*And* she's been at the Registrar of Deeds. She was there today. Rosie and I think she's working for her dad. Don't you see"—Laurel grabbed Elizabeth's arm and squeezed, as if trying to force her mother to understand and share her concern—"if it gets out that a big developer is putting together something for a multimillion-dollar resort, land prices'll go out of sight and owners will hold out for top dollar. But if people think she's just another dreamer who wants a place in the mountains—"

"Whoa!" Elizabeth broke into Laurel's increasingly impassioned outburst. "Do you really think Amanda's been buying property? You do realize that land purchases are published—don't you think folks like Sallie Kate would notice one person buying lots of adjoining properties?"

"Well, maybe she hasn't made her move yet," Laurel insisted. "Maybe she's going to work with lots of different realtors and make all the purchases right at the same time. I don't know what exactly it is, but she's up to *something.*"

Elizabeth was amused to see her daughter's lower lip thrust out just as it had when Laurel was an obstreperous toddler, thwarted in some ambitious plan.

"And another thing, Mum, why does she have a box at the post office? I know she gets a lot of mail here, mixed in with yours and Ben's—what does she need a post office box for—unless it's for mail she doesn't want you all to see?"


"The girls concocted this conspiracy theory all because they saw Amanda coming out of the Deeds Office. Apparently she didn't see them, so after she was gone they went into the office themselves. One of Rosemary's friends from high school works there, and she told Rosie that Amanda had been in quite often but she—the friend, I mean—didn't know what Amanda had been looking for. And then later, the girls were passing the post office and through the window they saw Amanda unlocking one of the rented postal boxes."

*Christmas cards—Sandy and good old hairy-assed Don, one from that car dealership where I was pricing a four-wheel drive, bills, junk, more bills*—Phillip raised his eyes from the stack of letters he was sorting through to see Elizabeth studying him, waiting for a response.

"Sorry, sweetheart." He dropped the letters onto the kitchen table, gave her a lingering hug, and looked over her shoulder at the pots on the stove. "I don't get it; the other night they were all having so much fun together—I was thinking how well Amanda fit in. I would have sworn your girls really liked her."

"Me too." Her lips brushed his cheek and she returned to her dinner preparations: assembling a salad, cracking the oven door to check on the heating bread, stirring the thick mass of spicy black beans, lifting the lid of the pot where rice was simmering.

Phillip sniffed the rich aromas greedily, hoping that dinner would be soon. "Can I do anything?"

Elizabeth turned a harried eye on him. "Make a suggestion. How can we find out what Amanda's up to?"

"Oh." He snagged a cherry tomato from the container on the counter and popped it into his mouth. "I meant do you want me to set the table or open some wine. But as for Amanda and her suspicious activities, why don't they just ask her?"

"Laurel said she was going to. They've all gone in to Asheville to listen to music at some pub tonight. I expect before the evening's over Laurel will find a way to work it into the conversation."

Elizabeth was chopping a large red onion with careless speed, her face screwed up against the fumes. He laid a gentle hand on her shoulder. "Lizabeth, what do *you* think about Amanda? I sure wouldn't figure her for some kind of corporate advance man—you just have to look at her and Ben together. He's happier than I've ever seen him."

The frenetic chatter of the knife on the cutting board slowed, then stopped. "That's true. And that's what makes even the *possibility* that she's not here just because of Ben so disturbing. I don't think he can survive another heart-break."


"She acted kind of funny, Mum." Laurel poured a second cup of coffee and joined her mother and sister at the table. "We were at the pub, all sitting around with our beer, and when the band took a break I said, kind of joking-like, 'So, Amanda, Rosemary and I saw you this morning coming out of the Deeds Office. We waved but you didn't see us. Are you going to buy property in Marshall County?' "

Elizabeth pushed aside the pile of Nola Barrett's papers that she had been studying. Her girls. *Almost like old times, both of them in their flannel pajamas, here at the breakfast table together.* Laurel's uncompromisingly red hair was a tousled mop around her angular face, while Rosemary's usual sleek, low ponytail had been replaced by two braids. *Just like she used to wear it when she was five. I swear, it's hard to believe she's... my god, she'll be thirty-one next month! And Laurie just turned twenty-six. Amazing.*

Tearing herself away from happy nostalgia, she addressed the present. "And what did Amanda say?"

Rosemary looked up from the book she'd been reading as she nibbled at a muffin. "She didn't say anything for a moment, Mum. You know how unflappable she usually is? Well, it seemed to me that she was rattled by Laurie's question. She had that deer-in-the-headlights expression for an instant and then she recovered, took a sip of beer, and said something about historical research and that she had a relative who she thought might have owned property in the Ransom area."

"And then the fiddler started up again and that was the end of it." Laurel yawned widely. "Ben and Amanda left not too long after that, and Rosie and I went down to my studio and ended up going to a Christmas party over at the Wedge." She flashed a devilish grin at her sister. "I wish you could have seen Rosie boogeying down with Rafiq. She made such an impression on him that I think he's in love again—"

"But what was really interesting to me, Mum," Rosemary overrode her sister's tale, ignoring it out of existence, "was the way Ben was acting—all protective of Amanda—as if she were a..." The professor of English struggled to find the perfect phrase, frowned, and resorted to the inevitable. "...a bird with a broken wing. But I still wonder..."

Rosemary heaved a sigh and craned her neck to look at the pile of papers in front of Elizabeth. "What's all that? Are you writing a book, Mum?"

She reached for the top pages and began to peruse them. "Oh, this is what you were telling me about—the stuff that crazy old lady wrote."

"Not that old, nor that crazy." Elizabeth pulled the photocopy of the map from the folder at the bottom of the pile and pushed it across the table toward her daughters. "You'll like this—it's a copy of a map of the river from the mid-1800s."

The two heads bent together as the sisters marveled over the spidery calligraphy and delicate delineations. "Look, there's Sill's Slough—and it shows a big house near the river there. And there's that creepy old house at Gudger's Stand. But there's no bridge—"

"I've seen this map before..." Laurel's head jerked up and she turned a puzzled face to Elizabeth. "It was..."

Closing her eyes, she drummed her fingers on the table to aid her memory. "I know—it was in the Troll's house. In a frame on the wall."

Elizabeth shoved her chair back and jumped to her feet. "Wait a minute! Let me see that map." Peering over her daughters' shoulders, she jabbed a finger at the name on the foot of the map and the inscription—*Thos. W. Blake fecit ~ 1861.*

"It just means Thomas W. Blake made this map in 1861, Mum." Rosemary's tone was professorial. "*Fecit* is Latin for—"

"I know that much Latin, sweetie. Four interminable years in high school. But I didn't make the connection till now." Elizabeth stared at the words, thinking hard. "Girls, I think we need to take the Troll a little neighborly Christmas cheer—maybe some of that pumpkin bread I made yesterday. It's time to talk with Mr. Thomas W. Blake—the Fifth."

# Chapter 21

## *Echoes in an Empty Room*
### Saturday, December 23

It was a room full of echoes. *Look at these nice flowers Lavinia has brought you. Lavinia has brought you. Nice flowers Lavinia has . . . and how could one know which of the echoes was the first utterance and which were merely the repetitions, the bounced shadow-sounds? And if you repeated yourself, as they said that you did, did you repeat yourself? Then who was to say what was repetition and what was not?*

*Did Cousin Randall come to them as he came to you, angry and shaking his cane, sputtering and choking as he tried to speak? Choking as you are choking now. Take it away, away.*

*Who stands at my bed foot, whispering in a terrible voice, Let justice be done? Oh, wake Duncan with thy knocking! Wake! Wake!*

"Wake up, Nola. You're having a nightmare, I do believe."

The fingers grasped her shoulders, shaking her, breaking her, waking her. Nola Barrett moaned and struck out with all her feeble strength.

They flitted in and out, changing, always changing. One offered her juice, *too sweet, too sweet, Kool-Aid, aidez moi, no,*

*NO, not the pill, willy nilly, the pill will make me nil, will I, nil I, I will be nil.*

"Do you hear me, Nola? Open your mouth. I want you to swallow this down right now and stop this nonsense."

*Non sense, I am making non sense. No, I will not gulp, gullible gull though I seem. No pill, no pill, the pill will make me nil.*

Fingers pried at her lips, held her nose, pulled at her chin, forcing her mouth open. *No, not again, I say no, not again.*

"Goddammit, you *bit* me, you fucking bitch!"

The savage pinch on her inner arm stung and throbbed, but the brutal hands released her jaw.

"Is Nola actin' ornery agin?" Another voice in the room, and a blob of pink and orange appeared in Nola's limited field of vision. It was accompanied by the acrid whiff of cigarette smoke that had become all too familiar.

"She's a little agitated, but I think she'll quiet down pretty quick now. I'm just going to wash my hands and then I've got to get out of here."

Water running, gurgling in the sink, water splashing. Rubber-soled shoes squeaking over the linoleum and out the door. The fat pink-and-orange blob sank into the chair by the bed. There was a *click* and the rush of canned laughter.

"Let's watch us some TV, Nola sweetie. You want the rest of your nice juice? No? Well, I'll just finish it up then."

Summoning all her strength, Nola Barrett turned in her bed to face the wall, opened her mouth, and silently spat the white tablet from her mouth. Her trembling hand scrabbled its way unsteadily over the pillow till her fingers touched the sticky object. Concentrating all her will on the disobedient fingers that seemed to belong to someone else, Nola began to push the pill slowly, inexorably toward the edge of the mattress.

‿

Phillip's eyes narrowed. The thin figure climbing into the truck parked below the old stand was familiar. As was the purple jacket and the dark red hair. *And the big fella at the wheel must be the boyfriend Lizabeth mentioned, Rocky or some such name. Wonder what they're up to?*

The truck was parked near the foot of the road leading up to the old house and almost in front of the brick building inhabited by the man the Goodweather girls had called the Troll. Phillip brought his car to a stop on the shoulder of the road at a discreet distance and pulled a map from the pocket on the door, unfolding it almost to its full extent and holding it up to cover most of his face.

*I'm just another lost tourist. A little out of season but those two aren't paying me any mind. Looks kinda like they're having an argument.*

The driver was facing straight ahead, shoulders hunched, both hands gripping the steering wheel of the idling truck, while the thin young woman was turned in her seat to face him. Her hands darted and gesticulated. The driver sat unmoving as the silent tirade grew to a climax. At last the young woman's hands dropped out of sight and Phillip saw her abruptly turn away. For a moment the occupants of the truck were frozen in their respective poses, then the driver stirred, exhaust poured from the rear of the truck, and it pulled out into the empty road, made a slow U-turn, and chugged away toward Dewell Hill.

From over the top of his map, Phillip could see that Nola Barrett's niece was still staring out her window, her pale features set in an angry scowl. On the rear window of the truck cab a white decal showed a plump kneeling cherub and the words *Our Angel—Little Ricky—2004–2006.*

The truck had just labored round the hairpin curve above the old stand and out of sight when Blaine's cruiser

appeared. Hastily Phillip refolded the map into an approx-
imation of its previous size. He started his car and slowly
followed the sheriff up the road to the old house.

Only a litter of twigs and small branches remained of the
tree that had blocked the road on the day of Nola Barrett's
suicide attempt. The two vehicles jolted over the ruts and
pulled to a stop at the side of the forbidding building. Phillip
cut his ignition and, seeing that his friend was pulling on
heavy gloves, tugged his watch cap down around his ears
before he climbed out of his car.

"I'd be interested to know who sawed up that tree,"
Mackenzie Blaine said, emerging from his car.

"Probably someone looking for firewood, don't you
reckon?" Phillip shivered and looked up at the old house,
trying to imagine its towering chimneys plumed with
smoke. In its usual fickle fashion, the weather had moder-
ated. The recent snow had vanished and the temperatures
were moderate forties and fifties. Still, it was chilly, up on
this hill above the river.

"Could be. They certainly hauled it all away." The sheriff pointed to a confusion of heavy-treaded tracks. "But
there'd be no need to come all the way up to the house if
what they wanted was just the firewood."

"Well, hell, Mac, maybe they were just curious about
this old place. Lizabeth says there're all kind of stories
about it—not just Nola jumping or the old man getting
murdered, but going way back—"

Blaine waved a dismissive hand. "I know, I know, the
drovers' gold, the Union gold, the Confederate gold—why
is it that people always want to believe in buried treasure?
C'mon, Hawk, let's take a little tour of this gracious
home."

At the padlocked back door, Blaine yanked off one glove
and reached into his pocket to produce a key, from which
dangled a yellowed tag. "Miss Barrett had the place locked

up after old Revis's death. She had a key and the sheriff's office got one—in case of emergencies.

"Of course," he said, removing the padlock and pushing open the back door, stepping carefully on the rotting steps as he did so, "this key was accessible to anyone in the office at one time or another—there could be copies all over the place."

The pale light of the bleak winter day struggled through the filthy windowpanes to produce a wintry twilight. A rusting gas range and an open-doored, empty refrigerator, both heavily coated in dust, made clear the nature of the room.

"Through here's what used to be the barroom—back when Revis was running this place like a kind of private club for anyone willing to pay a couple of bucks to join for a night."

The big space boasted a motley collection of chairs and tables, many overturned, a battered pool table, and a crudely constructed counter on which sat a lone shot glass beside two empty beer bottles. A magnificent fieldstone fireplace dominated the end wall, its wide opening boarded over. On the stone hearth squatted a malevolent-looking wood heater made from an oil drum.

"The other end of the house is the same—another big fireplace. That was where the old man mostly lived. It was the family quarters even back when this was a real inn. This would have been where the customers ate—and likely the cooking was done in the fireplace. The kitchen we came through would have been a later addition."

"This is an amazing building, Mac." Phillip looked from the wide-planked floor to the massive logs that formed the walls. "Why the hell hasn't someone—"

"Miss Nola refused to talk about this place after the old man died. Locked it up and, far as anyone knows, never set foot in it again . . . until she came back here to try to kill herself."

The sheriff moved to a door on the inner wall. "Back here's a kind of hall with stairs to the second floor. Of course, there's the outside stairs too. And on the other side of the hall is Revis's living quarters. We'll have a look at it later. You can see from the inside how it was put together—what they call a dogtrot plan. Basically, it's two log rectangles with an open area between them covered over by one roof. Then at some point the open area got closed in."

The central hallway was thick with shadows and Mackenzie switched on a high-beam flashlight he pulled from his jacket pocket. "Watch your head going up those stairs. Low clearance."

At the top of the stairs, they found themselves in a narrow hallway running the length of the house. As Mackenzie shone the flashlight down the hall, Phillip could see doors on either side and, at the end, another boarded-up fireplace. The sheriff swung his light around to reveal an identical scene on the other side of where they stood.

"Six rooms on this side and six on the other—so this is where the paying customers slept." Phillip pushed open the nearest door, which squealed in protest.

A stained and sagging mattress on a metal frame, a straight-back chair, and a table with a chipped and rusting white enamel basin crammed the tiny space. Any storage needs were met by a row of nails along the unpainted wood of the inner walls. A kerosene lamp, its oil long ago evaporated to an amber stain on the glass reservoir, stood on the broad windowsill, completing the bare necessities offered by the cheerless room.

"Not strong on amenities but I guess the drovers didn't mind—this would have—"

"Drovers? Hawk, back when this was a drovers' inn, this upstairs was nothing but two big open rooms. The drovers rolled up in their blankets and slept as close to the fireplaces as they could get."

Phillip could see a smile playing about his friend's face as he continued.

"These partitions came a good bit later. And this wasn't any tourist court, good buddy." Mackenzie snorted. "Probably another reason Miss Nola didn't like to talk about it. For years and years this place was pretty much a whorehouse."

# The Drovers' Road VII
## Driving Hogs

*I confess, said the Professor, to an overweening curiosity. What did you, a simple—I beg your pardon, an inexperienced country lad, think of Mr. Patton's fine hotel and its languid denizens? In those far-off and golden days when I was still in funds, I spent a month among the lotus-eaters at that hostelry, attempting to ingratiate myself with a wealthy widow.*

*At first, she was entranced with me, hung on my least syllable. But her meddling friends intervened. When I think that but for the calumnies of others, I might now be consort to Mrs. Rupert Radnor of Philadelphia and a valued member of Main Line society . . . But, alas! 'Twas not to be. The slings and arrows of outrageous fortune have brought me low, marking me as the prospective bridegroom of Miss Nettie Mae Nobody of Nowhere, North Carolina.*

*The Professor blew his nose loudly into a once white handkerchief, then waved a hand at his cell mate. Forgive my bitter garrulity, Lydy. Tell me your impressions of Warm Springs.*

*As usual, the young man had waited philosophically for the mostly incomprehensible soliloquy to end, seizing on those few words that had meaning for him and paying no more attention to the rest than he did to the maudlin singing issuing from the neighboring cell. When the Professor had carefully folded his handkerchief and resumed an attentive attitude, Lydy took up his account.*

*Well, sir, the folks at the ho-tel hired me on to help with the horses and mules they kept for folks to ride. And I hadn't been there much more'n a week when the head man told me I was to be a groom and ride out with the rich folks when they went the next morning to see the sunrise from the top of Rich Mountain. Them furriners was a sight on earth. They changed their clothes three and four times a day. And oncet or twicet a day they would waller in them great marble tubs, a-hopin to git cured of everwhat hit was that ailed them. I tell you, Professor, they was as idle a gang of folks as ever I seen.*

*I will say for them that they was free with their money but, still and all, I was right happy when it came time for the droves to commence. As the air begun to cool and the leaves to turn, the rich folks packed their fancy clothes into great trunks and piled into the coaches so as to be out of there afore the roads was full of critters and the dust they raised and the droppins they left fouling ever inch of the way.*

*They kept us fellers busy there at the hotel for another few weeks as they had to have everything just so afore closing for the winter. But soon as my job there was done, I hired on with a great drove of hogs bound for Greenville, South Carolina.*

*Forgive me the solecism, but might I inquire as to your remuneration? Your salary?*

*The Professor's question was met with a blank stare and he amended his query.*

*I meant to ask, what was your pay for this grueling journey?*

*Lydy's face brightened. Well, sir, hit was thirteen dollars and found—meanin that the owner paid fer our meals at the stands. Hit was easy money, to my way of thinkin. Hogs is clever critters. They take some humorin but once they was on the road, they would move along at a right smart pace without offerin to stray. We had great long whips that we cracked right often to keep the beastes from loaferin but they weren't much else to do most of the time.*

They was a friendly, talksome feller named Shelton, took it upon hisself to walk near me and tell me all manner of things. He'd gone with many a drive and knowed the road well. And one of the first things he showed me, not a mile upriver of Warm Springs, was the place where a drownded man had been found some months afore.

Hit was a young feller, Shelton told me, and the spring floods had beat him about on the rocks of the river so bad that hit took a time afore anyone could put a name to him. They had laid him out in a shed a good ways from the tavern but when the weather begun to turn warm, the innkeeper said he would have to go in the ground as an unknown fer he'd not keep much longer. A man who had stayed at Gudger's Stand allowed as how he thought from the hair on the corpus's head that hit could be the Ramsey boy who had worked for Ol' Luce and was said to be courtin his daughter.

One of the other fellers who was trampin along nearby ups and says, Naw, I heared hit was Ol' Luce's wife that boy was ruttin atter. Shitfire, that black-eyed piece'd make a preacher lay down the Book iffen he could lay—

But just then we come to a side-ford, where the mountain reaches down to the water so steep and rocky that the road has to run through the shallows. Hit took all the hollerin and whip-crackin we could do to push them hogs through the water and back onto the road oncet hit took up on land again. The river is fearsome strong and swift. Iffen a hog loses his footin in the side-ford or makes for the deeper water, he can be caught up by the ragin current afore you can hardly spit.

Keep them beastes close, hollered the boss. I'll not have another lost in Sill's Slough.

When we had got through the side-ford and the hogs was back in the muck of the road, Shelton sidled up to me. You ever heared of the Dakwa, boy?

There never was a man liked to talk as much as ol' Shelton.

Lydy caught himself and cast a sly look at his cell mate. *Reckon you and him might be kin, Professor?*

*And what is this Dakwa?* the Professor asked, ignoring the gibe.

Shelton said that *hit was some kindly of great fish that the Cherokees talked of. Hit was supposed to live under a big rock there at Sill's Slough and hit would grab a man or a beast and suck hit under.*

*Last year,* said Shelton, *when we struck that side-ford they was a big old spotted hog got into the deep waters. That hog struck out for the other shore, swimmin like one thing and then all to oncet he commenced to whirl around in the water, a-squealin and sputterin like maybe something was bitin on him.*

And then ol' Shelton he pointed back at a place in midstream where the water seemed to run kindly contrary around some jaggety rocks. *Hit was right there that hog went under,* says he, *and, though we waited and watched for the better part of an hour, hit never did come back up. Reckon hit was the Dakwa what et that hog.*

The Professor waved aside the tale of the river monster. *A fable, Lydy, a story to amaze and entertain children. Press on. I would hear of your return to Gudger's Stand.*

*Well, sir, first I must tell you of the place we stayed that night. Hit was at the Flores Stand we put up and there I come to learn of the Melungeons. The Melungeons and Mariah of the Flowers.*

# Chapter 22

## *Troll Trove*
### Saturday, December 23

"So you ladies are interested in my honored forebear, the man who drew this map? If you like, I can show you an article he penned for *Harper's New Monthly Magazine* in 1858."

With a courtly flourish, Blake motioned them to a sagging leather couch that bore the scratch marks of countless cats. He moved to a low bookcase, ran a finger lightly along the spines of the books on the top shelf, and pulled out a tall leather-bound volume.

The Troll, as Elizabeth persisted in thinking of him, had not appeared surprised to find the three Goodweather women at his door but, on being shown the copy of the map, had even invited them into the old store building that was his home to see the original and to answer their questions. He had immediately recognized Laurel, asking what she was currently working on, and, though his breath was redolent of alcohol, his manner was impeccable.

Elizabeth had dismissed her previous suspicions and, resolving to learn what she could from this odd individual, followed her girls through the door of what had once been Wakeman's Mercantile & Supply. *We'll chat about the map and whoever it is Blake's named after and then I'll try to get the conversation around to the bones in the silo and whatever it was that went on down here eleven years ago.*

Beyond the door lay a large, high-ceilinged space, evidently the main living quarters of the Troll. *A curious room,* Elizabeth thought. *Something between an old-time general store, an artist's loft, and a museum. With touches of Grandmother's living room.*

Deep shelves lined the walls, but the assorted merchandise of a general store had been replaced, for the most part, by books and storage boxes. A gaunt yellow cat reclined languidly on a high shelf near the woodstove, while a pair of white-pawed tabbies shared a dilapidated basket tucked between stacks of paperbacks. Two glass-fronted display cabinets heaped with antique tools and farm implements formed a divider between the front two-thirds of the long room and the kitchen area at the back. If, as seemed likely, there had been counters, they had been removed to allow for the motley assortment of furniture.

"My great-grandfather was fascinated by the people of this region. He wrote numerous vignettes that found publication in the periodicals of his day. This has always been one of my favorites."

The ancient hickory bark seat creaked as Blake seated himself in the high-backed chair opposite them. He opened the book to a page marked by a yellowed envelope, adjusted his glasses, and began to read.

*"We proceeded with all dispatch along the Buncombe Turnpike but were forced by Old Sol's departure from the heavens to arrest our voyage at Flores' Stand. Though less commodious than most inns or 'stand houses,' it is an hostelry far surpassing all others in wild beauty and Lucullan fare. The innkeeper, Ish Flores, is a swarthy man of a somewhat forbidding countenance but his gentle nature becomes evident whenever his dark eyes rest on his wife, the lovely Mariah.*

*"Our first glimpse of this dusky beauty was as we filed into the long low room filled with rustic tables and benches for the*

*entertainment of travelers. Through an open door at the back of the room, we could see a spacious garden, a veritable cornucopia of fruit and flower. Beyond it lay a snug stone house, the living quarters of our hosts, as I learned later. A wide path led from the house through the garden, and down this path came a veritable vision! Taller than many men, she carried a willow basket laden with rosy-cheeked peaches and her waving black hair cascaded unconfined almost to her knees. There were white flowers at her brow and a smile of transcendent beauty welcomed our weary company."*

Blake passed the open volume to Elizabeth. Engravings decorated the printed pages—one entitled *Mariah of the Flowers.* The woman was just as he'd described her: smiling, stately, with an exotic beauty that seemed totally incongruous with the time and place.

"She's lovely," Elizabeth murmured, lingering over the illustration before handing the book to Rosemary, who peered intently at the portrait.

"Does your great-grandfather say where this Mariah and her husband were from?" Rosemary asked, offering the book for her sister's scrutiny. "Flores seems like a strange name to encounter at that time in western North Carolina. And she's so unusual looking—not Native American, with that wavy hair; not African-American either. Where was their stand?"

Blake answered with smug satisfaction. "Just a few miles downriver, as a matter of fact. The little stone house he describes still exists, though the stand is gone. My ancestor was evidently fascinated with the Floreses. He made frequent visits to them after his marriage. The Flores people were Melungeons."

Elizabeth frowned. "Melungeons . . . I think I've heard that term but—"

"They're a people of mixed race; the name may come from the French word *mélange.*" Thomas Blake removed his glasses, breathed on the thick lenses, and began to polish them with his shirttail as he continued his explanation.

"Some ethnologists call the Melungeon people tri-racial isolates—a mix of African-American, Caucasian, and Native American who've maintained a distinct identity over the years—but there are other, more romantic theories—a hypothesized connection with Portuguese explorers or shipwrecked Carthaginians intermarrying with Native Americans."

Laurel looked up from the picture of the dark-haired woman. "Awesome! And they lived near here? Are there any people like that still around? I've sure never heard of anyone called Flores in Marshall County. And I've never heard of Melungeons."

"The people who identified themselves as Melungeon seem to have been concentrated in east Tennessee. The Flores couple evidently came to Marshall County from that region by a rather circuitous route. It speaks well for the tolerance of the region that these two who were, after all, people of color, should have prospered as landowners and innkeepers. I've tried to learn more of them but there's very little—and I haven't been able to trace any descendants."

He held up the yellowed envelope he'd taken from the book. "This is a transcript of a letter my honored ancestor sent to his brother after his marriage to a Ransom girl. It contains the only other reference to Ish and Mariah Flores that I have discovered."

Blake resumed his glasses and unfolded the closely typed pages. He quickly skimmed the first page, moving his lips slightly as he read. "Hmm...no...this first part isn't relevant—suffice it to say that he was resigned to his marriage and equally resigned to the fact that he and his untutored mountain bride would be an embarrassment to his wealthy family in Charleston."

The Troll's eyes twinkled behind the thick lenses. "The Blakes seem to have been of some consequence in that fair city before the War Between the States. The fact is, my esteemed progenitor was a remittance man—as long as he stayed away from Charleston, he received a quarterly allowance from his family."

The thin onion-skin pages crackled as Blake turned them over. "Yes, here it is. He refers to '*a Melungeon family—those strange dark people of mixed race who insist that they descend from the intermarriage of early Portuguese explorers with indigenous peoples. The Flores, whose stand is just downriver from Gudger's Stand (of which more later) is owned by the swarthy Ish Flores, a self-proclaimed Melungeon. His equally dusky wife, Mariah, is a noted herbalist and bee mistress. She makes fragrant, clean-burning, beeswax candles, a vast improvement upon the tallow candles and bear oil dips that most households employ. Mariah is also renowned for her honey wine—a potent libation that must be identical to the metheglin of Olde England.*

"'*The comely Mariah is a veritable Pomona—her vegetables, fruits, and flowers are horticultural marvels. She says that these all derive from seeds and slips given her by an old man she and Ish encountered in their travels before coming to this county.*

"'*I give you Ish's own words: "We come out of Tennessee along a trail the Cherokee used, just us and our old piebald mare, heavy-laden with our household goods. Up on the bald some call Max Patch the weather turned wicked and Mariah was took bad with a fever in her lungs. She would surely have perished had not a man called Suttles, a true good Samaritan on a white mule, found us there and made us welcome at his place, the warmest snuggest cabin-house you ever did see. We stayed with this fine man for quite a little time and when Mariah was better and able to travel, he gave her seeds and starts of some of the plants we have here. Hit seems like they always bloom fuller and their flowers are brighter and the fruit sweeter—*"'"

"Excuse me, Mr. Blake, what was the name of the man on the white mule?" A jolt of recognition had shot through her at the mention of Max Patch; Elizabeth once again felt the dizzying sensation of being on the other side of the mirror. *Even this room, a jumble of old and new, and this man,*

*Thomas Blake, reading to us the words of Thomas Blake of a century and a half ago.*

The present-day Thomas Blake looked up from the typescript. "Suttles—a not uncommon name, I believe. Interestingly enough, some of those very fruit trees mentioned here still survive around that little stone house. I hike down there occasionally to, as it were, commune with the spirits."

He folded the pages carefully and returned them to the envelope. "That's the sum of what Great-grandfather Thomas had to say about the Floreses directly. But from passing references in his writing, I am led to believe that he saw their place as an idyllic refuge from family life. He and his wife had thirteen children and they all lived on the upper floor of this very building, after his father-in-law erected this establishment and put him in charge." The Troll gestured at the venerable oak rolltop desk behind him. "That was his, as were many of the volumes in the bookcase beside it. I wonder what kind of shopkeeper he made. I suspect that my great-grandmother Nettie Mae must have been the business mind of the two—I have some of the account books from their time and they are in a precise feminine hand—not the dashing scrawl of his writings."

"That's so cool—that you're living in the same place where your great-grandfather lived—I'll bet you feel really close to him." Laurel's look of wide-eyed wonder glanced over the framed photos on the wall, groups of dark-garbed, unsmiling individuals. "Do you write too? This is an awesome place for a writer."

Thomas Blake was silent for a moment. Then, his eyes fixed on nothing in particular, he said, "I tell myself I'm writing a great antiwar novel, the next *Red Badge of Courage* or *Catch 22*, but I fear—I'm very much afraid that what I'm really doing is drinking myself to death."

# Chapter 23

## *Converging Threads*
### Saturday, December 23

A whorehouse—here in bone-dry, Bible-thumping Marshall County? Go on, Mac, pull the other one! The church ladies would have raided this place with pitchforks."

Mackenzie Blaine wiped at the dusty glass of the window and peered out toward the river. "Well, I guess it was more like a house of accommodation, not actually a bordello or whatever they used to call them. From what I've been told, when the railroad came through and the big cattle drives ended, whoever owned the stand put in these partitions to turn the drovers' inn into a regular hotel. Thing was, there were better hotels not too far off, in Ransom or, going the other way, in Hot Springs.

"So before long, this turned into the area's no-tell motel—fellas wanting to get drunk away from their wives' eyes and still have a bed to pass out on, fellas slipping around on their spouses, couples looking to break the Seventh Commandment in more comfort than a hay barn allowed—that sort of thing. And there were usually a few country girls hanging around downstairs where the bootleg beer and liquor was sold, girls who were hoping to get together enough money for a ticket out of the mountains. They weren't quite hookers; they called themselves waitresses—but most any man with a few dollars and a need on him could find company for the night.

"And when the passenger trains quit running, old Revis kept on selling liquor, and there were still plenty of under-age young folks and boozy old lowlifes to keep him in busi-ness. No one even bothered to pretend that this was still a hotel, but anyone could slip the old boy a few bucks and get the use of one of these rooms for the night, no questions asked. It went on like that till Revis got himself killed. Then Miss Barrett locked up the place and threw away the key."

Phillip looked at the stained mattress, then at the bolt on the door. "Where the hell was the Marshall County Sheriff's Department when all this was going on?"

The sheriff shrugged. "Well, I'd guess they were likely getting a taste of Revis's profits. Or some action, on the house. Or both. But I don't know that for sure. One of the old-timers told me that the Holcombe brothers mainly saw Gudger's Stand as a convenient way of knowing where the criminal element on this end of the county was likely to be on any given night."

"So are we looking for something, Mac, or what? I ap-preciate the tour and all; it's an interesting old place—but why are we here?"

"We're here because all the threads *lead* here. Revis died in the room below us; Miss Barrett jumped from the porch out there; the preacher's suicide note mentioned that silo across the road; there were human remains in the silo... even that Hummer someone burned up ties in with the stand, since it belonged to the developers who want to buy this place. But I just can't seem to get a fix on how all these things are connected."

As he spoke, Blaine turned away from the dusty window and gave Phillip an embarrassed half-smile. "Hell, I don't know, Hawk, I guess I came here looking for inspiration—maybe hoping the house might tell me something...or you might get an idea. And then there's the time element—if the county commissioners go through with the taking people are whispering about, that company young Holcombe's friend owns is likely to gut this place and turn it into a lodge or god knows what—if they don't just burn it down and put up something on top of the ashes. If there's anything to find here, this could be our last chance."

Phillip moved to stand beside his friend, bringing his face close to the windowpanes in an attempt to see the fields that lay by the river.

"You forgot the other thread, Mac—that alleged gang rape in the old school bus. That bus is right over there— and didn't the woman say she'd been drinking just before? Maybe she'd been."

*Sweet Jesus, what is she up to now?* The thought interrupted his sentence, but then he resumed. "Mac, did you notice Elizabeth's jeep down there in front of that old brick building? And, yep, there they are—Lizabeth and the girls coming out the door. What the hell are they doing down there?"

Mackenzie's response was succinct and surprising. "Investigation, I have no doubt. Open the window and holler at your lady friend, Hawk. Ask her to join us. Maybe the house'll talk to *her.*"

"Why does Mackenzie want to see me?" Elizabeth asked as she made her way past the sheriff's cruiser. "Will it take long? The girls are in a hurry to get back to the farm. I was going to run them back home, then go see Nola."

Phillip lifted open-palmed hands. "You got me, Lizabeth. I don't know exactly what Mac wants. But you were saying the other day that you'd never seen the inside of this old place. Now's your chance and with two armed escorts to keep the ghosts away." His face relaxed into a cheerful expression. "Tell you what, why don't you let the girls take your car on back to the farm and you come with me? We could grab a bite somewhere first and then I'll take you to see Miss Barrett."

As she followed Phillip along the back porch to the door, Elizabeth noticed, with a familiar pang of revulsion, the dangling rubber dolls. Their once pink bodies were dappled with black mildew, and they shuddered and danced on the weathered clothesline. *It's the vibration of our footsteps that's making them jiggle—that's all. Maybe I could just pull them down and never have to look at them again. Maybe—*

But Phillip was opening the door and motioning her in. "Look at the size of these logs, sweetheart. And wait till you see the fireplaces!"

She stepped through the door into the little passageway and was assailed instantly by a confusion of sensations— cold dry air, carrying the scent of decay and rat droppings; the loom of the giant chestnut logs to either side of her; and the ceiling pressing claustrophobically low, mere inches above her head. There was hollow silence in which the pounding of her own pulse seemed amplified till it could be mistaken for the heartbeat of the old house itself.

Dizzied, *it's coming from the light outside into this dark stuffy little hall,* she put out a hand to steady herself. The slight curve of the log met and accepted her hand, its polished smoothness speaking of the many other hands, long gone to dust, that had slid over it. Closing her eyes, she seemed to hear the tread of heavy boots, the scrape and whine of a fiddle, the laughter of drunken men and women, accompanied by a phantom whiff compounded of sweat, whisky, and tobacco.

"Lizabeth, are you all right?" Phillip's voice brought her back to the present.

"I'm good. Just trying to get adjusted to the dim light. *Here and now, Elizabeth, here and now.* Where's Mackenzie? I want to find out if I'm in trouble."

"In here." The sheriff's voice emanated from the open

door to the right. As she entered the room, Mackenzie
Blaine turned a wry look on her and gestured to the tarnished brass bed in the corner. "Thought as long as you
were out *investigating* things, Elizabeth, you'd be interested
in the scene of a crime. This is where Revis died, back
in '96."

*It's odd. The first time I met Mackenzie, when Miss Birdie
was trying to find out about Cletus, I really disliked him. And he
thought I was just a nosy woman, trying to second-guess the authorities. Which, I guess, I was . . . am. But now that I've gotten
to know him as a friend of Phillip's, I can understand his point of
view a lot better. And, for whatever reason, at least he no longer
treats me like a meddling idiot. What was it Phillip told me he
said—Miz Goodweather has that blasted woman's-intuition
thing going for her, plus the instincts of a snapping turtle—she
won't let go of a problem.*

"Hey, Mackenzie, how nice of you. I've always wondered what this place looked like inside. But what're you
and Phillip doing here?"

She was surprised at his candor as he explained the various threads of the several unsolved cases, concluding with
". . . and they all lead to Gudger's Stand. So I thought
Hawk and I'd come here and brainstorm a little about how
or if all these cases connect. Maybe get some inspiration
from the place. Then, what d'ya know, Hawk looks out the
window and there *you* are, coming out of Blake's crib. And
I figure you've been asking questions and I also figure he
may have told you more than he'd tell me. So, what have
you learned from our resident eccentric?"

Before replying, Elizabeth looked around the lifeless
room. The mattress had been stripped bare; two lumpy
ticking-covered pillows had been tossed casually at the foot.
To one side of the vast stone fireplace, a vinyl-covered recliner extended its footrest, almost touching a cheap television atop a flimsy metal stand. Strips of foil on the
rabbit-ears antenna suggested that reception had been poor.

"Okay, Mackenzie, I *was* asking some questions. But really it was more about an ancestor of his way back. Mr. Blake has a wealth of information about the mid-1800s. But he's not inclined to dwell on the recent past."

"No, he wouldn't be," Blaine agreed. "He's probably killed enough brain cells that the recent past is just a blur." The sheriff was moving cautiously around the room now, inspecting first the battered chest of drawers, then the contents of an ancient trunk that stood at the foot of the bed. "I don't know why I bother; after this long if there was anything incriminating, the murderer would likely have gotten rid of it."

"I thought you said the place had been locked all this time," Phillip broke in. "And only Miss Barrett and the sheriff's department have the keys—"

"Exactly," said Mackenzie Blaine. He opened a door on the farther wall. "Three—no, four—small rooms through here, one leading to the other. Stacks of magazines, no furniture. Probably kids' rooms, in the days when the whole family lived in this end of the building."

"Is there a bathroom back there?" Elizabeth knew what a rare commodity indoor plumbing had been in the county at least until the seventies, when there had been an effort to nudge homeowners and landlords toward installing septic tanks.

"No bathroom, not nohow, not nowhere." Blaine grinned at her. "There's an old zinc tub hanging on the back porch. And down that path behind the house is what used to be an outhouse, till it burned. When I was doing some research on this place and Revis's death, I came across a reference to the fire trucks responding to a call from here. The old outhouse was on fire and it was completely destroyed. It was written off as a prank. And Revis didn't have long to be inconvenienced by its loss, because he was dead a week later."

Phillip laid a hand on her arm. "Lizabeth, did that Blake

fella mention that Miss Barrett's niece and her boyfriend paid a call on him this morning?"

Elizabeth stared at him. "How did you know that? Yes, he did, just as we were leaving. Said it was a red-letter day, with so many young women calling on him. And then he said something about a bond he shared with Nola's niece. A *sad* bond, he called it. And something about hoping there would be time to see justice done. But then he kind of went all distant and very politely hustled us out the door."

"Blake's funny that way." The sheriff removed a glove and began to run his fingers along the top of the rustic mantel. "He was hanging around when we were removing those remains from the silo. Finally I went over and asked him if he remembered anything unusual going on around the silo eleven years back. Stupid question, I know, but his reaction was pretty interesting. His eyes started to tear up, behind those Coke-bottle-bottom glasses of his and he kind of muttered something about bad boys running wild that year. Then he shuffled away, still mumbling to himself. I thought I caught the words 'One more.'"

# Chapter 24

## *Desperately Seeking*
### Saturday, December 23

Elizabeth followed Phillip and Mackenzie through the old house, silently listening as Mackenzie pointed out the original structure beneath the recent accretions. The odd feeling that had come over her on first entering the hallway had gone, but the strange sense of *almost* hearing the sounds and *almost* smelling the odors of a time long past teased and danced just at the edge of her consciousness. *It would be so easy to close my eyes and imagine what it was like—but I don't really want to. I don't think this was ever a happy place, in spite of all that laughter.*

The solid reality of the two men beside her and the unchecked flow of their speculations and theories were a comforting anchor to the present as the three of them came once more into that claustrophobic hall and passed quickly through the door to the back porch.

As Mackenzie turned to snap the padlock back into place, once again the dolls, shivering and twisting in the chill breeze, caught her eye.

"Mackenzie, I have a favor to ask."

Neither Phillip nor the sheriff so much as smiled at her request. Mackenzie gently cut the wretched little dolls down, handling them gravely to her, one by one. *This is ridiculous—but I can't just leave them here. Maybe when we pass by the collection center*— But she knew that, after years of seeing the dolls not as lifeless rubber toys but as piteous tormented creatures, she couldn't toss them into a bin to lie amid rotting garbage. No, no more than she could have thrown away the much-loved toy dog that had been her bedmate for much of her childhood and now reposed in state in a trunk with her grandmother's wedding dress. *The Velveteen Rabbit syndrome appears to work, not just for inanimate objects you love, but also for ones you pity.*

"Thanks, Mackenzie, I really appreciate it. These things have given me the creeps for years. It'll be nice not to have to see them hanging there anymore."

She shoved the trio of dolls into her denim shoulder bag, trying to act as if they were just some litter that she would eventually dispose of in a responsible manner. *I'll probably have to bury the bloody things with bell, book, and candle—my god, Elizabeth, are you on your way to becoming a very strange old lady or what?*

"Take your time visiting Miss Barrett." Phillip pulled into a slot in the Layton Facility's parking lot. Cutting the ignition, he reached behind his seat, pulled out a small newspaper, and flapped it open. "I picked up the latest issue of the *Guardian* and it'll keep me occupied for a while—I'll be interested to see what kind of coverage they gave that public meeting where the Hummer got torched. Plus I always get a kick out of the letters to the editor. All the news that fits, as they say."

"I probably won't be long—Nola tries hard to communicate but it wears her out way too quickly." Leaning over, Elizabeth swiped his ear with a hasty kiss before heading for the Layton Facility's front door.

᠎᠎᠎᠎᠎᠎᠎᠎᠎᠎᠎᠎᠎

*Alone, alone, all all alone. Michelle, not belle, horribelle
Michelle. Stay away all the day—*

Nola Barrett lay motionless in her bed. Behind her
closed eyes, unruly thoughts swooped and darted like startled birds, buffeted by the blare of the television and the
unwelcome odor of untouched and congealing food on the
tray beside her bed.

A soft voice was riding on the raucous sound of the chattering, mindless box that flickered on the wall. "Hey, Nola,
it's Elizabeth."

Nola opened her eyes. *A friend in need, a friend indeed.*
Elizabeth's tall form stood beside her bed, stretching out a
hand.

*I will not be nil. I will not—* Focusing all her attention
and willpower on the inert mass that was her limp left arm,
Nola struggled to clasp Elizabeth's hand. *Find the words!*

As Elizabeth's strong hand took gentle hold of her trembling fingers, Nola bent her will to calling forth and order-
ing the words that beat against the bars of her mind. She
clung to the calloused hand and croaked, "No pills, I will
*not* be nil!"

Panting with the exertion of forcing her tongue along an
uncharted path, Nola pulled Elizabeth's hand toward the
farther side of her bed and guided it to the hidden tablets.

"Whose pills these are, I do not know." It was easier to
let the poet help her speak, but now she must form her plea
unaided.

"What's this, Nola?" Elizabeth pulled loose the small
white tablets and peered at them. "Are you spitting out your
pills?"

"They. Are. Ill."

Each word was a battle to be fought, a child to be
birthed in slow, agonizing labor. But Elizabeth's blue eyes
were intent and Elizabeth was listening ...

"Pill. Makes. Nil."

Elizabeth seemed to be considering. Would she understand? One more effort must be undertaken. Beat back the circling, swarming, scattering, chattering words and choose.

" 'Throw physic to the dogs; I'll none of it.' "


"Nola was trying very hard to tell me something about these." Elizabeth held out the pills for Phillip's inspection. "She's evidently trying to avoid taking them. These were stuck to her bedspread—like they'd been damp from her mouth and as they dried, they stuck."

Phillip took one tablet between his fingers and held it to the light. "You know what these are?"

"Not a clue—my pill taking doesn't extend much beyond an occasional ibuprofen. And Nola sure couldn't tell me."

"It's an Ambien—a pretty heavy-duty sleeping pill. I know about it because it gets used some recreationally and by meth users trying to come down. Maybe we should check the Internet when we get home. Seems like there was a big flap not long ago about some weird side effects associated with Ambien. Who's Miss Barrett's doctor?"

"I don't know. Remember I told you about Dr. Morton— the brother of that pastor who shot himself—they were visiting her soon after she went in to the facility. But Dr. Morton told me right out that he wasn't Nola's physician— he was just there as a courtesy to the family."

Phillip frowned. "What family do you suppose he was talking about?"

Elizabeth shrugged. "I assumed he meant his brother— who, I guess, was Nola's pastor—had asked him. But it's an odd way of putting it." A thought struck her. "That neighbor of Nola's, Lee what's-her-name, told me that Nola had slammed the door in the pastor's face a few days before she jumped. I wish I knew what that was about. But the thing I'm trying to figure out, Phillip, is whether I rat on Nola—do I inform the people back in there that she's not taking her meds—or—"

"I'd hold off on that, sweetheart." Phillip tossed the folded paper aside and started the car. "Let's find out some more about Ambien first. It's just a sleeping pill, after all. It's not going to be life-threatening if she misses a few."

There were errands to do before returning to the farm—a few last-minute groceries and a stop at the gas station. Phillip popped the hood of his car and got out to confer with the always taciturn Jim Hinkley. "The engine seems a little off and I want to see what our local car wizard thinks. Shouldn't take too long, though."

As the two men lost themselves in the study of the car's workings, Elizabeth idly picked up the copy of the *Guardian*. Not much of interest. The report on the meeting sounded like a commercial for development; the burning of the Hummer was dismissed in a paragraph as a "fire of unknown origin." The letters to the editor were better—a fairly evenly divided representation of those for and against development in Marshall County.

On to the classifieds . . . real estate, shockingly expensive. *I can remember when land at a thousand dollars an acre was considered over the top, now . . . good grief, not quite a whole acre and they want $50,000! . . . $149,500 for 5.39 acres . . . thank god Sam and I moved here when we did . . . sure couldn't afford to buy here now . . . cars . . . job opportunities . . . "Need man with chain saw" . . . who doesn't? . . . "Two Wedding Gowns for sale, Size 12, Size 16, never used" . . . wonder what happened? A story there, for sure.*

She looked up. Now Phillip and Jim Hinkley were in the work bay of the garage, and Jim was holding a dirty-looking cylinder in his hand. Phillip seemed entranced, peering at the object and poking at it with one finger.

She sighed and turned a page. Birth announcements . . . a "Lordy, Lordy, Debbra's Forty" ad beneath the photo of a gap-toothed little girl wearing a majorette's outfit; a

"Seeking Information" ad. *"Will anyone with information on the whereabouts of Spencer (aka Spinner) Greer, last known to be in the Ransom area in October, 1995, please contact Boxholder, PO Box 1066"*—ah, the Norman Conquest—*"Ransom, NC"*... It was familiar; the same ad, offering a substantial reward, had appeared intermittently in this paper for years. *Another story waiting to be told.*

Her eyes wandered on to the next page... *after-Christmas sale... moving sale... Wait a second—the address. The other ads like that had a Tampa address, that's why I noticed them in the first place.* She flipped back to the previous page. *Box 1066, Ransom, NC.*

"It was the air filter. Took a while to find the right one, but while he was looking, Jim actually chatted with me a little bit. Asked how I was liking the county, talked about the weather and stuff. I felt honored, first time he's actually talked to me. And then he showed me pictures of some fish he caught last summer."

Elizabeth looked up, confused. Phillip was behind the wheel again, the hood was down, and Jim Hinkley was back in the work bay, doing something with a tire.

"What? Oh, right, I remember when Jim finally started talking to me, I felt like I'd been let into some exclusive club. It was a great feeling."

"You sure were lost in that newspaper. Do you even read the classifieds?" Phillip had an amused look on his face as he pulled back onto the road.

"I always do—there're interesting little hints of stories." She told him about the unused wedding dresses and they speculated on the meaning—two jilted sisters? One bride with weight-gain issues?

"And here's an ad that shows up every so often, someone looking for Spencer or Spinner Greer. Only I'm pretty sure that before, the box to reply to was always in Tampa, but now it's in Ransom."

"Maybe this Greer's the one who ran out on the girl

with the wedding dresses. And she's moved here to hunt for him in person and she's brought the dresses with her." Phillip's grin widened.

"Well, she's hung on to those dresses for a long time— the ad says 'last known to be in the Ransom area in 1995.' But it's definitely a theory." Elizabeth folded the paper and tossed it to the back seat. "Or what if he promised to marry *both* sisters—"

"Hold on, Elizabeth. When did it say this Greer was last in the area?"

The silly game was over: Phillip's face was serious now. Elizabeth reached for the paper again.

"I think it was '95 . . . yes, here it is, October of '95."

Phillip didn't reply at first. Then in a voice of great weariness he said, "Probably just a coincidence. But October of '95 is when that gang rape is supposed to have happened."

"And you're thinking. . . ?"

He took a deep breath. "I'm thinking the two are connected. Hell, Lizabeth, I'm thinking it's all connected."

# The Drovers' Road VIII
## Love Lies Bleeding

The road was churned to mire with the passing gangs of cattle and hogs and still Lydy didn't come. Drove after drove come and went, and whenever I found the chance, I asked for news of Lydy but none had seen him. Then a man with the last bunch passin by stopped to bargain with my daddy over some lame hogs they was lookin to get shed of. Daddy got them hogs cheap and, bein pleased with his bargain, told me to give the man some of the fried peach pies I'd just took from the fire. When I handed them over I asked my old worn-out question one more time. I didn't hardly wait for an answer and was on my way back into the house when the man spoke up. Why yes, says he, they's a feller meetin your description in the drove that's behindst us. He took him a big bite of that hot fried pie and grinned at me, allowin that hit'd likely be several hours before that drove got to Gudger's Stand.

I found me some little jobs to do in the upper rooms, sweepin and such. Up there I could keep watch from a window or the porch and be the first to catch sight of the next drive comin. Down below I could see Belle, piddlin about in the little patch of special herbs and flowers she tends, sweepin around in that fine green skirt she'd had on when the stagecoach brought her back last month.

᠁

*To tell the truth, I had been sorry to see my stepmother come back. I'd been hopin that Belle might of found a richer man than Daddy at the Warm Springs and run off with him. But on the very same day Lydy had rode off settin high on that wagon, back she come on a stagecoach. Hit was good-bye to the one I loved and hello to the one I hated, near bout in the same breath.*

*Daddy was there at the door to greet the passengers and help the ladies down when he looks up and it's Belle, holding out her hand to him and stepping out of the coach. I'm back, Lucius, says she, I'm back and I've found a cure. You'll see—I vow I'll give you a son for a proper heir before a year passes.*

*She cut her eyes at me when she said them last words, and I had to turn away for I wouldn't have her see me cry. Daddy looked to have forgot all the hard things he'd been sayin about her whilst she was gone and was leadin her into the house as if she was some great lady. And from that day on, I knowed Belle Caulwell for what she was—a witchy woman and my bitter enemy.*

*I was sweepin the big room where the drovers slept when I seen the first signs of dust raisin far down the road. My heart leaped in my bosom to think that soon I'd see my Lydy again and I flung down the broom and made for the stairs, hurrying to my room so's to smooth my hair and put on a clean apron.*

*I tie the apron strings and run outside, meanin to be waitin on the porch when Lydy comes in view. But all to once I find that first I must visit the necessary house. Hit comes on right much these days, now that my belly's commenced to swell. So I run back to the place, tryin to make haste for all the while I can hear the squeals and grunts of the hogs and the ho-o-o-yuh! ho-o-o-yuh! calls of the drovers and their whips just a-snappin.*

*I come back round the corner of the house, fast as I can, and take the steps to the porch two at a time. They's a world of hogs all across the road, rarin and slaverin to get to the lots where the corn wagons are waitin and Belle is standin there, right in their path, like someone who don't know what a mean, hungry hog can do to a body.*

*Then I see Lydy, off to the side, and I holler to him but he's already makin for Belle. She just stands there like she was a tree planted in the road. She doesn't so much as twitch a finger as the hogs rush to either side of her. And now Lydy's beside her, pushin her behind him. He cracks his whip and sends the brutes away from her. I call to him again but the commotion is such that he doesn't hear. I see Belle lay her white hand on his shoulder and for a minute it seems to me that she is claimin him for her own. Then that white hand begins to slide down his back and he turns to catch her just afore she falls to the ground.*

*I watch as he carries her to the house and I call out to him a third time but his head is bent over her and still he doesn't hear. I lay my hand against my belly, hopin that the babe I carry can't feel my pain.*

# Chapter 25

# *Potluck*
## Saturday, December 23

*T*his is something different, Phillip thought. *Over a year and this is the first party Lizabeth and I've gone to together. For a long time I figured she didn't have any friends other than Sallie Kate and Miss Birdie.* He glanced over at Elizabeth, behind the wheel of the jeep. She had paid special attention to her appearance, replacing her usual diminutive gold hoops with earrings shaped like golden leaves and rooting through her closet to uncover something special to wear. She had emerged with a blue turtleneck sweater, *periwinkle blue cashmere,* she'd said, *a gift from her sister,* a black wool vest, heavily embroidered with green vines and red flowers, and a pair of new-looking black corduroy jeans.

"I have to get up my courage," she'd told him, twisting her long, dark, silver-shot braid into a crown around her head. "I've avoided this party ever since Sam died. But Helen Nugent called and badgered me till I said yes, we'd come. And she was right; it's time you met some of my friends."

There had been no time to follow up on the questions raised by those pills found on Nola's bed and by the ad seeking information about Spencer Greer. Just a rush to change clothes, gather up the chocolate pound cake Elizabeth was taking to the potluck, and, with a reminder to Rosemary and Laurel about feeding the dogs, hurry back out the door.

As the jeep wound around the unpaved mountain road that was a continuation of Ridley Branch, Elizabeth briefed him on what to expect.

"I think you'll like the people who'll be at the party—they're all very individualistic but easygoing. This is the community Sam and I kind of fell into when we moved here—a real mishmash of back-to-the-land hippies, artists, craftspeople, professionals, and blue-collar types. The main thing we have in common is that we all made the choice to come here. At one time, there was a potluck get-together almost every weekend, but now it's more like a few big parties during the year. The Nugents' Christmas party is one of the standards."

"Tell me about the Nugents. Have they been here long?"

"Oh, yes—they're old-timers among us newcomers—they've been here since the sixties, ten years before the first wave of transplants, twenty years before Sam and I bought our place. Jeff and Helen must be in their early seventies now. Jeff has this white beard that make him look like Santa Claus, and Helen is—well, she's a wiry little woman who looks like a piece of sun-dried leather. She's hard to describe because she's always moving."

Elizabeth had fallen silent as she steered the jeep up the driveway and pulled past a large, new-looking barn into an open field that was crowded with trucks and four-wheel-drive vehicles. Two women, heading for a path leading up the hill, paused to wave, and Elizabeth tapped her horn in acknowledgment. The shorter and stockier of the pair stared briefly and unabashedly at Phillip, before flashing a smile and giving Elizabeth an enthusiastic thumbs-up signal. Then the two hurried up the path toward the tall building whose lights twinkled through the trees.

"Maxie and Thelma—Thelma's the short one who evidently approves of you. They live on around this road. Nice folks. Thelma's a potter and Maxie makes incredible art quilts—real high-dollar stuff that sells through galleries. They've been here almost as long as I have."

"What about the folks giving the party—the Nugents?" As they walked toward the big house, from which could be heard the sound of music and many voices, he began to wonder what he could have to talk about with this artsy-craftsy crowd. "Are they artists too?"

"Not as such—I'd say they were artists of life, though— they raise these gorgeous Angora goats and sell the fleeces to handspinners and they have incredible gardens and an orchard of heirloom apples. And they're working with a program to introduce a blight-resistant chestnut to the forests. We'll come back in the spring when you can see what they've done here—the farm itself is a work of art."

Light streamed through the many-paned windows that had been cut into the log walls, etching geometric patterns on the broad deck that stretched to one side of the converted barn that was the Nugents' home. Taking a deep breath, Phillip followed Elizabeth through the front doorway into the warmth and swirling sound of a party in progress.


It was odd to be back at the traditional Christmas party. Odd that it was Phillip at her side, not Sam. For a panicked moment she felt like turning tail, but, with a welcoming cry of "Elizabeth! I'm so glad you came!" a wiry little person separated herself from a group of chattering women and bustled toward them. Beaming with pleasure, Helen Nugent reached up to hug her and Elizabeth felt the strength of her thin arms. *Helen doesn't change,* she decided. *She looked just like this ten years ago and she'll probably look the same at ninety.*

"And you must be Phillip. I'm Helen. It's so nice to

meet you at last." Her tanned face crinkled. "Of course I've heard a lot about you—all good, naturally." Taking the basket Elizabeth was carrying, she said, "I'll put this on the table. You two go get yourselves something to drink—the keg's back that way, on the kitchen porch. Jeff's back there too, Elizabeth—he's looking forward to seeing you again."

The big open space—a comfortable art- and book-filled living area flowing into a no-nonsense farm kitchen tucked under the bedroom loft—was filled with people: familiar faces, a few new faces, some faces that seemed familiar but she couldn't put a name to. They threaded their way through the throng toward the kitchen area, stopping for Elizabeth to greet an old friend, to exchange hugs, to introduce Phillip. He fielded questions about his teaching position at AB Tech and his previous job as a police detective in the coastal town of Beaufort. "No, Bow-furt, North Carolina, not Bew-furt, South Carolina."

Her friends and acquaintances seemed to be remarkably well informed about Phillip. *I shouldn't be surprised—after all, Sallie Kate and Harley know all about him and they socialize a fair amount. The newcomer community grapevine is evidently alive and well.*

When at last they reached the back porch, where the keg and an assortment of open bottles of wine were drawing a crowd of thirsty partygoers, Jeff, in a crimson sweater, his beard like a white waterfall rippling down his chest, came forward to engulf her in a bear hug.

"We've missed you, Elizabeth. I don't count running into you in town once every few years as seeing each other. I know," he said as she started to speak, "we're all busy with our farms or our work year-round. Thank god for Christmas; at least it gives us an excuse to party." He put both hands on her shoulders and stood back to examine her. "You look good, Elizabeth. And I hear Full Circle Farm's going great guns. We're proud of you, girl."

ॐ

"Let's find a quiet place to sit and eat—I'm about talked out for the moment." Elizabeth balanced her laden plate atop her glass of wine and scanned the living room for possibilities. Most of the sofas and chairs were already occupied, and little groups of people sat along the raised stone hearth that extended across one end of the room. "How about the stairs?"

They perched a few steps up the peeled log staircase and began to enjoy their food. The potluck fare was much as it had always been, thought Elizabeth—a quirky mix of earnest vegetarian entrées, heavy on brown rice and lentils; some really inspired casseroles, equally vegetarian, but sinfully tasty with herbs and garlic and cheese; wonderful salads; crusty homemade breads; barbecued ribs; skewers of chicken satay; and a spicy sausage roll she recognized as Maxie and Thelma's signature dish.

"This is quite a mix of foods—kind of like the folks." Phillip's fork hesitated over his plate, wavering between a delectable chicken satay and a jalapeño pepper, stuffed with cream cheese, wrapped with bacon, and hot off the grill. "They all seem pretty nice."

"We *are* pretty nice." Elizabeth looked up from her plate to see Thelma and Maxie claiming spots on the steps just below. "Even if some of us get a little loud at times."

Thelma looked over at a raucous cluster standing around the counter that separated kitchen from living room and shook her head. "They're arguing about the proposed plans for Gudger's Stand—it's a damn shame if the county commissioners let that company go through with that gated community."

"Hey, Thelma; hey, Maxie. It's good to see you all. This is my friend, Phillip Hawkins. Phillip, Maxie and Thelma Rudicek-Greene."

"Pleased to meet you." Phillip nodded at both women.

"So, do most of these folks oppose development at the old stand?"

Maxie, a comfortably plump, comfortably middle-aged woman with graying brown hair, set down her glass of beer. "I think all of us here are opposed to that kind of development—exclusive gated communities, huge, ecologically unfriendly second homes—*anywhere*. But Thelma and I and all the old river guides feel particularly strongly about Gudger's Stand. There's so much history there and it's the perfect site for a county park. If RPI gets its way, the rafting companies and all the other paddlers are going to have to find another put-in site. People are really upset!" Maxie's soft brown eyes flashed uncharacteristic fire.

*It's like seeing a . . . a fluffy bunny stamp its feet,* thought Elizabeth, noting the flush of anger on Maxie's cheeks.

Thelma laid down her fork. "Hell, the county commissioners just want to get shed of responsibility for that place. It's gotten a bad reputation ever since the old man was killed. And then this thing of a body in the silo . . . they're probably wetting their pants at the thought of having to deal with some new scandal."

"Someone told us that you were a friend of the sheriff." Maxie turned to Phillip. "Do you know if they've identified the . . . the remains yet?"

"Not yet—these things take time. And between the holidays and the fact that this isn't recent, it'll be a while before they know anything."

Elizabeth studied the two women, remembering when she and Sam had first met them, out for a walk on Ridley Branch. *Almost twenty years ago. They'd just moved to their place and weren't sure how neighbors would take to a same-sex couple. I remember we got to talking and Thelma said they'd had a carload of drunks come up their drive, hollering that they wanted to talk to the dykes.*

"I came out the front door with a shotgun in my hands and fired it into the air once. Got their attention for sure.

That car set a record for backing down a steep winding road. And now I always have a handgun with me," the Thelma of long ago had told them.

Thelma had changed the least—still stocky, her dark brown hair still close-cropped. A few lines at the corners of her eyes. *And the tattoos are probably still there on her back and arms.*

The change in Maxie was more obvious. She had been in her mid-twenties when the two had moved into Marshall County—a slender, quicksilver nymph whose sun-streaked brown hair fell past her waist. More than one male had been smitten at the sight of her, but Maxie's hazel eyes never strayed from Thelma—her avowed life partner.

*And now she's a motherly-looking, slightly dumpy woman. Ay law, as Birdie says. When I remember how the guys used to carry on over her . . . and to no avail.*

"I'd forgotten you all used to be river guides. How long ago was that?"

Thelma's brow furrowed. "We guided for River Runners from when we first moved here in '89 till . . . it was five or six years, I guess. Finally we reached a place with my pots and Max's quilts that we couldn't give up the time in the studio—not to mention the fact that it's damn hard work paddling one of those big rafts and we weren't getting any younger. The whole scene started kind of changing too—or we did. Just got too old and too responsible for the drinking and the dope every night."

"It was six years," Maxie answered quietly. "Our last summer was '95—before old Revis died. Don't you remember, Thelma—that last time we went to one of the parties down by the bridge and that guy tried to rape me?"

# Chapter 26

# *It's All Connected*
### Sunday, December 24

W hat time is it?" Elizabeth yawned enormously as they walked hand in hand down the path toward the jeep, following the bobbing beam of Phillip's flashlight. Lights twinkled like fireflies in the field below them as other departing guests headed for their cars.

"Twelve twenty-three." The words were punctuated with a yawn even larger than hers. "Your friends are a hardy lot." Phillip looked back to the big house. It seemed to hover above them, emanating light and music, a giant ship, manned by extremely friendly aliens. "We aren't first to leave, but not the last by a long shot."

"It could go on another hour or so, but I'm done in." Elizabeth stopped and pulled him to her. "Are you glad we went? That stuff Maxie and Thelma were telling us—wouldn't you say it could be connected—"

He kissed her lingeringly and held her to him. "Lizabeth, I enjoyed the party a lot more than I thought I would. I like your friends and I hope they're going to be my friends. But those two women—that story—well, it's given me a lot to think about."

"It was sometime in October—the last party of the season," Thelma had said. "Guides from all the companies always had a big bonfire and a combined picnic, campout, cookout, all-day, all-night, hoop-de-do down in the field by the bridge. There'd be a lot of drinking and a fair amount of weed but it was always a good vibe; me and Max had never had any trouble in the years before. Oh, there'd always be some guy who was sure that if she'd 'give him a chance,' he could turn her into a 'real' woman, but it was more of a standing joke than anything ugly.

"But this time Max was talking about, the party got crashed by a bunch of jerks who'd been up at the old house, drinking at Revis's so-called private club. At first they seemed okay; they'd brought some bottles of tequila and were passing them around and everything was cool. Then this one guy starts putting the moves on Maxie. I had a pretty good buzz going and I was just sitting on this log, watching the whole thing. I knew my girl back then, just like I know her now, and I was sure she wouldn't be crawling in anybody's sleeping bag but mine. So it was just kind of humorous to see this guy try and impress her. I was watching the whole thing like it was some fucking sitcom."

Thelma had taken a swig of her beer and wiped her mouth with the back of her hand. "Anyhow, I'd gone off behind a bush to take a fast pee and just then this prick tells Max oh dear, he hadn't realized how late it was. He's got to leave because his mama's not well and he promised to get home before whatever time it was. Sweet Baby here was such an innocent back then that when he told her he forgot to bring a flashlight and would she help him find the way to his car, she fell for it."

Maxie had blushed and looked away as her partner continued the story. "Luckily I came back to the fire just in time to see them heading off into the dark, so, not being as trusting as Max, I followed after them. It didn't take long; once they were away from where the party was going on, the bastard grabbed her and put one hand over her mouth. When I caught up, he was pulling her toward one of those abandoned cars that used to be down there. I always carried a little Beretta back then—a dyke had to be careful in some company—and I pointed it straight at his crotch and told him what was going to happen if he didn't let Maxie go."

Thelma had laughed richly and reached out to ruffle her partner's hair. "I should have shot the sorry fucker's dick off, but there would have been too many complications. The minute he let go of Maxie and slunk off into the dark, we got our shit together and headed for home. That little experience was another reason we dropped out of the whole rafting scene for good."

"Maybe you should have shot him, Thelma." Maxie's quiet voice had been grim and her expression steely. "When we heard about them finding that body in the silo—was it just last week? I remembered that night and I wondered if it could have been Bam-Bam. Remember, we never did find out where she went."

Elizabeth and Phillip had fallen asleep while discussing the implications of the missing girl; the story was still in Elizabeth's mind when she awoke in the chilly light of Christmas Eve morning. James had wedged himself tightly between her and Phillip, and Molly too had sought the additional warmth of the bed, preventing Elizabeth from stretching out her legs.

"Phillip," she whispered, "are you awake?"

There was no answer. His back was uncommunicative, a blank comforter-covered wall.

"Phillip?" she persisted.

"Uhmm?"

"Are you going to call Mackenzie first thing and tell him about what happened to Maxie? And about this Bam-Bam person?"

"Uhm-hum." He tugged the covers higher, dislodging James from his nest and disturbing Molly who stood and, with a reproachful look to Elizabeth, circled twice before curling up once again at the foot of the bed.

"Thelma said that Bam-Bam was a guide with River Runners. I know those folks; I'll call Debbie and see if they have any record of her. With a name like Bam-Bam, they should remember her."

"Uhmm."

"I know it's probably nothing—Thelma and Maxie said that guides came and went all the time. But it all goes back to that October of '95. Isn't it possible that the bones you found in the silo are this girl? And what if the guy who grabbed Maxie was part of the rape? They said 'a bunch of guys who'd been drinking up at the stand.'"

"Uhm-hum."

"And what the *hell* should I do about those pills Nola's not taking? If it's the nursing home overmedicating her, there's no sense talking to anyone there. And I don't trust Tracy, who is, I suppose, Nola's guardian at this point."

There was a long exhalation of breath and Phillip rolled over to face her. His eyes were shut but the suspicion of a smile played about his lips as he reached for her.

"Come here, Sherlock."


"Okay, I understand that Christmas Eve is probably not the best time to start bugging Mackenzie about all these things that happened over ten years ago. But I just did a little Google research on those pills Nola's been spitting out."

Phillip looked up from his book as Elizabeth emerged from the office clutching a printed page. "Listen to this, Phillip. Side effects from Ambien can include hallucinations, delusions, altered thought patterns, poor motor coordination . . . there's more, but some of this could certainly apply to Nola."

She thrust the printout at him and waited for his response.

Outside, a light snow was drifting down, fat feathery flakes giving silent promise of a white Christmas.

They were alone in the greenery-bedecked house, but for the dogs. Laurel and Rosemary had gone down to help Ben and Amanda with the ongoing care of the greenhouses, full of tender seedlings and cuttings that required watering.

"And then we're going in to Ransom," her daughter had told them. "A friend of Ben's is having a kind of open house we're all invited to. I know, Mum"—Rosemary had held up a forestalling hand—"yes, it's snowing. But I looked at the weather on the Internet and it's just light flurries till after midnight. We'll be fine. And Amanda doesn't drink at all, so she'll be the designated driver. If you want, we'll take the jeep so we'll have four-wheel drive."

He had watched the play of conflicting emotions on Elizabeth's face. It was clear that she didn't want the kids driving in snow—even a light sprinkling was enough for her to postpone all but the most urgently necessary travel. What was it she called herself—a Weather Wimp?

It had also been clear that she wasn't going to protest. *She'll just stay on edge till they're all back safely. Add that to Nola's pills and what her friends told her about the missing Bam-Bam—sweet Jesus, what a name—and she's going to be bouncing off the walls the rest of the day.*

Phillip took the page that was waving under his nose and glanced at it. "You're right, Lizabeth, some of it *could* apply to Nola. But isn't it also possible that Nola's behavior is the result of her fall? Or whatever it was that caused her to jump in the first place?"

The set of her jaw told him that she wasn't convinced. For the sake of peace, he hastened to say, "But I'll get hold of Mackenzie about this on the twenty-sixth—we'll have a better shot at getting his attention then; same with the other stuff."

Her tightened lips relaxed and he was relieved to see a lopsided smile appear. "Sorry, Phillip, I'll let go till Christmas is over. You're right; it can't hurt to wait a day or two. Besides, I need to go do some cooking for tomorrow. And polish Gramma's silver."

She pulled the printout from his fingers, folding it as she made her way back to the little office. "I'll just make a quick call to Debbie at River Runners first and ask about Bam-Bam."

Phillip shook his head and returned to his book. *She's hopeless. I guess I just have to wait till she runs down.*

In a few moments, Elizabeth was back. "I called their house. All I got was the answering machine playing 'God Rest Ye Merry, Gentlemen' at me."

Phillip closed his book. "Miz Goodweather, I take that as God's way of telling you to relax." He stood, causing an instant eager response from the dogs, who crowded around the door to the mudroom, anticipating his next words.

"Come on, let's go for a walk. I'll polish Gramma's silver for you when we get back."

# Chapter 27

## *God Rest Ye Merry*

### Monday, December 25

Idon't get it—it says, 'to Phillip from Fifi and a guy who digs chicks who dig chicks.' What the... Who's Fifi, anyway?"

He looked around at the others gathered there on the so-fas before the blazing fire. Laurel was standing by the huge Christmas tree, fulfilling her traditional role of distributor of presents; Elizabeth was on the love seat beside him, reading glasses pushed up on her head and pen and paper at hand to record gifts from out of town so that thank-you notes could be written. Rosemary, Ben, and Amanda occupied the larger sofa, but none of them had been given a present yet—only him.

They were all watching him expectantly as he examined the brightly wrapped rectangular package that was obviously a book. No answers were forthcoming, however, so Phillip shrugged and began to remove the red yarn bow.

"Not yet!" Laurel's urgent cry stopped him and he looked at Elizabeth for guidance. *What now?*

The Goodweather Christmas was in full ritual progress. The household had awakened with the sunrise and hurried into jeans and sweaters or flannel shirts. Laurel had been dispatched to feed the chickens with the eager accompaniment of Molly and Ursa, while Rosemary saw to the filling of the various bird feeders near the house. Phillip had raked the still-warm ashes from the fireplace, brought in wood, and built a new fire while Elizabeth set the table.

"Merry Christmas!" Ben's voice had rung out as he and Amanda came through the door. Ben carried a basket, heaped high with some last-minute additions to the pile of presents under the big tree.

"Merry Christmas!" Amanda had echoed, setting the large glass bowl of ambrosia she had brought on the dining table, and "Merry Christmas!" Elizabeth had called from the kitchen, the sound of her voice wafting, it seemed, on the mouth-watering aroma of the cheese strata she had just taken from the oven.

*At least breakfast was straightforward enough,* Phillip mused. *No weirdness there.*

"We've always tended to chores and eaten breakfast before opening presents," Elizabeth had explained. "When the girls were little, we'd get up around five-thirty or six, and first thing of all, they'd have their stockings and the unwrapped presents that Santa left. But we like to take our time with opening the presents from each other."

*Evidently,* he thought, looking at them all as they watched him studying the still-unopened package Laurel had handed him. All the other gifts remained beneath the tree and no one moved to claim them.

"Phillip, I'm sorry—I forgot you wouldn't know about our little game." Elizabeth motioned to her daughter. "Laur, give me one of mine. Then Phillip can see what we're up to."

As Laurel rooted around in search of the appropriate gift, Elizabeth asked, "Did Ben tell you about this thing we do, Amanda?"

"Oh, yes, he even got me to help with some of the tags for his gifts to you all." Amanda curled her long legs gracefully under her. "I think it's a wonderful idea—at home my—" She brought her hand to her mouth and coughed.

"Excuse me, I guess it's the dry air. Anyway, my parents always let me just rip into presents so fast I didn't have time to really appreciate what I was getting. This sounds like a fun way to slow things down."

"Laur, get Mum the squishy one in the paper with the holly on it. It's an easy clue." Rosemary pointed at a lumpy package.

Laurel picked it up and put it in her mother's lap. Elizabeth squinted at the homemade gift tag, then adjusted her reading glasses and read aloud: " 'To Mum from the man nicknamed for the old cut on his cheek, the man who lost the high card.' " Phillip looked around. Every last one of them was grinning, except Elizabeth, whose face was serious. She appeared to be working out a problem of some kind. *Weird.*

" 'Old cut on his cheek' " . . . Elizabeth spoke slowly, as if thinking aloud. " 'Cheek' as in 'face,' Rosie? Or . . ."

"Face, definitely face." Rosemary's own face was full of delighted anticipation. "And an old cut would become a . . . ?"

"Scab?" Elizabeth hazarded.

"Close . . . later it would be a . . ."

"A scar? Oh, I've *got* it!" Elizabeth's face lit up with sudden glee. "Scarface! Right?"

Rosemary nodded. "Now, if Scarface loses the high card . . ."

"And aces are high! So Scarface minus the ace is *scarf!*" She untied the ribbon and carefully set it aside, then tore open the flimsy paper.

"Oh, Rosie, one of your gorgeous hand-knit scarves! And the beautiful yarns, so many shades of red! Thank you, sweetie. And what a terrific puzzle!"

Elizabeth draped the long scarf around her neck and turned to him. "Do you see how it works? The tag is a clue to help you guess what's inside."

"Well, I'm pretty sure this is a book. But I don't see where Fifi or this other stuff—"

"But the game is to guess the title or the subject or the author of the book. Or all three."

He looked at her and saw a plea in her bright blue eyes. *Please, be part of this. Part of us.*

Running a hand over his head, he grinned. "Jeez, a fella has to be a detective to open presents with you guys. But I think I get it. You all do a few more before I try mine, okay?"

Amanda's package appeared to be another book. *These are some reading folks—I'd say at least half the packages under the tree are probably books.*

" 'Almost a fact and more than a smile.' " The smooth beautiful brow creased minutely in the least hint of a frown. " 'Weed out the capsicums and find a female's spheroid toy.' Wow, this is tough."

She looked toward the love seat. "It's your writing, Elizabeth, isn't it? Any hints?"

"You're looking for three words—start at the end: 'a female's spheroid toy.' "

"A ball?" Amanda's voice was tentative.

"Whose ball?" Elizabeth insisted.

"Hers . . . the female's . . . her ball. Her ball . . . is that it? An herbal? I've been wanting one so I can look stuff up."

"But *whose* herbal?" The glee in Elizabeth's face was infectious.

Amanda grinned back at her. "One of the most famous, of course. Culpeper's. Brilliant! 'Weed out the capsicums'— cull the peppers." Her elegant fingers began to remove the wrapping and then stopped. "But what's the other part: 'Almost a fact and more than a smile?' "

"I'm pretty proud of that." Elizabeth lowered her eyes in assumed modesty. "It tells what *kind* of copy of Culpeper's Herbal it is."

There were blank looks all round and then Rosemary's

quiet voice said, "It's a facsimile copy—*'almost a fact'*— F-A-C—and *'more than a smile'*—S-M-I-L-E with an extra *i.* "

She nodded at her mother. "Good one, Mum."


And so it had gone till the last clue had been unraveled, explained, applauded. *It's really the game that's the big deal, more than the presents. The game and the time they take to appreciate each other's puzzles. I like that.*

And he had acquitted himself well, with the cheerful help of broad hints. *Damn, they've got me doing it.* The gift from Fifi had resolved itself into a copy of *The French Broad,* by Wilma Dykeman. It was from Ben and Amanda, and Ben had talked him through the clue, beaming with pride at his own cleverness. After that, Phillip had managed to puzzle out the other tags attached to the modest pile of gifts that had come to him.

It had been a pleasant day. *A terrific day.* He had dreaded being asked to carve the turkey, not wanting to seem to take what had been Sam's place. But there hadn't been a turkey. Instead there was a trio of roasted ducks, burnished golden brown, which Elizabeth had skillfully and quickly sliced and disjointed. A pan of dressing: an exotic mixture of bread cubes, herbs, onions, and celery, dotted with andouille sausage, pistachio nuts, and kumquat slices; thin bright green beans; and a lettuce-and-citrus salad garnished with jewel-like pomegranate seeds accompanied the ducks. Champagne with the meal, then coffee and a creamy white dessert that Elizabeth had said was "Gramma's Charlotte Russe."

"I don't think I'll need to eat for a week," he groaned, dropping onto the sofa and falling back against the cushions.

Elizabeth looked up from the three open books which

she seemed to be trying to read all at once. "You survived it—the full family folderol."

"It was great, Lizabeth, the way Christmas should be." His eyes were closing of their own accord. "Family..."

Elizabeth jerked awake and the book that had been on her lap fell to the floor as the telephone's shrill ring ripped through her contented, semicomatose, post-Christmas-dinner doze. *Turkeys have tryptophan that makes you sleepy; I wonder about ducks. Quite a few glasses of champagne and some port probably contributed.*

She pulled herself up and hurried to the phone. Phillip, stretched full length on the sofa, slept on. The house was very quiet, Ben and the three girls having set off to enjoy the sunset from the top of Pinnacle. Ursa and Molly had followed them out the door, but James had only shivered and settled deeper into the cushions on the love seat.

Snatching up the phone, she greeted the unknown caller with all the cheerfulness she could muster in her befuddled state. "Merry Christmas!"

"And tra la la to you, Lizzy." Gloria's voice was cold and there was a suspicious slurring to her words. "I'd been hoping my only child might call on Christmas Day but as he couldn't find the time—"

"No fair, Glory. Ben tried twice this morning to get you and there was no answer."

"Oh. Well, Jerry and I were at the club for brunch—they do a magnificent buffet—and we just got back. Jerry and I have reconciled, thank you for asking. Oh, and thank you for the wreath—*very* charming. So clever of you. I hope the blouse I sent is something you'll wear. Your wardrobe is so *drab*—a little glitter now and then will perk you up."

"Thank you so much, Glory! I love the color. Coral is

one of my favorites." *And if I can pick off the bloody sequined flamingo, I might actually wear the thing.*

"Wonderful. Now let me speak to Ben; Jerry and I are on our way to a party and he fusses if I leave my cell on."

"Good for Jerry. But Ben and Amanda and the girls have gone up the mountain. There was a lovely fluffy snow yesterday and they were hoping to get some pictures of the sunset from the top—"

"God! Hiking! How *dreary* of them. Well, give them all my love. . . ."

A thought struck Elizabeth. "Glory, wait a second! I was wondering, do you happen to know anyone named Greer who lives in Tampa? I know it's a big place and all, but—"

"In a minute, Jerry!" Gloria was evidently speaking to her husband in the next room. "For heavens sake, this is my only sister and it's Christmas! In just a goddamn *minute!*"

*Wonder how long this reconciliation will last?* Elizabeth waited.

"Greer? Hmmm. It *sounds* familiar but I can't quite place it. Charlie Greer? No, that was Charlie Weir. Oh, of course! Greer was the name— Hang on, Lizzy. I have a call on the other line."

*You have a call on* this *bloody line,* fumed Elizabeth, but rather than hanging up, as she usually did when Gloria put her on hold, she gritted her teeth and practiced patience. At last Gloria returned.

"I swear, that woman can't dress for a party without having to find out what all her friends are wearing. If—"

"Greer, Glory. Do you know someone named Greer?"

"Well, Lizzy, I was trying to tell you. Spencer Greer was the name of the man Amanda's mother, Ronnie Lucas, used to be married to. It was such a tragic— *All right, Jerry! Here I come!* Sorry, Lizzy, Jerry's about to stroke out. We'll talk later."

# The Drover's Road IX
## The Dark Enchantress

*So you returned at last to Gudger's Stand. The Professor laid aside the month-old newssheet that had wrapped a handful of sugar cakes in Nettie Mae's basket. And there you found . . . ?*

Lydy looked up from a dispirited examination of his filthy, broken fingernails. Looks like that jury'd git done before now. What was that you said?

*My young friend, be heartened by the delay, not downcast. It is, I believe, a propitious sign. Tell me of your return to Gudger's Stand.*

Well, hit was a quare thing. When we was nearin the stand, I was of two minds. I weren't yet ready to leave off travelin round and seein new places but I was as eager as a billy goat in rut to lay down with Luellen again. But somehow, when I finally did see her, she weren't to my taste no more.

Oh, she was still soft and pink and that yaller hair was shining but I seen right off that she was breedin. And when she run to me and grabbed at my arm, why, I begun to think of one of them basket fish-traps the Indians used to make. We had one, back to the home place. Them traps is wide at one end and the fish, he swims in, thinkin all along that he kin turn and swim back out everwhen he wants to. So he keeps on a-swimmin, farther and farther in, and the trap keeps gittin narrower and narrower till that fish is stuck, not able to turn, not hardly able to move.

*It's been said by some*, the Professor hesitated as if reluctant to *commit an indelicacy, that is, the* hoi polloi *are of the opinion that you fell in love with Belle at first sight and that was your reason for spurning the fair Luellen, the young woman who was carrying your babe beneath her heart.*

The Professor laid his hand on his chest, frowned, and moved it lower. *A vile phrase: mawkishly sentimental and anatomically inaccurate,* he muttered to himself.

Lydy spat in the direction of the noxious waste bucket. *Now here's a thing to consider, Professor. How's a man to know whose babe a woman's carrying, unless he's kept her locked away and solitary for nine months and more afore the child is born? Luellen vowed hit was mine but I knowed she hadn't been a maid when first we lay down together. And then I come to find out that her and that Ramsey feller, the one who'd went away right afore I come to Gudger's Stand, the same one what those fellers had said was found drownded in the river, they'd been layin up together for some little while. And from things Belle told, that baby could have been got by several fellers.*

*No,* Lydy hardened his face and leaned back against the bricks of the wall behind his bunk, *Luellen wanted to give her baby a name and she flat tolled me in with the promise of a share in Gudger's Stand iffen we wed—tolled me in like tolling a hog with a handful of corn, tolling him right to the butcher.*

*Of course, one is sensible of a man's distaste at finding himself on such a lee shore. Indeed, I am keenly in sympathy with your aversation to such perceived trammels, but after all, my young friend, did not the inducement of the eventual proprietorship of Gudger's Stand outweigh so small an impediment as a child not of your getting? Many a man would gladly raise a whole brood of cuckoos for such a prize.*

*Reckon that man hadn't held Belle Caulwell in his arms nor had her lay her white hand upon him, claimin him fer her own.*

Lydy spoke without heat or rancor, merely a bald statement of fact, fact as immutable as the sunrise in the east.

*Ah, the pulchritudinous Belle, the dark enchantress. The Professor straightened, his eyes alight. At last we come to Belle. Of course, I saw her during the early stages of your trial. Until my father-in-law-to-be had me incarcerated, I, like many others of this benighted county, followed the proceedings assiduously. Belle Caulwell was, of course, the cynosure of our interest: the beautiful, bereft widow, sitting there in the courtroom, her dark head bent to her needlework during the doleful proceedings, her classic features like marble as she gave her evidence. And of course I heard the whispers . . . pray, Lydy, tell me more of this enchantress.*

*The young man looked toward the heavy cell door beyond which the sound of heavy boots could be heard. Ye hear that? Could be the jury's done decided and the bailiff's come fer me.*

*He sat up, tense and expectant, then slumped back as the sound of footsteps died away.*

*Maybe they done decided to let me rot.*

*The Professor waited silently for a moment, then spoke in a confiding tone. Nettie Mae told me it was said that Belle could charm wild creatures with the sound of her voice, that men and beasts alike were ensorcelled by the sinuous melodies she wove.*

*Lydy stared at the other man, his eyes dull. Women-folk says a lot of things, don't they? Now Belle could sing and that's a fact; she'd sit weavin at that loom of hern and the lonesome sound of her songs would twist all around and amongst above the clack of the loom. As fer charming wild critters, she did have her a tame bird, one of them great black and white peckerwoods that has a call like a crazy woman's laugh. She didn't keep hit in no cage neither; alls she had to do was to step out the door and call fer hit and here hit come, flapping out of the trees to light on her shoulder and whisper in her ear with hits cruel white beak.*

*But I reckon what you're wantin to know is about me and Belle. I might as well tell you the way of it. That first night I was back at the stand, I had made me down a pallet in the hay barn, where I had slept before. But Luellen's daddy looked at me hard and said, Son, you'd best sleep in the common room afore the fire where you kin stay warm. I figured Luellen would likely find a way to slip out durin the night and though, like I done said, she weren't so much to my taste no more, still I weren't agin layin with her. So, think I, I'll make fer the hay barn atter a time and see if she's a-waitin fer me.*

*But I done what her daddy said. I took my place afore the fire with the other drivers. I was some fuddled for Ol' Luce had been mighty free with the applejack. Afore long I had gone off into a deep sleep filled with troublesome dreams of men turning into hogs and a great fish monster swallowin them whole. And then I was one of them hogs and the monster had me in his cave and there was blood rainin down the walls.*

*I was thrashin about, tryin to get free of the fish-trap I'd run into, when there was a hand on my shoulder and the feller who'd been sleepin next me was shakin me awake.*

*Goldarnit, Lydy, you're like to wake the house. You got yourself all snarled up in that blanket and you're kickin like a young mule.*

*I come awake and at first hit was like I was back in that dream where the walls was runnin blood. Then I seen hit was only the light from the fire makin them so red.*

*Thankee, friend, I whispered. I'll step outside and get my head clear.*

*I crept out as quiet as I could, pickin my way between the sleepin men all around the fire. Outside, there was bright moonlight and I decided to lay me down in a little grassy hollow near the barn, where I could watch fer Luellen. I flung my blanket down and stretched out, the cool air washin over my face, takin away the feelin left by that worrisome dream. I was layin there, watchin the moon ridin high above the world, when all to oncet a dark shape comes betwixt me and the moon. I see from the skirts that hit's a woman and I feel myself getting hard.*

*Luellen? I says, and the woman kneels down before me. And then her hair is a dark cloud, blotting out the moonlight and her honey breath is in my mouth and in my nose and the hummin sound of her words is filling my ears and her white hands are moving on me and I am Belle Caulwell's creature forever more.*

# Chapter 28

## *Let Nothing You Dismay*
### Monday, December 25, and Tuesday, December 26

Elizabeth sat at the dining table watching the reflected pinks of the dying day fade on the snowy peaks along the eastern horizon. A new gardening book, filled with glossy photo layouts of heartbreakingly beautiful English gardens, lay open before her.

"You always write your thank-you notes on Christmas Day?" Phillip took the chair at the other end of the table, motioning to the little stack of sealed and stamped envelopes at her elbow.

"Not always—but within a few days. I'd rather get it over with than have to keep reminding myself."

"And it's something to keep your mind off all the other things you're worried about, am I right?" His tone was light but his expression was serious. "Lizabeth, are you going to ask Amanda about this Spencer Greer connection?"

She shut her eyes. "I want to. I really, really want to. But for one thing, I don't think I should mess up Christmas Day for everyone by getting into something that may lead god knows where. And for another, I think I ought to wait till I can hear the rest of whatever it was my sister was starting to tell me. It'll be midday tomorrow before Glory'll answer her phone, so I'll just have to contain myself."

The sound of boots stamping on the front porch roused

James, and he responded with a high-pitched peal of barks but did not leave his snug corner of the love seat.

"You guys should've come. We got some amazing shots of the sunset!" Laurel burst through the door, followed by the two dogs and Ben and Rosemary. The girls headed for the fireplace, shedding coats, gloves, and hats as they went. Ben, however, left his outerwear on.

"What've you done with Amanda?" Phillip asked when it became obvious she was not out on the porch.

"She was feeling pretty zonked and went to the cabin to take a nap—said to tell you thank you for everything, Aunt E." Ben came to the table. "She really enjoyed herself— said she wished she'd grown up in a family like this. I was going to give my mom a quick call and get some leftovers to take to the cabin, if that's okay."

"Take what you want, Ben. But your mom called while you were up the mountain. She said she was going to a party—you'll have to try again tomorrow."

Ben's eyes rolled. "I expect she was pissed too—in both senses of the word."

Elizabeth hesitated. "Well, she—"

"Don't bother, Aunt E. I know how she is. That's another thing Manda and I have in common—parents that suck."

Elizabeth awakened to feel a hand on her shoulder. Sleepily she rolled over and reached for Phillip, only to find his side of the bed empty.

"Lizabeth, I've got to go. Mac just called. The old house at Gudger's Stand is on fire. I need to go give him a hand."

She forced her eyes open. In the partial light from the hall, she saw Phillip zipping his jeans. She tried to focus on the bedside clock and its luminous dial: 1:34. She sat up.

"Just go back to sleep, sweetheart." Phillip was settling his handgun into its holster. "I'll give you a call as soon—"

"I'm coming with you." Elizabeth jumped out of bed, yanked open her closet door, and began pulling on warm clothes. "Please?"


"My guess is arson. Once they get the fire out, I'll be real surprised if we don't see evidence of a propellant."

They had found Mackenzie Blaine by his cruiser, watching as hoses from an assortment of fire engines pumped water through the broken windows along the front and back of the house. When they had first turned onto the bridge, Elizabeth had winced at the sight of the historic building, its lower windows alight with bright flames and heavy smoke spiraling from it into the night sky. But that had evidently been the peak of the fire's activity, for by the time they were across the bridge and climbing out of their car, the flames had winked out and only the smoke remained.

"Not what you'd call a professional job though," the sheriff explained. "A real arsonist would have gone for something that would smolder away unnoticed long enough to take hold. Likely whoever it was broke a window to get in, dumped some kerosene on the floor downstairs, then got out and tossed a match through the window. Made a big flare-up inside, mainly down at the far end, where Revis's bedroom was, but those thick floors and walls just laughed it off. Anyhow, Blake called 911 when he saw the first flames. The fire departments were here in record time."

In the glare of the lights from the various emergency vehicles, the old building squatted—an apocalyptic vision of an inn for demons and lost souls. Smoke poured from its shattered windows and hacked-open doors, taking form briefly in the wavering beams of light, then obliterating itself against the moonless sky. The firemen, vivid in their yellow turn-out gear, moved back and forth before the house, crisscrossing in and out of the beams, like figures in a silent movie.

With a sick feeling of déjà-vu, Elizabeth saw a dark shape clutching something in its arms emerge from the door on the upper gallery, stagger to the railing, sway, and drop to the floor as smoke, like a vengeful ghost, roiled and billowed after it.

"Phillip! Mackenzie! There's someone up there!"

The two men had been watching the road as yet another fire engine arrived from yet another volunteer fire department. Instantly they swung around to follow her horrified gaze and pointing finger.

"I don't see anything." Blaine's voice was skeptical. "All the smoke and these lights moving around probably made it look like—"

But a hoarse cry had gone up from the firemen on the ground as two yellow-clad figures, both protected by breathing apparatus, burst through the door that gave onto the upper gallery. The two figures swiftly picked up the crumpled body by its shoulders and feet and disappeared back into the smoke-filled interior.

"Who the hell was that?" The sheriff was already jogging toward the house.

Phillip hesitated, looked at her and started to say something, then seemed to think better of it. He turned away and followed Mackenzie Blaine up the drive.

Elizabeth waited for a moment, shivering in the cold air. Then, reasoning that she would only go a little closer, not near enough to get in the way, she followed Phillip.

She stopped, however, at a barrier that had been set up to keep onlookers at a safe distance. On the frozen ground, she saw a little huddle of firefighters, Phillip and the sheriff among them. They were clustered around the recumbent form of the rescued person, and the sheriff was squatting down, evidently speaking to whoever it was. A discussion of some sort was taking place, and the figure on the ground appeared to be attempting to struggle upright.

All around her were first responders and a few other individuals who didn't seem to have any function, milling about on the edge of the scene. "Fire junkies," she had heard Phillip call them, men—it was almost always men—who would drop anything at the report of a fire on the scanner and come to watch.

"They get some kind of thrill, watching stuff burn. Some of 'em end up being arsonists—if there aren't enough fires to satisfy them, they'll set some. Lots of forest fires probably start that way."

The skinny, slack-jawed young man in the faded brown heavy coveralls who was staring intently at the busy scene around the house, could he be responsible for this? As she watched, he elbowed the bulky form beside him.

"Well, I was the one told them about that feller in there. They was so busy gittin' the hoses in place after they busted in the doors and winders that they didn't see that light moving around upstairs. Finally got one of them old boys to listen to me and quick as they got the flames dousted, they went in after him. What the hell he thunk that he was doin'..."

"Musta had a reason; something in there he didn't want burned up." The big man in the camouflage jacket spoke slowly, as if weighing each word.

*He sounds familiar.* Elizabeth sidled closer, but the big man had turned away to beckon to someone behind him. "You come tell him we was the first ones here—he don't want to believe me."

*What was it Phillip said, back when Dessie's house burned? The obvious suspect in any fire is the first person on the scene.*

She watched as a second camouflage-suited hulk hove into view. The skinny young man reached out to slap the newcomer on the shoulder.

"Shee-it, son! Y'uns must sleep in your car with the

scanner on. I be damned if you and Marval ain't beat me again."

A roar of raucous laughter went up from a cluster of fire-fighters. Elizabeth strained to see what was happening and was rewarded with the sight of Phillip and Thomas Blake. Blake was clutching a sturdy cardboard box to his chest and walking, somewhat unsteadily, toward her, oblivious to Phillip's supporting hand under his arm. As they reached Elizabeth, the Troll halted abruptly and peered into her face. The unmistakable alcoholic fumes of his breath assaulted her and she drew back, but not before seeing the contents of the box—a pile of old clothes, freshly stained with birth fluids, and a scrawny black cat, curled protectively around three tiny black kittens.

"Miz Goo'weather, your servant. 'S a bitter cold evening for a gen'lewoman to be out. I beg that you will join me and my kin' frien' here in my abode for a li'l groggin of nog—'scuse me, the smoke has befuddled my tongue—a noggin of grog."

He swayed and his attempt at a courtly bow almost dislodged cat and kittens from their nest. Hastily Elizabeth made a grab for the box.

"Let me take her for you, Mr. Blake. Of course, Phillip and I would love to join you for a groggin of—a noggin of grog."

# Chapter 29

# *Tea and Small Talk*
## Tuesday, December 26

This is one strange scene, thought Phillip as he sat in the cluttered living area beside the Troll. *It's 3:05 in the mother-loving a.m. and she's back there in this old drunk's kitchen, making tea and small talk like things are normal.*

"I'm warming a little milk for Mama Cat while I'm back here—is that all right?"

Phillip looked at Blake, who seemed now to be almost completely recovered from his brief exposure to the smoke and flames. The walk through the cold air back to his home had cleared the last of the alcoholic slurring from his tongue, and he had been profuse in his apologies and almost manic in his conversation.

"I do appreciate your solicitude, good sir," he had said as Phillip steered him toward the brick building. "May I have the pleasure of knowing the name of my supporter? Hawkins? Ah, a venerable surname from Mother England—one recalls the redoubtable admiral, Sir Francis Drake's own cousin, who comported himself so bravely in the time of the Armada."

Blake had continued on in this garrulous strain as they entered the building that was his home, explaining how he had happened to notice the pregnant cat's absence and had gone outside to look for her in and under the junk cars that stood around the building.

"Some heartless person abandoned the poor creature beneath the bridge only a few days ago. I saw her and brought her in but she is not yet accustomed to me and my other friends."

Blake had gestured at the seeming dozens of felines that prowled about the room and crouched or curled on every available surface. "It was obvious that the moment of her *accouchement* was fast approaching and I knew she would be seeking a place to nest. When I saw the flames up at the Gudger house, my heart sank—I felt a pang, first of apprehension and then of certainty, that she had sought refuge there. After calling 911, I dashed up the hill, having first taken the precaution of wetting a blanket to shield myself from the flames. I mounted the steps, taking them two at a time, and plunged through the open door—"

"The door was open?" Phillip interrupted.

Blake nodded. "The back door, yes. Wide open. Puzzling, as it's been padlocked for years. I confess, in my haste I neglected to note whether the padlock had been forced or—"

"Excuse me, Blake—I need to give the sheriff this information." Phillip stood. "Lizabeth, I'm going to step outside and see if I can raise Mac on my cell. He needs to look for that padlock. Back in a few."

It had been maddening. He could see the sheriff, not a hundred yards away, moving about in the lights of the fire trucks as the weary crews packed up and prepared to leave the old inn, could see him but, in the ever quirky mountain conditions, could not get a cell connection. Remembering at last that the sheriff had called the bridge a "dead zone" as far as cell phones were concerned, he had plodded back up the hill, only to learn that Mackenzie had found and bagged the padlock.

"It hadn't been forced—but it had been tossed over in those brambles. Pure luck that it caught my flashlight's beam when I scanned the area."

Fingerprints would be unlikely; they agreed on this. "And since there's no way of knowing who might have made copies of the key in the past..." Mackenzie had sighed. "It's a dead end, Hawk. All we can say is it probably wasn't just random mischief."

"What about Blake? He was first on the scene. You know—"

But the sheriff was shaking his head with weary certainty. "I don't think so, Hawk. That individual's what you might call a troubled soul but he's no arsonist."


"I put the box with the cat and her babies in the bottom of that big cupboard back there and left the door open. Maybe that'll make her feel safe. She's had plenty to eat and drink and the babies are all nursing again." Elizabeth handed Thomas Blake a mug of steaming sweet tea. "I hope this is all right. I thought we could both use something hot."

Gently pushing a gray and white cat off the woven seat, Elizabeth took the tall straight-backed chair near the sofa. Blake, his face pasty white behind the smeared soot, slumped wearily over his tea.

"That was really brave, to go looking for that poor cat. Not many people would risk their lives that way."

He waved aside her words. "I fear that mine was a spirituous bravery—had I not been quite inebriated I would never have attempted so foolhardy a rescue. But still, one small good deed in a naughty world..."

A single tear traced its way through the dirt on his cheek. He drained his tea and tried to rise. "Mrs. Goodweather, I must ask to be excused. I have arrived at that stage of my drunkenness where I become tediously lachrymose. If you would forgive me, I think I shall retire."


"He insisted on going upstairs to his bedroom but, Phillip, he started crying so hard, he could hardly see to stagger. In the end, I helped him up this claustrophobic enclosed staircase—there's a door to it back in the kitchen area—and got him to his bed. He flopped down, still weeping, and began babbling all kinds of disconnected stuff. It was really hard to listen to—I have a pretty low tolerance for maudlin drunkenness and I was about to make my getaway when he said, very clearly, 'Of course, Spinner was gay. Poor boy, he just wasn't ready to admit it.' "

"You sure he said 'Spinner'?" Phillip had his arm around her as they walked back to the car. On the hill above them, two cruisers from the sheriff's department remained and the fleeting beams of flashlights behind the shattered windowpanes showed that Blaine and his men were still at work, searching for evidence that might explain the blaze.

"Oh, he definitely said 'Spinner.' Absolutely. So I sat down and waited. He was talking about all kinds of stuff but he kept mentioning Spinner. It seemed to be tied in with the abandoned cat—something like he had a weakness for helpless and abandoned creatures but he's been more successful with cats than anything else."

"So what all did he say?" Phillip unlocked the car. "Did you ask him where Spinner was now?"

"I tried to. But he launched into a long story about how he'd always been an outcast and that gave him a fellow feeling for other outcasts. He said he'd failed his family when he was forced out of the service."


Thomas Blake had tossed to and fro on his rumpled bed in an agony of confession that had brought no catharsis. "It was the calamitous termination of my military career that taught me to seek oblivion in a bottle. I tried to help a young corporal under my command, and ended by destroying us both. He was grieving at the loss of a comrade killed in a training mishap. And I, instead of telling him to buck up and be a man and a soldier, I, soft, foolish Thomas, put my arm around him to comfort him. I swear that was all."

Blake seemed to have forgotten her presence as he continued, words tumbling over one another as they escaped him. "I only made it worse for him. A self-important fellow officer, coming upon us at that moment, chose to misconstrue the situation. Rumors began to fly and my commanding officer was eager to be rid of me. And when I was discharged and returned home, my parents' shame was so deep that they would have almost nothing to do with me. And so I drink."

Blake had lapsed into silence, broken only by gasping sobs. When the worst of the crying jag had passed, Elizabeth spoke. "I'm so sorry, Mr. Blake. I wish I could help you."

They were just words but she found that she really meant them, even as she wondered if, after so many years, help was *possible* for the Troll.

The storm of drunken sobs passed. Blake lay still now, flat on his back, his face hidden in the crook of one arm.

"Mr. Blake," Elizabeth said gently, "you mentioned someone named Spinner. Was his last name Greer?"

His reply had been muffled. "Greer? Possibly . . . it has a familiar sound. Spinner was an outcast too. But he vowed to face what he was and what he'd done like a man. I applauded his resolution and urged him to take the final step."

Blake lowered his arm and gazed up through his smeared glasses. "I thought he had done the thing; I believed him redeemed and safe; but I have recently learned that he reneged on his promise. In the end, I fear he was as big a coward as I—he ran away."


"And then Blake just fell asleep—or passed out. So I came downstairs to wait for you."

Phillip was preoccupied for a moment with adjusting the car's heater. When at last it was working to his satisfaction, he said, "Mac told me some more about Blake's past. Evidently this episode Blake mentioned—him with his arm around the soldier—well, it seems the soldier *was* gay and some of the roughnecks in his unit, once he'd been written up, decided on a little retaliation for quote 'besmirching the honor' unquote of their unit. Things really got out of hand. The young man was beaten severely and sexually assaulted with a—with an object, as well."

He reached over and gave her hand a reassuring squeeze. "I'm sorry, sweetheart; it's ugly. But it goes a long way toward explaining why the poor guy stays drunk all the time."

# Chapter 30

# *Emerging from Darkness*
## Tuesday, December 26

The words came and went too quickly. Just when she had one forming at the tip of her tongue, it swirled away. *Like those fortune-telling eight balls my classmates brought to school*... Yes... No... Sometimes... Maybe... Wait and See... Never... The words and thoughts floated lazily up through her murky consciousness and disappeared again before revealing themselves.

*And that is a simile—using the word "like." It is not a... not the other one where the comparison is direct. If I said "My mind is a fortune-telling eight ball," that would not be a simile but a... a...* The word swam away, laughing over its shoulder at her. Years and years of teaching the basics of poetry and composition to bored freshmen, drilling into them the simple terms, and now she couldn't even remember... was it "dactylic"? She was sure there were three syllables: *dah, dah, dah.* No, dactylic was meter: the waltzing three-beat of "THIS is the FORest primEval/The MURmuring PINES and the HEMlocks." The elusive word peeked out at her, then dodged away.

"Here's you your juice, Nola, and your pills. Sit up like a good girl... or do you need a helping hand?"

Nola struggled to obey. She'd learned that Michelle's "helping hand" was harsh and left dark bruises on the tender flesh of her inner arm. But she said nothing, staring straight ahead, letting her jaw hang slack. From the corner of her eye, she could just make out the other figure standing *like lurking death* near the closed door. Without her glasses, it was difficult to be sure, but when she heard the voice, her question was answered.

"I brought some more of her meds. You should have enough now for the rest of the month. After that—"

"Do you guys realize it's almost nine-thirty! Mum, you never sleep that late. And where did you guys go last night anyway?"

As Elizabeth and Phillip made their somewhat shame-faced entrance into the living room, Laurel turned from the sketch she was doing of her older sister to glare at the late-risers. Rosemary, her dark hair falling like parentheses on either side of her serene countenance, was elegantly sprawled across the love seat by the fire, engrossed in one of the books she had received for Christmas.

At the sound of Laurel's voice, Rosemary looked up with the somewhat bemused expression of the reader who must make the not-always-welcome transition from the enthralling world on the printed page to the mundane demands of the here and now.

"Morning, Mum...morning, Phillip. There's coffee made and I brought the bowl of ambrosia up from the basement refrigerator. And we filled the bird feeders and let the dogs out. Where *did* you all go? I heard the jeep going down the road in the wee hours this morning, so I came downstairs to see what was happening—"

"And while it was nice that you left a note, Mum, 'Back soon' doesn't really cover the ground, now does it?" Laurel added a few more lines to her sketch, frowned in an accusing manner, and erased them.

"You're right, sweetie. But we were in a hurry and there just wasn't time to explain."

Feeling properly chastened, Elizabeth began to describe the events of the previous night while Phillip headed for the kitchen in search of coffee.

"Then the old house didn't actually burn down?" Laurel squinted at her sketch. "Rosie, would you put your head back the way it was . . . down a little more . . . there."

Rosemary complied and, still holding the pose, asked, "So, how do they think this fire got started?" The question was directed at Phillip, returning with a mug in one hand and a plate in the other.

"It was probably deliberate but—"

"Like that Hummer that burned up—maybe it was the same people—trying to scare off the developers." Laurel broke into Phillip's reply, only to be quashed by Rosemary's quiet voice.

"That doesn't make any sense, Laur. Why would the people who're trying to *save* the old stand from the developers want to burn it down? I think it's more likely it was some bored teenagers 'hoo-rahin' around,' like Miss Birdie says. They'd just see a creepy old house, not a historical landmark."

*Creepy old house.* The words echoed in Elizabeth's head. *Someone had called it that not long ago. Someone who—*

"Wait a minute. Nola's *niece* said something about the sooner they tear down that creepy old house, the happier she'd be. And now that I come to think of it, that presentation by those developers—by RPI—about their plans for the Gudger's Stand property—it talked about a historic *re-creation.* I'd been assuming they were going to turn the old stand into the centerpiece of their development but—"

"You could be onto something, Lizabeth," Phillip said. "What if it was in RPI's best interest to get rid of the stand house—not have to hassle with preservationists and folks like that who wouldn't go for major changes at the Gudger house? It's happened before—a piece of property that was inconveniently historic and too expensive to restore or maintain *and* in the way of progress suddenly burns to the ground."

*The day after Christmas is not the best time for getting information,* thought Elizabeth as she looked at the list she had made:

1. Nola/Ambien
2. Call Gloria re Spencer Greer
3. Bam-Bam?—call Debbie at River Runners

Phillip had left shortly after breakfast. "I told Mac I'd come back and give him a hand with looking around the Gudger place again. And I'll stop in and check on your drunken friend—he probably feels even worse than I do this morning."

For once the little office was empty—the girls had already checked their e-mails and had gone to visit Miss Birdie. There'd been no sign of Ben and Amanda this morning, but that was not unusual. Only the dogs were there, crowding the floor of the tiny room with their sleeping bodies.

Elizabeth studied the brief list, trying to decide what to do first. *Nola—she's my main concern at the moment.* Phillip had spoken with Mac as promised and Mac had suggested that she call Adult Protective Services.

"There's nothing he can do, Lizabeth. You have to go through Social Services and, yes, they're probably closed today. Why don't you go visit your Miss Barrett this afternoon and see how she's doing? If she's been overmedicated, but has started refusing the pills, she may be able to communicate better now. And if that's the case, maybe she'll be able to take charge of her own affairs again."

*I hope so. Wouldn't it be great to walk into that awful little room and have the old Nola look at me and say "Get me my glasses and get me out of this ridiculous place! And what* butcher *is responsible for this travesty of a hairdo?"*

She put a question mark by Nola's name and wrote down the number of Social Services after it, with the admonishment "CALL!!!"

*Bam-Bam. God, what a dreadful nickname. At least, I sincerely* hope *it's a nickname.* Elizabeth punched in the numbers for the proprietors of River Runners and was rewarded with an almost immediate answer.

She began to explain who she was and what she wanted but was interrupted as soon as she mentioned Ben's name.

"Oh, hi there, Elizabeth. How are Ben and that gorgeous girl of his? Tell them we're goin' to do another moonlight run on the twenty-eighth, if the weather cooperates. How can I help you?"

As Elizabeth had expected, Debbie remembered the girl named Bam-Bam. "She was a good guide. Small, but tough as nails. We were hopin' she'd come back the next summer but never heard from her. No surprises there—most of the folks who work for us are free spirits—they like to keep movin'. Still, she left without botherin' to pick up her last week's pay. She was hitchin' and probably got a chance of a good ride with someone at that last party and didn't want to wait around till the next day. Of course, considerin' she took with her a really good down jacket I'd lent her, I guess we're even. But, damn, I still remember that jacket—almost brand-new, green and purple—really nice lookin'."

Bambi Fleischaker was the girl's real name. Debbie had checked her records to be sure of the spelling. *F-L-E-I-S-C-H-A-K-E-R.* Elizabeth carefully tapped the name into a Google search and was rewarded with a mixed bag of information ranging from the search for extraterrestrial intelligence to the Alaskan Malamute Annual and several sites devoted to unusual baby names.

And one site called "Bambi, Come Home."

# The Drovers' Road X
## Love Medicine

I slipped out to the barn as soon as the house was quiet, thinking that Lydy would be lookin for me in our old place. Up in the haymow where the pallet was waitin, I stretched out to wait, smilin to myself at how easy it had been. Lydy had took the applejack from my own hand, like Mariah had said he must, and he had drunk it down in one swaller, never tastin what was in it.

When first I'd had sign that I was with child, I'd gone to see Mariah. Though they was Melungeons, Mariah and her man was well thought of in our part of the county and she was known to be a good hand with herbs and cures. She had helped me back of this when my courses begun and I had such pains every month that I had to take to my bed. Mariah had give me a tea brewed of raspberry leaves and willow bark, with honey from her bee gums and hit had stopped the pains almost to oncet.

So now I made my way through the woods, along the trail that ran above the drovers' road. Hit was more steep-like and twistin amongst the rocks and trees but at this time of the year the drovers' road was deep in muck and no place for a single girl to travel on anyways.

I found Mariah in her little stone house, strainin honey into the heavy brown crocks she had. Like always, she had flowers in her hair and like always she was happy to see me.

Lulie, she says, openin out her arms and smilin that way that *always makes me wish I'd known my mother. I walk into her arms and as I feel her warmth, I bust out bawlin.*

*What is it, Lulie? she asks, when I can talk again. She puts her big hands on either side of my face and looks into my eyes, like she is seein my inside thoughts. It's not the monthly pains this time, is it? And before I can make answer, she says, No, I see. Quite t'other way round.*

*Mariah, says I, I don't know what to do. He hasn't spoke for me yet and I fear he may not.*

*Her dark face was grieved as she spoke. Lulie, you've not come here thinkin I'll rid you of this child? I know what the talk is but that's a thing I will not do.*

*I had knowed that, but hit had been at the back of my mind that she might help me that way. It was whispered that my step-mother Belle had once rid a girl of the bastard she was carryin but then the girl had bled to death. That girl had been sickly to start with and she'd likely have died anyway, is what was said. But Belle was still in Warm Springs and even had she been to hand, I could never have gone to her with my secret.*

*No, Mariah, I'll not ask for that. But I've heard you can make a drink that will bind a man to a woman forever more. That's what I want of you.*

*She cast her eyes down and stood silent for a minute. Mariah, I said, if I can't marry Lydy, all that's left for me is to fling myself into the river. I'm beggin you, fix me that love medicine.*

*Hit's a powerful thing, she warned me. And oncet hit's done, hit can't be undone. You got to think on that. Lulie, if the boy don't want to marry you and your daddy casts you out, you can come here. Me and Ish'll care for you like you was our own.*

*Them two had never had children but Mariah mothered any sick or lame creature that came their way. She had nursed me through the summer complaint the year I was born for Belle hadn't had no idea how to care for a baby.*

*But I kept on a-beggin and swearin to throw myself in the*

*river till at long last Mariah agreed and told me what I must do. I was to dig the root of the little three-petaled woods flower that bloomed white in the spring. I knowed which one she meant and where there was a patch of them, though the pretty white flowers was long past. Next I was to wash the root in spring water and lay it to dry in some dark place. When hit was bone dry then I could crush it into a powder.*

*My granny said that it should be a Friday when you crush the roots and Friday midnight when you mix it with the honey, Mariah said.*

*Did you ever use this potion? I asked and her eyes went to the open door. Out there was Ish, bent over hoein the garden rows. He seemed to feel her lookin at him and straightened up, a great white smile on his brown face.*

*Only oncet, said she.*

*I had done like Mariah told me and the little bottle of love medicine was hid away in my feather tick against Lydy's return. Truth to tell, I'd almost forgot hit, thinkin I might not have need, thinkin maybe Lydy would come to me on his own. But after I seen him save Belle from the hogs and carry her into the house, all unheedin of my call, a cold fear come over me and I unstitched the tick and got that little bottle out.*

*I held it up to the window, letting the last rays of the settin sun stream through it, lightin it up with a yellow glow. Put it in his food or drink at night and give it to him with your own hand, Mariah had said. Make sure he takes all of it and make sure you lay with him afore the sun comes up. As soon as that happens, he'll be yourn forever more.*

*The moonlight sifted through the logs of the barn, making bars acrost my body and the sweet-smellin hay beneath me. I lay* there, eager for Lydy and eager for the lovin that was to come, the lovin that Mariah had said would bind him to me for all time. To me and to this baby, I thought, layin a hand on my belly. I shut my eyes and begun to picture the years to come, me and Lydy with our fine family—runnin the stand and bringin up our boys to do the same. I fell asleep picturin them so clear, standin afore me like stair steps, from the tallest to the least un . . .

But my dreams was different. It was me in the river and Lydy on the bank, standin there where he had first helped me with the washin. He was laughin an evil laugh as he watched me bein carried downstream, wavin my arms and hollerin fer him to save me. My skirts was heavy with the water, twistin roun my legs and pullin me under. I tried to kick free and then I heard the grunt and squeal of the great fish monster Daddy used to tell of and I hollered out.

I woke all to oncet and lay there blinkin, happy to find myself not in the river but still all a-tremble. So I sat up, fearin to fall back to sleep and back into that evil dream. My heart was poundin in my ears and at first I didn't hear the sounds outside the barn.

But when the thumpin in my head had quieted and I was full awake, I heard the small little noise in the grass and peered through a crack betwixt the logs, thinkin to see Lydy comin to me, my own true love.

Hit was the bitterest sight my eyes had ever seen. They was down there in the moonlight, Belle and Lydy, ruttin like a pair of hogs. I seen them and hit was black bile in my mouth to know what I had done by usin Mariah's love medicine.

# Chapter 31

## *Missing Persons*
### Tuesday, December 26

"The number you have dialed is currently unavailable. Leave a message at the tone."

Elizabeth made a face at the telephone, then, in obedience to the beep, began to speak. "Phillip, I found out some stuff. That Bam-Bam girl Thelma and Maxie were telling us about—her name was Bambi Fleischaker. And there's a whole Web site about her—her parents have been trying to get in touch with her for years. It said they last heard from her in the spring of '95 when she was hitch-hiking through West Virginia. I'm wondering if maybe Bambi ended up here—in the old silo."

She clicked off the telephone and sat, the instrument still in her hand. *God, what a grim message to leave. And that poor girl's parents—all this time not knowing where their daughter was... or if she was even alive. Like whoever it is looking for Spencer Greer.*

Elizabeth glanced at the clock on the computer. *Quarter of twelve. Surely Glory'll be up by now.* With a sigh of resignation, she punched in her sister's number.

"I *told* you, Lizzy. Amanda's mother was married to a Spencer Greer before she married Lawrence Lucas. Of course, I never *met* this Greer; Ronnie was a widow when she and the little boy moved to Tampa. She met Lawrence through mutual friends and Lawrence fell in love with her. Very romantic—you know she's every bit as good-looking as Amanda *and* she hasn't let herself go like some people I could mention. Anyway, Lawrence was completely smitten and they were married within a few months. Lawrence offered to adopt the boy but Ronnie wanted him to keep his father's name—apparently Ronnie'd been quite in love with this Greer and might have remained a grieving widow forever if not for the financial security Lawrence offered.

"Then Amanda was born a few years later and they were a happy little family. Of course, Lawrence has more money than God on a good day, so there were no problems *there*. The boy was quite attractive and evidently very intelligent—did well at school and all that. Little Amanda absolutely worshiped him—of course, he was a good deal older. Let's see, Larry and Ronnie married in '80—the year Ben was born—and the little boy must have been six or seven at the time. I remember him at the wedding, standing up beside Ronnie in his little white suit, so darling. So there were eight or nine years between the two children, but in spite of that—"

"Glory, what was the tragedy you mentioned yesterday?" *God, she's getting as bad as Aunt Dodie, the way she runs on.* Elizabeth switched the phone to her other ear and began to doodle on the list in front of her as her sister continued, undeterred.

"Oh, the tragedy—that's what I'm getting to. The boy *died* when he was only nineteen. He was traveling in South America or Africa or one of those *awful* places and there was a horrible accident or maybe it was one of those *gruesome* diseases they have. Lawrence and Ronnie flew wherever it was and brought the ashes home. Yes, that's it, it must have been a highly contagious disease—I know there was a reason he had to be cremated. So there was a small family service and that was that. They never speak of him now. I believe it broke Amanda's heart. We all think it's why she's turned out to be so odd."

"And the father of this boy, this Spencer Greer, are you sure he's dead?"

"Well, really, Lizzy! When a woman moves to town, a woman with connections to some of the *best* families, let me add, if that woman says she's a widow, I, for one, don't demand to see a death certificate. Of course he's dead."

Elizabeth stared at her list. The three items were almost obliterated by her spiraling doodles. *So why, if Spencer Greer is dead, is someone looking for him? And who's paying for this ad?*

Amanda. Who else? Previous ads had said to respond to a post office box in Tampa; this most recent one bore a Ransom address. Amanda had moved here from Tampa. *Quod erat demonstrandum. And didn't the girls see her checking a post office box in Ransom? Part of her supposed tie-in with her father's development companies, according to Laurel.*

"But it doesn't make any sense," she explained to James, who was watching her intently, waiting to see if she was going to go to the kitchen and fix some lunch. "Even if Spencer Greer is alive, what would it matter to Amanda?"

Instantly, an answer presented itself—fantastic, but—*Okay, say Amanda's mother wasn't a widow. Say she wasn't even divorced. That would make her marriage to Amanda's father bigamous and so maybe Amanda got wind of that and—*

"Baloney, Elizabeth! You're turning this into a bloody soap opera." She stood, stretched, and started for the kitchen, accompanied by the usual retinue of hopeful dogs. Resolutely ignoring the remains of yesterday's duck—*there's enough for us both to have some tonight since the kids are going out*—she made a cheese-and-chutney sandwich on one of the leftover rolls, absentmindedly tossing slivers of sharp cheddar to Molly, Ursa, and James in turn.

*Besides, the ads have been appearing for years,* she thought as she took her plate to the table—*if they first started in '95, Amanda would have been... what did Glory say, Amanda was born a few years after Ben... eighty-two from ninety-five... no way. A thirteen-year-old girl placing ads in an obscure out-of-state town looking for her mother's previous husband? Get a grip, Elizabeth; there has to be another explanation.*

A visit to Nola would be just the thing, she decided, to extract her fevered imagination from the tales it was attempting to spin. The day was clear and cold enough that a little snow still dusted the ground, but there was no wind and the air felt wonderful—invigorating rather than punishing.

A stop at the mailbox yielded a few late Christmas cards, a letter for Ben from someone in Delaware... *and that, Elizabeth, right there is one reason Amanda might choose to get her mail in town. So Ben's nosy aunt doesn't know all her business.*

As usual, her trip off the farm included various small errands to be done: *Dumpsters, gas at Jim Hinkley's, go see Nola, deposit those checks... I can take care of all that, pick up some groceries, and, just like James James Morrison's mother, be back in time for tea.*

As Elizabeth neared Nola's room, she realized that the picture of a completely recovered Nola, tapping an impatient foot on the floor and demanding to be released, was tantalizing her and speeding her pace. The sound of a cheerful voice in the room ahead lifted her hopes.

"That's okay, Michelle. You go on and take your break." The voice was familiar but not Nola's. It continued on. "I wish you could have seen them this morning. Those rascals PC and Opie were playing with my knitting and unraveled half of what I'd done yesterday."

A bulky form hurried through the door, almost colliding with Elizabeth. "Oopsie, didn't see you there! Go right in, her and her neighbor's having a little visit."

The aide didn't linger but hurried down the hall, pulling a pack of cigarettes from one pocket and a cell phone from another. With a brief prayer to Whatever or Whomever that Nola might be better, Elizabeth stepped into the room.

*No change.* The disappointment was like a blow. Nola lay on her bed, mouth slack, eyes glazed. She didn't seem to register Elizabeth's entrance, but lay unmoving. Only the labored rise and fall of her chest betrayed that she was alive.

Like the voice, the silver hair and bright blue eyes of Nola's visitor were familiar. *It's the neighbor... what was her name... Lee something?*

"Well, hello there, Miz Goodweather. Remember me—Lee Palatt? I guess I've about worn poor Nola out, telling her about my kitties."

The sweet-faced woman stood, looking ostentatiously at her watch. "I've got to be running along now—due at a meeting for the spay-neuter clinic volunteers."

She leaned over the bed, raising her voice slightly. "You just rest and get better, Nola. I'll be back to see you soon."

As Lee Palatt turned to leave, she threw Elizabeth a meaningful look, nodding toward the door and mouthing the word *Outside.* Elizabeth glanced at Nola, then followed the other woman out to the hall.

"Poor Nola! Have *you* seen any improvement? I don't know; it seems to me she's losing ground. I'm surprised that so-called niece of hers isn't around more—they were here and then they were gone. She *says* she's a nurse at a hospital in Raleigh and can't get any more time off. They managed to clean out that little house pretty thoroughly, I'd say." Lee Palatt's words dripped disgust. "Selling off everything they can...

"But it's an odd thing—last night I saw a light in Nola's

house, moving around like a flashlight. I thought it might be those two back for something they'd missed, but when I looked I didn't see any vehicle. I'll tell you this: whoever it was, they were definitely looking for something. Good grief, look at the time! I've got to run!"

# Chapter 32

# *And One Found Hiding*
### Tuesday, December 26

The woman on the bed had not moved, but as Elizabeth took the chair beside the bed, her head turned. Closing her gaping mouth, she slowly winked one eye. In a hoarse whisper, she said, "E-liz-a-beth. I. Am. Here."

A great surge of joy swept over her and Elizabeth grasped her friend's thin hand. "Nola! Oh, thank god! Let me go get someone—they need to know you're yourself again. They—"

"No!" The fierce whisper was accompanied by the tightening of Nola's fingers around hers. "No! Not yet! Not until his...accounts are closed. Don't tell. Promise me... don't tell. Elizabeth, come back in...two days. Give me time to find out who...wants me quiet."

"Nola, what do you—"

A voice from the doorway spoke. "You're wasting your time—Nola's done quit talking."

The chubby aide came into the room, a can of Mountain Dew in her hand.

"They just shut down like this sometimes," Michelle explained, taking a long pull at the can. "Miss Nola, she's one of the lucky ones though, so many friends still coming to see her every day, even if she can't talk and don't recognize no one."

"Oh, but she—" Elizabeth felt an urgent tug on her hand. She turned to see Nola, once again gap-mouthed and staring. The hand that had crushed her own so tightly a moment since fell limply to Nola's side.

"—she seemed like she knew me for just a moment there." Elizabeth stood to leave. "But I guess I was mistaken. Tell me, does Nola recognize Mrs. Holcombe? I expect she comes pretty frequently."

"Almost every day. She don't stay long but she always has a little something for her Nola."

It was impossible to get the poem out of her brain. Milne's verses about James James Morrison Morrison Weatherby George Dupree had been a favorite with the girls as children, especially Laurel, who would shriek with delight at the tale of the naughty mother disobeying her three-year-old son and the dire consequences thereof. *She hadn't been heard of since.*

The words flowed automatically without any effort of memory, as if they were following a well-worn groove. *Which is why, I guess, it was easier for Nola to communicate with memorized lines rather than have to come up with new sentences. But now she's making her own sentences. Why doesn't she want anyone to know she's better? Why is she pretending to be worse? Is this just another aspect of her illness? Paranoia? Delusion? "Not till accounts are closed"—what was that about? And "come back in two days"?*

Elizabeth slowed the jeep in front of the bank, trying to decide if she wanted to attempt parallel parking in the ridiculously small space left between a battered blue Chevy pickup and a massive black SUV, both of which had parked over their allotted lines, when a familiar tall, slender figure with a long flaxen braid caught her eye. Amanda was on her way into the lobby of the post office.

Feeling ridiculously like Nancy Drew, Elizabeth slid her car *(no sporty roadster, more's the pity)* into a fortuitously empty space beyond the bank, leaped out, and hurried to the glass doors that gave a view to the post boxes. Amanda was there, fitting a key into one, though what the number was, Elizabeth could not make out. The lock appeared to be stiff and the key turned with difficulty, but at last the little metal door opened, revealing a jumble of letters and flyers.

Eagerly Amanda reached into the box and pulled out her mail. Elizabeth took a deep breath, pushed open the door, and stepped into the post office. A quick glance confirmed it. Amanda was standing before an open Box 1066. The one in the ad—the Norman Conquest date made it impossible to forget.

"Hey, Amanda." Why did her voice sound so accusatory? "I need to talk to you."

"Elizabeth!" Amanda whirled, letters in her hand. "I didn't see you. I was just—"

"Amanda, I want to know about Spencer Greer." The words were sharp and impulsive. Somehow all of Elizabeth's reluctance to pry, her disinclination to get involved, had been swept aside. There was none of her usual careful self-editing and weighing the consequences—the words were coming of themselves. "It may not be any of my business, but Ben's my nephew and I need to know that you came to the farm because of him, because you care for him in the way he cares for you. I need to know...oh, bloody hell, Amanda...I need to know that you're what you say you are. I will *not* have Ben hurt again."

Amanda stood immobile, staring in amazement at her. Elizabeth was abruptly aware of her own flushed face and of the fact that her voice had become increasingly shrill as she harangued the unsuspecting young woman. *Oh god, have I just made everything worse with that little tirade? Will she tell Ben that his aunt is too bloody crazy and thank you but no thank you, she's outta here, so much for the idyllic life at Full Circle Farm?*

Then, slowly, Amanda's face crumpled and tears began to slide over those perfect cheekbones.

"Amanda, sweetie, please, I didn't mean..."

Amanda shook her head and in a choked voice said, "It's fine, Elizabeth. I understand. It's just...I think I'm crying because I wish that my mother had cared about Spinner as much as you care about Ben."

# Chapter 33

## *Spinner Greer*
### Tuesday, December 26

"S pinner Greer was . . . Spencer Greer is my brother. My half-brother. I'm trying to find out where he went."

They had moved from the too-public post office lobby to Elizabeth's jeep. Amanda, seemingly relieved to be sharing her secret, had been more than forthcoming. The words had poured out of her.

"When I was little and just learning to talk, I couldn't pronounce 'Spencer.' So he was Spinner to me and, eventually, to everyone. It suited him, in a weird way. He spun from one enthusiasm to another—music, theater, tennis— he was good at everything but nothing held him for long. It was like he was always looking for something that would be *It*, whatever It was." Amanda paused to blow her nose. "I was only seven when he went off to prep school. But he sent me funny postcards and letters all the time. And when he was home, on vacations, he was just wonderful. It was Spinner who taught me to ride a bike, to roller-skate, to swim. He had all the patience in the world with me, and I absolutely idolized him and lived for the times that he was home."

"He sounds like a wonderful brother." Elizabeth reached out to touch the girl's hand. "But, I have to confess, Amanda,

I talked to my sister this morning and asked her about Spencer Greer. Among other things, she said that your brother had died in an accident or of some illness. Did she have that wrong?"

Amanda drew a shuddery breath and turned to face Elizabeth. She was calm now; only her reddened eyes hinted at the storm of emotion that had just passed.

"I was away at summer camp, actually a camp here in the mountains near Brevard, when it supposedly happened. The director called me into her office and told me, oh very kindly and gently, that my brother was dead. She said that my parents felt that it would be best for me not to come home but to stay at camp. All she could tell me was that Spinner had caught some terrible disease and had died quite suddenly. I knew that he was taking a year off from college to travel—I'd had some postcards from different places."

Amanda's soft gray-blue eyes brimmed with tears again. "I still have the postcards—all soft and fuzzy on the edges from being handled so much. I spent most of the last month of camp on my bunk, crying and reading and rereading those cards—Atlanta, Asheville, Charleston, Baltimore, Boston, New York—Spinner said he was looking for a place he belonged."

"When camp was over, I didn't fly home with the group of Tampa girls; instead, Papa came for me in the car."

Amanda looked out the window, watching the few pedestrians hurrying along Ransom's nearly deserted sidewalks. "It was the strangest, most surreal experience, Elizabeth. For once, Papa wasn't in a big hurry. He took me to Asheville to see the Biltmore House and to Cherokee and then we went to a big amusement park near Charlotte. It took almost a week to get back to Tampa, and all that time he let me cry and carry on and talk about Spinner. And I did too, all the way through North and South Carolina and Georgia. But when we got to Florida and stopped in

Lake City to spend the night, Papa said that when we got home, I was never to mention my brother's name again.

"'You're going to have to be very grown up now, Mandy,' he said. 'Your mama isn't dealing with this loss very well. Any mention of Spencer is painful to her, so I want you to promise me not to talk about him with her—it's easier for her right now just to carry on as if Spencer never existed.'

"So I came home to a house where there was absolutely no trace of my brother. Instead of his room with the dark green walls covered with posters and the jumble of books and magazines and tennis clothes, there was a guest room—all shiny yellow and white and smelling of fresh paint. Nothing of Spinner was left—even his furniture had been replaced.

"My mother was changed too—a different hairstyle, a new hair color, and her face that had been soft and sweet had become thin and brittle. She hugged me, asked how camp had been, and then, before I could even get out the placemats I'd woven for her, she excused herself to go lie down. 'A little headache,' she said.

"She had headaches all summer, and after that summer, my life was a succession of boarding school, summer camp, boarding school, summer travel, holidays with my parents but almost never at home." Amanda's brief laugh was humorless. "Wherever home was. When I came home the first Christmas, they had moved to another, fancier house and it got harder and harder to remember Spinner. I felt like I'd lost everyone—Spinner was gone, Mama and Papa weren't the same, and I didn't know anymore who I was."

"According to my sister, you were on your way to becoming quite well known as a model. That's an achievement a lot of young women would envy."

Amanda shook her head. "It's all smoke and mirrors, that world. There I'm just a hanger for the clothes. What

I do now—actually creating beauty with my hands and brain—is much more satisfying."

She looked at Elizabeth and her eyes shone. "After so much unhappiness it's been like a miracle to find myself here. I'm finally doing something I love, with someone I love. Don't worry, Elizabeth—I'm totally serious about Ben. He's the best thing in my life since Spinner, and in a way it's because of Spinner that we ended up together."

Elizabeth raised her eyebrows. "I don't understand."

"It happened last year, when I was staying with my parents for a few weeks until they left for Palm Springs. They always have this huge bash just before Christmas—you know, several hundred of their closest friends. Anyway, I was getting dressed for the party and managed to trash the only pair of pantyhose that would work with this really short dress I was wearing. So I went down the hall to my mother's dressing room to see if she had any. Guests were already beginning to arrive and Mama and Papa were both downstairs and I was frantically pulling open drawers looking for pantyhose."

Amanda held up the little handful of flyers and junk mail she had taken from Box 1066. "This is the only kind of mail I've gotten so far. But I keep hoping for an answer to my ad because of what my mother had hidden from me—a manila envelope marked 'Amanda' and it was full of letters to me from Spinner—all but one were unopened and most of them were postmarked either '94 or '95—*two years* after he was supposed to have died."

# The Drovers' Road XI
## The Fine Thread

Many would deem it an auspicious augury when the jurors' deliberations are prolonged.

Lydy paused in his endless circuit—a ludicrously curtailed three steps away from the window wall and three short steps back—to glance dismissively at his cell mate. Then he shifted his attention to the square of gray sky visible through the bars. The despairing slump of his shoulders suggested that he did not share the Professor's optimism. He stood for a moment longer, then turned to continue his pacing.

The Professor closed the small leather-bound book with which he had been attempting to divert himself and returned it to his breast pocket. Even Homer's sublime words, he muttered, pall upon too frequent perusal.

Lydy, I beg of you, my young friend, relate to me more of your peregrinations. I collect you continued on the Drovers' Road after your brief return to Gudger's Stand; it was at a later date the unfortunate events leading to your incarceration occurred, if I do not mistake. Pray, tell me of your journey to South Carolina.

At last the restless pacing ceased and Lydy dropped down on his bunk. He leaned forward, resting his elbows on his knees, his big hands drooping.

We was on our way early the next morning. I'd not had a word alone with Luellen but from the way she wouldn't look at me when she was serving out the breakfast, I come to think she must *have suspicioned what had passed betwixt me and her step-mother. Belle weren't about that morning—and we had had but a few words the night before. But, like I said, I knowed that now there was nothing for me with Luellen. Right afore we left, ol' Luellen come sidlin up with a poke of fried pies for me and begun to say something but I made out I had to be on my way and left her standin there with that little calico poke still in her hand.*

*Belle's scent was on me yet as we took to the road and I looked back to the house, where I seen her standin on that upper gallery, that dark hair of hern like a storm cloud around her head. She didn't throw up her hand nor make nare sign but I felt the pull in my loins as if she'd bound me to her by a fine thread.*

Lydy closed his eyes. *God help me, I feel hit yet, a-drawin me to her.*

The Professor cleared his throat. *I have little experience of these stock stands. On my journey from Charleston to Warm Springs, I had occasion to put up just outside Asheville at a fine hostelry was called Sherrill's Tavern. It, so I was told, served as a stock stand in the fall and winter months. But as I was there in the early summer, the custom was, in the main, from the Albany coaches. I found it a most commodious inn, set among pleasant fields, only somewhat marred by the muddy condition of the road leading to it. On the day I arrived, there had been a heavy down-pour that morning and all the male passengers were obliged to re-move from the stagecoach and push.*

Lydy roused from his reverie. *I just called to mind a quare thing I heard about at one of them stands. They was a feller there named Aaron come in whilst we was there with a great pack of goods on his back: sewing notions and fripperies fer women-folk, razors and pocketknives fer men and all manner of things fer sale. He was a funny little dark-complected feller and he talked the quarest you ever heard. A man told me this Aaron was from someplace over the water and that most of the year he traveled the back roads where there weren't no stores. He was said to be a Jew,* like the ones in the Bible, but he didn't wear no long robe, just an ordinary black coat and britches like anyone.

He was a talky feller and he got to tellin about where all that he'd traveled and what all that he'd seen. He said as how he had come through South Carolina back in the spring and in a place called Mount Airy he seen two yaller-skinned brothers, joined at the breast by a band of flesh. They was born that way, he said, in some far-off land and hadn't one never took a step without the other one had to come too.

Now this Aaron told hit fer a true story and I might of believed him till he went on to say these brothers was married to two sisters and they had two houses and took hit in turns to pass a night in each house. He said they had any number of young uns, though wasn't none of them joined nowhere. I believe he must have been a liar though. You can't trust a furriner to speak the truth.

As a matter of fact, Lydy, I believe your peddler was alluding to Chang and Eng, the renowned Siamese twins. I myself, some years ago—

A thump of boots and the rattle of the chain that secured the door of the cell interrupted the Professor's observation. Lydy stiffened expectantly as the door creaked open a cautious few inches. A grizzled face appeared in the crack and a rough voice said, Lydy, there's three of us out here come fer ye and ever one of us armed. You step out and come along peaceable like and they won't be no trouble. The jury's ready with the verdict.

# Chapter 34

## *Something Like Fate*
### Tuesday, December 26

It was arson, all right—see how they set the mattress on fire—slashed it and the pillows open so they'd burn better—but at the moment I'm fresh out of motives." Mackenzie Blaine rubbed his hands together and stamped his feet in an effort to warm them. The interior of the Gudger house seemed, somehow, at least ten degrees colder than the out-of-doors. "What d'ya think, Hawk? I suspect you and your lady friend mighta been discussing the subject."

Phillip looked around the wreck of the bedroom. The half-burned recliner lay on its side and the ratty little television's tube was shattered. The old trunk's lid was open and its interior was a mass of charred clothing. Every drawer had been wrenched from the chest of drawers and dumped into the center of the room to make another pile of tinder for the arsonist's kerosene.

Burn marks stretched across the floorboards of the bedroom and into the little hallway, marking the fire's path. The stench of the wet, charred wood and plastic and cloth was strong, and he knew that it would linger in his nostrils and cling to his clothes for hours.

"Lizabeth did suggest that both Miss Barrett's niece and those RPI development folks would be happy not to have a historic building on their hands. You know how it is—once the historic preservationists get a bee in their bonnet about maintaining a place's authenticity, all of a sudden there're miles of red tape to untangle and everything has to wait till every single interested party has had their say and made their appeals. What if someone figured the place would be more useful as a development *without* the historic building? You said something like that yourself, back before Christmas when you were showing me around this place."

The sheriff kicked disconsolately at a jumbled heap of debris. "I know I did. And I've been quietly checking into the whereabouts of all those parties on the night in question. The niece and her boyfriend say they were back in Raleigh, but I haven't been able to confirm that yet. And the RPI bunch all have alibis—hell, they were every one of them at a big do up at the Holcombe place, along with most of the politicos and movers and shakers of the county. Of course—"

"Of course that doesn't mean shit," Phillip reminded him. "Folks like RPI don't personally commit arson—they hire it done. But this was such a godawful *amateur* job—no, it doesn't make any sense."

"Nope, none of it does." With a last look around what remained of the bedroom, they traced the blackened trail of the fire through the little hallway and into the onetime barroom.

Mackenzie Blaine led the way to the back door. "The RPI folks say it's radical environmentalists. Kind of a convenient catch-all phrase, like 'outside agitators' was back in the civil rights era. But there was a letter in the paper from some group called Black Bear Watches saying they'd torched the Hummer in protest of RPI's plans. Only thing is, no one's ever heard of this group.

"Way too many unanswered questions, Hawk. Why'd Miss Barrett jump? Why'd Payne Morton kill himself?

Whose bones are those in the silo? Who's the damn mole in my department?"

"About those bones," Phillip trailed Blaine out the door onto the back porch. "Does the name Bambi Fleischaker ring any bells for you? She was a young woman who evidently went missing around that same October as the alleged gang rape occurred. Elizabeth is thinking that's who it was in the silo."

As they began to follow the overgrown path around the house, looking once more for anything that might be a link to the incompetent arsonist, Phillip briefly outlined the story told by Thelma and Maxie, with the addition of the new information about the Bambi website. Mackenzie Blaine listened without comment till Phillip had finished, then began to shake his head slowly.

"First of all, I've been going through the records—all the missing-persons reports and inquiries starting in mid '95—and these records are what you might call badly incomplete. Of course, the department wasn't fully computerized—hell, until Miss Orinda either retires or explodes because someone inadvertently lights a match around her, it's not going to *be* fully computerized. Anyway, the paper records were damaged in some flooding a few years ago and there're whole sections stuck together or washed clean of ink—it's a god-awful mess."

Blaine prodded with his boot at a mound covered with leafless vines and dead vegetation. The square outline of a rusted metal roof lay half-buried in the pile of dirt and charred rough-sawn timber. "This must be what's left of the outhouse that burned a little before Revis was murdered."

Feeling somewhat aggrieved, Phillip exclaimed, "What's the matter with you, Mac? I've just given you—no, *Lizabeth*'s just given you a nice little late Christmas gift to pass on to the medical examiner. When they get around to looking for names to go with those bones, you hand 'em

Bambi Fleischaker. Once that's confirmed, we can start looking for the murderer."

"'Fraid not, Hawk. I talked to the ME's office this morning. They won't be doing a full workup for several weeks yet, but the young lady I spoke to let drop one interesting bit of information. She said that the ME took one look at the pelvis and said the bones were definitely male. So our skeleton's not your Bambi."

"The letter that had been opened was postmarked San Francisco and written in December of '93, almost six months after Spinner supposedly died. He wrote that he wanted me to know that he was alive and that eventually there'd be a way for him to see me. There was something about breaking a promise to Papa and that he should never have made that promise."

Amanda was shivering as she told the story—how she had snatched up the letters and run to her room to read them, only to be interrupted by her father's voice calling to her to come downstairs.

"I pulled on a silk top and a long velvet skirt—I never *had* gotten those pantyhose—and shoved the most recent letter into the skirt pocket. Once I made my appearance downstairs, I thought I could slip away and read it.

"As I went down the stairs into the crowd of people milling about the entrance hall, I knew that I was no longer the same person who'd climbed those stairs an hour before. Mama and Papa were in the hall welcoming guests, and when Papa beckoned to me, I can remember looking down at him—at *them*—and wondering if I'd ever really known them at all. They seemed changed too. Mama's face was more like a mask than ever, and the sound of talk and laughter and the smells of dozens of heavy perfumes and the odor of the food that was being laid out in the dining room all rushed up at me. I remember thinking that if I could just get through the party, then I'd do whatever it took to find Spinner."

Amanda tilted her head as if to gauge the reaction to her tale. Elizabeth nodded. "You didn't run screaming down the stairs, waving the letters to confront your parents in front of the assembled company like someone in a soap opera. I completely understand. That Southern Lady thing of never washing family linen in public dies hard, thank god. So you waited."

Amanda nodded. "I did. And I was rewarded for it. If I'd made a big scene that night, the party would have broken up and I might not have met Ben."

She had played her part, meeting and greeting at her parents' side. Finally, when the stream of incoming guests had abated and the crowd had scattered to various rooms throughout the house, Amanda had slipped outside, past the swimming pool to the garden house, where clusters of candles in hurricane lamps flickered invitingly. None of the guests had yet found their way to this secluded spot and she took advantage of her solitude to pull out the letter, rip it open, and read the last message her brother had sent her.

"He said that Mama and Papa still hadn't come round and he doubted now that they ever would. But he wanted me to know that he was buying some property in the mountains and hoped to settle down there. I had read just that far when Ben walked into the garden house."

"Had you met him before that? I know Gloria was doing her best to get him interested in, as she put it, 'the right sort of girl.'"

"No, I'd been away for some time, doing photo shoots here and there. Mama had mentioned Gloria's handsome son and how I would just love him, so naturally I was ready to dislike him. The minute I saw him I knew who he was. But, like you say, the Southern Lady stuff dies hard. So I introduced myself and asked all the right questions and before I knew it, we were having a great conversation even though I was dying to finish reading that letter."

Amanda's perfect face blossomed into a disarming lopsided grin. "Fate or karma or something led me to Spinner's letters. But fate or karma wasn't done with me, because when I asked Ben what he did, he said he was getting ready to go back to his aunt's farm where he lived, a farm in the mountains of North Carolina. 'Near a little town called Ransom,' he said. 'You've never heard of it.'

"Oh, but I had. The letter in my pocket was postmarked Ransom, NC."

# Chapter 35

# "I Have No Heart"
### Tuesday, December 26

S o you came to Ransom to look for your brother."
Amanda nodded. "It was all so perfect—I was
tired of modeling and ready to find out what I
really wanted to do with my life; I was attracted to Ben—
after the men I'd known, he seemed so real—and I thought
if I came to Ransom, maybe I could find someone who'd
known Spinner—or maybe even find Spinner himself. In
that last letter, he said that he'd bought property here and
wanted to build a little cabin.

"Ben and I spent a lot of time together in the last few
weeks he was staying in Tampa and it just kind of worked
itself out. And here I am." Amanda's guileless eyes said
that this was the simplest thing in the world.

"Did you ask your mother why she hid the letters from
you?"

"I did. When I'd read all the letters, it was clear that
something Spinner had done had turned Mama and Papa
against him. I didn't know what it was, but they had made
the choice to never see him again and to pretend to everyone—even me—that he was dead.

"The day after the party, Papa was away and I went to
Mama's room. I knocked on the door and she opened it but
just stood there, blocking my way. I told her how I'd found

the letters. And she just looked at me and said, 'Have you? I should have destroyed them long ago, but I couldn't.' It was awful. That brittle mask she'd worn all these years just crumbled away and she looked so terribly old and defeated. And then she told me.

"Do you know what it was, Elizabeth, what terrible thing Spinner had done that made them pretend he was dead? He told them he was gay—and so they killed him."

Amanda was weeping now, but the story continued to spill out. "Mama said Papa had promised Spinner a lot of money if he would stay away from me—Papa didn't want me 'contaminated.' And Mama went along with the whole phony story.

"I yelled at her that she was heartless, to do that to her own son and to let me grieve for him when she knew he was alive. She just said, 'Yes, I think I have no heart.' And then she closed and locked her door, leaving me standing in the hall."

"Amanda"—Elizabeth felt near tears herself—"I think I can show you that your mother tried to get in touch with Spinner—she wasn't entirely heartless. And I can take you to someone who knew him."

"And so we went right away to Thomas Blake's place and pounded on the door but no answer. I guess even a troll must have to go get groceries sometime."

"Yeah, when I got done with Mac, I went down to Blake's place but couldn't rouse him. One of those junkers out front was missing, so I figured, same as you, that he'd gone somewhere."

Phillip watched as Elizabeth pulled open first one drawer and then another in the old secretary. He had returned around six to find her deep in a storage closet, from which she emerged, a spiderweb caught in her hair, eager to tell him all about her encounter with Amanda.

"Anyway, I told Amanda we'd go see Thomas Blake tomorrow when she got back. She and Ben and the girls were going in to a movie tonight, and they were all going to stay at Laurel's place. *And* I told her I could find one of those earlier ads seeking Spencer Greer. I'm pretty sure it's in a newspaper I saved."

As Elizabeth resumed her search through the bottom drawer of her secretary, Phillip looked toward the kitchen. No pots on the stove, no tantalizing smells. He took a seat on the sofa and immediately James hopped up to try to lick his face.

"Sounds like you've had a full day, Lizabeth. No, James, no tongue!"

He nudged the small dog gently to one side. "Have they been fed? I can take care of that if—"

She was on her knees now, searching through the neat piles of manila envelopes, old tax returns, bundled correspondence, and other odds and ends. Her long braid dangled over her shoulder and she flipped it impatiently out of the way.

"Thanks—but I fed them the minute I got home. If James is telling you otherwise, he's lying."

She pulled out a neatly folded newspaper with a startling five-inch headline: "Y2K: THE END?" and got to her feet. Passing by him, she ran one hand gently over his head. "And I'm going to feed us too. There's a salad already made in the refrigerator and in about fifteen minutes we're going to have some very elegant sandwiches with the leftover duck, okay?"

"Better than okay. Sounds great. You want a glass of wine now? I stopped to get some champagne for New Year's and they had good deals on some other stuff. There's a nice red from the Biltmore Winery—what was that Ben said the other night—'a naïve little domestic . . .'?"

" '. . . but I think you'll be amused by its presumption?' "

Yeah, I think that's from an old *New Yorker* cartoon—it's part of the family language now."

Elizabeth turned on the light in the dining room and pulled out her chair. "What did Mackenzie want you for? You're not officially working for him yet, are you?"

"No, the job doesn't start till January twenty-second—I forget why that particular date. Anyway, Mac wanted to go through the fire scene again."

He was uncorking the naïve little domestic and describing the desolation of the ruined house when she interrupted his somewhat leisurely narrative.

"You say the mattress was ripped open and all the drawers and things dumped out?" She looked up from the yellowing newspaper on the table before her as Phillip handed her a glass filled with the deep red wine.

"Yeah, it was one helluva mess. The arsonist must have thought that stuff'd burn better than it actually did—all those old clothes and things were likely damp and moldy. You remember how that whole place was—hadn't been heated in years."

He took his own glass to the other end of the table. "Mac says he's stymied. Nothing's adding up. And by the way, Sherlock, it looks like the Bambi thing is a dead end. The bones in the silo were a male."

He could see the struggle of conflicting emotions crossing her face. *She's glad it wasn't her friend's friend; she's disappointed her lead wasn't the right one. But she's going to stay cool.*

"Really? Well, so much for Sherlock. I'll just hope Bambi got where she was going. But they're looking at the bones already? I thought it was going to be weeks or months before they got to them." With delicate care, Elizabeth turned a brittle page of the 2000 Millennium Edition of the *Marshall County Guardian.*

"No, they haven't really started; evidently that was just an off-the-cuff comment the ME made—nothing official."

He watched as she turned another page and ran her finger down what looked to be the classified ads.

"I'm glad this got saved—all the fuss there was about the Millennium. If I ever have any grandchildren, maybe their kids would get a kick out of reading about how panicked a lot of people were and what dire prophecies were floating about what would happen when the second hand hit twelve on that crucial moment when the twentieth century became the twenty-first."

Her finger continued its search, up and down the columns of newsprint. "To tell the truth, when the New Year and the new century rolled around, Sam had only been dead for a couple of weeks and I wasn't opening the mail except to pay bills. The magazines and newspapers piled up for a few months till Rosemary came home one weekend and sorted them—and me—out. It was her idea to save this so-called historic edition."

Her finger stopped and stabbed at an ad. "Here it is—I thought I remembered right. 'Spencer Greer, or anyone with knowledge of his whereabouts, please contact Box holder, P.O. Box 4973, Tampa, FL 33629. Generous reward offered.'"

She refolded the newspaper carefully. "I'll check at the library to see how soon after '95 the ads started; I'm almost positive this wasn't the first one. I remember they came around like clockwork, three or four times a year."

"And Amanda didn't know her brother was alive till a year ago; is that what you said? So . . . ?"

"So it almost has to have been her mother. Which means she may not have been quite as heartless as Amanda thinks."

# Chapter 36

# Who Is Little Ricky?
## Wednesday, December 27

The schoolhouse clock out in the living room had just struck midnight. His eyes had drifted shut and the book in his hands was slipping toward the floor when Elizabeth's voice at his side brought him back to consciousness.

"I've been thinking, Phillip."

He closed the book, laid it on the bedside table, and watched her through drowsy eyes. She had just emerged from the bathroom, pink with the warmth of the hot bath she invariably soaked in before bed. She unpinned her braid, shook it out, and began to brush her hair—long, dark, silver-highlighted waves that smelled of something sweet and fresh—herbal shampoo, she had told him.

"Maybe the fire at the stand was a cover-up. You said the mattress and pillows were cut open and drawers pulled out. Maybe someone was looking for something. What do you law enforcement types call it—'tossing the place'? And when they found what they were after—or didn't find it—they tried to set a fire to cover their tracks."

"Lizabeth, what would anyone be looking for?" He shoved one pillow aside, laid the other flat, and settled into it with an appreciative grunt. At the foot of the bed, James moved over to Elizabeth's side and curled himself into a tight little ball. "That building's been empty for years now, and according to Mac, half the county probably had access to the key. If there was anything valuable, it's long gone."

She cracked the windows, letting a thin cold finger of air into the room, then climbed into bed beside him, pulling the covers up high and turning off the reading light.

"Before the whole thing with Amanda today, I went to visit Nola. And, just like you said, she's improving. But now she's putting on an act."

He lay in the dark, lulled by the rhythmical breathing of Ursa and Molly on their beds and trying not to drift off as Elizabeth described Nola's strange behavior and the neighbor's observation of a bobbing light in the little stone house. Elizabeth's words came in slow phrases, as if she too were teetering on the edge of sleep.

"Lee Palatt...didn't think it was the niece...they'd cleaned out the house and gone back to wherever it was... said it was like someone looking for something."

Elizabeth's words sounded farther and farther away. He forced himself back to wakefulness to ask, "When was that? Tracy and what's-his-name—they were around a few days ago. I saw them at the bridge."

A long silence met his question and he became aware that Elizabeth was asleep, her breath slow and regular. With a sigh of deep content, he spooned his body around hers and felt himself slipping into blissful unconsciousness.


Blissful unconsciousness gave way to strange dreams— once again he was climbing up the silo, his headlamp flashing dizzyingly in all directions. Once again as he achieved the topmost rung and looked down into the echoing interior, his stomach lurched in protest.

Turning away, he saw again the light dancing over the surface of the river and illuminating the winter-bare branches of the ancient trees that lined its bank. Then, overcoming his reluctance, he brought the light to bear on the shining white object below—seemingly hundreds of feet below. *I'll never make it down there without falling. What the hell was Mac up to, making me climb all this way?* Then, without warning, as he focused his attention on the objects he had been sent to find, it was as if a camera zoomed in, carrying him in a giddy swoop to the bottom of the silo. He found himself standing beside a small tombstone of gleaming marble, topped by a cherub of the same material. The cherub's face was somber and with one chubby hand it pointed to the words carved on the smooth surface of the stone: *Little Ricky~2004–2006~Our Angel.*


"You were dreaming pretty hard last night."

Returning from letting the dogs out—or, in James's case, *putting* the dog out—into the drifting snow of another cold morning, Elizabeth was surprised to see Phillip still in bed, the covers pulled up to his chin and his eyes fixed on the ceiling. The frown of concentration on his face suggested deep thought. At last he spoke, posing a question to the air.

"Who's Little Ricky?"

Elizabeth dropped a kiss on his forehead. "What is this—Trivial Pursuit? Okay, I'll play. Little Ricky was the kid on *I Love Lucy*. Gramma used to love to watch the reruns. Do I win something?"

His expression was unchanged as he continued to stare at the ceiling. "Last night, right before you fell asleep, you mentioned Nola's niece and her boyfriend or whatever he is, Rocky—"

"Actually, his first name is Stone."

"Whatever. The thing is—"

She was relieved to see his face lighten as he interrupted himself to ask incredulously, "Sweet Jesus, did I just say '*whatever*'? Hanging around all these twenty-something types is ruining my vocabulary. Listen, Lizabeth, I had this dream . . ."

As Phillip recounted the dream and its origin, Elizabeth listened eagerly, with a steadily growing conviction that this might be leading somewhere.

"What were the dates on that decal you saw on Stone and Tracy's truck?" she asked.

"2004 to 2006. Same as on the tombstone in the dream."


The snow had diminished to a few drifting flakes when Elizabeth, a bucket filled with food scraps in the crook of her arm and a jug of hot water in her hand, picked her way carefully down the steep road to the chicken house. With her other hand she wielded a metal-tipped walking stick. The Christmas snow, packed by the passage of her car, was ice-slick in places, and she was forced to proceed crabwise along the shoulders, where a fresh coating afforded a modicum of traction. Cleated boots helped some; her walking stick helped some more. But past experience had taught her that inching along like an old lady was the best way to avoid a fall.

The chickens were still huddled on their perches in the dimness of their house, and they muttered sulkily as she flung open the door to reach the feed can. She scattered the mixed grain on the hay-covered floor, then checked the nest boxes. A single forlorn egg rested in one—frozen solid, a crack running from top to bottom.

Elizabeth tossed the scraps from the chicken bucket onto the frozen ground within the wire enclosure, eliciting a fluttering rush as the birds hurried to investigate. The stainless steel bowl of water was also frozen solid, so she kicked it upside down, poured a little hot water over it to loosen the ice, then righted the bowl and filled it from her jug. The hens instantly abandoned the duck carcass—the last vestiges of the Christmas Day meal—that they had been squabbling over and ran to dip their beaks in the steaming water. Only the rooster, Gregory Peck, stayed by the remains of the duck, picking up and dropping choice bits of meat and making inviting sounds to his harem.

"You're such a gentleman, Gregory." *And handsome too.* The proud scarlet comb and great crescent spurs, shiny green-black tail feathers, a white body, densely speckled with black and bronze, curving copper-colored saddle feathers—it wasn't the stereotypical red-rooster coloring but quite distinctive.

As she stood admiring the strutting bird, an image flashed into her mind. *Red rooster . . . a stuffed toy rooster in Nola's cupboard . . . and toys and children's books. I wondered who they were for. If Stone and Tracy had a child, it would be Nola's nephew or niece. If that was Little Ricky, then now that child is dead. . . .*


"It seems like more than a coincidence—Tracy shows up and Nola tries to kill herself. What if the news of Little Ricky's death was the reason . . . the catalyst?"

Phillip swept the snow from another step before answering. Elizabeth stood on the stone path below him, snow-flakes frosting her hat and jacket. Her eyes were dancing with excitement and the tip of her nose was red with the cold.

"Before you go working out some big theory, Sherlock, don't you think you ought to find out for sure who Little Ricky is? The truck I saw could have been borrowed and it could have been someone else's Little Ricky. Those toys you saw could have been for . . . say, some charity thing."

"I know." The excitement dimmed. "I need to find out for sure. But I have a real feeling the nursing home won't give me Tracy's phone number. And I *can't* ask Nola—if my theory, as you call it, is correct, mentioning Little Ricky right now could set her back, just when she's begun to come out of her madness or whatever it was."

She hurried up the stairs to the porch, the empty chicken bucket clanking on her arm, then turned. "No, I think I need to talk to Nola's old friend Lavinia and see if she can't fill in some of the blanks. And I'm pretty sure I know where to find her today."

# The Drovers' Road XII
## The Silver Needle

*Alone in the tiny cell and lost in a waking dream, the Professor relived the halcyon days of his journey from Charleston to Warm Springs. The bright-eyed widow he had met at Sherrill's Tavern, the liberality of her charms, the turtledove dulcitude of her every utterance—all suddenly vanished in a cacophony of hoots and jeers. The Professor started awake to hear once again the rattle of the chain and the squeak of the door.*

*It could have been no more than an hour since Lydy had been removed to the courtroom, but the man who stumbled back into the cell and dropped onto his bunk might have been decades older than the callow youth who had been escorted away.*

*His face was void of expression, bloodless lips pressed tight together. For a long moment he stared straight ahead. And then he spoke, as one continuing a narrative after some trivial interruption.*

Now, one of the last places we stopped on the Drovers' Road was Lester's. Hit was Micahjah Lester owned that place, though it was his wife what run it, far as I could see. She was a great hugeous woman, had six black hairs growin out her chin. She could pick up a drunken drover and fling him out the door thinkin no more of hit than iffen he was a cat. They was a quarrelsome lot there at Lester's, and all the talk was of states' rights and abolition and se-cession.

Lester had him some slaves what worked around the place and

*he kept talkin big about how the government hadn't ought to take a man's property from him and how folks in the South had ought to han—*

*Lydy swallowed the word and began again.—Had ought to run out all them thievin abolitionists. Ol' Lester, he had him a news sheet and he begun to read aloud from it about how one of them abolitionists, a feller named John Brown, had gathered together a band of white and Negro alike and had broke into an armory. Him and his men killed several white men and captured a number more. But then the army was called out and all the abolitionists that wasn't killed was captured. And then they was tried and they was . . . they was done away with.*

*Lydy, my friend. Please, allow me . . . The Professor extended one hand and tried to look into Lydy's eyes. But their blue depths were glazed over and the young man carried on with his account, not heeding his cell mate's attempt at communication.*

*Now when Lester said as how North Carolina ought to fight for states' rights, even if it meant breakin off from the Union, a lot of us allowed as how hit sounded like we'd be fightin to hold on to slaves didn't none of us have and that hit didn't make no sense fer a poor man to fight a rich man's war. Folks was beginnin to take sides and git all riled up but right then Miz Lester come in and tole her husband to shut up speechifyin and come to bed.*

*That raised a laugh and several fellers made low jokes about Lester and his wife, but we all lay down to rest without no more quarrelin. Hit was a peaceable enough night, though those fer and those agin se-cession never did agree. And the next mornin, atter we'd et and got the hogs back on the road, them hateful little boys of Lester's hid in the bushes alongside the road and rocked us as we passed by. One of them rocks caught me on the head and raised a great pump knot. I would have gone atter that young un and blistered his hide fer him but we had to keep them hogs a-movin.*

*The Professor, unable to control his curiosity, leaned across the narrow span of floor and grasped the young man's arm. Lydy, for the love of God, what happened in the courtroom? he implored.*

*For a moment Lydy's dulled blue eyes lightened as he shook off the importunate hand. Then, relapsing into the strange torpor that seemed to have him in its thrall, he answered the Professor's question.*

*She was there, settin up at the front, still stitchin on that black and purple quilt and I could feel each of them stitches like hit was a silver needle in my heart. The folks fell quiet and the foreman gave the verdict but Belle, she never looked up oncet, just put in some more stitches.*

*So I set there, waitin for the judge to speak my sentence and watchin Belle, all the time feeling that thread drawin tighter. The judge called out my name loud and strong and told me to stand. I did, never takin my eyes from Belle, waitin to see would she say ought when the judge passed sentence. I had thought she might.*

*Then I seen Loyal Revis, the new-elected sheriff, walk over to her and bend down and whisper something in her ear and just then the words roll out from that ol' judge's mouth.*

*And then Belle looks up at the sheriff and smiles, the same way she had one time smiled at me.*

# Chapter 37

## *The Funeral Feast*
### Wednesday, December 27

I found her in the room where they keep the pay phone.... Well, how was I s'posed to know? Believe me, I like to drop when I seen her. Here I'd just stepped out for a smoke and her sound asleep when I left. I swear I wadn't out of that room more'n five minutes—ten at the outside. *You* know she ain't been off that bed 'cept when I get her in a wheelchair and roll her around or when I can get her onto the commode.... No, she had just set in the wheelchair and pulled herself along usin' her feet.... No, I don't *believe* she had made any calls."

Parked in the sun on the barren little patio, Nola sat slumped in the wheelchair. She let her mouth hang slack as she listened to the one-sided conversation, but inwardly she thrilled to the sensation of being keenly aware again, of taking in every detail of her surroundings, of being able to find the *words*, the blessed *words*.

On her left a few ugly concrete planters lined haphazardly along the edge of the patio were crowded with plastic flowers: muddy-toned jonquils and peonies incongruously sharing space with gaudy poinsettias. Faded plastic chairs were pulled up to a round glass-and-iron table that sprouted a stained and drooping green-striped umbrella. *A dreary spot, like the rest of this horrible place.*

But the fresh air, bracingly cool even in this tiny sun-trap, was a revelation: a blessing and a delight after the eternal choking fug of the overheated nursing facility. Nola took deep greedy gulps of it, savoring its keen edge. She looked up, past the sterile concrete and plastic, to feast her eyes on the clear sky that had miraculously appeared as the early morning snowfall ended. The unblemished blue square above her head was of piercing azure intensity. As she stared into its depths, tears of joy sprang into her eyes.

> *... and the living air,*
> *And the blue sky, and in the mind of man:*
> *A motion and a spirit that impels*
> *All thinking things ...*

*Thinking things. I am a thinking thing again. And those lines are Wordsworth's and they are from "Lines Composed a Few Miles above Tintern Abbey."* It was all she could do to keep from letting out a wild hoot of laughter, from bringing the fat Michelle to heel with a well-aimed word.

*I wanted to die but I was wrong. Wrong to seek death when I should have sought retribution. After all these years ... But now ... which one wants me drugged and out of the way? To whom is Michelle speaking? If I knew that ... I must wait.*

"Yes, I been giving her the medicine like you told me. Yes, the full dose, mornin' and evening." Michelle swung around, her piggy eyes coming to bear on Nola. "She's quiet as can be now—looks like she'll be ready to go back to bed and stay put.... Oh, I *will* ... now that I know what this naughty girl might get up to. You just leave it to me."


The final lugubrious strains of the organ died away as the funeral director stepped to the front of the chapel. He raised one manicured hand for attention.

"The family of Payne Morton wishes me to thank all of you for your many kindnesses during this trying time. Mrs.

Lavinia Holcombe, godmother of the deceased, has asked me to say that there will be a reception for all our departed brother's friends and family at her house on Holcombe Hill immediately following this service."

Elizabeth gathered up her winter coat and purse and filed out of the pew to join the others heading toward the parking lot. Just ahead of her, two broad-beamed women kept up a whispered running commentary.

"It broke his mama's heart that Payne's own church wouldn't have the service there, but the elders come down strong against it, it being suicide."

"And then not even to have a casket nor a real funeral... But there wadn't nothing left of his head but the face—like a watermelon had rolled off the truck and busted flat open was what I heard."

"Now, Racine, you coulda gone all day without tellin' that."

"You're going *where?*" Phillip had given her an incredulous look when she appeared in the living room in her going-somewhere-serious clothes. Black wool pants, black low-heeled boots, a lavender turtleneck, and a black blazer had been hastily unearthed, and she had twisted her hair into a knot at the nape of her neck.

"To the Good Shepherd Funeral Home. There's a memorial service for Payne Morton at eleven."

"I didn't think you really knew—"

"We spoke on the phone. And then I did meet him once at the Layton Facility." Elizabeth had held out the latest issue of the *Marshall County Guardian,* folded open to the obituaries page. "The family will receive visitors with a reception at Holcombe Hill afterwards. Evidently Big Lavinia was his godmother."

"And...?"

"And I hope that in the general flow of reminiscence that

goes on after funerals around here, I might pick up some information about Nola. She went to his church and I would imagine a lot of her fellow churchgoers will be there. And of course, there's Big Lavinia—Nola's oldest friend. It would be a chance for me to have a word with her—to see if she knows about Little Ricky."

Cars and pickup trucks were parked all along the edge of the sweeping drive that curved past the white-pillared house on Holcombe Hill, and a steady stream of people climbed the stone steps and passed through the red-painted double front doors. Elizabeth pulled in behind a gleaming new Mercedes and joined the others making their way up the drive to the house.

"Welcome . . . thank you for coming . . . Susie darlin', the family's back there in the den and I know they'd want to see you . . . welcome . . . so good of you to come . . . oh, Mary Ellen, I just have to hug your neck . . . welcome . . ."

In the broad entry hall stood Big Lavinia, dispensing hospitality to all comers. As she took Elizabeth's proffered hand, her eyes narrowed and then, almost instantly, she made the connection. "Miz . . . Goodweather, wasn't it? My poor Nola's friend. But I hadn't realized you were acquainted with the Mortons?"

Mercifully the press of people behind her prevented further conversation. Mumbling something about having met the pastor recently and wanting to pay her respects, Elizabeth was released to move on to a second line before the table in the center of the hall, where an immense arrangement of white lilies loomed over an open visitation book.

She took her place in *this* line, wondering if coming to the funeral and reception had been a good idea. *Surely Miz Holcombe will leave the door eventually and I'll get a chance to ask about Little Ricky.* As it came her turn to sign her name, she glanced quickly down the signatures, recognizing name after name of county politicos, educators, professionals, businessmen—the spectrum of the well-to-do and well connected. *I wonder, are they here because of the Mortons or because any event at Holcombe Hill is the place to be? Pastor Morton seemed much more . . . more of the people.*

As she scrawled a semilegible signature, a name a few lines above hers caught her attention. HOLLIS NOONAN, the bold black pen strokes proclaimed. *That's the guy who spoke at the meeting, the developer who wants the Gudger House. And the doctor, the brother of the deceased—he's a partner in the company—RIP—no, RPI. As are the Holcombe brothers, or at least the younger one, according to Ben.*

She moved on, caught up in the flow of mourners who seemed drawn to a large doorway on the left. A matronly woman at her elbow beamed. "You're Elizabeth Goodweather, aren't you? I met you at that quilt exhibit you put together for the library last year. It's real nice to see you again!"

The smile faded as the woman recalled the reason for this event. She lowered her voice slightly and continued. "Quite a turnout, don't you think, for poor Payne? Did you know him well?"

When Elizabeth explained that she was only an acquaintance, the woman seemed relieved to be able to speak more freely. "Well, of course, some are saying he always did have a dark side to him. There was that trouble back when he was still in school, but though there was a lot of talk, nothing ever came of it. And he really seemed to find himself when he went to seminary. You know, his family's quite well off but he always lived on his pastor's salary. He and his wife and those two darling babies just barely scrape along. And what she'll do, I can't imagine. Though I expect the family'll convince her to accept some help now."

The tide of funeralgoers had swept them into a large formal dining room. There a long linen-draped table was covered with an assortment of buffet offerings. Elizabeth's new friend smiled delightedly and picked up a plate. "I never *can* resist funeral food! There's Nell Bledsoe's Co'-Cola Ham . . . I reckon someone got Sadie to make all those little biscuits. And I know Big Lavinia will have had her Mexican girl make a flan . . . ooh . . . and that looks like Kaye's chocolate Kahlúa cake down there—only the best thing you ever put in your mouth! You better get you a plate—I expect they want us to keep moving on through—we'll find us a spot to perch back in the family room."

*Oh, boy, do I feel like a . . . what was it that friend of Sam's used to call himself . . . a schnorrer? I hardly knew the deceased and I'm getting a free lunch. But Miss Lady here is just what I was hoping for—one of the talkative kind.*

Following Miss Lady down the table, Elizabeth helped herself to some of the special dishes so loudly praised by her companion. She took a ham biscuit and several ladylike little sandwiches, a scoop of what was described as "Aileen's Macaroni with Four Cheeses—you've already put on two pounds just by looking at it."

*Maybe something green,* she decided, starting to serve herself from a huge bowl of baby spinach leaves decorated with jewel-like dried cranberries and toasted pecan halves.

"I'm surprised anyone'd bring that—it was just a few months ago people were dying from *E. coli*–infected spinach. One of our own congregation lost a precious little nephew. They pulled that stuff right out of the stores for quite a while." Miss Lady took a serving of three-bean salad. "I heard even washing won't get the germs off. Wasn't it the saddest thing—all the good little children dying from eating their spinach."

Elizabeth hesitated, then bypassed the vinaigrette-glossed leaves and followed Miss Lady into an adjoining room. *A nephew,* she thought.

"Are you talking about—" But she was speaking to the woman's back and her words went unheard.

The big room was swarming with people, eating and talking. A buzz of conversation was steadily growing louder as newcomers added their voices. Comfortable overstuffed sofas and chairs brimmed with people; the long stone hearth of the fireplace provided seating for more. Others stood, a plate in one hand, a glass in the other, hopelessly looking for a surface to put something down on.

"The window seat. Those fellas are getting up now. Let's us scoot over there and grab it."

Again Elizabeth followed her chance acquaintance, admiring the decisive action with which the older woman cut out two teenage girls, cell phones to their ears, who were making for the same spot.

They had just settled when the sound of shouting was heard from the front hall. Instantly, heads swiveled to the doorway and all conversation stopped except for one very deaf old man who went on with his reminiscence unhindered.

The roomful of people listened in stunned silence to the ensuing antiphony.

"Respect for the dead?" In the hallway a woman's high-pitched voice rose to a manic shriek. "You make me *laugh!* Let me tell you about that so-called—"

"...of course, Payne's folks still have Pritchard—now *that* boy's done 'em proud." The aged man, sitting in a wingback chair and addressing the young woman who occupied the ottoman before him, thumped his cane for emphasis, not seeming to notice his audience's lack of response.

"God *damn you all!*" The unseen woman's shrill voice broke into gasping sobs. Murmuring and a movement of feet could be heard, and those nearest the door craned their heads to get a better view. The rest stayed fixed in their places, waiting for the woman's crying to stop.

"I saw how he'd failed in the past little bit," the old man

asserted. "Couldn't hardly get through his sermon and mumbled worse than usual."

"No, you bitch, I *won't* leave quietly! I have things that need to be said in a public place. And all the people who need to hear them are here, all except for that dead hypocrite— he made a solemn promise and then took the easy way out. Just because you're a Holcombe, you think—"

There was the sound of a scuffle, a wail of anger and frustration, the opening and closing of a door, and Lavinia Holcombe's voice was raised in clear, calm tones. "Please listen, all of you. I want to ask that we just go on as we were, in respect for the departed and for his family. This unfortunate young woman has obviously been drinking. My men are escorting her off the property. Please, let's all forget this unfortunate incident; there's lovely food in the dining room and the Morton family is receiving close friends in the den."

The hubbub of voices resumed, louder than ever as the deaf old man in the armchair drew his monologue to a close. "Poor fella, I wish he could of seen how many turned out to pay their respects and that he could of heard all the fine tributes. Once we're gone, memories is all that's left."

# Chapter 38

## *Overheard at a Reception*
### Wednesday, December 27

W ell, what in the name of goodness was *that* all
about? And who in the world *was* that?"

"No one I know—woman must not of
been in her right mind. She looked like a crazy thing—that
ugly dyed hair every which away. Big Lavinia handled it
good though, don't you think?"

"Holston said those big fellers just took hold of that
woman's arms and scooted her out the door and down the
driveway. He said he went out on the porch to see what was
happenin' and there was a truck at the foot of the drive,
looked like it was waitin' for her. They took her right to it
and put her in the passenger side. One of 'em went round
and said something to everwho was drivin' and then Holston
said that truck took off like a bat out of you-know-where."

All the interrupted conversations had been resumed—
with a new subject and, if possible, at a higher volume.
Elizabeth's seatmate had deserted her, presumably in search
of fresh information, to join a group of women who had just
come in from the entrance hall.

Finishing the last bite of the macaroni and cheese—a far,
far better macaroni and cheese than she had ever tasted—
Elizabeth took her empty plate and went in search of someplace to dispose of it. As she moved carefully around the

knots of people, scraps of conversation caught her attention.

"I don't believe they could have heard her. The whole family's back in the den and the door's shut. See, over there where Hollis Noonan's standing? Big Lavinia told him to make sure they don't get overwhelmed by too many people coming to say a word. I heard Payne's mama was all to pieces and his poor little wife is just barely managing to hold up for the children's sake."

"Well, it's a blessing they *were* back there. To think of someone carrying on like that—"

"If Hollis isn't the best-lookin' thing I ever saw . . . I just *love* that gorgeous blond hair. You know, someone told me he's set up a trust fund for Payne's little girls. Of course, he won't miss it, the money he's got."

"It's wonderful the way those boys have all kept up their friendship. I can remember them spending vacations here and how all the girls were after Hollis and that other boy— what was his name? He's the only one of the group that hasn't stayed in touch. Big Lavinia said he's moved out west somewhere."

"You remember that skit they did at the festival the first year—pretending to be a rap group? I just about died laughing. What did they call themselves—'5 Bad Boyz'— 'boyz' with a *z*? Something like that. And those awful baggy pants and all that tacky jewelry! I think Big Vance and Big Platt like to had a fit when they saw Little Vance prancing around like that. And I know Jana Lee Morton skipped Book Club the next day, she was so embarrassed. She said it was those outside boys had the idea."

"Well, it's a sad time for them now, losing one of their number in this terrible way. But you see how they just draw together when times are bad—that's the test of friendship, I always say."

Elizabeth moved unnoticed among them, lingering on the outskirts of first one group, than another. Most of these people, the so-called important people of the county, were strangers to her. Here and there was a familiar-looking face—someone she'd seen at the library or the bank or the post office—but not anyone she could put a name to.

One group was crowded around a long table that stood against the wall of windows. Everyone seemed to be studying the items laid out on display, so Elizabeth drifted over to see what they were looking at.

All manner of memorabilia lay tastefully arranged on the dark blue tablecloth, accompanied by identifying labels. At center was a large framed photo of the deceased, Payne Morton, one hand raised in exhortation as he stood in the pulpit. Smaller pictures showed him in the varied aspects of his life: with his parents on the day of his ordination; with his wife and two small girls on a picnic; umpiring a girls' softball team; posed with his brother, holding up the head of a trophy buck.

The late pastor's worn Bible lay open at Psalm 139, and one of the older men in the group bent to peer at several heavily underlined verses. He began to read, running his big finger along the lines,

" 'O Lord, thou hast searched me and known me' . . . Amen to that . . . then it skips some . . . 'Whither shall I go from thy Spirit? Or whither shall I flee from thy presence?' "

He shook his head sadly. "Now that's the truth—you can't hide from the Almighty. Brother Payne was a good somebody and folks all thought the world of him but I believe he must have had some turrible secret eatin' at him to cause him to take his own life."

Elizabeth moved to the end of the table, where a thick scrapbook lay open. A newspaper clipping titled "5 Bad Boyz Wow Crowd" was pasted beneath a glossy photo of young men in rap gear. She leaned down to study the faces. Even though they were much younger, with sneering expressions meant to evoke a streetwise toughness, she recognized the Morton brothers and the Vance Holcombe as well. Hollis Noonan too was little changed: the same long blond hair sweeping across his face, half-covering his assumed scowl.

She leaned closer. The fifth member of the group had his head turned half away, but something about him, the fine features, the pale hair—

"Happier times, Miz Goodweather, happier times."

Lavinia Holcombe appeared at her elbow, her black bulk effortlessly cleaving the throng. "Have you been to see poor Nola recently? I haven't been able to with all"—she swept one be-ringed hand in an inclusive gesture—"all this."

"It's a lovely reception, Miz Holcombe. But such a sad occasion for you—I understand you were Pastor Morton's godmother?"

"Yes, indeed I was." Big Lavinia extracted a wisp of lace and fine linen from a hidden pocket and dabbed at her eyes. "More than that, the Morton boys were like my own. From grammar school on, Little Vance was well nigh inseparable from Payne and Pritchard. Back and forth between the two houses all the time. I would have sworn I knew the Morton boys as well as I know my own. Yes, it's quite a loss."

She tucked the handkerchief away and looked toward the door where Hollis Noonan stood guard. "Have you seen Nola recently? I know you've been such a good friend to her."

"I saw her just yesterday, Miz Holcombe." It was all that Elizabeth could do to keep the excitement out of her voice. "And that reminds me—"

"How did you find her? Did you see any change? Any improvement?"

Elizabeth hesitated, trying to avoid a direct lie. *A silly quibble, as I'm sure Ben would point out. A lie is a lie is a lie.*

Big Lavinia was waiting for an answer.

"No," Elizabeth replied, assuming a thoughtful look,

"no improvement that I could *say.* Maybe she seemed a little calmer but—"

"Did she try to talk to you—recite poetry like she was doing?"

On firmer ground here, Elizabeth shook her head. "No, no poetry at all. But Miz Holcombe, I had a question. Does the name 'Little Ricky' mean anything to you?"

She was surprised to see tears welling again in Big Lavinia's eyes. "Oh my, yes. Yes, indeed. Little Ricky was Nola's nephew. Tracy's child. He died only a few months ago and it absolutely devastated Nola. Oh, she held it in for a time but then when Tracy came for a visit and the baby wasn't with her, I think it all finally sunk in and just sent Nola off the deep end. I'm afraid his death has affected Tracy's mind too. It's the only reason I can find for her behavior today."

# The Drovers' Road XIII
## The True Account

*BANG! BANG! BANG!* Once again, the Professor was
torn from his dreams. The ragtag mob that had derived its simple
pleasure from shouting out lewd catchphrases and dire predictions
to the newly sentenced man had at last grown weary of the sport
and dispersed. Now the sounds were of hammering and the terse
grumbled instructions of the carpenter to his apprentice.

Groaning to find himself in the dank cell rather than in the
soft embraces of the dream widow, the Professor blinked and sat
up, bringing the thin blanket up around his shoulders as protec-
tion from the chill air of the bleak January morning.

Across from him, the young man slumped on the edge of his
bunk, just as he had been when the light faded to darkness the
evening before.

*My young friend, the noise has awakened you—*

*I ain't slept,* was the simple reply. *I been thinkin.*

The wounded stupefaction of the previous day was gone, replaced by a nervous energy. Lydy's right leg jigged uncontrollably
and his usual slow speech had become a frantic outpouring. From
hand to hand he tossed the small stone that had accompanied
Nettie Mae's bundle of provisions.

*I done said what had to be said at the trial and I'm content
with how it come out but now I want you to set down my story
the way it really happened. That way, iffen I burn in Hell, yet
there're be a true account of what happened at Gudger's Stand.*

*The Professor shook his head, trying to clear away the last cobwebs of sleep. It would be an honor, my young friend, to be accorded your confidence.*

*He patted at his breast pocket and drew out the stub of a pencil and a little leather-bound copy of* The Odyssey. *I had already made some few notes taken from your tales of life on the Drovers' Road. A fortuitous plethora of blank pages at the close of this immortal epic have made it possible for me to keep a rough journal of my sufferings while incarcerated. But willingly shall I devote what space remains to your revelations. It seems quite apposite: your wanderings, Belle, the Circe who charms man and beast. Indeed, there are a number of these chance parallels that strike the—*

*I want you to write down these words.* Lydy raised his voice to cut off the spate of literary conjecture. *Then, seeing he had gained his cell mate's attention, he continued on in a subdued tone, one the men hammering and sawing outside could not overhear.*

*I ain't afraid to die for the death of Lucius Gudger. Hit could be that I'm to blame. But I did not murder his daughter Luellen. And this I swear to, as a man facin eternity.*

*. . . and . . . this . . . I swear . . . The Professor paused to rub the pencil point against the rough brick wall in an attempt to sharpen it . . . as a man . . .*

*The way of hit was this: When the drive reached South Carolina, we was paid off and I set out to walk back to Gudger's Stand. Without the hogs, a feller can make a good sight better time and take to the ridges instead of follerin the river. I hadn't yet made out just what would happen when I got back—all I knowed is I was being pulled, ever minute, by that thread with Belle at the other end.*

*Quite a dilemma. The girl you do not wish to wed, with child—her stepmother, the woman you wish to bed, with spouse. Shall we omit the account of your return travels—these blank pages are not inexhaustible—and come to the crux of the matter? What of Luellen, whose bloodied nightclothes at the riverside told a grisly tale? What of her murdered father, whose gory remains cried out for revenge?*

Lydy wiped his face. *Professor, when I come back to the stand, my only thought was to stay near Belle. The preacher weren't due till the new year . . . but you know that . . . so I let hit be thought that I would marry Luellen. My only thought was to have more time with Belle. And hit seemed that was her thought too for she come to me every night, slippin into the little lean-to room where I lay apart and drawin the bolt behind her. Ol' Luce was drinkin right much those days and, so she said, sleepin sound.*

*What of Luellen?* The busy pencil paused and the Professor lifted inquiring eyes. *Was she cognizant of this liaison? Did she know about you and her stepmother?*

Lydy shrugged. *Reckon she must of. But she never spoke of it, just spent her time sewing clothes for me.*

He looked down. *These ones here what I got on. Hit may be she thought oncet the preacher had done his business, Belle would let loose of me. I kindly thought hit myself. But hit all changed on that last night, a few weeks atter I'd got back.*

The Professor licked the point of his pencil and turned over a page. *Ah, yes, the fateful night. Pray, proceed.*

*They was several travelers at the stand for the night and Belle and Luellen was kept busy cookin and servin. The new sheriff was there likewise and from the way he talked to Ol' Luce, I could see he'd been there a time or two before. He said he planned to ride the road to the Tennessee line, makin himself known at all the stands and wherever there was a few houses.*

*That was an unlucky chancet, for had the sheriff not been there that night, I'd not be here now. Howsomever, that night at table was the last I seen of Luellen and the last time I saw Ol' Luce alive. Him and the sheriff was still drinkin and playin cards when the rest of the company took to their pallets. I never seen Luellen atter supper that night. She was always goin early to her bed, sayin she felt puny. And when they shown me her bed shift, all bloody and torn, I could only shake my head and swear I didn't know nothing of it. They made out I had kilt her first and flung her in the river afore goin atter Ol' Luce.*

*I had been dead asleep when come a scratchin at my door. I waited, thinkin it was Belle, but when the door stayed shut, I got up and looked out. In the dark of the big room, there weren't nothing but the empty tables and benches and the glow of the dyin fire. It seemed like hit was near mornin but hit was yet black dark outside.*

*A little sound come to my ears like the creak of the big front door chinkin and closin. I got my boots from where I had left them to dry by the fire and went outside to see who it was.*

*Ol' Luce was layin there on the stones. He'd already been bad drunk when I went to bed and at first I thought he'd likely pitched down the stairs. I made to pick him up thinkin to carry him inside but his head rolled back and it was then I seen the great wound in his neck. I put my hand to it and the blood was sticky and cool and I stood, tryin to think what can have happened . . .*

*And then comes Belle, weepin and wringin her hands. O Lydy, what have you done, cries she. And I hear feet a-clatterin down the stairs and men callin out and I light out for the steep woods, Ol' Luce's blood still on my hands.*

# Chapter 39

## *Ragged Edges*
### Wednesday, December 27

Amanda called. She and Ben'll be back around three. Evidently Rosemary and Laurel have hot dates in town. They're staying at Laurel's another night." Phillip came into the room, trailing the cord of a power drill behind him. "And I rehung those doors that were scraping the floor. So, how was it? You find out anything?"

Elizabeth dropped the mail on the table. "Little Ricky *was* Nola's nephew. And he was one of the children who died from that *E. coli* outbreak back in the fall. Big Lavinia thinks that's what triggered Nola's suicide attempt. But the most interesting thing was Tracy—she showed up at the reception after the funeral, carrying on like a banshee, shouting that Payne Morton took the easy way out."

"Because . . . ?"

"I don't know—something about a promise he'd made. She was hustled out of there pretty quickly, as you might imagine." She flopped onto the sofa, startling James, who had been napping at one end. With a reproachful look, he slipped to the floor and joined Ursa and Molly on the rug.

"Phillip—that note the pastor left, do you remember what exactly it said?"

"Nope." He coiled the cord neatly around the drill and returned it to the bucket of tools by the front door. "But I have a copy, for what it's worth."

He disappeared into the guest room, where most of his clothes and sundry items had been stowed, awaiting a final decision on where he would be living in the coming year. In a few minutes he was back. "Here you go, Sherlock. The pastor's last words. Good luck to you making sense of them."

Picking up the bucket of tools, he whistled to the dogs. "I'm going down to the lower place; Ben asked me to put out some more hay for the cows. C'mon, pups, let's go for a walk."

There was an instant joyful response from Molly and Ursa, who rose and shook and made for the door. James didn't move.

The copy was faint but legible. A wavering gray shadow like a backward *L* showed the raggedly torn edges of the original. The straggling phrases that the pastor had written in his last moments were disjointed and poignant—almost like a poem, Elizabeth thought.

> *After eleven years of agony and guilt*
> *I am ready to pay the price*
> *she was willing. God help me,*
> *it was an accident. God help me,*
> *I can no longer live*

She stared at the copy, an uneasy feeling growing in the pit of her stomach. "Punctuation," she muttered.

" 'I can no longer live...' " There was an echo in her memory. *I can't go on...* A mystery... Agatha Christie?... A suicide note on a scrap of paper...torn edges. She scowled at the page, trying to decipher the source of her uneasiness. Her lips moved, trying different combinations of words and phrases. Still scowling, she reached for the phone.

ᴔ

"May I speak with Sheriff Blaine, please? This is Elizabeth Goodweather calling."

The husky croak at the other end told her the sheriff was on another line and it would be a few minutes and then relegated her to the limbo of Hold. Elizabeth drummed impatient fingers on the dining table.

"Sheriff Blaine here."

"Mackenzie, this is Elizabeth Goodweather. I—"

He broke in. "Is there a problem?"

"No, not as such. But I wanted to ask you something. You know the note Payne Morton left? Well, Phillip showed me a copy he had and something about it doesn't seem right—"

"Ah, Elizabeth, could we—"

"No, really, Mackenzie, I think this might be important. I would have run it by Phillip but he won't be back for almost an hour, and I really want to hear what you think about this. The punctuation in the note's all wrong."

"Elizabeth, that note was written by a man about to kill himself." There was a distinct hint of irritation in the sheriff's tone. "He's not likely worrying about—god, what was it that old bat Miss Darien used to get me for?—comma splices, that's it."

"Mackenzie, please! Get the note and look at it."

There was a heavy sigh. "Okay, Elizabeth. But it's only because I hope you invite me to dinner again soon."

He was back at the phone in minutes. "Okay, Miz Goodweather, I'm looking at the note. What's your point?"

"Well, in the first place, look how neat the writing is. The handwriting isn't any last-minute scribble—every letter is perfectly formed—"

"Before you ask, yes, we've checked it out; it's definitely Morton's writing."

"But the thing about the *punctuation* is that it's in kind of random places. It wouldn't be so strange if he'd left it out altogether—or used dashes instead of commas. Particularly since these aren't sentences at all—"

"I don't think I follow you." The weary resignation in Blaine's voice warned her that it was only his friendship with Phillip that kept him on the line.

"Okay, look at the note, where the two edges are ragged, like they'd been torn."

"They *were* torn. Lots of people use scrap paper."

She ignored him. "Now what if the original, *untorn* note had read something like:

*I am ready to pay the price of my silence. He told me
she was willing. God help me, I believed him. He told me
it was an accident. God help me, I believed him.
I can no longer live with this lie. I must confess."*

There was a silence.

"Say that again," said Mackenzie Blaine.

She said it again.

"Or something along those lines," she added. "You see how it could work. And the way the paper was torn, there could have been lots more at the end. And he would have signed his name if—"

"—if this was a letter, a confession. Instead of a suicide note." The sheriff spoke slowly, as if struggling to process thoroughly this new point of view. "And what you're suggesting is maybe someone didn't want Morton to confess, so they killed him—"

"—and tore out just enough of the letter to make it *sound* like a suicide note—"

"—and that would be where the thing about the silo came from."

There was a long, pregnant pause and then the sheriff said, "I won't say you've convinced me, Elizabeth; the whole thing's seriously sketchy. But I will say I'll follow up on it. Happy now?"

ು

*There was a definite click on the line, just before Mackenzie hung up. Probably old whatsername in the front office, listening in. Now there's a woman who undoubtedly knows where all the bodies are buried. What a great job for a blackmailer, if she were so inclined.*

Elizabeth picked up the stack of Nola's papers she had been working her way through—notes for the novel, copies of old newspaper or magazine articles, and the more prosaic ledger books from the stand, dating back to the end of the 1800s. Prosaic, but fascinating for the picture of an era.

The words "A Modern Day Circe" caught her attention and she paused at a copy of an old letter to the editor of *Harper's New Monthly Magazine*—from Thos. W. Blake, Junior.

*8th January, 1899*

> *My dear sir,*
>
> *Inasmuch as my dispatches from the Carolina Mountains have found favor with your readers, from the earliest in 1858—my sketch of a Melungeon stand-keeping couple—and proceeding through the troubled years of the lamentable War that pitted brother against brother to the Modern Day to the coming of the Railroad to these hidden wilds, I make bold to propose yet another sketch, set in the same by-gone day and rustic demesne as my first.*

### Notes on a Modern Day Circe
by Thos. W. Blake, Junior

As the Turn of the Century approaches and I cast my gaze back two score years to my earliest days in these majestic mountains that will one day receive my bones, I am reminded of a time long distant when I was privy to the ramblings of a convicted murderer and I am struck, once again, by the singular qualities of the woman who, I make no doubt, led him to his ruin.

How I came to be in the company of young Lydy Goforth is a matter over which I shall draw the kindly veil of Time. His name has become a part of the lore of these mountains, thanks in no small part to the ballad I penned, now popularly considered to be of his own production. As if an illiterate agrestic could have— But I digress. My position in the community, my wife, my children—any of these are sufficient cause for me to avoid the smallest mention of my connexion with Lydy Goforth.

I shall, therefore, limit my remarks to Belle Caulwell—a woman whose fatal beauty had the power to transform a simple rustic lad into a beast, capable of the last extreme of violence. Pale of face and black of hair and eye, her exotic countenance was oft remarked upon in this land of blue-eyed folk. I have not been able to trace her antecedents—it is said she appeared at Gudger's Stand as a child of thirteen, unaccompanied and unable (or unwilling) to say from whence she came. I could believe she had ridden on a dragon's back straight from Aeaea, the island home of the original Circe, were it not for the fact that Belle spoke in the mountain brogue rather than Archaic Greek.

I have questioned more than one venerable in our community concerning Belle and all are agreed that we shall look upon her like no more. One aged farmer had tears in his eyes as he recounted his memories of Belle at her loom—how the drovers lingered ensorcelled as the sinuous thread of her song rose above the thump and clack of her loom.

The women-folk have a different tale. They call her pale skin "sallow" and speak of the "heathen" fashion in which she let her black hair fall loose and unconfined. They will allow her to have had a fine figure—a tiny waist, a deep bosom—but that is all they will allow. One ancient crone, lest constrained in her converse than others, whispered that Belle was known as one who could rid a girl of an unwanted child, through use of herbs and potions. "And she had an instrument, a silver rod with a hook on one end—" but at last modesty prevailed and the beldame would go no further.

The sound of the door opening called her back to the present, and Elizabeth looked up to see Amanda smiling apologetically. "Is it too late to go see that guy—the one who knew my brother?"

# Chapter 40

## *Dead End*
### Wednesday, December 27

Thomas W. Blake was leaning on the parapet of the bridge, staring down into the turbulent river that swirled and eddied around the ice-covered rocks. He seemed oblivious to the approach of Elizabeth's car, continuing his morose study of the churning water without looking up.

Elizabeth pulled to one side and, leaving the vehicle running and Amanda inside, she got out and went to stand beside the strange figure. "Good afternoon, Mr. Blake. I was just reading a copy of one of your grandfather's letters—about a modern-day Circe. I found it in some of Miss Barrett's papers."

"Good afternoon, Miz Goodweather. Yes, Miss Barrett and I have, at times, combined forces in research. And, to be strickly accurate, tha's *great*-gran'father."

The courtly bow was somewhat clumsy and the words were slightly slurred, but Blake seemed happy enough to see her, so she persevered.

"I wondered if my friend and I could ask you some questions."

A lordly wave of his gloved hand, the gracious gesture only slightly impaired by the holes in the gloves' fingertips.

"Ask what you will; I am yours to command. At leisure, one might say."

"Do you think . . . that is, would you mind if we talked in your house? It's a little cold out here for me. And I'd love to see how the cat and her babies are getting along."


Mother and children seemed to be thriving. Still in the same box, but with a clean towel for bedding; still in the big cupboard, the little family was a picture of domestic contentment. Amanda crouched over them, crooning with delight and stroking the kittens' tiny heads with a careful finger.

"They're precious—do you think Ben would like a kitten? Or would it be a problem with your dogs?"

"Probably not." Elizabeth ventured a cautious caress of the mother cat's thin side and was rewarded with a buzz of pleasure. "The dogs are pretty laid-back."

Thomas Blake stood watching, swaying gently. He had put a kettle to boil, unearthed three clean mugs, and bestowed a tea bag in each, as well as a generous tot of vodka in his own. His eyes did not leave Amanda.

"I'm sorry, Mr. Blake, I haven't introduced you all. This is my friend, Amanda Lucas. Amanda, Thomas Blake."

Elizabeth was struck suddenly by the absurdity of the formal introduction: the grizzled, slightly drunken man in his ancient, begrimed clothing and thick-lensed glasses bowing over the hand of the tall, exquisitely clean, exquisitely beautiful woman in the midst of this tumbledown, cat-crowded abode. *It could be a scene from* Beauty and the Beast *or maybe* Phantom of the Opera.

But the two played their parts solemnly, and when the kettle boiled and the mugs were filled, Blake ushered them to the living area of his warrenlike dwelling.

"You say your name is Lucas? And your home is . . . ?"

"I live on Elizabeth's farm. But I'm originally from Florida."

Amanda's impatience overcame her manners and she set her mug down on the table at her elbow, sloshing hot tea on a sleeping tabby's tail. With a yowl and a sideways twist of its lithe gray body, the cat jumped to the floor, where it began at once to groom itself. "Mr. Blake, Elizabeth thought that you could tell me something about my brother. His name is Sp—"

"Spinner Greer. Yes, the resemblance is extremely strong. I was confused by the different surnames." The thick glasses glittered at her appraisingly. "Yes, my dear, you're very like."

"Mr. Blake, I haven't seen Spinner since 1993. My parents told me he was dead. But recently I found letters from him, written in '94 and '95. And the last ones were from Ransom." Amanda's eyes were imploring. "Please, do you know where he is? I know he bought property here . . . up on Bear Tree Creek. He said he was going to build a cabin."

The man nodded. "Spinner had great plans. Your brother was enraptured with this county and its history. He used to stop in to visit and read through some of the documents and historical material I've held on to—and I grew quite fond of him. The poor boy seemed eager for a confidant and I was happy to give such advice and moral support as were within my poor powers.

"But no." Blake shook his head. "I'm so sorry. I can't help you. I haven't seen your brother in years. Nor have I had any communication from him since our last meeting in . . ." He paused to consider. ". . . yes, in 1995."

Amanda's lips parted, then without speaking she slumped back in her chair, bitter disappointment in every line of her body.

"Mr. Blake"—Elizabeth gently stroked the calico cat which had just jumped onto her lap and was happily kneading her denim-covered thighs—"Amanda's been advertising in the *Guardian* for months, looking for information about her brother. And there were similar ads before that, going back for years. Why didn't you ever respond?"

Blake drew himself up and replied. "In the first instance, dear lady, I never read that provincial rag. In the second, had the advertisement somehow been brought to my attention, what could I have had to say? I had no information. One day the young man was here. He had come to bring me a Christmas libation and had stayed to help me drink it. The liquor loosened his tongue and soon he was pouring out his heart and soul—the next day he was gone, never to return. When weeks and months passed, I realized that he had repented his decision and, embarrassed by the confidences he had shared, had decided simply to move on. So many of them do."

"And you have no idea where he might have gone?"

Amanda's hopeful question hung in the air as Thomas Blake considered it.

"He had spent time in New York and in San Francisco as well. He claimed to regard both with loathing. But like the dog that returns to its vomit, he may have capitulated to the siren call of the lifestyle. And, of course, the medical options in those cities would have been far more extensive."

"I don't understand." Amanda crossed her slender arms and hugged herself as if struck by a sudden chill. "Spinner wasn't sick."

Thomas Blake drained the last of his vodka-laced tea. "My dear, but of course he was—the last time I saw him, he'd just learned that he had AIDS. And after all this time with no word, I've come to believe he must have lost the battle."

# The Drovers' Road XIV
## The Iron Chain

I ran and climbed through the thickety woods like a wild thing
with hounds all a-slaver on its trail. They was a little light from
the setting moon and afore long signs of dawn begun to show in
the sky. I regretted my heavy coat and my blanket layin back in
my room, for hit was bitter cold. At least, thinks I, with only this
light snow, by the time the sun comes up, could be hit'll melt
away my tracks. For a time there, I made out that I could get
plumb away.

But when the sun had cleared the mountains and I found myself at the top of a long ridge with a choice of ways to go, something come over me and I couldn't run no more. Hit was like that
fine thread had turned to an iron chain and hit was draggin at me
ever step. And instead of slippin into the cover of the woods and
lightin out for a far place, I stood there and looked all around me.

The broom sedge was waving brown on the hill and the birds
that had been making such a racket, not a minute past, was still,
like as if a great hawk had glided over. I fell to my knees, wore
out with runnin and knowin that it weren't no use. The hue and
cry at the stand had begun as soon as they'd seen the body, and
though I had a start on them and knowed the land well, I was
afoot and they had horses and mules.

But surely, a man afoot could elude a rider in these steep and
precipitous hills. Surely a man like yourself—

Hit might have been a man could, Professor, but I had lost

*heart. For as I'd run, hit had come to me that hit must be Belle
had done this thing so as to be free for me. And the recollection of
Ol' Luce layin in his blood, his eyes starin, had plumb taken the
heart out of me. They'll not rest till they find someone to answer
for that, thought I.*

*I lay watchin the sky, like I had done that last day at my un-
cle's farm, and I wondered how come I to be in such bad case; hit
was like they was a spell on me and I couldn't run no more. The
clouds chased one another acrost the sky till they was plumb out of
sight and I thought of all the places I hadn't yet seen and so fell
asleep there in the broom sedge.*

*The sun was high overhead when they found me there with the
dry, brown blood on my hand, and I stood to meet them.*

*Boys, I said, holdin my hands high, I'll go with you. I ask
pardon for leadin you such a long, hard ways.*

# Chapter 41

# J'y Suis; J'y Reste
## Wednesday, December 27

Amanda's stunned expression and her indrawn gasp of surprise were immediately followed by the slam of car doors and heavy footfalls approaching the door.

Thomas Blake stood and bent to place a consoling hand on Amanda's shoulder. "I'm truly sorry, my dear. I had thought you must have known."

Ignoring the nearing footsteps, he moved back to the kitchen and Elizabeth heard the *glug-glug* of the vodka bottle. "Mrs. Goodweather, you said you're interested in the history of the stand. I have some items you might find of interest."

Blake emerged from the kitchen and started to pull down one of several shoe boxes on the top shelf of his tall bookcase. "Some copies Nola shared with me in happier times and some odds and ends I found at the bottom of the very box the little mother in there chose for her *accouchement*. I've not had leisure—"

The knock at the door interrupted his explanations and he returned the shoe box to its place. "Unwelcome visitors, I'm afraid, but I beg that you ladies will stay. I don't believe they will linger."

A thought seemed to occur to Blake as he wobbled

toward the entrance. "But perhaps their visit, destined though it is to failure, will serve another purpose." He pulled open the door.

"Gentlemen, punctual to the minute. Please, step in."

Elizabeth recognized them at once: Pritchard Morton, brother of the deceased Payne, who had been at Nola's bedside on her first visit; Vance Holcombe she remembered from the dais at the meeting at the high school; as well as Hollis Noonan, moving force of Ransom Properties and Investments, he of the annoying boyish grin and tossing hair, *god, he's doing it now,* who was coming toward her with outstretched hand.

Blake spoke up. "Mrs. Goodweather, may I present . . ."

*For a drunk and a recluse who looks like a homeless person, old Thos does have nice manners,* she thought, trying to mind her own as the sheaf of golden hair was flipped back into place.

"And this is Mrs. Goodweather's friend, Miss Amanda Lucas."

Elizabeth was forgotten as the newcomers turned to Amanda. They appeared to find her extremely interesting and she saw the glances the trio exchanged. *Well, she is pretty gorgeous; hardly surprising they can't keep their eyes off her.*

"Gentlemen, I have my answer."

All three men turned to look at Blake, who was standing very straight, bolstered, Elizabeth noticed, by the bookshelf at his back.

"Your offer—RPI's offer—was generous, nay, even munificent. But I do not choose to sell and abandon my family heritage."

"Your family heritage?" Noonan's boyish face was suffused instantly with anger. "I don't fucking believe this! You live in a derelict, flea-infested *dump* and we offered you—"

"Hollis!" Pritchard Morton barked out the word.

The effect was immediate. Noonan's furious expression changed to one of mild concern adorned with a self-deprecating smile. "My horrible Irish temper. Ladies, please forgive me. Blake, my associates are prepared to sweeten the offer to the tune of—"

But Blake was shaking his head. "I've made my decision. Double, triple, quadruple the sum—my answer remains. I do not choose to sell."

Noonan's face reddened and he opened his mouth but shut it again as Vance Holcombe began to speak.

"Tom, you've known me and my family and Pritchard's family all your life, right? We all go back a long ways and we all want what's best for the county, wouldn't you say?"

Blake swayed, took another sip from his mug, and nodded. "That's right. But do we agree on what's best? Ay, there's the rub."

The three exchanged glances again. "Maybe it would be better if we came back another time, when you don't have guests," Morton ventured. "I feel that you haven't really considered what the offer could mean to you."

"Gentlemen, you have my final word." Blake's eyes were half-shut. "In the immortal words of the Comte de Mac-Mahon at Sevastopol: *'J'y suis; j'y reste'*—here I am and here I stay."

"We'll see about that." Noonan's voice was under control but his hands, Elizabeth noticed, clenched into white-knuckled fists, betraying his emotion. "The county commissioners are drooling over the thought of turning this whole area into the centerpiece of the new, revived Marshall County. They're willing to authorize a taking for the stand property; when we tell them how this dump will blight the whole project, I think they'll go along with us on condemning this eyesore. They're not going to let one pathetic old drunk stand in the way of a plan that has so much to offer the county."

Noonan looked at his watch. "You can have another

twenty-four hours to come to your senses. Then we'll be
back with a revised and considerably sweeter deal. If you
don't see fit to accept it," a shrug was accompanied by the
toss of the head, "then we'll go to the commissioners."

Motioning toward the door, Noonan summoned his
friends with a glance, then flipped the boyish charm back
on. "Ladies—Mrs. Goodweather, Amanda—I apologize
again."

His eyes slid to Amanda, who was sitting quietly, stroking
a purring ginger cat. "Have we met somewhere? Your face
is so familiar. Chapel Hill? Or maybe—"

"She's Spinner's sister, you fool!" Blake spat out the
words, all pretense of civility gone. Still propped up against
the bookshelf, the older man continued. "The resemblance
is striking. And she's trying to locate him. Perhaps one of
you can tell her where he is. After all, you were friends and
comrades, all five of you."

The memory of the picture of the 5 Bad Boyz flashed
into Elizabeth's mind. *Of course! That was why that fifth one
looked so familiar.*

Amanda rose abruptly, dumping the ginger cat from her
lap. "You were his friends?" She moved closer, looking from
one to another of them. "He wrote to me from Ransom in
December 1995—he said he was going to build a cabin.
But there were no more letters. Please . . . where did he go?"

# Chapter 42

## *The Accounts of Randall Revis*

### Wednesday, December 27

Phillip could hear the music as he opened the front door—the true mountain sound, with only a guitar to accompany the singing and then a fiddle sobbing wildly on the occasional break. There seemed to be two voices, male and female, handing the verses back and forth. The woman's clear sweet voice was taking its turn, the poignant words throbbing with anxiety and the pain of love.

> *I see a dust cloud and the stock drawing near;*
> *I see a tall figure; it must be my dear.*
> *My heart's pounding faster; oh, will he be kind,*
> *When he finds that there's two where he left one be-*
> *hind?*

And now the man was singing—a lonesome, haunting sound—the sound of a man who sees his doom ahead and goes willingly to it.

> *Who is this dark woman in the midst of the road?*
> *She beckons me to her; oh what does this bode?*
> *Her eyes are deep pools and they're drawing me*
> *nigh.*

*She lays her hand on me and for her I would die.*

*Luellen comes to me and I turn aside—*

"You're back." Elizabeth punched the button to halt the tape in the boom box. She wiped her hands on her apron and hugged him heartily.

"Yep, Ben and I went in to the tractor place. He's decided I have potential as a tractor monkey and wanted me to be familiar with the parts department and the guy who runs it—Ben says there's a lot more use in the tractor but it's at the age where little things keep breaking or wearing out." He sat on the cushioned bench and began to unlace his boots. "Saw your car there at Blake's. Was he able to tell Amanda anything about her brother?"

"Nothing good." Elizabeth ran through the highlights of the visit, ending with Amanda's appeal to her brother's old friends.

"They all three seemed embarrassed by her question. They said they hadn't really seen that much of Spinner in the last few months he was in Ransom. Kind of insinuating things about his being gay—one of them said Spinner had made a lot of different friends recently, and one of the others laughed and said, 'Yeah, they were *different*, all right.' "

"Did they have any idea where her brother'd got to?" He picked up the empty plastic tape box lying beside the boom box and read the penciled notation: *Songs of Love and Murder by Josh and Sarah Goforth.*

"Not really. One of them kept making these snide comments about Spinner going somewhere 'more appropriate to his lifestyle'—New York or San Francisco or 'one of those places with lots of his kind.' "

He listened as she described Blake's rejection of RPI's offer and the threat of a county taking, then asked, "Has the county ever done that before? *Can* they do it?"

"I don't really know." Opening the oven door, Elizabeth pulled out a cast iron skillet of cornbread. She turned out the fragrant cake onto a bread board and began to fill bowls from the steaming pot of chili on the stovetop. "Sallie Kate seems to think it's possible. And if the Holcombes want it to happen, I expect it will."

"Thomas Blake let me borrow a box of Nola's papers. He said he'd been helping her with research for her novel and she'd given him a lot of her copies from original sources so he could piece together his family's history. And he said some more stuff that pertained to the stand had just turned up. It was at the bottom of the box where the cat had her kittens—more historical records of some sort tucked under the old clothes."

They were settled before the fire with their after-dinner coffee, feet comfortably propped up on the big cedar chest in front of them. With a delighted cry, Elizabeth lifted out a page from the box on her lap.

"Look at this one! It's a copy of an old newspaper article about the same murder as that ballad I was just playing."

She held up the paper and began to read with exaggerated dramatic emphasis, skipping down the columns of close-packed print. *"An Account of the Recent Terrible Murders at Gudger's Stand . . . the flight and capture of the desperate drover boy Lydy Goforth . . . the mute witness of the ensanguined snow . . .* Now there's a word for you; they don't do journalism like that anymore. . . .

*". . . hapless young girl dragged to the riverside . . . bloodied night garment ripped from her frail body . . . footprints that told the sordid tale . . . matching the home-cobbled cowhide boots belonging to Lydy Goforth . . . peculiar pattern in the setting of the nails and a crescent-shaped indentation along the side of the left sole. High Sheriff Loyal Revis, fortuitously on the scene, was the first to note these telling details, and it was he who led the hardy band of trackers, some deputized on the spot, in pursuit of the*

*young man who was at last captured, the* blood *of his victim* still
on his hands."

She finished with wide eyes and a melodramatic quaver,
then grinned and handed the copy to Phillip. "Quite a
story."

Phillip studied the page. "Simpler times. I bet Mackenzie
wishes his cases could be solved that easy." He handed the
page back to her. "What else is in there?"

Elizabeth began to remove the papers and clippings.
"Odds and ends is what he said. Let's see . . . more newspaper articles . . . a little privately printed genealogy of the
Blakes and Wakefields . . . copy of another newspaper article
about a bridge being built at Gudger's Stand to replace the
ferry . . . a bunch of little books tied up with a string . . ."

She undid the knot and spread out the books—pocket-
sized ledgers, their gray-green cloth covers stained and
worn. Picking one at random, she opened it. The endpa-
pers were covered with penciled jottings. On the first page
were the initials "R.R." and the date "1990–1993."

Elizabeth began to page through the book, trying to
read the cryptic notations that accompanied various sums.
"Look at this, Phillip. It must have belonged to that old
man, Nola's uncle."

*What was it Nola had said? Not till his accounts are closed?*

Phillip glanced over her shoulder. "It looks like the private account book of a small-time loan shark." He took the
book. "See how the same sums occur every month—and if
a month's skipped, there's added interest."

He flipped through the entries. "Very, very small-time,
payments of five or ten dollars—the highest recurring pay-
ment is twenty-five from someone he calls 'Trucker 2.'"
Phillip handed the book back to Elizabeth. "The old guy
ran an illegal drinking establishment—he probably picked
up a little on the side lending money out till payday—
something like that."

Elizabeth took up another book, the one marked

"1994–1996." The same small amounts, as Phillip had said, received from the unknown debtors: Four-Eyes, The Gimp, Trucker 2, Cat Man. She moved on—July, August, September. Some debts evidently were paid—Trucker 2 disappeared, as did The Gimp—and new nicknames appeared: Sandals, Beach Boy, Cave Girl.

"Not exactly riveting reading." She flipped rapidly through the pages. "I wonder if Cat Man is Thomas Blake?"

Suddenly the pattern made by the repeated five- and ten-dollar notations shifted. "Phillip, the numbers get a lot higher, beginning in October of '95. There're new names and they're paying one or two thousand apiece."

"So they are . . ." He frowned at the names. *Holy Joe, Kildare—who were these people?*

"You know, Lizabeth, I'm thinking this doesn't look like loan-sharking."

She nodded. "But it does look like blackmail, doesn't it?"

# The Drovers' Road XV
## And Faithful Beyond

The hammering of the day before had been replaced, as the morning hours wore on, with the increasing clamor of a gathering crowd. Lydy lay motionless on his narrow bunk, not even turning his head when the rattle of the chain announced the opening of the door.

A rough voice proclaimed, Professor, here's your broadsheet. Printer's got three little boys hawkin copies to the crowd and they're sellin like one thing.

The Professor took the sheet that was thrust through the narrow crack. The hand withdrew, the door shut, and there was the familiar sound of the lock and the chink of the chain being replaced. Holding the hastily printed broadside to the light, the Professor pursed his lips as he scanned the inky lines, then offered the rough sheet to his companion.

Here, my poor boy, is the account based on your trial. The version of the unhappy events that you swore to in court. The printer has labored all the night to have this ready for your . . . for your perusal.

The young man glanced at it briefly, then returned his gaze to the featureless winter sky beyond the barred window. I ain't no hand to read. I'd take hit kindly was you to say it over for me.

The Professor cleared his throat. Of course, if it will afford you some modicum of satisfaction. The title is, as you wished—
*The Most Lamentable Story of Lydy Goforth, Composed by*

*Himself on the Eve of his Hanging for the Grewsome Murders*
*of the Standkeeper Lucius Gudger and his Fair Daughter*
*Luellen—Anno Domini 1860.*

*When Lydy made no response, the Professor took an oratori-*
*cal stance, holding the rough sheet at arm's length, and half*
*singing, half intoning, began to recite the hastily composed verses.*

> "Come all ye good people and hear my sad
>      tale;
> My time it draws nigh and my soul it doth
>      quail.
> I'd have you take warning, take warning of
>      me
> If murder you've done, then you must pay
>      the fee."

*An abrupt gesture from Lydy silenced him. I believe I don't*
*want to hear it atter all. If you wrote hit as I told you, hit'll do.*
*Long as I know that you have the true story wrote down some-*
*wheres else.*

*There was a sudden roar from the crowd outside and once*
*again a rattle and clank and the door swung wide. Three armed*
*men stood there, and beyond them a shifting crowd, all craning to*
*see the prisoner emerge.*

*Lydy, you got to come on now.*

*The burliest of the three stepped forward but Lydy waved him*
*back. Swinging his feet to the floor, he stood, his hands clenched*
*at his sides. Professor, I thank ye kindly for your company and*
*charge you to keep to our bargain.*

*The Professor laid a hand over his heart. Faithful till death.*
*Choking on the word, he brushed his eyes with the back of his*
*other hand. And faithful beyond.*

*And faithful beyond, replied Lydy, opening his hand to let the*
*smooth stone fall to the floor.*

# Chapter 43

## *The Biter Bit*

### Wednesday, December 27, and Thursday, December 28

So if Revis was blackmailing these people—what are the names? Kildare, Pretty Boy, Holy Joe, The Fairy Queen, and Little Big Man—in October and November and December—"

"The Fairy Queen didn't pay in December," Elizabeth put in. "And the payments from the others each went up by five hundred dollars."

Phillip ran his hand over his head, then pointed a warning finger at her. "Don't say it. Is there an entry for January?"

She flipped ahead. "Revis's accounts for '96. Only January is filled in and it looks like The Fairy Queen is off the books—there're just the four names. But the rate they're paying is up—two thousand dollars each for two of them, and three thousand each for the other two."

"And by February, Revis was dead. The classic mistake of a blackmailer—ask for too much and the victim—or victims—can turn desperate."

Elizabeth looked back to the page for October 1995 and ran her finger down the names. "It started here—and this is when Mackenzie's anonymous letter-writer says she was gang-raped and when Bam-Bam dropped out of sight. Could be a coincidence but somehow I doubt it. The payments increase in December—was Revis just greedy? Or did something else happen?"

Phillip's quiet answer was like a knell. "December's also the last time anyone heard from Amanda's brother. You realize, don't you, Lizabeth, whose bones those probably were in the silo?"

She nodded silently and pointed to the December entry. "The Fairy Queen," she whispered. "Spinner."

"That leaves four possibilities for Revis's murderer—"

"The Bad Boyz." She put her hand to her mouth. "Cletus said that they were bad boys who put him in the bus with the naked girl."

"I'm not sure I follow you—bad boys?"

Elizabeth moved her finger to another entry. "Now there're only three—Holy Joe's gone too—the so-called suicide."

The night-duty aide was moving quietly around the room, tidying the other bed, where she had dozed, and collecting the romance novel and puzzle books that had kept her company through her shift. Nola watched through barely opened eyes and made her plan.

*This one'll leave a little early, as usual, and Michelle will get here a little late, as usual, and there'll be time.*

She could see the aide glance at her, so she maintained her gape-mouthed pose of deep sleep. The aide stepped over, leaned down, and gently pulled the sheet up a little higher. She stood and studied her client.

*Benevolently? I think so but dare not trust her.* Nola began to snore slightly. *Don't overdo it. Just enough to convince her that I'll be asleep and out of trouble for another hour or so.*

After another moment, she heard the diminishing squeak of rubber-soled shoes on linoleum. Cautiously she opened her eyes and saw with relief that her door was pulled almost shut.

As quickly as she could manage with limbs stiff from disuse, Nola Barrett pulled herself out of bed and hobbled across the room in search of her glasses. In one hand she clutched four white tablets.

"Good morning, Miss Nola! You want me to help you to the potty? . . . What a sleepyhead you are. I believe I'll just turn on the TV to help you wake up a little so you can have some nice oatmeal when your breakfast comes."

*She almost caught me. If only I could have had a few more seconds to stir it in thoroughly.* Once again stretched out on the bed, Nola continued her imitation of sleep. She could hear Michelle's heavy footsteps moving from the television to the plastic-covered reclining chair, and she could hear the chair's sigh of protest as Michelle sat down.

"Ooh, here's some good juice just goin' to waste again."

The television clicked on and a woman's voice said, *"More later on the blizzard lashing the Plains; we're going now to Bret on the beach at Waikiki—tough assignment, Bret!"*

"Umph, reckon that juice woulda tasted better cold. It must of settled or something."

A sigh and Michelle sat back. There was the rattle of the cart delivering breakfast trays in the hall.

"Just set it there. I'm lettin' her get her beauty sleep." Retreating footsteps and the sound of a lid being removed.

"Oatmeal, toast and jelly, scrambled eggs . . . maybe I'll just taste a corner of this toast . . ."

The weather report droned on, segueing into something Nola recognized as Michelle's favorite show—people yelled at one another and accused family members of heinous things while the audience cheered and booed like a crowd in the Roman Coliseum, watching the barbarians tear each other to pieces.

Michelle, who usually accompanied this show with a running commentary, was silent. Nola waited a little longer,

then opened her eyes. The young aide was limp in the reclining chair, a half-eaten piece of toast drooping from one
hand.

With a grim smile, Nola Barrett sat up and slipped on
her glasses.

*It worked. Now if he can only manage to do as I directed. He
has to get here before they come for the tray.*

Phillip dragged the navy watch cap from his jacket pocket
and put it on, pulling it well down over his ears. "I'm going
in and have a talk with Mac. These little account books will
give him something to think about." He tucked the parcel
under his arm. "It all comes back to that old house and the
things that went on there. I'm thinking Mac's going to be
very interested in the three Bad Boyz still standing."

"I bet he will." Elizabeth reached for the chicken bucket
and the scraps of last night's meal. "After I do my chores,
I'm going in to check on Nola. She told me not to come
back till Friday but I just don't feel easy about her. Of
course, if she's still going on with that phony act, there's not
much I can do. But maybe I can get that aide to leave us
alone long enough for me to ask some questions."

Michelle slept on. Nola took a last look at the clock on the
wall, removed her glasses, and lay down to wait. *What are
the chances he'll do it? I should have asked Elizabeth. But how
well do I know her? She might have balked ... have felt it her
duty to stand in my way. But where* is *he?*

The door was pushed open again and a familiar voice
spoke. "As you desired, dear lady, punctual and sober. And
I've brought the items you specified."

# Chapter 44

## *Star-2-3-0-0*
### Thursday, December 28

*S*he specifically told me not to come back till Friday. Is she going to be angry if I just check on her? But what if she's in danger from whoever was trying to keep her doped up?

The interior monologue repeated its dreary loop as Elizabeth parked her car and picked her way across the icy parking lot to the entrance of the Layton Facility. She was aware of a subtext to that monologue, running concurrently but, as it were, on a slightly different frequency. *This is a woman who tried to kill herself. Why do I believe she's acting rationally?*

At the front door she was surprised to see Thomas Blake, evidently on his way out. Blake was courteously holding the door open for a thin old man bent over a stout walking stick. Catching her eye, Blake nodded and waited.

Without a word to Blake, the thin old man hobbled through the door, brushing past Elizabeth as she waited on the porch. Something about the old man, *was it a scent? his gait? the set of his shoulders?* made her look more closely.

Stiff new overalls, a heavy jacket, and an insulated cap with earflaps protected him from the bite of the air, but he had taken the extra precaution of swathing his lower face with a plaid wool muffler. Mirrored sunglasses added a bizarre touch, and as he glanced briefly at her, Elizabeth saw her own reflection. *You're staring at the poor guy, Elizabeth. Cut that out.*

"Mornin'," she said, nodding in his direction and looking away almost at once.

With a muttered and indistinguishable reply, he shuffled away, moving slowly but purposefully toward the parking lot.

"Mrs. Goodweather, good morning!" Blake's voice rang out in cheery tones. "Well met! I've just been calling on our friend."

*How does he do it? Drunk as he was yesterday afternoon, here he is, out and about this early.*

"How *is* Nola?" Elizabeth asked, stepping into the warmth of the lobby. "I just thought I'd come by for a minute."

Blake let the door swing shut. "I found her much the same, I fear, quite unresponsive. I'm afraid, though, that your trip is in vain. You won't find her in her room. An aide just collected her and wheeled her away for—what was it? I believe the young woman said hydrotherapy."

"Really?" Elizabeth glanced at the clock on the wall. *A little after ten.* "Well, since I'm here, I guess I'll wait."

A thought occurred to her. "You know, I've been wondering about Nola's uncle—there was some of his stuff in that box you lent me and it got me to thinking about his murder. I read about it in the paper back then, of course, but I don't remember anything much except that he lived alone and that the stand had come down in his family. I guess *you* knew him fairly well, being his nearest neighbor and all."

Blake's quick look was guarded, but he replied, "I knew him slightly. He was not the easiest of neighbors. But, as you are undoubtedly aware, his establishment was a convenient source of beer and liquor. And, as you have surely surmised, I did, on occasion, have recourse to his wares, grossly inflated though his prices were." He raised his hand to the keypad by the door, preparing to tap in the code that would release the lock. "I'm sorry I cannot offer more information. I have an appointment that must be honored."

"Of course, please, don't let me keep you. Just one more quick question—did anyone ever call you 'Cat Man'?"

The steel-rimmed spectacles glittered at her. "As a matter of fact, that was the appellation the river guides bestowed on me years ago." Blake punched in the code to release the entry lock. "It was kindly intended and preferable to 'the Troll,' wouldn't you agree?"

With a civil nod, he hurried out the door and Elizabeth turned to make her somewhat shamefaced way to Nola's room.

The door was shut. After tapping at it and receiving no answer, Elizabeth pushed it open. *I'll just wait here till they bring her back from her hydrotherapy, whatever that may be.*

Inside the room the television was chattering away, and before it, a figure swathed in a shawl slumped in a recliner chair.

"Nola?" But even as she spoke Elizabeth saw that it was the aide Michelle—sound asleep.


After twenty minutes of sitting on the foot of Nola's bed and listening to Michelle's adenoidal breathing compete with the dubious entertainment of a talk show, Elizabeth had had enough. She moved to the door only to be met by an awning-bedecked juice cart blocking the way.

"'Scuse, please." A sleepy-looking woman entered the room carrying a pitcher of ice and a paper cup filled with a noxious-looking purple liquid. Depositing the cup on the tray table at the side of the sleeping Michelle, she glanced at the unconscious form and spoke loudly. "Here's your juice, Miss Barrett."

"That's not Miss Barrett; that's her aide." Elizabeth

tried to contain the indignation she felt—on behalf of Nola and every unfortunate enduring the anonymity of institutional care. "Miss Barrett's having hydrotherapy."

"Not today, she ain't. The hydrotherapy unit's out of whack. They got it all pulled to pieces this very minute. Two fellers been working on it since eight a.m."

"No, Nola wasn't scheduled for hydrotherapy today. Let me see—no, there's nothing at all." The woman behind the desk looked up with a reassuring smile. "You know, these senile cases wander some; it's just the nature of the illness. But they can't get out—all the exits have keypads or alarms. She's probably in one of the other residents' rooms—some of these old dears will go crawl in bed with the first man they come to. The widows, you know, they miss their husbands."

She lifted a phone and spoke into it, then turned back to Elizabeth. "We'll do a room-by-room search in each wing—if you'll just have a seat in the living room at the front, I'll let you know when Miss Barrett's back in her room."

As she sat on the shabby imitation Queen Anne love seat, waiting to hear that Nola had been found, Elizabeth found herself gazing at the keypad by the front door. "Press Star-2-3-0-0. Please do not open door for residents."

*Thomas Blake said Nola'd been taken away for hydrotherapy. Did he misunderstand? Who came and got her? And why?*

As she stared out the door at the parking lot, its pavement now wet and shining with melting ice, the image of the thin old man Blake had held the door for flashed before her. Mirrored sunglasses, muffler, gloves, hat pulled well down—*that could have been anybody*—*that could have been Nola!*

Minutes later she was pressing Star-2-3-0-0, shoving open the door, and sprinting for her car.

# The Drovers' Road XVI
## To Speak a Word

I was at the back of the crowd the day they hanged Lydy Goforth. Like many a woman there who'd not have it known that she'd turn out for such bitter sport, I wore a sunbonnet and kept my face hid. Folks had come on foot and in wagons from all around to see the end of the murderin drover boy and, though a murdered woman, I passed unnoticed in the throng.

Lookin back atter all these years, I sometimes think that maybe I could have stepped forward and spoke a word that might of changed things but then I know that it had to fall out as it did. Besides, though I knew for a certainty he weren't a murderer, it was him had flung me aside for that black-eyed Jezebel and he was the one had brought shame on me. How could I, with a belly too big to hide under my shawl, have stepped up to the scaffold and said, Here I am. I ain't dead.

Belle was there, in her widder's weeds with the black veil hidin her face. She was setting in a wagon druv by the sheriff's brother-in-law and the sheriff's sister was at her side, pattin her hand and whisperin in her ear. I reckon she could have spoke a word too, though her belly didn't show yet.

I heard the woman next me tellin her husband that the sheriff was plum foolish over that huzzy and was like to marry her, breedin though she was.

Her man told her not to be an old cat. Hit does my heart good, said he, to see a woman strong for retribution—bearin witness like that at the hangin of her husband's murderer.

I almost said something at that but recollected myself and moved away from there to where I could see better.


Ish and Mariah had took me in when I run off. I never told them just what happened, though I believe that Mariah suspicioned, for she didn't treat me the same as before. But I was a woman comin near to my time and that was enough for her kind nature.

I had hid in the woods till I heard the sheriff and the other men takin after Lydy, goin up the mountain, then I slipped along a rocky trail through the woods, careful to leave no sign. When I come to their stand, they was in their little stone house and I saw Mariah's dark face at the window. She flung open the door afore I could call out and folded me in her warm arms. Nor did she ask the first question as to why I come to be there at first light—she just put me into their bed which had a feather tick and blankets that smelled of herbs from her garden. She gave me a bowl of venison stew and some of her honey wine to drink and told me to go to sleep.

Don't tell no one I'm here, Mariah. Will you promise? I said and she promised solemn though I think that later she come to regret it.

And now I stood watchin as the men brung Lydy to the scaffold and one of them climbed up the steps behind him. The sheriff called for quiet and asked if Lydy had aught to say. He stood straight, castin his gaze round the crowd, lookin kindly surprised that all these folks had come together because of him. Then I seen his eyes light on the wagon where Belle sat.

He stared the longest but she made no sign and he said no word. They laid the noose around his neck and I turned away.

# Chapter 45

## *At Large*
### Thursday, December 28

The thin old man with the mirrored glasses—that must have been Nola! She looked right at me. Blake could have brought her the clothes and now he's driving her... where? And why? Why didn't she just tell the people in charge that she was herself again?

Elizabeth pulled onto the road leading to Dewell Hill and down to Gudger's Stand. *What did Nola say—"Not until his accounts are closed"? Does that have anything to do with those entries that must be blackmail? What the hell is she trying to do?*

Everyone in the world seemed to be out on the road today, and most of them were driving too slow. Elizabeth ground her teeth as she saw one of the county's snowplows pull into the line of traffic ahead of her, lumbering along at a stately twenty-five miles per hour. Passing on this narrow two-lane road was illegal as well as almost impossible, but she found herself inching closer to the car ahead of her and eyeing the oncoming lane of traffic with an eye to opportunity.

None came, but at last she reached the turnoff for Dewell Hill and sped down the winding road. *Nola's cottage, I ought to look there first. Or could he have taken her to her neighbor's place? I need to check there too.*

Nola's stone house came into view, cold and lifeless in its bleak winter setting. Elizabeth pulled up in front of Lee Palatt's house. Two fat, long-haired cats stretched out on the stone front steps, taking advantage of the noonday sun. They watched Elizabeth's approach with mild interest, one of them going so far as to stand up, rub against her jeans, and trill a greeting mew as Elizabeth banged on the door.

It opened almost immediately and Nola's neighbor peered out. "My heavens . . . I thought you might be from the sheriff's office. Mrs. Goodweather? Is something wrong?"

"Nola seems to have disappeared from the nursing home. It's possible that . . . a friend came and got her. I wondered if maybe you might have seen her."

Just as she stammered out her news, Elizabeth was hit with a sudden realization: *What if this woman's in on it? She may know where Nola is and not tell me. Or could she be hiding Nola?*

"Nola disappeared? I thought she was dying! Are you sure?" Lee put one hand over her heart as if shocked by the news and then, looking closely at Elizabeth, stood back and beckoned her in.

"Why don't you come have a cup of tea . . . or maybe a bowl of soup? I was just finishing my lunch." Without waiting for an answer, she turned and led the way to the back of the tiny house.

Elizabeth followed. *That seemed like genuine surprise. But she could just be a good actor.* From the living room, she could see into an immaculate little bedroom, where an orange tabby draped himself languidly across a blue blanket at the foot of the bed.

In the kitchen, a table bore a half-full bowl of soup, a half-eaten grilled cheese sandwich, a glass of water, and an open book—*a solitary lunch. Surely, if Nola were here—*

"I haven't seen anything of Nola—but if she's improved enough to go missing, at least that's good news. But of course she wouldn't have come here. Please, have a seat."

Lee Palatt set a spoon and a bowl of soup before Elizabeth. The enticing aroma floated up to her, reminding her it was past her lunchtime. *Five minutes. Have the soup and then go find Nola.* "Why'd you think I might be from the sheriff?" she asked between spoonfuls.

"Well, I called them over an hour ago. These two old men had just walked up to Nola's back door and broken it open, bold as you please." Her hostess sat opposite her, well launched into her story. "Now, that niece of hers has pretty well cleaned out everything except Nola's old clothes, so there's nothing to steal. I guess those two found that out, because they weren't there long. By the time I called the sheriff's department and got back to the window, they were gone."

Lee's pleasant face was pink with indignation. "They got clean away and small wonder! You know, that woman who answers the phone at the sheriff's department was downright rude! Said they had enough to do without following up on every call from nervous old women living alone. Well, I told her—"

Elizabeth put down her spoon. "Lee, thank you for the soup. It was delicious but I have to go now. Let me give you my number; if Nola were to come here, you could call me."

Lee looked up in surprise. "Oh, she'd never come here—I told you she has a thing about cats—absolutely can't be around them."

*So she'd hardly go to Blake's place either. But still, I have to go take a look, just to be sure.*

The clutter of derelict vehicles in front of the old brick building seemed much the same—some on blocks, long years past use; others on their own tires, looking more or less capable of locomotion. *Why didn't I pay attention to what he was driving back at the Layton Facility?*

Elizabeth parked and headed toward the door. One old truck appeared to be the popular favorite among the cats, and its hood was covered with lounging felines. As she passed by it, she laid a hand on the hood—still warm. *Aha! The Troll is in!*

Repeated knocking finally had its effect. Thomas Blake pulled open the door and stood staring blearily at her. The smell of alcohol was strong. "Miz Goo'weather. We meet again."

"Yes, we do, Mr. Blake. Where's Nola?"

He blinked. "Nola? Surely—"

She pushed her way past him into the building and called out, "Nola! It's Elizabeth. I want to help you stay out of that horrible place. If you're afraid of someone, I'll take you to my house. Please, Nola—"

"Belie'e me, she's not here. Sh—severe allergy to cats precludes her visiting my—"

She whirled on him and grabbed the front of his flannel shirt, pulling him close. "Listen, goddammit, I want to know where Nola is. I'm afraid she's in danger from whoever it was keeping her drugged in the nursing home. I think they're afraid of something she knows—something that could destroy them."

"Please, no violence." Blake looked down at her hands, still clutching his shirt. "Strongly . . . deplore violence."

She released her hold on him; he swayed and staggered to the sofa. A cloud of cat hair rose as he collapsed onto the sagging cushions.

"I told her to trust you—more dependable than a drunk . . . but she had made up her mind. And when Miss Nola makes up her mind, she's a . . . a ver'tible force of nature. Not to be deterred."

He made a sweeping motion with his hand and repeated himself. "Not to be deterred in her quest. So when she had me take her first to her house and then back to Jim Hinkley's, I did not protest. Mine not to reason why—"

Elizabeth frowned at Blake. "Why the hell would Nola want to go to Jim Hinkley's gas station? And where is she now?"

Blake lay back, his eyes drifting shut. "As to where she is now, I could not venture to guess. But I rather suspect that her reason for having me chauffeur her to Jim Hinkley's was so that she could retrieve her car."

# Chapter 46

## *A Woman Alone*
### Thursday, December 28

I don't argue with Miss Nola. Sure, I was surprised to see her after all the talk there'd been but when she marched into the bay where I was greasing that old Chevy there and said her niece had made a mistake and she didn't want to sell her little car after all. I just said, 'Yes, ma'am, Miss Nola,' and went and got it. She said she'd stop in and settle with me later and in she got and off she went. That way. Toward town."

It was freedom; it was bliss; it was joy untrammeled to be behind the wheel of her car. To be in control of her body and mind once more. To breathe real air, not the exhalations of others, to see a changing landscape reeling past. Oh, free!

The sight of a police cruiser checked the flow of giddy exuberance, and Nola Barrett slowed to a sedate fifty-five. She took her eyes off the highway just long enough to admire the graceful shape of the Colt .38 revolver lying on the seat beside her. *What was it Mother used to say? A woman alone needs a gun. Your granny got this from a feller comin back from the First World War and she give it to me. You take care of yourself now, Nolyda, and take care of our girl when I'm gone.*

Nola wiped her eyes with the back of her hand. *I tried to, Mama, the best I could. The best doctors, the best nursing care. But what I had to do to pay for that ... Mama, sometimes I think you were right about Belle's curse on Luellen's line. We're at an end now—Little Ricky is gone and our Tracy will bear no more children.*

The soaring joy of moments ago vanished as completely as if it had never existed, and Nola Barrett drove on, feeling the bonds of her fate tightening around her. *And the last of Belle's evil line died at my hand. Endgame—no winner.*

*What now, Elizabeth? Nola could be heading to Ransom or to Asheville. Or to Charlotte or New York City or Timbuctoo. She's an hour ahead of you and could be in another state by now. Or she could have turned down a side road and be doubling back. What the hell is she up to?*

And is this rational behavior or the behavior of a crazy woman? Elizabeth didn't allow the words to form, but they hovered there on the edge of her inner dialogue. *Phillip— maybe Phillip could make a suggestion.*

The bypass shopping center was just ahead. She turned off the road and pulled to a stop at the edge of the parking lot. Her cell phone had slipped off the seat beside her, and she was stretching to retrieve it when a rap on her window startled her. She jerked upright, cell phone forgotten.

A pale, haggard face was staring at her, its lips forming words she couldn't make out. Purple jacket and wisps of hennaed hair showing beneath the fleece cap—Tracy, Nola's niece, was talking excitedly and motioning for her to lower her window.

"... just got in town and went straight to the nursing home. Those incompetent idiots had no idea where she was. I don't believe this shit. That neighbor said you'd been there looking for Nola; evidently you haven't found her."

"Get in, Tracy. It's too cold to keep this window down."

The young woman looked momentarily surprised, then, with a shrug of her bony shoulders, came around to the passenger side, climbed in, and continued her explanation.

"Naturally, I went to Nola's house, thinking that, if she could, that's where she'd go first. And I'm really afraid that's what she did."

Tracy continued, the words flowing in an unpunctuated stream. "In her bedroom in the middle of the floor were clothes I'd never seen her wear—overalls for god's sake and a doofus-looking fur cap with those ear things and a pair of mirrored sunglasses...I'd left a box of Nola's clothes in there and they'd been dumped out in a pile...I can't be sure but it seemed like some were gone."

She paused to gulp a breath. "Miz Goldwater what has me worried I mean really really worried is that the floor-board, the one with the knots that look like a pig's face, was pulled up. She used to keep a gun there. I'd completely for-gotten about it when Stone and I were cleaning out the place."

"A gun!" Elizabeth's mind raced, filled with dire scenar-ios. *Self-inflicted lead poisoning,* someone had said of Pastor Morton's supposed suicide. It was an ugly thought. "Tracy, do you think she's going to try to kill herself?"

The emaciated young woman turned weary eyes to her. "I'm afraid so. After all, she's already tried it once. It's the guilt she feels that drove her to it the first time. And I don't think anything can take that guilt away." Tracy closed her eyes. "I blamed her. I told her it was all her fault that Little Ricky died. And some of it *was* her fault. But I don't *want* her to die! She's the only blood kin I have."


Mackenzie Blaine closed the small account book and pushed it back across his desk to Phillip Hawkins. "Hawk, what can I tell you that you don't already know? This suggests a lot but it's worthless as evidence. I wouldn't be at all surprised to find—"

"I tell you, Sheriff's gonna want to see us. Me and Lonnie got something to tell him and we want to see him now!"

Loud voices from beyond the door, followed by a clumping of boots, interrupted the sheriff, who rose and went to his door. Pulling it open, he called out, "Miss Orinda, send them back right now!"

Sheriff Blaine resumed his seat. "That old—" He shook his head and began again. "She thinks she's Saint Peter at the gates. I believe she gets a kick out of making people wait. Would probably like 'em to make appointments—'I can give you a three-thirty on Tuesday of next week; the sheriff will be happy to discuss your burglary then.'"

More loud clumping, and a disapproving Miss Orinda ushered in two young men. Their boots, as well as their camouflage hunting pants and jackets, were caked with red clay and darker muck, and their faces bore marks of the same soil. The smaller of the two, wiry and intense, shifted his chewing tobacco to his cheek, then stepped forward.

"What me and Lonnie want to know is kin we get immunity if we tell about what we found?"

The two, it was revealed eventually, had decided to prospect for the legendary gold, said to be buried somewhere at Gudger's Stand by either Union or Confederate sympathizers or, alternatively, by a murderous landlord from the days of the Drovers' Road. "And me and Lonnie was thinkin', once them developer fellers gets to work, they'll be bullnosers and back-hole diggers all over, tearin' up everything. Well, shitfire, me and Lonnie said, let's go have another try afore them outside people git it all. And Lonnie said as how he'd heard of people hidin' stuff down the outhouse hole for wouldn't no one want to go lookin' *there* and so early this morning we took us some shovels and maddoxes and just commenced to dig there where that old outhouse used to be."

The two prospectors had been hidden from the road and, fueled by greed, beef jerky, Mountain Dew, and a certain amount of Mad Dog 20/20, had managed to remove the half-burnt remains of the old structure and begin to excavate the burned bits of debris that had fallen into the pit.

"We had got down almost six feet when we come upon it. First we seen the green and purple cloth amidst the dirt and then Lonnie says, 'Reckon why someone'd throw a nice jacket down a shit hole?' and then we seen the rest."

# The Drovers' Road XVII
## And This Was the Way of It

When the crowd roared, I set my foot to the road. They was a big family from over near Sodom took me up in their wagon and carried me past Dewell Hill and to the head of the trace leadin down to the river. They had come to town to trade and to see the hangin and they couldn't talk of nothing else. They had bought them a broadsheet with the ballad of Lydy Goforth on it and one of them who could read good would line out a verse and then all of them but the babies would sing hit back. I laughed inside myself to think that only I knew the truth of what had befell.

This was the way of it, the night before me and my daddy was murdered.

I was passin through the common room on my way to my bedplace. My back was achin and I was sore at heart too with watching Lydy makin eyes at Belle for two weeks and more. Daddy was drinkin with the sheriff and talkin loud. As I come nigh to him he called me over and said, in the hearin of all, Girl, I want you to know that they's goin to be another heir to Gudger's Stand.

He was grinnin and all puffed up and he poured hisself another tot of applejack. Yessir, Belle is breedin—goin to bear me a son. She's certain sure hit's a boy and that suits me fine—better'n leavin my all to a daughter what's a fallen woman.

You damned old fool, I cried out. Iffen she's breedin a-tall, hits

*Lydy's babe that Belle's a-carryin. She's been layin with him ever night—*

*And he rared back and with all the company watchin he caught me a blow that knocked me to the floor. I lay there a-gaggin, and holdin my belly whilst he said, You'll keep that lyin talk to yourself, Luellen.*

*Without thinkin I hollered, I'll serve you out for that blow, you old fool, and pulled myself up and run at him, a-hammerin at him with my fistes. The men there was all a-laughin as they pulled me offen him and hauled me to my room.*

*That un's a fair hell-cat, said one as he closed the door on me. B'lieve, was I Ol' Luce, I'd not turn my back on her ary whipstitch.*

*I lay there in the cold dark, burnin with anger at them all, seein a time comin when I'd be no better than a servant in what should have been my house.*

*I'll serve them out, I vowed, and fell asleep thinkin black and hateful thoughts.*

# Chapter 47

## *A True Lady*
### Thursday, December 28

The madwoman swung her car around the elegant circle drive at Holcombe Hill and came to a stop behind Big Lavinia's shining pearl-colored Cadillac standing empty at the front steps. *I was a coward before, blind with grief and my own guilt. But there are others to be called to account, others who bear even more guilt....* *"If you wrong us, shall we not revenge?"*

Shoving the revolver into the pocket of her long black coat, she left her car, keys in hand. As she passed the gleaming Cadillac, she stopped, then used her key to gouge a deep scratch in its formerly pristine paint. After regarding her handiwork briefly and finding it good, she climbed the steps and pressed the doorbell. Deep chimes sounded within the house. The madwoman waited, enjoying the warmth of the sun on her cropped head and breathing in the spicy scent of the evergreen swags around the doorframe. The high gloss of the double doors' red paint reflected the sun, and on every hand the most commonplace objects glittered in sharp relief. *A good day to be alive.*

"Yes?" One of the doors had opened and a dark-faced woman wearing an apron over her shirt and slacks was looking inquiringly at her.

"*Buenas tardes,* Juana, I'm here to see Lavinia."

When the woman hesitated, Nola Barrett gestured upward. "My hair—*mi pelo*—is different; that's why you don't recognize me. But you know me: I'm Nola Barrett. Now tell Lavinia I'm here."

With a last wary look, Juana stood aside to let her enter. "You wait," she said, and disappeared down the hall on whispering slipper-clad feet.

The madwoman hummed to herself, the words of the old ballad running through her head as they had run through her blood for all of her life.

> *I'm nearing the place where my journey will end;*
> *It's farewell to my comrades when we round the*
>     *next bend.*
> *I'll lay down my whip and—*

"Señora Lavinia say come back to Señor Platt's office."

Juana, reappearing noiselessly at her elbow, motioned toward the door at the end of the hall.

With her hands thrust deep in her coat pockets, the madwoman strode down the hall and into the room where her destiny waited.

Big Lavinia sat, *like some obscene idol, like a fat spider at the center of its web,* behind the massive desk. "Nola dear, my goodness, you had us all so worried. You really should have let them *know* you were ready to leave. The whole Layton Facility is in an *uproar* and poor Michelle is—"

Ignoring the honeyed words, the madwoman, a wild peal of bells sounding in her head, eyes half-dazed by the dancing lights that had begun again, withdrew the revolver from her pocket, cocked it, and leveled on the woman she had come to kill.

"There's my cell phone." Elizabeth pointed to the little device, lying at Tracy's feet. "I'll call the sheriff. We need—"

But Tracy was shaking her head obstinately. "I don't trust the sheriff. He works for the Holcombes."

"Mackenzie? Oh, no, Tracy, he's—"

"I asked for help and he never answered." The young woman's face was a mask of bitterness as she nudged the cell phone with her foot, pushing it farther away.

"What are you talking about?"

"I was raped—gang-raped—and like a fool I kept quiet. When I finally had the guts to tell about it, Sheriff Blaine wasn't interested."

Elizabeth sat speechless as, in a torrent of anger, the whole story gushed out.

"In high school I had a job waitressing at the stand weekends and summers. My mom had worked there when she was younger and I think Nola had too, though she denied it. She didn't want me there but my mom had just been diagnosed with MS and Nola didn't have the energy to worry about both of us.

"The pay was lousy but the tips were real good. In the summer the river guides were around and some of their clients too. And there were the regulars, mostly nice enough old guys who liked to have girls bring them their beer and burgers and maybe try to look down our tank tops when we put the beer on the table. And then there were the college boys..."

The noise in her head had built to a painful crescendo. Remembering her mother's instructions, the madwoman sighted along the barrel and drew a bead on Big Lavinia's deep bosom, reconsidered, then moved to her forehead. Big Lavinia's red lips were moving but there was no sound—only the roaring in her head.

The madwoman shrieked as pain exploded in her right hand. She looked down, aghast to see the pistol on the floor and Arval at her side, holding an upraised nightstick. At the same time, massive arms encircled her body and a huge beefy hand covered her mouth.

Through the diminishing roar, she could hear Big Lavinia's smug voice. "Platt always made such a point of having someone nearby during interviews. So many *angry* people out there, and quite a few lunatics too . . .

"No, Arval, I don't think we'll involve the sheriff; poor man, he has so much to do. And then there's his tendency to take investigations just a *little* farther than is quite desirable. Not to mention all the prying reporters we'd have coming around. A *true* lady's name is in the newspaper on only three occasions—announcements of her birth, her marriage, and her death. I certainly don't want the Holcombe name linked with *Nola's.* "

Big Lavinia was standing now and making her ponderous way around the desk. She stood gazing up at her would-be assailant, her piggy little eyes snapping with fury. "You common blackmailing slut. After all I've done for you and your bastard daughter and her bastard too. Oh, it's a proud heritage you all share—whores and huzzies and never a husband among you. As if I'd let you point a finger at my boy and his friends. Rape? Don't make me laugh— that girl was *giving* it away. And if her wanton ways finally caught up with her, she has only herself to blame.

"You boys, escort Nola out and lock her up in the old springhouse. You can take turns guarding her—it's awfully cold out there. Watch out, Marval; don't let her bite you. Arval, you'd better put her car in the garage for now and close the door."

As she was pulled along, Nola heard Lavinia say cheerfully to her employees, "Fair turns, boys. It won't be too long. I'll make a call and get some help so you two won't have to miss your movie night. As soon as it's dark, Little Vance and Hollis and I'll take over. Poor Nola, just *determined* to kill herself."

# Chapter 48

## *No Hope for Justice*
### Thursday, December 28

A t least I wasn't a virgin—that would have made it worse, I guess."

Tracy stared out the window at the shadows lengthening across the parking lot. "And like Nola said, some of it was my fault. I'd been flirting pretty heavy with this one guy...one of the college boys and he'd been so sweet; then I overheard him call me—well, something terrible. He was laughing about how I was so easy. It really hurt me and I ran outside so no one would see me crying." The young woman's voice choked then she went on.

"I was sitting down at the end of the porch drinking and crying and one of the other college boys came out—the quiet one who never flirted with any of the girls. He sat down by me and took hold of my hand. He didn't say anything, just let me vent.

"God, I was a drunken mess, nose running, mascara smudged, and carrying on about how much I lo-ooved that son-of-a-bitch who'd just called me a cheap little—" Tracy stopped short of the ugly word, glancing over at Elizabeth.

"Anyway, this guy pulled me up and said, 'Let's go for a walk.'" Tracy wiped her nose and went on. "We walked along the road by the river, up toward the river guides' campground, and I told him all about my family—my mom sick with MS and my uptight aunt. It was October but the weather was mild. I remember there was a moon because it and his hair were the same color. I had just started to notice how good-looking he was and was beginning to think that I'd been flirting with the wrong guy, when he started telling me about *his* family. Here we were, walking along holding hands and I'm starting to think about how nice it would be if he kissed me, when all of a sudden he tells me his family's disowned him because he's gay."

"Tracy," Elizabeth reached across to touch her companion's arm, "was his name Spinner? Spinner Greer?"

The young woman turned wide eyes on her. "I never knew his last name. But I had sex with him because he seemed so nice and I thought maybe..." She covered her face and her voice was muffled behind her fingers. "...this is how dumb I was: I thought I could *cure* him. I took him into a bus that some guys I knew had fixed up to live in and I lighted candles and...and I did everything I knew how to do. He was willing and the sex was okay but I could tell...it was like he was just going through the motions. And then we both fell asleep. I woke up to feel someone putting a gag in my mouth and something over my head where I couldn't see. They had hold of my wrists and ankles and were tying them down. And then it started."

His cell phone buzzed. Phillip stepped away from the group of men at work in the half-excavated pit at the old stand.

"Lizabeth? I can't hear you very well."

The words came in clusters interrupted by bursts of static. "...trying to find Nola...Layton Facility...gang-rape victim is...Mars Hill...tell Mackenzie...gun...A final blast of static announced that reception was at an end.

Phillip hit speed dial for Elizabeth's number but was re-

warded only with an invitation to leave a message on voice
mail.

"Lizabeth, call as soon as you get somewhere with better
reception. Or maybe it's *my* phone. I'm with Mac at the old
stand again. I think we've found Bam-Bam."

The road to Mars Hill was all but deserted and Elizabeth
pushed her luck, staying a steady ten miles over the posted
speed limit. She was on her way to the home of a retired
English professor who, so Tracy had said, was a longtime
friend of Nola's. "There's a chance she'll go there. You look
for Nola in Mars Hill, I'll make the rounds of her church
friends. I don't know what else to do."

Elizabeth had agreed to this plan—a definite long shot
but better than doing nothing—and gotten directions. And
as soon as Tracy had left the car, Elizabeth had retrieved
her cell phone and called the sheriff's department. A disinterested female voice had taken note of the missing Nola
Barrett. "Oh, yes, we've already been informed by the
nursing home. Thank you." The phone had crashed down
without further words.

Next she had tried Phillip, only to be frustrated by such
bad reception that she couldn't be sure if he'd heard a word
of her broken explanations. Giving it up, she had set out for
Mars Hill, replaying the story Tracy had told in such bitter,
chillingly matter-of-fact tones: the rapes, Nola's insistence
that they keep it quiet. "No one will believe you, Tracy. You
say you think it was that Spinner person and his friends—
and one of them Lavinia's boy. No, think of how your
mother would feel. Her life's a misery to her now; do you
want to make things worse? In any event, you'd just be accused yourself if you went to the sheriff with this story.
There's no hope of justice for us in this county. But I have
an idea. If we can't have justice, maybe we can get compen-
sation. We'll go speak to Lavinia privately."

*Lavinia.* Elizabeth took her foot off the gas and let the car slow. *Wouldn't Lavinia be an even older friend? Tracy sending me to Mars Hill to get me out of the way for some reason? Did Nola really have a gun? Lavinia.* The car slowed still more, finally coasting to a stop on the shoulder.

Elizabeth deliberated a moment longer, then made a U-turn and headed back toward Ransom... and Holcombe Hill.

# Chapter 49

# *Down by the Riverside*
### Thursday, December 28

Over and over, Elizabeth replayed the ugly story as Tracy had told it.

"I was there in that bus, tied to that filthy bed all night. When they finally left, I guess I must have passed out. The next thing I knew, there was a blanket over me and that old drunk who lives there at the bridge was untying me. He said someone had told him I was there but he wouldn't say who. Then he carried me back to his place and gave me some hot tea. He wanted to call the sheriff but I begged him to take me home to Nola."

*And Nola told Tracy not to report the rape.*

"I showered and scrubbed till my skin was raw, trying to get all the traces of those animals off me. And then Nola told me to get dressed and come with her.

"She must have called ahead, because they were all there—Big Platt and his brother the retired high sheriff, Lavinia and Little Vance. All lined up waiting for us."

*Nola knew Tracy couldn't prove anything—the girl hadn't seen anything and Nola had let her wash away any evidence that might have proved a case. But she marched in there and extracted enough money to send Tracy to nursing school and to take care of Tracy's mother all through her illness.*

꙳

The western hills were aflame with the rose and gold of the setting sun. From Holcombe Hill it was easy to see the dying of the day and the shadows of advancing night, but Elizabeth turned her back on the lovely view and hurried up the broad steps. Repeated ringing of the doorbell at last brought a response in the form of a squat Latina.

"*No estan aqui, nadie.* They all go out." The woman shook her head and repeated, "*No estan aqui.*"

"Did Nola Barrett come here today? *Una mujer...*" Elizabeth struggled to remember the word for "thin." "*Una mujer flaca,* with hair..." Using her fingers as scissors, she mimed a very short hair cut and added, for good measure, "Hair *muy negro y muy blanco.* Very black and very white."

A look of dawning comprehension grew on the dark face and the woman began to speak in rapid and, to Elizabeth, almost utterly unintelligible Spanish. She could make out only a few words: *la flaca loca*—the skinny crazy woman— and *al rio*—to the river.

The parking lot at the bridge was empty but for a nondescript midsized car, definitely not Nola's. Elizabeth drove slowly across the bridge, wondering what she had expected to see. *"Rio" could mean anywhere—on any river. But I immediately assumed—*

The flash of headlights off to the right caught her eye. *Someone's down there in that field where that old abandoned bus is. Oh, shit, now what?*

Once again she tried her cell. No joy. This area, here in the narrow gorge between two mountain ranges, was evidently the deadest of dead reception zones.

From the direction of the lights, she heard a high-pitched scream of despair.

꒓

Turning her car onto the overgrown dirt road, she could see in the rapidly forming frost the recent tracks of another vehicle. As the car bumped along the frozen ground, Elizabeth felt her body tense with cold and fear and adrenaline. *The scream. Was that Nola?*

The red glow of taillight reflectors winked at her through desiccated weeds, and she saw the outlines of two cars, both facing the river. The farther one she recognized as Nola's—the driver's door was open and the headlights were on. The other car, incongruous in this setting, was a big new-looking sedan *a Cadillac or something,* gleaming palely amid the scrubby undergrowth.

Immediately she turned off her own lights and eased her car to a stop. There was no sign of anyone in either car. But down by the riverside she could see movement as dark figures swayed and flickered in the headlights' beams. She switched off the ignition and quietly opened her door.

Moving cautiously through the dark, taking care to stay out of the fan of light cast by Nola's little car, Elizabeth edged closer to the river. A large outcropping of several waist-high boulders lay between her and the river, and she moved silently toward them. The people at the river's edge seemed completely unaware of her approach, blinded as they were by the car's lights and deafened by the roar of the river, unusually high and swift with the added burden of recent snowmelt.

On a flat ledge of rock that extended out into the rushing river lay a group of rubber rafts, evidently awaiting moonrise and the River Runners' planned moonlight trip. To one side of the rafts stood three fantastic figures, harshly illumined by the headlight beams. Nola, *it has to be Nola,* scarecrow-like in a voluminous black coat almost to her ankles, her piebald hair spiky in the wind, stood at the edge of the rock shelf, one hand gesticulating, her mouth moving in what must have been impassioned speech. Opposite her, a short broad figure swathed in a long pale quilted coat seemed to be equally aroused. The third figure, a man whom Elizabeth recognized as Lavinia's son Vance, stood a little behind his mother, clearly fascinated by the shouting match in progress.

Crouching behind the big rocks, Elizabeth listened. Snatches of speech came to her, tattered and shredded by the wind that swept along the river's gorge. "... *deserve to die ... no one will believe ... death of innocents ... foul and rotten underneath ...*" The accusations and recriminations whirred like bats through the night air.

Then Lavinia seemed to grow weary of the verbal battle. Gesturing to her son, she stepped back, like a tag-team partner bowing out. Obedient to his mother's command, Vance edged across the slick rock toward the still-ranting scarecrow that was Nola Barrett and seized her by the shoulders.

Instantly one bony knee shot up to catch him in the crotch, and Little Vance Holcombe fell gasping and moaning to the ground.

At once, Big Lavinia was at her son's side. Still keeping to the cloaking darkness, Elizabeth moved closer, in time to hear Big Lavinia bellow, "You bitch from hell, leave my baby alone!"

And now Nola was upon Lavinia, clawing at her face, dragging the big woman toward the water while shrieking in a banshee pitch, "Your baby? What about my granddaughter and *her* baby? What about the vile disease your son and his friends gave her—the disease that killed my precious Little Ricky?"

The two women swayed back and forth, locked together like lovers as they grappled at the water's edge.

And then Lavinia toppled, bringing Nola down with her as the pair continued to exchange blows.

"Vance, help me!" Lavinia croaked through the blood that was streaming from her nose and soaking the silky fabric of her coat. Her fur hat had been pulled off and her once carefully coiffed hair hung in limp hanks about her raddled face. "Help me! Get her off me!"

Elizabeth started forward, but without warning, strong arms were around her and a hand clapped over her mouth. A husky voice whispered in her ear, "I don't know who you are, but there's no need for you to interrupt the fun."

Painfully whimpering, Vance Holcombe was climbing to his feet as his mother continued to call for his help. Nola was up again, doggedly trying to pull Big Lavinia's great mass toward the edge.

"Stop her, Vance! Try to be a man for once!" howled Lavinia, beating at her one-time friend.

"Why don't you handle it, Mama, like you always handle things?" Vance was within reach of the two women now but strangely made no attempt to interfere.

Nola seemed oblivious to him, concentrating all her attention on the task of dragging a flailing, squirming Lavinia across the rock.

As Elizabeth struggled in the arms of her captor, she could not take her eyes from the scene being played out in the lurid illumination of the headlights. *Almost like slapstick comedy—but Nola's face—it's terrifying. I think she really must be crazy after all.*

The bone-white cheeks, the glittering eyes, the manic strength—all confirmed it. Miss Nola Barrett was doing her best to roll her benefactor of so many years into the icy turbulence only inches away.

Suddenly, Little Vance shot forward. Catching Nola off balance, he pushed her between the shoulder blades, launching her off the rock and into the boiling current.

"Nola!" Elizabeth flailed and tried to cry out but the brutal hand over her mouth muffled the protest. Elizabeth watched in horror as her friend bobbed, arms waving, briefly buoyed up by air trapped beneath her long coat. Nola's mouth opened in a silent scream. And then the current took her, sweeping her out of the narrow swath of light and downriver, into darkness.

# Chapter 50

## *The Bravest Thing*
### Thursday, December 28

On the rock ledge, Little Vance crouched at his mother's side. Lavinia, like an overturned turtle, was struggling to right herself. "Help me up, son, for pity's sake!"

Little Vance stood and extended a hand to his mother. Then, before she could grasp it, he put one foot against her back and rolled her off the edge of the rock, into the swirling waters.

"Good-bye, Mama. It's gonna sound so nice at your service, how you gave your life trying to rescue your old friend. Platt and I will both be proud."

Lavinia's face, surprise instantly succeeded by horror, stared up as she fought for purchase amid the rocks. One pudgy hand, diamonds flashing, clutched at the rock ledge.

Slowly, deliberately, Vance stepped on the trembling fingers. Again and again, until they released their hold on the ledge and slid away.

"You're full of surprises, Vance," Elizabeth's captor spoke, his words close to her ear as he trundled her, helpless in his pitiless grasp, out onto the ledge of rock. "So am I. Look what I have."

Vance turned a cold eye on them. "It's that woman who was with Spinner's sister. She'll have to go too." In the glare of the headlights his face was a nightmare mask, void of any emotion.

"Let's put her in one of these." The voice at her ear was amused and she was swung around to face the stack of waiting rubber rafts. "A nice touch, don't you think? This one and Miss Lavinia both drowning while trying to save poor crazy Miss Nola."

There was an arm around her neck now, cutting off her air, choking her. With her one free hand Elizabeth reached behind her, scratching, gouging. Long hair brushed her fingers and she grasped at it, clutching a few strands and yanking with all her might. There was a pained yelp and the pressure around her neck increased. Her last thoughts were of the hangman's noose.


A white Cadillac emerging from the dirt road along the river was an unexpected sight.

Phillip nudged the sheriff, who looked up from his notes. The ME had concluded her work and the remains had been removed from the old outhouse site. Phillip and Mackenzie Blaine were at the foot of the drive up to the old house, preparing to return to Phillip's car and call it a day—a long day.

"Why'd anyone want to take a big Caddy off road?"

"Probably kids, got Pop's car and going gallivantin'," was Blaine's disinterested answer.

The big car lurched onto the pavement and started up the road toward Dewell Hill. As its headlights swept across the sheriff's cruiser, it stopped abruptly, rocking with the impact of the brakes. The front doors flew open and two men leapt out and ran toward them.

"Sheriff Blaine, we just tried to put in a call for you but the reception—"

"What's the problem?"

"Oh, god! My mama . . . in the river! She's gone!"

Between gasping sobs, Little Vance explained, his friend supporting him with a sympathetic arm. "Miss Nola showed up at our house this afternoon. She was talking crazy and then she ran out and took off in her car. My mama was worried about her, so Hollis and I followed after Miss Nola. And Mama just had to come too. You know how close she and Miss Nola always were. Mama did everything for her."

Holcombe's face was white and his voice was unsteady but he continued on. "We followed her along that old road down there, honking and trying to get her to stop, but in her little car, she could go faster. When we caught up, Miss Nola had left her car and was standing at the edge of a big rock. Mama jumped out of the car and ran there and tried to reason with Miss Nola." Little Vance shook his head. "I can't—"

"Let me, Vance."

Phillip studied the second man. *He must have gotten into some briars, the way his face is all scratched. They both look done in.*

Hollis Noonan picked up the story. "The two ladies were on this big rock that stuck out into the river and it looked like they were hugging each other. Vance and I relaxed and thought it was all over and then either Miss Nola slipped off or jumped and Miss Lavinia went in too and then, out of nowhere, comes this woman with a long braid. She's yelling for Nola and when she sees her in the water, she grabs one of these little rafts that were there, pulled it to the water, climbed in and started off after them. Bravest thing I ever saw—and the stupidest. We yelled at her to paddle for shore while she could stop, but she was out of sight in no time. Of course there's not a chance in hell she'll get to them. Not sure how much chance she has either, if she makes it as far as Sill's Slough."

꒰ꜱ꒱

Her face was in the water and some of the water was in her nose. It was very, very cold. She seemed to be spinning in bitter, wet darkness.

Coughing and sneezing, Elizabeth tried to sit up, only to be flung down by a violent twist.

*Where am I?*

Her throat hurt and her head was aching. One of her hands was clenched in a fist, clenched so hard that it felt impossible to open. With the other hand, cold but still functioning, she explored her surroundings: an undulating rubbery floor, awash in several inches of icy water, a balloon-like wall, a saggy length of nylon rope.

*A raft. I'm in a bloody river raft!*

She was being borne along the raging white water, spinning like a pinball between treacherous rocks. Black trees loomed on either side of the dark river, but the sky overhead seemed to be growing lighter. Drenched and gasping, she clung to the wall of the raft, inwardly noting that it seemed much softer than it should, almost unpleasantly squishy.

*Oh, my god. It's losing air.*

A silver quarter-moon peeked above the trees on the right bank. As it crept higher, shedding cold light on her and the river, she saw, sliding back and forth in the water covering the floor of the raft, a paddle... *a blessed, blessed paddle. Now I have a chance—if I can get my other hand to work.*

The raft swirled and bucked in the rushing currents and Elizabeth, keeping low and bracing herself against the raft's side, tried to focus on her frozen hand, prying the cramped fingers open one by one. As the fingers reluctantly uncurled, she felt a wisp of hair plastered against her palm and, instantly, memory flooded back: Nola... Big Lavinia... and the other two.

With the hairs *so few... but enough,* pressed hard between

her thumb and forefinger, Elizabeth unzipped her jacket pocket and slowly, tediously, precisely, scraped the strands into the wet interior and pulled the zipper shut.

*Gotcha, you bastard! Gotcha!*

With grim determination she reached for the paddle.

# The Drovers' Road XVIII
## A Murder Tale

I come awake of a sudden, thinkin I had heard footsteps and the sound of the front door openin slow and careful. Maybe, thinks I, hit's Belle and Lydy slippin out to the barn. Iffen I can wake that ol' fool and take him to where they lay . . .

Not stoppin to dress, I pulled my shawl round me and went, barefoot and quiet as ary night moth, through the dogtrot and out to the porch. I quick looked toward the barn, thinkin to see the two of them movin along the path, but there weren't nothing but the moon on the snow and the black shapes of them ol' boxwoods. Just a dream, I thought and turned to go back to my warm bed. Hit was then I saw what lay on the path below the steps.

Looking back these fifty years and more, I marvel that I was so clearheaded and quick-thinkin in that dreadful moment. I stood there lookin at my daddy's body and at the long kitchen knife, silver sharp in the moonlight, and at the dark blood goutin slow from the dreadful cut acrost his neck—like a pig-killin, I thought, when they bleed the hog.

He weren't nothing to me, atter the way he'd done me afore all the company, and I have never yet in all these years shed ary tear for that old man. I just went on watchin the blood and thinking on what this meant for me and the babe I carried.

I knowed that Belle or Lydy or the two of them together must have done this thing. But hit was me who had quarreled with my daddy but a few hours since. Hit was me who'd hollered out be-

fore the sheriff that I'd serve him out. I made no doubt that they
would accuse me of comin upon my daddy, layin dead drunk and
helpless, and all in a passion, seizin up that knife and cuttin his
throat. And I might have done hit too, for he was hateful to me
and I was glad that he was gone. But someone had been afore me.

All this thinkin happened so fast that his blood was yet flowin
when I seen what I could do.

The house behind me was quiet. Hit seemed to me that the
murderer had likely gone back to bed and was layin there sleep-
less, waitin for someone to find the body in the mornin and then
point a finger at me. So I made a plan.

I hurried down the path to the river, pretendin someone had
aholt of my arm and was draggin me. I could see by the light of
the settin quarter-moon how the print of my bare feet showed
clear in the thin skift of snow on the path.

Oncet to the river, I turned and come back, takin long strides
and stayin close to the marks I had already left. Then I dried my
feet and crept into the house. I put on an ol' raggedy dress from
my scrap bag—a dress that wouldn't be missed. And then I went
and found Lydy's boots where he'd left them to dry by the fire.

Hit was so simple, I like to bust out laughin. With the boots
on my feet, I went to where my daddy lay and made sure to tread
in the blood and tromp all round, coverin my footprints. I
walked down to the river again, each step coverin the marks of
my bare feet returnin. I had ripped my night shift and dipped it in
the blood and now I flung it into a patch of brambles beside the
path. There was but the final set of tracks to make, back to the
house and up the steps, leavin bloody snow on the wood, and back
to the fireplace, where I took off the boots and left them for Lydy.

# Chapter 51

## *The Dakwa Waits*
### Thursday, December 28

It seemed to Elizabeth that she had been paddling for hours, always aiming for the nearer bank only to be thrust back, again and again, by the capricious, malicious current, almost to the middle of the river. She had negotiated several small rapids, just managing not to flip over. *But they're little ones—beginner stuff.* A low growl ahead reminded her. *That big scary one is somewhere up there—the one Ben and Amanda said the guides wouldn't run at night. Too dangerous.*

The ominous roar grew louder. In the distance ahead the moonlit river was a churning, turbulent field of solid white. The icy water sloshing in the bottom of the raft was inching higher and her frantic attempts to propel the clumsy, half-inflated craft toward the shore were continually countered by rapid streams flowing through the narrow channels among the rocks.

*This is fucking hopeless. There's no way I can get past that hydraulic up there. Ben said it takes a seasoned guide to run it at high water and I haven't a clue what I'm doing. If I overturn, I'll be sucked under, and that'll be the end of it.*

"A hollow under there the size of a car," the guide had said last summer, before carefully maneuvering the raft Elizabeth and Phillip were in through a series of rapid drops bounded on either side by protruding rocks. "Divers went down there a while back when there was an accident—some fool in a kayak. No PFD, no helmet, no experience—what can you expect?"

No PFD—personal flotation device. She remembered the raft trip last summer, how in a deceptively calm section of the river, the guide had allowed them overboard to experience the currents. "You won't be able to swim," he had warned. "What you want to do is lay back flat with your feet up and pointed downstream. Your PFD—your life vest—will support you. Remember, feet *up* and downstream—just go with it."

It had been blissful—being carried along effortlessly, enjoying the cold water on a hot day. And then the powerful hands of the guide, grabbing her by the shoulders of her life vest and whisking her magically back to the safety of the raft before the coming rapids.

The coming rapids—no life vest. *And if somehow I managed to get to shore, I'd be soaking wet, in the middle of the woods, in December. How long before hypothermia sets in?*

A cloud slid over the face of the moon, momentarily turning the river before her to unfathomable darkness—to a nothingness down which she was dashing as in some horrible nightmare. The roar ahead was louder still.

"That's the Dakwa, hungry for his dinner," the guide had said, part of the weary patter handed down from one guide to another and trotted out for the tourists year after year in hopes of eliciting tips at the end of the day. "Yep, Mr. Dakwa's belly's growlin', for sure."

A feeling of great weariness came over her. She was still mechanically paddling, still trying to propel the semi-inflated raft toward the nearer shore, but it was as if her mind was no longer engaged. Thoughts of surrender, of letting go, of giving herself to the river, of the peace that passeth understanding—

"NOOO!" she yelled, breaking the spell that the

constant hypnotic roar of the rapids had cast. "No, goddammit! If I don't make it, those murdering bastards will
get away!"

Digging her paddle into the water with renewed energy,
she turned her head to the nearer shore, trying desperately
to make out the outline of the trees against the sky.
Blackness reigned.

And then, in the midst of the black, too low, far, far too
low to be a star, shone a small yellow light. At the same moment, the moon emerged from the clouds, bathing the river
in its radiance and revealing close at hand a line of rocks
stretching almost to the riverbank.

With one last furious effort, she sank the paddle's blade
into the water, digging hard and fast. The raft inched closer
to the rocks, its unwieldy bulk veering and yawing in the
current.

It happened so quickly—she hadn't stopped to consider,
not even a *one, two, three, now or never* had crossed her
mind. One minute she was in the raft, reaching out to catch
hold of the edge of the nearest rock, and the next she was
underwater, her feet swept from under her and her body
falling forward, caught in the inexorable grasp of the river.

*Oh, god, I don't want to drown.* The water was so cold, so
swift. She fought to bring her feet back under her and
pawed wildly, trying to get her head above the surface.

*I have to breathe!* But still the black river held her in
its cold embrace. The memory of Nola—open-mouthed as
the water took her—flashed across Elizabeth's fading consciousness. For one nightmare moment the white face stared
at her, the pale lips moved, and a thin, bloodless hand beckoned.

*No! I won't!* Driven by mindless terror, Elizabeth thrashed
against the current, her lungs burning. *I have to breathe!*
Her flailing legs knocked against something hard; her
boots slipped down its smooth length. Frantically she tried
to catch hold of it, a miraculous, solid *it* in this eternity of

rushing waters. With a mighty twist of her body, she heaved herself forward.

A tree limb, a blessed tree limb, its rough bark slimy with long immersion. She clutched at it with both hands and *oh, mercy of mercies* it held firm, lodged by the water's force into a crevice in the rocks. She hauled herself along it till her head broke the surface and at last she could breathe. Clinging to the sturdy branch, her lungs gulping down icy air, Elizabeth looked downriver, just in time to see her abandoned raft tossed into the air.

Shuddering with cold and adrenaline, she began the tedious journey to the shore, dragging herself along the limb as the river tugged at her body—trying to break her hold, trying to win her back.

*I thought there was a light.*

The moon revealed only dark woods. Elizabeth inched her way through the frigid water to the cluster of rocks where the limb was wedged. Here, the river was only waist-high, but the current was so strong that she had to cling to the rocks to avoid being knocked down. Her hands were numb with cold and it grew increasingly difficult to hold on.

Creeping painfully along the slippery rocks, at last she reached a shelf—a slab of stone with less than a foot of water washing gently over it. With a ragged sob of relief, she dragged her weary, bruised body onto it and crawled to the rocky shore.

"Stand up, Elizabeth. Stand up and keep moving." Her voice was a hoarse whisper in the cold moon-brushed night, but her stubborn body obeyed the command. She forced herself upright and began to limp toward the dark trees.

*I thought there was a light.*

# Chapter 52

## *A Light in the Woods*
### Thursday, December 28

Moonbeams danced and shimmered through the bare branches above her head, confusing her sense of direction. *If I keep my back to the river and just go on walking, I'll hit the highway... eventually. But I have to keep moving.*

Elizabeth's teeth were chattering and her sodden boots felt like lumps of lead around the lumps of ice that were her feet. Already the sound of the river was growing fainter. *And if I can't hear it behind me, I could walk in circles.*

*I thought there was a light.*

Her soaking jacket weighed heavy on her body, a film of ice beginning to glaze its surface. She pulled off the sopping garment and tried to squeeze some of the water from it before thrusting her arms back into its icy embrace. Sitting down to remove her boots and wring out her socks seemed like a good idea, but she knew that once down, there was a strong possibility she wouldn't be able to get back up. Stifling a sob, she plunged blindly into the deep woods.

*I thought there was a light.*

The going was rocky and steep and the twisted tree roots over which she clambered made eerie patterns in such faint luminescence as sifted through the lacy winter branches. Only the knowledge that she must keep moving or die impelled her on into the unknown darkness. *Left, right, left, right, boots, boots, boots, boots, moving up and down again,* she drove her aching body forward.

And there was a light.

Its soft yellow glow beckoned from between two ancient trees, and Elizabeth broke into an awkward run, staggering and slipping on the frozen earth. The light was warmth, someone to help her, someone to do the thinking she was finding increasingly difficult.

A hunter or a camper? Who would be out on a frigid winter night? She thudded doggedly on. *Hunter, camper, soldier, sailor, tinker, tailor, it doesn't fucking matter. Just let it be someone who can get me out of here before I lie down and freeze to death.* She fought her way toward the beam, stumbling through the undergrowth, ignoring the brambles that slapped her face and pulled at her freezing clothes. The light burned steadily.

Then there was the cloying smell of boxwoods as she pushed through a mass of brambles into a clearing. At the farther edge of the open ground sat a small stone house, surrounded by the black shapes of ancient boxwoods. In its single window, a candle burned.

Summoning the last of her strength, Elizabeth plodded on numb feet toward this unexpected apparition. There were no more questions, only the overwhelming desire to be inside and near that light.

"Hello!" she tried to call out to make her presence known, but her voice failed her, producing only a strangled whisper. She raised a fist to knock on the rough wooden door, and it swung open at her first touch. Hesitating on the doorstep, she managed to croak out another weak "Hello?" and then, receiving no answer, stepped inside.

The caressing warmth of the fire burning in the stone fireplace enveloped her like a mother's loving embrace, and she crossed the puncheon floor in three steps to stand shivering on the hearth. Painfully, she began to pull off her frozen clothing.

There was no one in the tiny room. In one corner a wooden bedstead with a sagging mattress was piled with blankets, and she pulled one off to use as a towel. When she had restored the circulation to her hands and feet and dried herself as well as possible, she wrapped a second blanket around her and added another log to the fire. She sank into a rustic chair by the hearth and let the warmth sweep over her till, at last, the shivering stopped and she dozed, head nodding on her chest.

An enticing smell penetrated her consciousness and her head jerked up. *I was dreaming about beef stew. But I must have just dozed for a minute—that log I put on isn't even burning good yet.*

Still half asleep, she stood, noting the innumerable bruises, scrapes, and scratches on her arms and legs. The candle on the windowsill caught her eye, and she limped over to examine it. *Who would go off and leave a candle and a fire burning?*

A small wooden table sat beneath the window, and she stared in amazement. *Was that there when I came in?* A brown earthenware bowl, filled with a steaming stew, lay before her. So too did a wooden spoon and a dented metal cup, brimming with some amber liquid. A scent of flowers and honey hung in the air, deliciously entwined with the savory aroma of meat and onions.

*I'd better eat that before I wake up and it's gone.* The illogic of the thought almost made her laugh, but she seated herself at the table and plunged the spoon into the stew. In the window the candle burned steadily, sending out the sweet fragrance of beeswax.

The last gratifying, unctuous spoonful of the food was gone, and, still in a waking dream, she reached for the cup and sniffed at the contents—a rich mix of honey and alcohol. One sip and then another. *It must be honey wine—mead or, what was the old name—metheglin? Who was telling me about that not long ago?*

She swallowed the last of the sweet, strong drink, feeling its warming tendrils creeping through every fiber of her weary body. Her head swam with the warmth and the wine, and, happily overcome, she stood and lurched toward the bed.

*I've sat in the chair and eaten the food. As I seem to have fallen into a fairy tale, I might as well sleep in the bed.*

Unwrapping the blanket from her body, she spread it over the bed, then slid under the covers, falling instantly and gratefully asleep to dream of a black bear at the door that reared up and, shifting shape, became a smiling dark woman with flowers in her hair.

# Chapter 53

# *Footprints in the Snow*
## Friday, December 29

She woke to the smell of herbs and honey and flowers and the rough scratch of wool against her naked body. She lay still, waiting for something to make sense.

And then the memory of the raft and the river, the icy water, the light in the woods swept over her. *But I'm here, wherever here is. I'm alive.*

Opening one cautious eye, she peeked from beneath the gray blanket that she had pulled up over her head. A square of pale light—a single window, a table and a chair, a fireplace filled with ashes, a few simple shelves with crockery and tin cups. No sign of electricity, no sign of a phone. The air was frigid and her warm breath wreathed above her.

*How did I find this place? It must be someone's fishing camp. And why can't I remember anything?*

Before the cold fireplace, two ladder-back chairs were hung with her various garments, and her boots lay on their sides as if to dry in front of the nonexistent fire. *Obviously I took my clothes off. And had the sense to spread them out to dry. Did I build a fire?*

She rolled out of the bed, pulling the top blanket around her. The floor was icy cold as she padded over to retrieve her clothing, dreading the fact of the still-wet fabric against her body.

*But it's all dry! Or almost dry. I* must *have built a fire. But I can't remember . . .*

She dressed hurriedly, suddenly thinking of her family, of Phillip—they were probably frantic with worry. *I have to get to the highway—I can flag down someone, maybe they'll have a cell phone.*

The memory of how she had come to be in the river flooded her mind in an instant, vivid flashback. *Nola. Oh, god, Nola! And Big Lavinia . . .*

She pushed the dreadful pictures aside to concentrate on getting her feet into her still-damp boots. *Just get out to the road.*

In the back of her mind an echo whispered, *I thought there was a light,* and she glanced around the little room, in search of an explanation for the vague memory, already dreamlike, fading in the light of day. *No electricity, just a couple of kerosene lamps.* On the broad windowsill, a puddle of dried yellowish wax seemed to indicate the remains of a candle.

*Get going. You have no idea how long it'll take. But if this is someone's fish camp, there must be a road.*

It was with a strange reluctance that she opened the heavy door and stepped out into the pale morning light. *This little stone house probably saved my life. I was absolutely at the end of my strength last night but now—it's amazing, I feel wonderful—not even hungry.*

Pulling the door shut behind her, she stood on the broad flat rock that served as a doorstep and surveyed her surroundings. Far off through the trees, she thought she could glimpse the sparkle of sun on the river, though no sound of the rapids could be heard. A thin coating of snow lay on the ground, already beginning to melt as the sun rose higher.

Elizabeth blinked and wiped her eyes. A trail of footprints led from the clearing to the step where she stood.

*But . . . bare feet? Did I take off my boots and walk through the snow barefoot?*

She moved toward a particularly well defined print and turned to place her boot within it. *Within it.* The foot that had made the print was both wider and longer than her own.

Then she heard the characteristic rattle of a diesel truck, just beyond the house. With a final puzzled glance at the footprint, now little more than an ill-defined oval smear, she hurried around to the back of the stone house.

A shed, its bright lumber suggesting recent construction, and a narrow, lightly graveled road met her eyes. And a shiny red truck, making its majestic way toward her.

It rolled to a stop and a husky young man in brown insulated coveralls, an ear-flapped furry cap on his head, jumped out.

"Any chance you might be Miz Elizabeth Goodweather?" he called.

Her wide grin and vigorous nod answered his question, and he bounded to her, grabbed her hand, and shook it energetically.

"Praise the Lord, they thought you was drownded. They's search parties out fer you since first light. That's my daddy's fish camp there, so I said as how I'd search this part of the shore."

Restraining an impulse to hug the big man, Elizabeth beamed at him. "I'm so glad to see you—but tell me, there were two other women in the river. Have they . . . are they . . . ?"

He dealt with her question kindly, laying a big hand on her shoulder. "Ma'am, I s'pose they'll find 'em sooner or later. But I reckon more'n one miracle's too much to expect."

As they jolted down the gravel road, her rescuer slapped his forehead. "Doggone it, I told them River Runners folks I'd git their beacon for them and here I done gone and forgot."

And then they were on the highway, heading for the sheriff's department. Her rescuer—"Buddy Mace, ma'am"—looked at her curiously. "You sleep all right last night?"

When she assured him that she had, Buddy raised his eyebrows. "Reason I asked, my daddy always swears that place is haunted." He paused, considering. "No, that ain't the way of it. Not to say haunted, but more, he says, like there's spirits there—good ones."

Buddy's eyes stayed on the road. "Now I don't put no credit in such but I'll tell you a quare thing. My daddy used to be a real rip-roarer and he give my mommy a bad time ever since I can remember. But atter he heired this place and started spending time at the fish camp, seemed like he was more at peace with hisself. He'd come home from here with a string of fish and, iffen it was summer, he'd have picked some flowers for our mommy—they's a world of flowers grows around that place. Hit was oncet a part of one of them old stands, and they say, back before the War Between the States, hit was owned by some quare dark people. But they pulled up stakes and left, is what I heard."

# The Drovers' Road XIX
## The Widow Barrett

All these years of waitin and the house at Gudger's Stand is still held by Belle and Lydy's line, whilst I scratch out a livin at Dewell Hill. At least Belle ain't here no more to queen it over folks, for she died giving birth. Hit was a boy and she let on my daddy had fathered him, so it's that boy now holds title to Gudger's Stand, though he carries his stepdaddy's name of Revis. His birthin was hard with a long dry labor and Belle's death in a welter of blood at the end. They say she called down curses on many a one and that she bowed up like a cat and spat in the preacher's eye when he come to offer comfort.

And I have a new name, for Luellen Gudger is the poor girl betrayed and murdered by the wicked drover boy. They even have a song about it. I fear Luellen must remain dead lest the true events of that awful night come out. But my girl and her girl know the right of hit. They are sworn to keep the memory of our claim to that land alive.

It might have been better, I sometimes think, to have cut loose from here and go west with Mariah and her Ish. When the war started, folks begun to turn against the Flores and such-like dark folk. Some set about the story that they was escaped slaves. There was mutterin against them, livin on their own land and runnin an inn like as if they was white.

Then come a day when a traveler offered a terrible insult to Mariah and Ish struck him down, never to rise again. No one *saw, for the man had accosted Mariah in her house. But we feared it would come to light and we knowed what would be the outcome. That night, we gave his body to the river and we all slipped away, me and my baby Lyda and Ish and Mariah with all the household plunder they could load on their old wagon. Mariah wept bitter tears, to leave her tidy stone house and her flowers and her bees, and vowed that someday she would surely return.*

*By morning we was in Tennessee where no one knowed of any of us. That's when I became the Widow Barrett, a dead soldier's wife travelin with her babe and her two faithful slaves, goin to her daddy's home in Kentucky. We kept movin along, always west and north for it was our purpose to get to Illinois where there wasn't no slaves.*

*A long and hateful journey but the best deed I have done. When we parted at the great river, our tears flowed together and they begged me to come with them for they purposed to travel on, through the Free States, to the Far West.*

*But hit seemed to me then, as hit seems to me now, that a fine cord binds me and, was I to roam, hit would always be there, pullin at me, haulin me back. Hit's a slender cord, spun of black hate, red blood, and bitter betrayal, and it binds me and mine to the house at Gudger's Stand for all time.*

# Chapter 54

## *The Scene in the Library*
### Saturday, December 30

I f I live to be a hundred, I don't think I'll ever have a
happier moment than when I saw you getting out of
that big red truck."

Phillip pulled Elizabeth closer to him on the sofa. "And
the second happiest might just be the memory of the look
on Noonan and Holcombe's faces when *they* saw you.
Holcombe had been blubbering about his darling mama
and how would he survive without her and what a saint she
was, boo hoo. And then there's Noonan: the strong, take-
charge guy, on his cell phone or his—what are those things
called—Boysenberries? Flipping that damn hair out of his
face every few minutes and calling me *sir* all the damn
time—and here you come. God*damn* but those two saw
their future take a radical change the minute you showed
up! And then you start talking, and you show Mac that hair
you had in your pocket, and they're falling over themselves
to incriminate each other. I tell you, Lizabeth, it's going to
be a pleasure seeing those two go to jail."

He looked at her and she nodded and smiled sleepily,
then snuggled closer, laid her head on his shoulder, and
drifted off to sleep.

*And what would it have done to my life if you hadn't made it?*
With one careful finger he traced her eyebrows, dark and

decided with a sprinkling of silver hairs beginning to show, her small, neat ears, the line of her chin, the sweet curve of her parted lips. *I'm lucky to have her back ... and, by god, I'll quit making conditions. If she decides marriage isn't what she wants, then I'll take whatever I can have. But I don't want to lose this woman, ever.*

"Hey, Phillip, is Mum asleep *again?*"

Laurel and Rosemary had finished the dinner dishes and were taking their places on the little love seat. They both looked at him expectantly.

"She's plumb wore out, as my aunt Omie would say. After everything that happened to her, she had to spend a good part of yesterday explaining to Mac exactly what went down. And losing her friend like that—there's an emotional tiredness too."

Laurel winked. "Pretty sensitive for a cop—ex-cop— whatever you are."

Phillip nodded, then slid Elizabeth's braid free and laid it gently over her shoulder. "Soon to be a cop again—I start next month working for Mackenzie."

The sisters looked at each other and an unspoken communication passed between them. Then Rosemary asked softly, "Mum said she thought someone was overmedicating Nola—did that come out in all this incriminating I heard you say those two murderers were doing?"

"Matter of fact, it did. They dragged in Pritchard Morton's name—the doctor whose brother supposedly shot himself. They said Pritchard was the one supplying Big Lavinia with the pills and Big Lavinia was paying an aide to give Nola a lot more than she should have. Guaranteed to keep Nola confused and physically uncoordinated."

"Why? Why were they drugging her?"

"Once Lavinia knew that Tracy, Nola's supposed niece, wanted to press charges about the rape, I think she was scared Nola would start talking too and then her precious Little Vance would be in danger. I think Lavinia figured if they could keep Nola confused and crazy, they could eventually get rid of her with no suspicion—crazy old lady in a nursing home dies—friendly doctor around to sign the death certificate..."

"But why did Nola jump in the first place?" Rosemary wanted to know. "Why try to kill herself?"

"What Tracy told us, when we finally got her in and heard the whole story, was that Nola blamed herself for two deaths—Randall Revis—"

"I thought those *guys* killed Revis, so as not to have to pay any more blackmail."

Phillip nodded. "Yeah, Revis knew about the rape and was bleeding the Bad Boyz. But according to Little Vance, it was Noonan did all the killing: Noonan killed Revis because he didn't want to pay blackmail the rest of his life; Noonan killed Spinner because Spinner was going to finger all of them in the rape; and Noonan killed Pastor Morton because Morton at a rather late date developed a conscience and wanted to confess his sins to the authorities. Unfortunately, Pastor Morton's sins were so linked to Noonan's that Noonan couldn't let him talk."

"What about the other girl?" Laurel asked. "The one with the weird name."

"Bam-Bam? According to Little Vance, *her* death was an accident. Noonan got a little rough during sex and when she couldn't be revived, he dumped the body in the old outhouse and torched it. Evidently the other Bad Boyz knew about it—"

"But why did Nola feel guilty about Revis?"

"I can answer that." Elizabeth's eyes opened and she yawned. "I've always wanted to be part of one of those scenes where they sit around in a library at the end of a mystery and tie up loose ends. And here I'm sleeping through it...." She yawned again and sat up straight. "I think, from something Nola said, back when she was in the nursing home and mostly talking cryptic stuff, that she must have come in on the old man shortly after Noonan had beat his head in. Maybe Revis was still alive or maybe she *believed* he was still alive. In any event, she put a pillow over his face and waited." Elizabeth shuddered. "I thought of Nola as the sanest of women. But she was obsessed with the owner-ship of that property. There was a genealogy on her lap-top—it all ties in with that ballad about Lydy Goforth. . . ."

"Mum, did Nola actually have a claim to Gudger's Stand? Was the old man really her uncle?"

Elizabeth shook her head. "No. That was another thing that was in the genealogy. Evidently Nola's mother decided on a really practical approach to get the property back to their side of the family." A yawn overwhelmed her. "It's complicated—I'll print out the family tree later—but that horrible old man was Nola's father."

She yawned again and put her head back on Phillip's shoulder. As her eyes closed, she mumbled, "And the other reason . . . Little Ricky . . . tell them about . . . spinach . . ." A deep sigh escaped her and Elizabeth was asleep again.

"Spinach?" Rosemary's eyebrows were raised. "What *is* she talking about?"

Phillip settled Elizabeth more comfortably against his arm. Then he said, "That's the heartbreaker. The catalyst for all of this, the thing that sent Miss Barrett mad, was the death of her great-grandson—"

"Nephew." An academic precision was evident in Rose-mary's polite correction but Phillip shook his head firmly.

"Nope, Lizabeth found all this in that genealogy she was talking about. Tracy's mother was Lenore—Miss Nola's illegitimate child, born when Nola was in college. Nola and her mother managed to pass the child off as Nola's mother's and Lenore grew up believing she was Nola's sis-ter. That makes Tracy Nola's granddaughter—and Tracy was another illegitimate child, for what it's worth."

His face grew somber as he told the story. "So here's Tracy, victim of a violent gang rape in '95. She's sent away to boarding school and then to nursing school, all with the proceeds of the money Lavinia's paying Nola to keep quiet about the rape. Somewhere in this time, Lenore, Nola's daughter and Tracy's mom, dies and Nola's all alone, with plenty of time to think about what a rotten deal life has handed her.

"Now, fast-forward to 2002. Seven years after that night in the bus, Tracy has let herself trust a man. She and Stone move in together. He's the first and the only man she's been with since the rape. Things are going good and when she gets pregnant they're both ecstatic. And back home, Nola's thrilled—buying toys and clothes and books it'll take years for this baby, her great-grandson, to be old enough for.

"And when the little boy's born, it's all so wonderful, but then after about a year and a half, the baby stops growing and stops gaining weight. The doctors run a million tests and no one can figure out what's wrong till some bright intern thinks of testing for HIV.

"And that's it—Little Ricky has HIV. They test Tracy and so does she. She just hasn't had any symptoms yet. They test Stone and he's clean. That's when Tracy finally tells about the rape. Well, if only they'd known, there would have been prenatal testing but...

"So Tracy, who's carrying a real load of guilt now, decides to be the best mother in the world to this sick little boy. He's prone to colds, which can easily lead to potentially fatal pneumonia, so she's a demon with the vitamin C. He's severely immune-compromised, so she's Mrs. Clean incarnate; and he's generally puny, so she gets into health food, organic food, whole foods, natural foods, raw foods—"

Rosemary lifted a stunned face. "I see where this is going. When did Little Ricky die?"

"Back in September. He had just learned to enjoy the green smoothies his mother concocted to build his strength—pineapple, papaya, apples, and—"

"And raw spinach," Rosemary said softly. "The *E. coli*

outbreak. Little Ricky was one of the victims. It was the knowledge that her insistence on silence had probably caused her great-grandson's death that turned Miss Barrett into a madwoman."

"We brought in those two fellas who used to work for Big Lavinia this mornin'. Asked about a few things and among others, they admitted setting the fire at the stand. They said they'd been sent to find some little green-backed books and when they couldn't find them and saw what a mess they'd made, they decided to burn the stand down to cover up what they'd done." The sheriff looked at some papers on his desk and pulled one out. "Not the brightest matches in the box, ol' Arval and Marval. I told you that wasn't a professional job."

"How about the Hummer? They did a better job there."

"Nope, not them." Blaine passed a paper over to Phillip. "Manifesto of an ecoterrorist group committed to destruction of outsize SUVs. They're claiming responsibility."

The sheriff leaned back in his chair and swung his feet up on his desk. A smug smile tugged at the corners of his mouth. "By the way, Hawk, I've done a little early spring-cleaning at the department. A few of the holdovers from the previous sheriff are on their way out—I finally caught them in some questionable dealings—and praise god, Miss Orinda and her gut are retiring!"

"I thought you said she'd never retire."

"Well, she changed her mind." The smile widened. "I set a little trap for her—left some confidential paperwork about Arval and Marval, the blunder boys, on my desk and locked my office door. Told Miss Orinda I'd be gone for a couple of hours and left. I gave it a few minutes, then slipped back in and caught her in my office, sitting at my desk and going through those papers. When I confronted her she broke down—said she just wanted to protect Big

Lavinia's memory, that she's always done her best for the Holcombes.

"And that's why she stole Tracy's letter about the rape—*she's* the mole I was worrying about, Hawk. With Miss Orinda gone, we can all breathe easy." A delighted grin split Mackenzie's face. "I couldn't ask for a better way to start the New Year."

# Chapter 55

## *Breaking Up Christmas*
### Sunday, December 31

Breaking up Christmas" was what Elizabeth had always called it, after a fiddle tune of the same name, and from the first years of her marriage she had inevitably honored her grandmother's tradition of taking down the tree on New Year's Eve. "Bad luck to have it up in the New Year," Gramma had said as the tree went out the door and she turned to the preparation of collard greens, "to put greenbacks in your pocket," and black-eyed peas and hog jowl—all said to bring good luck.

*Well, Gramma, the black-eyed peas are simmering and we're taking the tree down.* Elizabeth circled the tall fir, carefully removing the few glass ornaments that had been her mother's, wrapping them in tissue, and restoring them to their compartmented boxes. Laurel, high on a ladder, was divesting the upper branches of their decorations and passing them down to Rosemary.

"It's like running a movie backwards," Laurel exclaimed. "A few weeks ago we pulled all this stuff out and"—she stretched to unmoor the rag doll angel from the topmost branch—"and now we're putting it back. And we do the same thing every year, but somehow it's not boring. It's more...more..." She paused, looking at the rag doll, whose prim mouth and lowered eyes seemed to suggest a secret. "... more *affirming*, if that's the word I want."

"The wheel of the year," Rosemary offered. "Always turning, the same thing coming around at the same time."

"And we always have the collards and the stuff for New Year's—it's like continuity with the past—with your Gramma, Mum. I never even knew her, but she's real to me because we keep her traditions."

Elizabeth looked around her shabby, beloved living room: inherited furniture *perhaps "passed-down" would be more accurate*, decorated with inherited scratches and nicks to which were added the wear and tear of her own family. The gnawed ends of the rockers on Gramma's sewing chair, *Dinah did that almost twenty years ago*, the burn on the dining table where Laurel had set down a hot skillet— everything told the story of their family.

And suddenly she thought of Amanda, beautiful, distant Amanda, alienated from her parents for their treatment of her beloved brother. *She has no family—unless she chooses to be part of ours. But she may be too deeply wounded. All she had was the memory of Spinner and now that memory is badly tarnished.*

"Have you girls talked to Amanda about her brother? It's bad enough that it seems almost certain those were his bones in the silo. But Tracy's accusation—that Spinner knowingly infected her with AIDS as well as setting her up for the rape—I know it must have hit Amanda hard. She's idolized her brother her whole life."

Laurel's face was serious. "Amanda's gone all quiet and withdrawn; even Ben isn't having much luck getting her to talk."

Finally all the decorations were in their boxes and the boxes were returned to the trunk. The tree had been dragged from the house to await use in a bonfire, and most *never all* of the fallen needles had been swept or vacuumed up. And the girls had taken the dogs on a hike to the top of the mountain.

The corner where the tree had been looked woefully bare, and Elizabeth pondered it thoughtfully. *Maybe I could find something to put there on the end of the table.*

She went to rummage in the closet where she kept seasonal odds and ends. A tall white vase caught her eye. *That would work, filled with evergreens* and she stretched to catch hold of it. As she pulled the vase down from the shelf, it dislodged a gourd she had decorated years ago. The big gourd fell, making a sharp *crack* as it struck the floor.

It was broken beyond repair. *It's just taking up space in the closet; toss it, Elizabeth.* But she hesitated, remembering the tedious chore of cleaning the basketball-sized globe to prepare its surface for the paint, scraping out the plump, dry seeds and papery membranes from the interior. Her fingers traced the incised lines of the mountains around the gourd's fat circumference and then the raptor soaring above the peaks. The acrid smell as her wood-burning tool bit into the gourd's smooth tan skin, the tiny sting of smoke in her eyes—it all came back to her.

*It's hard to just throw out something I worked so hard on*— she cradled the object in both hands, noting the thinness of the gourd's shell and the jagged crack that parted the sky and just touched the etched mountain rim of this little world. *What's that thing I read? Some people are process-oriented—getting all their enjoyment from the doing of a thing— while others are driven by the desire for the finished product. Well, I enjoyed the process of this for sure, and the product as well. But now . . .*

With sudden decision Elizabeth moved for the fireplace. The fire had subsided to coals. *This'll be better than putting it in the trash—more suitable, somehow.* With a wry smile at her own silliness, she opened the glass door, laid the broken gourd on the bed of glowing red coals, and sat down on the hearth to watch.

For a moment, nothing happened. Then transparent orange-and-blue flames appeared, licking at the base of the gourd. Elizabeth leaned closer, enthralled by the sight. Now, with a sigh, a soft *pumph* of sound, there was fire inside the hollow sphere, and a faint smell, fleetingly reminiscent of cooking squash, wafted toward her, only to disappear as the gourd was engulfed in flames.

The disfiguring crack widened, revealing the interior inferno. *This is beautiful!* she thought, as half of the gourd, now only a brittle charcoal shell, collapsed, leaving a black jagged wall pointing upward. This lingered, then, as part fell away, assumed a new shape.

*It looked like an Indian . . . and then like a pointing hand . . . and now it's a hanging man. You could use this, like tea leaves, to read omens. It doesn't matter what means you use—tea leaves, clouds, animal entrails—all you're really doing is freeing your subconscious to work.*

She was lost in thought, still staring into the fireplace, now returned to a slumbering bed of ashy coals, when Phillip came into the room.

"Lizabeth? You okay?"

With a start, she jerked back to the here and now. "I'm fine. I was just . . . freeing my subconscious."

*The hanging man. A sign of ill omen. Maybe that's why I always hated those damn baby dolls, hanging on the porch at the stand house. At least they're not there anymore.*

With a start, she remembered just where they were—in the bottom of her big, rarely used shoulder bag. *I was thinking about burying them but maybe that's a bit . . . a bit dramatic. What if I wrapped them up and put them in the trash? That way I wouldn't have to see their creepy little hands waving at me.*

As she pulled the pinkly obscene creatures from the bag, she noticed that the head of one was screwed round so as almost to face backward, giving the creature a particularly horrible, demonic look. On her way to the kitchen and the garbage pail, she fiddled with the head, trying to put it right.

It fell off in her hands and she made an involuntary sound of disgust.

"What *are* you doing to that baby doll, Miz Goodweather?" Phillip asked, watching with amusement.

Elizabeth didn't reply but stood looking into the interior of the headless toy.

"There's something in here," she said at last. "Paper."

A sheet of paper, folded and refolded, was wedged into the chest of the doll. She pulled it out, unfolded it, and scanned its contents.

"It's a letter from Spinner to Tracy, dated December 11, 1995."

> "*Dear Tracy,*
>
> *Please believe me that I didn't mean for that to happen—all the others. It was Hollis came looking for me and found you and me and then he called Vance and the Mortons. I wasn't part of it—what happened. Hollis made me stay and watch. He said it would make a man of me but I think it made me see that if that was being a man, I was happier to be what I am. I left town as soon as I knew you were safe—I told the Cat Man where you were and he promised to go get you out. If I'd been braver—but I wasn't.*
>
> *I'm back in Ransom now and I've tried to find out where you've gone but no one will tell me. Your uncle has promised to forward this letter and I've told him how important it is that you get it right away.*
>
> *Because this is the terrible thing I have to tell you—*"

Elizabeth looked up at Phillip, her eyes brimming. "He's writing to tell her that he's just found out he has AIDS and that she should go get checked right away."

"And Revis just kept the letter—maybe thinking to use it for more blackmail. God, what a sick—"

"Did you see the part at the bottom, where he tells Tracy about his little sister and how much he loves her and how afraid he is of losing her love because of being gay and having AIDS?"

Elizabeth stood and headed for the back door and the path to Ben's cabin. "I think we need to let Amanda see this letter—and then let Tracy know about it too."

When Elizabeth returned from the cabin, her face was shining. "Do you know what Amanda said, Phillip? She said, 'You've given me back my brother.'"

# Chapter 56

## *New Year's Eve ... with Distant Fireworks*
### Sunday, December 31, and Monday, January 1

Have you thought about it, Lizabeth?"
Bundled against the freezing temperature of the clear, windless night, Elizabeth and Phillip stood side by side at the porch railing. Behind them the rich strains of Yo-Yo Ma's cello reached out to enfold them in the caressing embrace of a Bach composition. In the distance beyond the river, a fireworks display was in progress, and the higher-flying rockets were gloriously visible. At that moment a glowing ball of cherry red soared heavenward, then opened into a golden-ribbed umbrella that released a shower of tiny red and green stars.

"Yes, I have—almost constantly."

Without taking his eyes from the sky, Phillip said, "I'd really like to start this year by marrying you, Elizabeth. But if you've decided it's not what you want, then we can go on like we are. If what you're getting ready to tell me is no, I'll accept that."

Elizabeth leaned against him. "Phillip, my love, I made up my mind, that day on Max Patch. Somehow, up there, I saw how ridiculous all my doubting and hesitating was.

And I haven't changed my mind. I want to be your wife—
for better or for worse, and all the rest."

The cello suite that had surrounded them ended and the
speakers hanging on the porch gave a little cough, then
slipped into a doleful mountain ballad.

*"Don't give your heart to nary man . . . "* The singer's voice
was raw with pain and longing.

Elizabeth turned a rueful face toward the speakers. "I
didn't know *that* was on the changer. Hardly appropriate
for the moment. She's so sad and I'm so happy."

"Happy's good." Phillip put his arms around her. "You
make me happy, Lizabeth Goodweather."

They stood at the porch railing, arms snug around each
other, and watched as the fireworks display in the distance
reached its climax.

Behind them in the empty house the telephone rang.
One, two, three, the muffled sound was lost in the mournful song that drifted on the cold air of the dying year.

*". . . for men ain't what . . . they oftimes seem . . . "* the singer
warned.

In the little office, the answering machine clicked on.
*"This is Full Circle Farm. Leave us a message."*

*"Hello, Elizabeth. It's Aunt Dodie. I thought it would be fun
to wish you a Happy New Year but I expect you're out at a party
or something. It gets harder and harder for me to stay awake till
midnight, but I've done it since I was a child, and just because
I'm eighty-three I see no reason to give in and go to bed. But the
television's so dull and I didn't feel like reading, so I decided to
pass the time by cleaning out the old gentleman's desk. It hadn't
been touched since he died and that would be—well, let me see,
he passed away back in '75.*

*"And here it is just a few minutes till ought-seven and in all
that time I haven't been able to bring myself to disturb the big old
rolltop desk in his study. Of course, all our business matters were
in the other desk, you know the one I mean, that tall glass-fronted*

*secretary in the parlor. The rolltop desk was where he kept his personal correspondence and the notes for the memoirs of his years in the Navy he said he was working on, though I'm well aware that most of the time he was in the den he was napping or reading those Hornblower novels. Poor dear, I know that time hung heavy for him after all those years of being in the thick of things."*

The sound of a sudden crash alarmed James, who had been curled comfortably in the office's big leather chair. His head came up. There was no repetition of the loud noise, and as the voice on the machine continued its flow, the little dog's eyes slowly closed and his head drooped till his nose rested on the chair seat. A soft snore emanated from the small furry body as Aunt Dodie rattled on.

*"Oh, excuse me, Elizabeth dear, I dropped you on the floor— or at least, your answering machine. Now, what was I . . . oh, yes, well, I was talking to an old friend the other day, of course at my age that's about the only kind there is, and I asked her what she was doing and she said she was putting her house in order— death order was what she said actually—so that her children wouldn't have to deal with her personal letters and things that might be meaningless to them after she'd passed on, though she's in perfect health as far as I know and younger than I by several years.*

*"But what she said got me to thinking that I'd do the same for my New Year's resolution and I realized that I ought to go through the old gentleman's desk—some of his Navy things might be of interest to the Maritime Museum in Beaufort and I could just burn the rest. So I began by taking things out and sorting them into piles—you know, newspaper clippings, documents, old photographs—and there was the sweetest one of you and Sam when you came through here on your honeymoon; I'm having a copy made and will send it to you; you both looked so happy, but oh dear, then I found the letter from Sam . . .*

*"And some of the things Sam said were so strange, and he had questions for the old gentleman about someone he was working*

*with whom he didn't quite trust—someone he called the Hawk—and—oh, thank goodness, there's the clock striking midnight—well, I've made it through another New Year's Eve. Happy New Year, Elizabeth dear. May it be filled with all the happiness you deserve."*

# Acknowledgments

My editor Kate Miciak's power to make me grow as a writer continues to amaze me. And now I'm thankful for her patience too. My wonderful agent, Ann Collette, is always a welcome source of advice, encouragement, and cheer. Someday soon I hope to introduce her to country life, up close and personal, bugs and tomatoes and all. Thanks to Deb Dwyer, my eagle-eyed copy editor, for her precision and for the nice comments. And once again, many thanks to Jamie S. Warren Youll for the great covers.

Cynthia Niles gave pharmaceutical advice and Marianna Daly, MD, and Polly Ross, MD, provided information on HIV/AIDS. I appreciate their help and hope I got it right.

The people of Hickory Nut Gap Farm and Sherrill's Inn, one of the few stands still in existence in my area, were a great resource. Many thanks to Cindy Clarke for suggesting I visit and for showing me around, and to John and Annie Ager for allowing a stranger to wander through their house and imagine it as it had been.

The Vance birthplace in Weaverville, NC, a pioneer farmstead with a five-room log house reconstructed around original chimneys and furnished to evoke the period from 1795–1840, helped me to visualize the world of Lydy Goforth.

430                    ACKNOWLEDGMENTS

Thanks to old friend Dayton Wild, a link with the past. When Dayton told me how his father (older than his grandfather—you work it out) had told him stories about the Drovers' Road, it gave me goose bumps and helped to make the past a little more real.

And I'm eternally grateful to all the fans who share stories with me or just tell me to keep going. Thanks to SFC Robert A. Myers (ret.) whose vivid reminiscence of a Melungeon couple he had known inspired Ish and Mariah Flores. And to Larry Suttles, who won the right in a library raffle to name a character. He asked that I use the name of his late father who had lived up on Max Patch and was a great plant propagator. "Maybe he could still be alive in your story," Larry suggested, and that gave me an idea. . . .

The following books were useful to me in working on this novel: *History of Buncombe County, NC,* F.A. Sondley, LL.D. (The Reprint Company Publishers, Spartanburg, SC, 1997—repro of 1930 ed.); *The French Broad,* Wilma Dykeman (New York, Holt, Rinehart and Winston, 1955); *Folk Medicine in Southern Appalachia,* Anthony Cavender, (The University of North Carolina Press, Chapel Hill, 2003); and *The Kingdom of Madison: A Southern Mountain Fastness and Its People* by Manly Wade Wellman, University of North Carolina Press, Chapel Hill, 1973.

# About the Author

Vicki Lane has lived with her family on a mountain farm in North Carolina since 1975. She is the author of *Signs in the Blood*, *Art's Blood*, and *Old Wounds*, which was chosen as a Book Sense Notable Book. She is currently at work on an addition to her chronicles of Elizabeth Goodweather's Marshall County, *The Day of Small Things*.

"Vicki Lane writes of Appalachia as if she'd been driving up our hills and through our hollows her whole life.... In showing us how memory lingers like a smoky mist across the mountains, Lane reminds us again that the past never completely dies."

—Margaret Maron, award-winning author of *Hard Row*

If you enjoyed Vicki Lane's
*IN A DARK SEASON,*
you won't want to miss any of her
haunting novels of suspense set in Appalachia.
Look for them at your favorite bookseller.

Read on for an electrifying early look at her next novel.

# *THE DAY OF SMALL THINGS*

by
Vicki Lane

*Coming soon from Dell*

# The Day of Small Things
## Coming soon from Dell

## *The Beginning*
### *Dark Holler ~ 1922*

On the evening of the third day, her screams filled the little cabin, escaping through the open door to tangle themselves in the dark brooding hemlocks that loomed above the house. The weary midwife, returning from a visit to the privy, glanced up at the mournful trees and shuddered.

"Seems them ol low-droopin boughs is just a-holdin in the sound. And all that pain and misery—hit'll linger there till ever wind that stirs'll be like to bring it back—all them cries a-flutterin round the house again like so many black crows."

Pausing to adjust her long skirt, the midwife frowned at such an unaccustomed flight of fancy. "Law, whatever put such foolishness into my head? I'm flat wore out, and that's the truth—how else would I come to think such quare things? But hit's a lonesome, sorrowful place fer all that and a sorrowful time fer poor Fronie. Her man not yet cold in his grave and her boy tarryin at death's door—ay, law, hit's a cruel hard time to birth a child—iffen hit don't kill her first.

For days the woman had labored. For almost forty hours she had clung to a fierce, tooth-clenched silence, broken only by an occasional low groan or an involuntary gasp as the pains came on anew. But at last her stern control had shattered, giving way to a frenzy of sobs and curses as the contractions grew in strength. And still the child would not be born.

Hurrying back into the small log house, the midwife pulled on the clean muslin apron that was the badge of her calling. The screams broke off and the expectant mother lay panting on the stained and stinking corn shuck tick, her breath coming in hoarse rasps. Long dark hair, carefully combed free of tangles in vain hope of easing the birth, fanned out in damp strands around her death-pale face. The anguish, the fear, the anger that had passed, like a succession of hideous masks, over the laboring woman's gaunt countenance, was momentarily replaced by an otherworldly absence of all emotion.

Then a great ripple surged across the huge belly swelling beneath her thin shift and the woman's face contorted once more. Her cracked lips opened to scream but nothing more than a strangled croak emerged. Gasping with pain and frustration, the woman twisted her misshapen torso from side to side as she clawed at her heaving belly.

The midwife caught at the woman's hands and held them till the contraction passed. "Hit'll be born afore sundown or they'll be the two of 'em to bury," she whispered to the frightened girl standing at the bedside.

"I ain't never seen no one die, Miz Romarie. My daddy, he was already gone when they fetched him home from the loggin camp." The girl's wide eyes brimmed with tears. She turned her face, ashen in the fading light, to the midwife. "Miz Romarie, I'm so a-feared . . ."

The midwife patted the girl's thin shoulder and then reached for the bottle of sweet oil that stood on a nearby stool. "We ain't got time fer that now, Fairlight. You catch hold of yore mama's hands whilst I see kin I turn the babe and bring hit on. Hold 'em tight now, honey."

*Black night had come and owls called out amid the sighing of the hemlocks as the exhausted woman looked without pleasure at her red, squalling infant. At last she spoke. "Hit'll allus be the least un, fer there won't be no more. Reckon that'll do fer a name—call hit Least."*

# The Burying Ground
## Tuesday, May 1

Today me and Luther put an end to that girl. All that was left of her is under the talking oak at the yon side of the burying ground. Luther said that it must be so and he ast that I give my solum promiss never to speak that name no more nor to think on them other things. And he give me this new book to write in and said that I must burn the old ones. We got all our life ahead says he—a fine new begining and when you got a mess a young uns about the place youll fergit all this hateful bizniss.

As her finger traced the straggling words, Birdie Gentry's lips moved silently. The pages of the composition book were yellowed and crisp with age but the words, penciled in childish printing by a determined hand, were clear. The old woman read on.

I'll not be sorry to fergit that poor crazy girl and what she done—but ... Dark scribbling blacked out several lines before the printing continued. There, I like to brok my solum promis alredy. So insted Ill write of the fine new house Luther is naming to build for us down near the

*road where the sun shines all day and ther aint all these
old dark trees that moans in the night wind. Luther has
already cut and hauled the timber—*

The abrupt *brrr* of the telephone sounded from
the living room. Birdie closed the journal and laid it
gently atop a stack of similar books then, moving
slowly, she pulled herself up and began to hobble
toward the other room in response to the insistent
ring, muttering as she went.

"I'm a-coming, you worrisome thing! Holler all
you want to, this ol' arthuritis won't let me move no
faster,"

"No, Dor'thy, I cain't do it. I made a solemn promise
and I've held to it, all these years. But I'll help you
any way I can, 'ceptin' fer that. Tell me, have you
heared atall from the young 'un since she took him
away?"

The voice on the telephone grew louder and more
agitated and Birdie listened without further comment, only shaking her head in sympathy with her
cousin's lamentations. Finally she broke in.

"Dor'thy, you and me both know Prin ain't a fit
mother. But if the Social Services lady ain't goin'
to . . . Now, don't take on so . . . we'll find us a way to
git Calven back to you. I'll think on hit and pray
on hit too. . . . Yes, I name to go up to the cemetery
this evenin', soon's I have my bite of lunch. I'm
a-goin' to pick up all them ol' wore-out flower arrangements and such and make the place look nice
afore Bernice's boy comes to weed eat round the
stones. . . . Naw, they ain't no need fer you to come . . ."

At last the call drew to a close. Birdie replaced the

receiver and sat motionless on the edge of her chair, her mouth pursed as she struggled to order her thoughts. Finally she roused herself and reached for the Bible lying on the crocheted doily by the telephone. Placing the book in her lap, she laid her outspread hands on the worn black leather and whispered, "I cain't do it without You help me, Lord. . . . In Thy Holy Name, I ask it."

Closing her eyes, she waited, head cocked as if listening to a distant voice. Then, eyes still shut, Miss Birdie cracked the Bible. One hand, index finger extended, hovered briefly in the air above the open book then fell like a stooping hawk to rest on the words below.

Birdie opened her eyes and peered at the verse her finger had singled out. Frowning, she adjusted her glasses.

"Zechariah 4:10, is it? *'For who hath despised the day of small things?'*" The old woman leaned closer to the Book. "Lord, You ain't speakin' very clear today. But my finger was touchin' on some of the ninth verse too . . . let me see . . . *'and thou shalt know that the Lord of hosts hath sent me unto you'* . . ."

Birdie lifted her head to fix the ceiling of her living room with a bright blue gaze. "Well, who you goin' to send me, Lord?"


The hickory staff dug neat pockmarks in the hard red earth as Birdie made her way along the path that wound up the wooded slope. Dangling from the crook of her elbow, a pair of black plastic garbage bags provided a rustling accompaniment to the brief huffs of her breath and the steady thump of her footfalls. The narrow, little-used trail ran beside a rusted barbed wire fence that marked the upper limits of an overgrown field thick with locust and poplar saplings amid brambles. A bright clump of coral-red fire pinks at the foot of a gray leaning post caught her attention and elicited a nod but Birdie kept on, following the trail into the woods.

In the dappled shade beneath the new-leafed trees, whole colonies of trillium, both white and pink, carpeted the rich mountain soil, while along the banks of the rocky stream, lavender phacelia and wild geraniums danced against the stern gray boulders. Beyond the tumbling froth of water the deeper purple of dwarf iris and wild larkspur dotted the steep wooded slope.

Birdie stopped, leaning on her staff and breathing in the rich woodland smell. *They's some things don't change, thank the Lord. That fine loamy smell of the dirt and the clean mint smell of the branch and the songs the water sings as it goes a-hurryin' to the river and the birds calling out and the wind a-stirrin' the trees. Hit's all the good things of life itself. I pity the city folks ain't never been in a mountain cove in May time.*

She stood a few minutes longer in rapt appreciation then, mindful of her purpose, resumed the climb. Soon the path curved to the right and a few more minutes brought her into a small clearing. A log barn topped by a rust-red tin roof stood below a line of dark hemlocks that swayed in the freshening breeze. Nearby, a lone fieldstone chimney stood amid a thicket of well-grown locust trees stood. Two lichen-crusted apple trees lifted twisted branched beyond a row of ancient looming boxwoods and Birdie's nose wrinkled as the shrub's characteristic aroma reached her. *Whyever You come to make them bushes smell like an ol tom-cat's been a-sprayin' em, I do not understand, Lord. Was it me, I believe I'd a found a nicer smell. Reckon hit's just another one of them mysterious ways of Yourn Preacher's allus talkin' about.*

Birdie gave a quick glance at the chimney. For a few seconds her sharp eyes followed the faint trace of a path leading from near the old chimney into the hemlocks. She stood bemused, lost in her thoughts and memories. Then, recollecting herself, she turned away to follow the upward trail into the first of a series of old fields. *Let it go. Atter all these years, cain't you let it go?* The words were a drum beat and her steps kept time. *Let-it-go. Let-it-go.*

As she climbed the old woman could see dark clouds gathering above the scrub-filled abandoned fields. She could scent the coming rain but still she continued her slow, purposeful progress to the family burying ground atop the hogback ridge. *Let-it-go. Let-it-go.*

At the summit Birdie paused briefly to catch her breath. Around her, gravestones and markers of all sorts and ages dotted the gentle crest of the ridge. Ignoring the more recent granite markers, deep-carved with names, dates, and bible verses, and their faded arrangements of artificial flowers, Birdie stumped doggedly on to the older section of the graveyard where modest sand concrete memorials and white painted slabs commemorated the dead of an earlier time. Here and there single plastic flowers were jabbed into the soil of these older graves but Birdie passed on without a glance, making her way to the far edge of the mown ground.

Only a narrow strip of tall grass and weeds divided the cleared hilltop from the forest of poplar, oak and beech, their leave lacquer-bright with the vibrant new greens of the season. The old woman's eyes narrowed in concentration as she moved beneath the canopy of a great oak. Scanning the thick growth at her feet, she thrust her staff into the long grass, sweeping it aside to uncover a homemade lozenge of white-washed concrete, set flat and all but lost in the rising tide of late spring. On the rough surface the date 1939 showed, etched by an unskilled hand just beneath the single word—"LEAST."

Miss Birdie Gentry leaned on her stick and studied the stone, lips moving soundlessly, tears dimming her bright blue eyes. *Many a year, law, yes, many a year. But hit weren't right—*

The babble of a familiar high-pitched voice broke into her reverie. Hurriedly, Birdie wiped her face on the sleeve of the man's shirt she wore over her loose house dress. With one sneaker-shod foot, she quickly pushed the hank of grass back to cover the little marker. When it was hidden once again, she made her way back among the graves where she began to pick up the tattered floral arrangements and jam them into a garbage bag.

*Well, so Dor'thy come along atter all. But reckon who it is she's talkin' to?* Her cousin's chatter floated up the hill, every word clear now. A light rain began to fall and Birdie stretched out her hand to catch the drops.

"She *said* as she'd be up here, cleanin' off the graves and gettin' ready for Decoration Day. All them old wreaths and such to gather up and get shed of. I *told* her to let me do it—you know Miss Birdie's gettin' up in years—eighty-five this October—and not so spry as she once was—but will she listen? And now it's come on to sprinkle. Well, I reckon it'll pass off right quick. How long did you say it was since you seen your aunt?"

There was a soft murmur—an unknown woman's voice. Birdie frowned and craned her head to catch the words but heard only Dorothy's cheerful reply.

"I declare, won't she be tickled you come at last!"

At that moment, Dorothy and her companion came into view. Dorothy, her familiar stout person clad in knit slacks and loose top, was a few steps in front of a slightly younger woman. Birdie studied the newcomer's face carefully, looking for some clue to her identity.

*Ay, law, now which one can that be? Many nieces as I got that I hain't seed in a great time . . . this un here, what age would she be? Hard to tell the way they dye their hair and all. And of course, some folks just naturally hold their age real good. Blue eyes, wiry built . . . I wonder—*

"Birdie Gentry, what in the world are you doin', standin' out in the rain like that? Why don't we go set in my vehicle till it lets up? And why in the world didn't you bring your truck and come by the road 'stead of walkin' all that way through the fields. I declare—"

Ignoring Dorothy's scolding, Birdie smiled and nodded at the other woman. "My mamaw allus said that hit was a fine thing to git wet in the first rain of May—that hit would keep a body healthy all the year."

The unknown woman stepped forward, her face blossoming into a lop-sided smile that was oddly familiar.

"Aunt Birdie, you probably don't remember me. I'm Myrna Louise—Lexter and Britty Mae's youngest daughter. The last time I was here was 1959—I was only sixteen then so I don't expect you to recognize me now."

*Lord, she sounds like a Yankee,* thought Birdie, looking for some hint of the teenager she dimly remembered. *But pore thing, she cain't help it—livin' up there in Dee-troit all this time with Yankees all about. Come to that, I believe she married one. But she does favor Lexter right much, now I come to look at her.*

The little woman extended her arms. "Myrna Lou, honey, come here and let me hug yore neck. What took you so long to come home?"

# Least
## Dark Holler ~ June 1930

The yard dog speaks and I look up from the peas I'm shellin. They's a woman and a girl coming up the road and Mama takes the bowl of peas from me and jerks her chin at the door. Go on, she says. Through the house and out the back way. Git you a hoe and go to work on them beans. I'll call you when the folks is gone.

I duck my head yes ma'am and go quick like into the house. But onct I'm to where Mama can't see me, I stay near the window so's I can hear them talk. Mama don't never talk much 'cept for when she's a-tellin me what to do. And now that Fairlight's run off and got herself married, they ain't no one to talk to me, bein' as Brother's as close-jawed as Mama.

Come git you uns a chair, says Mama as the woman and the girl start up the rock steps. I hear the mule-ear chair's hickory bark seat squeak like there's mouses in hit as the lady sets herself down.

Ooo-eee! she says, now hit's been a time since I come up here to Dark Holler. Like to forgot what a climb hit is. But I had in mind to git up to the burying ground and tend to my mamaw and papaw's graves. Come Decoration Day, I'll be goin with Henry over to the Buckscrape to where his people lie. Fronie, tell me, was that your least'un I saw just *now, scootin into the house? Law, she's growed like one thing. Don't she go to school? Lilah Bel here's in the third grade now and readin like one thing. Hit beats all, the way she took to learnin.*

*I skooch close to the window and careful-like peek around the edge to look at the girl who can read. Fairlight taught me my letters and C-A-T cat and H-A-T hat but then she went off. Mama don't hold with me learnin to read, is what I heared her tell Brother. Hit'll just aggervate them funny spells she takes iffen she gits all tired out with tryin to learn more 'n she's able.*

*The girl who can read is taller 'n me and she has the darkest eyes and straight dark hair cut short like girls in the wish book have theirs. She has picked up the bowl of peas and has set in to shellin them without noone tellin her to. Mama looks at her and nods her head. You don't know what it is, Voncel, to have a young un what ain't right. No, she ain't able to go to school—takes these funny spells now and again. And then Mama leans closer to the visitor lady and whispers, She's just simple and that's the truth. And it worries her to be around folks. But we git on. Now tell me, Voncel, was you able to bring me them rug patterns?*

*I see that the girl named Lilah Bel is looking right at the window where I'm peeking out. I stick my tongue out at her then I jerk back outta sight and go quick and quiet out the back way. My special hoe, the light one with its blade worn down like a piece of the moon, is leaning gainst the logs there on the back porch and I grab it and take the little path through the dark whisperin trees to the bean patch.*

*I make haste along the narrow trail so's I kin get them beans hoed and Mama won't get ill at me. And then I hear the drums and see the edges of their world.*

*Hit's allus that way—first the drums and the lights and then they show themselves. I step off the path and hunch* down low so's I kin crawl up under the droopin branches. Hit's under that biggest one of them old groanin trees where they have their nest. I hunker down there and listen to their sounds. Then I make a picture in my mind and the little things begin to creep out.